Waiting Game

Claire Kinton

Claire Kinton

Ghostly
Publishing

First published in Great Britain in 2012

Ghostly Publishing, 34 Bakers Close, Plymouth, PL7 2GH

Published in Great Britain by Ghostly Publishing –

Visit www.ghostlypublishing.co.uk for more information

Connect with the author at
www.ghostlypublishing.co.uk/ClaireKinton/

ISBN-10: 1-909587-25-7
ISBN-13: 978-1-909587-25-0

For my Mum & Dad

In life we all have an unspeakable secret, an irreversible regret,
an unreachable dream and an unforgettable love.

(Diego Marchi)

Claire Kinton

ACKNOWLEDGMENTS

Let me start by thanking the one man who knows me best and who has continued to sit patiently by my side, night after night, as I painstakingly punched out Dead Game, Waiting Game and End Game. Mr. Kinton, you're, as always, my watchman and in so many ways, my keen confidant, secretly believing in everything I do, yet never overly animated when it comes to testing the merchandise – I thank you, your presence and confidence makes every day an adventure and a blessing.

Secondly, I would like to thank, from the bottom of my heart, a truly gifted lady, my editor and writing mother, Jo Field. She has been with me from the very beginning of my publishing journey, never changing my voice, understanding every concept I have thrown at her and totally grasping the impression I wish to etch. She gets me!

I would also like to show my gratitude to Neil Trigger, your passion for your authors is so evident, your unwavering faith in my work is so motivating and your drive and creativity is truly inspiring.

There are just too many others I need to thank when it comes to my zest for storytelling and putting the second part of this trilogy together; but let me finish by saying a huge thank you to every person who has picked up a copy of Dead Game, read it, enjoyed it, even reviewed it – I spilt a little of my soul onto every page of that book and I hope my message never leaves you. Likewise with Waiting Game, may your troubles be eased, knowing, with every adversity, there is an education and with any education, there is understanding and with understanding, there of course, comes freedom.

AUTHOR'S NOTE

WILL LOVE CROSS ETERNITY TO FULFIL ITSELF?

When we die there are always people left behind, suffering, roaming lost, and trying to live, some it seems merely waiting for their turn to follow; their turn to end the agony of loss.

Death of those we love opens a wound that no one will ever really heal. It creates a hunger, not as in a hunger for food, more an agonising hunger of the spirit that will smoulder incessantly deep inside, the passage of time eating away at every cherished memory. When we find ourselves at this point, when the pain we feel is our only fuel for the journey ahead, here lies the test to find out whether our mission on Earth is finished or whether we can somehow find fulfilment in the absence of those who can never be replaced.

Every life is like a novel with the ending ripped out. Nobody really knows what is to come. My last story, Dead Game, followed Lance Corporal Archie Fletcher as he crossed the bridge to the other side of life, his journey through Transit was seemingly a game he was obliged to play. Waiting Game now follows Sarah Walker, Archie's soulmate, who must continue stumbling through life without him. Her journey is harsh and lengthy: it is a story of denial, compromise and acceptance. It is a long trek and a fragile heart that travels it. Compelled to move forward whether she wants to or not, Sarah's scars run deep, but just how far will she go in an attempt to assuage her loss?

CHAPTER ONE

AUGUST 2003
PAIN; FUEL FOR THE JOURNEY

People shoved past Sarah as she collected her hand luggage. Hot and flustered, she moved to the entrance of the main terminal, fumbling at her neck for her St Christopher.

"Don't underestimate yourself Sarah. You can do this," she told herself, fighting back tears as she shuffled through Heathrow security. "Don't look back ... you're fine … just keep walking."

The scene that greeted her proved too much. The vast sea of artificial lighting, the pungent blend of duty-free perfume, jumbled with freshly brewed coffee, and the hoards of passengers closing in on her, they were nothing in comparison to the gaping hole resting in her chest. All alone she staggered a few steps further into the chaos. Then the realisation of what she was about to do grasped her around the throat. She had swallowed it down hard a thousand times that morning, but now it got the better of her. That lump had been poised, hovering, waiting for the moment of comprehension and here it was. As though an oncoming steamroller impeded her path, Sarah's stagger ground to a halt. A fever rushed through her and with a shiver she turned back, looking past security, beyond the passport control queue, catching the steady eye of her mother, Patricia, still waving, still crying.

"I won't cry," Sarah whispered to herself, but her tears were already tumbling. "You've saved for this for years, you've dreamed of this for years. This is it now … slightly delayed, but still, this is it. Spread your wings and let the fairy in you fly." Sarah's thoughts fought gallantly to gain back control from her emotions. Nervously she twirled her pendant's chain around her index finger. "So why are you crying?" she murmured to herself angrily, whipping away tears with her shoulder, smearing black mascara across her white T-shirt. "You promised yourself no more tears; today was to be the end of tears." She grimaced at herself then squeezed out a smile for her own benefit. She'd no doubt her mother would not be able to see it. "Breathe!" Her breath remained firmly drawn in, as slowly she lifted a hand and waved then, exhaling, turned back to face Terminal Three head on.

Knotted inside and bleary-eyed, Sarah battled the crowds. Still, the rest of her journey to Gate 41 was easy. Avoiding duty-free, she headed for Costa and bought a café latte. No one bothered her tucked in the corner of the coffee shop, as she sat head down with her nose in the Rough Guide to Thailand. Infesting thoughts drowned each page, the words were rhythmically read, but there was no understanding or care taken to value them. She had too many tender emotions throbbing through her to heed instructions on how to find a hostel.

Her flight to Bangkok was called early. Salvaging her passport and boarding card from the nape of her knapsack, Sarah's eye caught sight of a tattered envelope, an unopened letter which she took with her everywhere. She would read it later, she thought, as she slipped away from Costa and into the sea of passengers headed for the boarding gates. As she walked her legs shook, the travelator a little respite. A queue had already formed to board flight MA001, a queue Sarah shied away from.

Finding a clear corner in the departure lounge to sit, she stared wide-eyed out of the floor-to-ceiling window overlooking the Malaysian Airways jumbo jet she was about to board. Any romance she'd held for flying was dead, her psyche had successfully twisted her longing thrill for travel into a loathing dread. She was terrified.

"You get yourself on that plane Miss … if you don't you'll regret it for the rest of your life," she told herself. "Why are you freaking? Hundreds of planes take off and land safely every day. Just because Archie's didn't …." Sarah's jaw locked at the mere thought of her cousin's name, her eyes filled and she felt the hole in her chest burn. The vision of the plane before her became a haze, she closed her eyes and let the second bout of tears that day spill. Conscious she was losing it and that the queue to board was shortening, she dashed for the ladies toilets, where she could hide and compose herself.

A month had passed since her cousin Archie's plane had nose-dived into the Persian Gulf, his funeral only a week ago and yet night after night, without fail, Sarah's nightmare of his aeroplane falling from the sky haunted her. It always started with that. Then a void of space accompanied by the steady echo of hollow footsteps; then more darkness; next, a vision of Archie's bronzed childish face, always smiling, his arms reaching out to her, but before she could grasp him, before she could replenish the hole throbbing inside her and become whole again, the image of his face would turn away. Then more darkness. Occasionally, if the nightmare lingered and she could not wake herself, she'd catch another glimpse of his face fading, although whenever he appeared a second time, he looked different somehow. He was not the boy she had grown up with, for she knew every tooth in that boy's head. This was a young man, who was alike to Archie in every way except in his maturity and his smile, which now bore a chipped front tooth.

The final call for flight MA001 was made whilst Sarah splashed her face with ice cold water in the ladies. "It's your trip of a lifetime, get a grip girl. Life is for living, so get on and live it," Sarah scolded, looking at the image before her in the mirror. Her mousey hair, in pigtails, was now fuzzy and wet, she had mascara all over her face and T-shirt and her skin was blotchy red. "What a mess," she muttered as she flattened down her fuzz with damp hands.

Then she heard a clink. Her ears pricked as she stared at her reflection. The clink was followed by a tinkling sound. She grappled at her neck as the chain she wore unravelled and began its decent towards the plughole. "No! Oh please no." She threw the chain to one side, ripped the plug from the sink and stared into the hole. Precariously balanced on an inner rim of the plughole was her St Christopher. "Don't do this to me now. I need that," Sarah stuck her pinkie carefully towards the pendant, desperately trying to tease it away from the drop. It teetered away from her. She withdrew her finger and looked back at her mirror twin. "Okay … calm down. It's just a bulky piece of metal with a picture on it." She sniffed in hard. "One half of it also happens to belong to Archie and it's coming with me on this trip or I'm not going."

Sarah closed her eyes, remembering the day she had given the St Christopher to Archie outside his house. He, just turned eighteen, had announced he was joining the Army. That day could have been yesterday. It was then that he had given her the letter, which she was prohibited from opening until after his death. At the time, the very thought of him being killed had made her feel sick and she had quickly shoved it away and deliberately forgotten about it. Yet now he was dead, she still couldn't bring herself to open it. Another flashback kicked in; of the horrific day they'd been informed of the crash and Archie's death. That day felt like it happened centuries ago, how could it be only a month? She had found the pendant on the stairs at 23 Eversely Avenue, Archie's home. Drunk at the time, completely baffled as to how it came to be there, for she had never seen it away from Archie's neck since she'd given it to him all those years before, she had been forced to suppose he had accidently left it behind. She had picked it up and firmly trusting the myth of St Christopher, had worn it religiously ever since. She sniffed again, wiping the sweat away from her top lip.

"It's not going down that hole," she muttered. Focused now, Sarah slowly yet somewhat shakily prised the pendant from its awkward position and flicked it into her hand. "Gotcha."

"This is the final call for flight MA001 to Bangkok. Could Miss Sarah Walker please make her way to boarding gate 41 immediately? This flight is now closing."

Jolted into action, Sarah shot out of the toilets. She didn't look out of the window at the waiting aircraft, her head was down, her breathing short. She slipped St Christopher into the top pocket of her dungarees and boarded.

Disrupting the already settled passengers, Sarah found her seat in the far righthand corner of the plane, another corner for her to disappear into. The aircraft backed out of its hold as she sank into the cramped seat. Putting her backpack on her lap, she stared out of the window at the tarmac. The flight attendant didn't waste any time, the comforting Asian music that had greeted her, along with two hundred and fifty sets of irritated eyes, disappeared. A safety video was playing; Sarah didn't watch. She blocked it all out, staring hard at the oncoming runway. The pilot stopped the plane, set for takeoff. The engines began to rev, louder and louder. The courage Sarah had felt that morning had drained away, all desire to be lifted into the air was gone; she fidgeted in her seat, her stomach in knots. The fever that had washed over her in the airport returned with a vengeance. For the first time since Archie's death she became urgently aware of her heart pounding in her ears. In fact she thought it may spiral into her mouth. How she longed for Valium!

"Please God keep me safe … please God keep me safe …" she muttered under her breath whilst clutching her chest. The plane began to move slowly at first then speeded up, progressively faster and faster. Still mumbling, Sarah's gaze fixed on the world outside hurtling by, until the engines reached a deafening climax. They bounced once, her stomach twisted. Then they were in the air. The ground descended as the plane climbed into the blue. Her fate for the next thirteen hours now lay in another's hands. "We're up. I did it. Okay, now breathe and re-lax." Sarah sighed, finally allowing her eyes to close. However her heart did not calm down and her pale, cold hands gripped onto the armrests fiercely, her fingernails digging in; knuckles white. She sat like a statue, rigid, barely breathing, feeling woozy and dazed. It wasn't until the man beside her poked her shoulder that she opened her eyes again and took a deep breath of the filtered air.

"'Scuse me, Miss, the lady wants to know if you wanna drink," said the man beside her in a strong Australian accent, his eyes far too close to Sarah's head. She didn't move an inch, her gaze instantly rapt on the miniature television that was set into the seat in front of her. An image of their plane slowly inched away from England.

"Just water thanks," Sarah mustered, her head spinning as she tried to focus. The Australian shifted back and the flight attendant passed over her drink and moved on. Tentatively, Sarah kissed the water. She didn't want to overdo it. Her stomach ached and her chest was agony. Any fast internal motion may cause an eruption.

"You okay?" the man next to her asked, swigging a beer, Sarah could smell it. "You look a bit green." She couldn't bring herself to turn, that meant eye contact and further conversation, neither of which she was up to or in any way desired.

"I'm fine, thanks. Just tired, that's all."

Getting no other response, the man turned back to his female companion on the aisle.

The flight dragged by minute after minute. Sarah barely moved, her water still clutched in nerveless fingers. She refused headphones and dinner. Outside turned from brilliant blue to purple then black. The sun had set on the other side of the plane. People were closing shutters and reclining, quietly nattering, taking blankets and drinking nightcaps. For what felt like hours Sarah remained frozen, her eyes never leaving the mini television set in front of her, the plane edging over the eastern part of Europe. Her body was cold and aching. She could, however, feel the curious stare of the fellow passenger beside her from time to time, his bulk too close for her to feel any ease.

No one disturbed her throughout the first half of the flight. There were no comprehensible thoughts or vivid impressions springing into her mind, she was blank inside. She wanted to feel blank inside. It hurt to feel or even think. Her new adventure seemed futile: there was no excitement anymore, just a bone-deep emptiness and the electronic image of her plane nudging across the globe slowly imprinting itself into her mind's eye. The cabin was dark now, bar a handful of overhead spotlights for as many readers. Sarah's eyes were beginning to burn as the plane flew thirty thousand feet above Russia. She couldn't sustain being awake for much longer. Her lids drooped and her shoulders pushed back hard into the seat. She had been rigid for such a long time that her attempts to relax shot excruciating tension up her neck causing her head to pound again. Pain from every angle seemed to be haunting this trip, emotional and now physical. Surely sleep would put an end to her living nightmare.

CHAPTER TWO

JULY 2003
IS SLEEP BALM TO A TROUBLED MIND?

There was nothing peaceful or rejuvenating about Sarah's sleep, which she fell into reluctantly. Each nap she had taken since Archie's death felt like a slice of her own death. As she began to drowse she was lulled torturously into another of her recurring nightmares: Archie's funeral.

***

Trembling, she sat in the middle of a crammed pew. Not daring to look about at the magnificent cathedral with its splendid stained glass windows and hundreds of devastated mourners, she gawked at the tattered tissue she fumbled in clammy hands.

"This can't be happening," she thought to herself, shaking her head. The cream and green floral print of her dress swam before her eyes; the family had asked mourners not to wear black, for this was to be a celebration of Archie's life, but be that as it may, Sarah felt pitch black to her very core. "Why God … oh why? Why have you taken him?" she whispered. "He was barely a man. He's left so many dreams behind."

Printed on the order of service, sitting untouched on the bench in front of her, was Archie's photograph, which eagle-eyed her every move. It was a photograph Sarah had taken in his parents' garden, whilst they were having a barbeque, three days before he was killed. He had been home from Iraq on R and R and was readying to return to Kuwait the very next day. His chiselled face was tanned and toned, his mousey hair cropped short, his smile even and pearly white. His blue eyes were a clone of Sarah's own; looking at them was like glancing in a mirror.

"God, we loved him so much, how could you do this to us? He was my best friend…" She couldn't look at the photograph, it hurt too much. To look at it would make the event real, it would force her to face the end, and she couldn't; she wouldn't. Just knowing the photo was watching her suffer was enough to splinter her heart into a thousand pieces all over again.

Then the dreaded beat of steady footsteps began and the unbearable echo of sobs started bouncing round the cathedral walls. Sarah's hand rose to her tear-soaked face and she knew it was her own uncontrollable cry she could hear. Desperate to contain it she held her breath, but this only made her whimpering louder. It was all she could hear, bar the footsteps of the coffin bearers. Strong arms wrapped around her on either side, they were of no comfort, their only worth was to get her on her feet whilst Archie's coffin was brought in.

She felt like such a fool standing there sobbing behind her Auntie Jo and Uncle Robert, Archie's parents. None of the front row moved or even murmured. Her cousins, Helena and Stewart, Archie's sister and brother, stood strong side by side. It appeared to Sarah that his family were like four stone statues, totally motionless. She desperately wanted to reach out and touch them, to comfort them. They looked so incomplete being only four, they didn't seem real. In the dream she knew they were real because she could smell their scent and hear their tight and shallow breathing.

Robert stood the tallest in a beige linen suit, his thick crop of once black hair now turned silver, his left hand in his pocket, Sarah guessed ready to retrieve his inhaler if he suddenly struggled to breathe, his asthma always worse when he was stressed. Beside him, his wife Jo, in a tan skirt suit, her fair hair now turned ash. Helena, whom Sarah stood directly behind, was dealing not only with the loss of her brother but with double-grief, having lost her first love James, who was on the same flight as Archie had been. Naturally bleach-blonde she looked immaculate wearing a sage green, A-line skirt and white blouse. Stewart, who at only eighteen was a good head taller than his elder sister and still growing, wore a suit, a pale grey one that Sarah knew had once belonged to his big brother, Archie. They stood so close there was barely an inch between them. It seemed that any word, contact or movement might create a weakness, their mask could not be broken or their strength to stand and see the day through would crumble. Sarah wondered how their tears did not fall, how could they be that strong when she felt so weak? Maybe it was fear; that if they shed a single tear they would never stop weeping. She didn't think her own tears would ever stop.

The footsteps in the aisle became louder the closer they got and each breath Sarah took was shorter and more uneven, until she felt it was impossible to draw breath at all. As she mopped up her tears with her drenched tissue, a convulsive gulp of air caused her to gasp, her hand clutched to her throat and as she tried desperately to inhale, she wheezed, "I can't breathe …"

***

Abruptly she was yanked from her nightmare by a firm shake on her shoulder. "You okay?" asked the passenger beside her, his voice croaky with drink and tiredness. It seemed Sarah had disturbed his sleeping with her talking and sobbing. Too tired herself to be embarrassed, she apologised, took a couple of deep breaths taking back control of her breathing, nodded to her fellow traveller and closed her eyes again.

Attempting to suppress dreaming, Sarah forced herself to stay awake. For a while she was back on flight MA001, listening to the relentless buzz of the engines, silent tears still pouring down her face. The plane shuddered. Sarah squeezed her eyes shut tighter. She didn't know which way to turn. Reality seemed just as desperate as her dreaming. Stirring in her seat gave her tortured emotions slight relief, but it would never change the fact that Archie was dead and no matter how hard she tried to pull herself completely away from her dream, she just couldn't. She tried to open her eyes, but sleep blurred her sight; she tried to sit up, but a strange pressure seemed to push her deeper into her seat. In a semi-conscious state she was a slave to her dream, as though someone or some force wanted her to relive every moment and emotion of that day and no matter how hard her mind tried, she could not rouse herself from it. Exhaustion won, forcing her to slip from reality back into the dream world, where she was again swallowed by a vortex of agonising memories and emotions.

***

Even in her subconscious, the day proved to be scorching, yet prickling goose bumps covered her from head to toe.

She was outside the cathedral now, the sun beaming down from high up in a cloudless sky; not even the whisper of a breeze to help dry her tears. Hundreds of shadows, all belonging to Archie's family and friends, hung like phantoms everywhere on the concrete ground. A solo bugler sounded the Last Post and rifles were fired. Sarah jumped with each shot, watching the sea of phantoms merge as they embraced one another for comfort. There was always a strong, motionless arm clamped around her shoulders, but different from the arms that had held her inside the cathedral. The person to whom these arms belonged was inconsequential, it could have been anyone who held her; she didn't care. Her head was so crammed with disbelief and sorrow it felt as though it may burst at any given moment, she wished it would burst. The ache in her chest felt like someone had thumped and winded her, she physically could not stand up straight for the pain.

Each time Sarah's mind flinched away from the dream, behind closed eyelids she caught a glimpse of the green digital image of her plane, which was now lasered into her mind's eye. Then, as if the turbulence of the plane and the turbulence of her own subconscious had fused, Sarah's mind seemed to flicker from the plane's digital image back to the merging shadows of mourners on the ground. Back and forth her awareness shifted with no let-up. Slowly the shadows disappeared, one by one, until only her own was left, totally unsupported. The noise of the plane's engines merged into her nightmare and above her there appeared from nowhere the silhouette of an aircraft, slowly growing larger and larger as it headed for the ground where she stood, alone and numb outside the cathedral. The dark shape grew quickly and soon covered the sun completely, causing the outline to distort and engulf the earth beneath.

Bewitched, Sarah watched, as her own shadow was swallowed up by the plane's. Her vision drew into a pitch black void where nothing was visible except a small pinprick of brilliant white light in the distance. Just as the plane's shadow had done, the pinprick of light grew. Slowly, a white figure appeared in the black void. For a moment Sarah thought it was her own shadow again, until she saw the figure had a face, a very recognisable face. It was Archie.

"I'm sorry," Archie said. His face, unshaven, was forlorn and younger. His usually cropped, army-styled hair was thick and bushy. He stood beside her, in what looked like a large puddle of water. Sarah could see their reflections in it.

"What for? Why should you be sorry?" Sarah asked. Her eyes struggled to look at his face in case it disappeared, her arms desperate to reach out to him and feel him for real.

"Sarah, I'm sorry I couldn't save you. I understand now why you had to die."

"No … I didn't die Arch, you did." This was the first time Sarah had spoken to Archie in a dream and although she didn't like the way the conversation was going, she was petrified he was going to disappear. A part of her knew she was dreaming and yet it all felt so real. She daren't move. A single shift in her consciousness would throw her straight back onto flight MA001 over Russia. She wanted to remain exactly where she was for an eternity. Archie's reflection in the water drew closer to her. She thought initially he was moving towards her, but then she realised it was the water rising. Once she understood this, the water quickly flooded them and quick as thought they were both completely submerged, their hair floated wildly around their heads as opposing currents pulled them apart. Their arms stretched out to one another desperately grappling, Sarah could feel herself screaming under the water.

"Please … stay with me … please don't go, Arch. No … follow me."

***

The aircraft hit a pocket of turbulence shaking the plane with such force that the breathing apparatus dropped from the overhead compartments, startling everyone onboard. Sarah woke from her nightmare in a full-blown panic attack.

"ARCHIE!" she screamed.

As if winded, she thrust forward with a painful gasp. Her half cup of water spilt, soaking her lap. The aircraft was alive but dark. Perplexed initially and still with the agonising mincing pain in her chest, Sarah rubbed at her eyes, adjusting to the gloom and dabbing her lap with the only thing to hand, a pathetic paper napkin. The image of the plane still trekked across the screen in front of her, covering Asia now, her destination finally in sight; on screen it was only inches away.

"Please God keep me safe. Just a bit further little plane, we're nearly there, stay up … please … just a little longer." More tears sprang into Sarah's eyes as she rubbed Archie's St Christopher through the pocket of her dungarees that covered her chest. Forcing her mind to think of something else she swiftly switched her gaze from the aircraft in front to the tiny ashtray in the armrest. The nicotine monster living in the pit of her stomach growled. It had been nearly twenty-four hours since her last drag. Her gaze moved on to the tired looking flight attendants who were hurriedly trying to settle the passengers and put away the fallen emergency breathing kits.

Sarah leaned over the snoring man and his mate beside him and grabbed a passing attendant by the arm, looking earnestly into her eyes for a sign of hope.

"Don't worry," insisted the stewardess, her voice was shaky, Sarah wondered if it was through adrenaline and fear or just simply tiredness. "It was just an air pocket. Try and go back to sleep."

Sleep was the last thing in Sarah's mind. She could not entertain even the thought of it. Unless … looking at the intoxicated man beside her she asked, "Could I have a large Gin and Tonic please?"

CHAPTER THREE

AUGUST 2003
WHEN YOUR HEART IS TROUBLED, TAKE HEED OF THE SUN

The International Terminal at Don Muang Airport was the first glimpse Sarah had of exotic Siam. Her flight landed at 10.35 Bangkok local time. Sarah had slept through the landing and not even stirred when her neighbouring passenger roared and cheered, with beer in hand, at touchdown. It had been the same tired flight attendant who had plied her with gin only a few hours before that helped her, as one of the last remaining passengers, off the flight.

Hung-over, on autopilot, relieved to have her feet on firm ground yet frighteningly unprepared and unaware of the chaos that awaited her at immigration, Sarah slowly navigated her way through the queues to passport control. 'Bangkok, August 2003' was stamped into her passport. She had made it.

An inner strength had risen inside her and like a puppet on a string she effortlessly retrieved her backpack from the conveyer-belt and as though she'd walked the same route for years, she headed for the south end of the arrivals concourse in search of a licensed taxi. She'd heard enough rumours about travelling in Thailand and was not about to make the easy mistake of getting in an unlicensed cab.

The automatic doors swung open and in that one small step, Sarah left the world of crisp, filtered air-conditioning and hit a stifling wall of oppressive heat. It was akin to walking into a sauna on full whack. There was not a cloud in the sky, the sun was still climbing to its summit, it was just past eleven in the morning and the atmosphere felt heavy and close, like a good thunderstorm was well overdue. Feeling a strong desire to gasp in more air, Sarah flung her backpack to the ground under the airport canopy. She would have been first in line for a taxi had she not given in to her nicotine monster so readily. Lighting up, it took only two drags before she felt physically sick. Her head spinning as the blood rushed to her head, screeching 'poison' every pump of the way. She crashed down onto her luggage, beads of sweat springing to her forehead.

"My god, this is unbearable, there's just no oxygen here," she said ironically to her cigarette. She forced herself to take another three drags, trying to ignore the fact her head felt like it would explode if she inhaled the toxic smoke one more time. Poised for her fifth drag she admitted defeat and stubbed it out on the ground.

Quickly flicking through her Rough Guide to Thailand, she found the first reasonably priced guest house on the page. It said it had small clean rooms and was in the Banglamphu district, a short walk from all the major sights in the Ratanakosin area. Perfect. She snapped the book shut and shoved it into the side pocket of her backpack.

There was not much of a queue at the taxi rank and taxis were filtering in rapidly, creating an orderly line of multi-coloured cars, ready for the masses of tired passengers. Flagging down a yellow and black number-plated car, she threw her bag onto the back seat and slid in next to it. Haggle artfully, get a price first, Sarah reminded herself.

"Lek Guest House, Khao San Road, please. How much?"

"Welcome to Thailand Missy. 400 Baht, I take you to Khao San Road, Lek Guest House," the Thai driver insisted, his voice kind and gravelly. He looked about a hundred years old, his English was pidgin but understandable and he had the happiest brown eyes Sarah had ever seen, a huge contrast to her own weary, bloodshot blue eyes that with one horrified glance in the airport mirror, she had hidden behind aviation sunglasses. His eyes seemed to be laughing; they were so beautiful, sparkling with so much life. Surely it should have been the other way around – her, the young Western backpacker, off on her adventures. Uncontainable envy flickered across Sarah's face.

"Sorry, 400 Baht is too much," Sarah retrieved her bag from beside her and went for the door.

"In the time you have left, Sarah …" he paused.

Sarah frowned, stopped, the door slightly ajar. How did he know her name? Had she misheard? She didn't turn back to him, she waited, her hand resting on the door handle.

"Why you follow your pain and attachment?" he continued. "They will only cause you more confusion and delusion. Don't do dat, Sarah. Use this jealousy you feel now as practice to crush the pain. You will see him again, you know dat."

"How do you know my…? What did you…? " Sarah shook her head in an effort to clear it. Was she still dreaming? Taking a deep breath in hope of stifling any lingering irritation, she turned back to the taxi driver. "Sorry, what did you just say?"

"400 Baht," the man's brow furrowed.

"I'll pay you 200 Baht to Khao San Road and that's it." A weight from deep inside Sarah's torso started to stir then lift. Was this excitement rousing? Was this man some sort of guru psychic? He had more to say and Sarah knew it, but could she bear to listen?

The man smiled a broad gummy grin and shook his head. "Oh no Missy, you pay 350 Baht please?"

"250?" Sarah sat back and looked into the Thai man's big brown eyes, hoping for just a trace of his obvious happiness to be transferred over to her. Squinting behind her brown-tinted sunglasses she gave him a closed smirk, her best effort at a smile.

"Ahhh," he paused a moment still staring at her face then, as though seeing he had hit the limit, "Okay den Missy, 250 Baht I take you to Khao San Road, Lek Guest House." Still staring, his smile dropped, "You sure you wanna go Lek Guest House?"

Panicking Sarah asked, "Why? What's wrong with Lek Guest House?"

"It on Khao San Road … noise too much." Cupping his hands over his ears the elderly Thai taxi driver, who appeared to have only one tooth in his mouth, shook his head and muttered, "Misses no sleeping at Lek Guest House."

For the first time in a very long time Sarah laughed. She could not believe such an ancient looking man was working, let alone could hear anything, she presumed he would be half deaf at least because he looked half dead, his beautiful brown eyes were the only sign of sparkling life.

Sarah knew jetlag would kick in shortly, so sleep would have its way with her, whatever the noise and when awake she needed any distraction to stop her from drowning in her own melancholy thoughts. She was here to see

Thailand, Bangkok – Venice of the East, the exotic city that never sleeps. If music drummed all night long, she'd be there not missing a single beat.

Smiling a big and beautiful white smile she said, "Thank you, Mister...?"

"Niran-Atid," he informed her.

Sarah clocked the photo identification attached to the dashboard, an artificial blue lotus flower hung from the rear view mirror. "Mister Niran-Atid – but I'm sure Lek Guest House will be perfect."

Without another word Niran-Atid pulled away from the curb. It wasn't long before they hit the Bangkok onslaught of traffic.

"What was it you were saying a moment ago, Mister Niran-Atid, about my pain causing me confusion?" Sarah tried to make eye contact with him in the mirror, but he stared on at the road in silence. "Mister Niran-Atid," Sarah said a little louder, thinking he had not heard her.

"Nothing more healing than silence," he replied.

It was a slow 25km drive from the airport into the city. The land was vast and flat, the traffic horrendous. After over an hour of listening to nothing but the constant chainsaw drone of hundreds of tuk-tuks outside, Sarah plucked a map out of the seat pocket in front of her and stared at Bangkok's labyrinth of routes.

"Keep it," said Niran-Atid spying her in his mirror. "You get to any part of city with that map. It complicated and you go slowly on road. Eight million Thai live in Bangkok and we all drive at same time it seem." He waved at the heavy traffic sizzling outside the window. "Use boats; they quiet and cheaper. Or maybe you try walk some place, but be careful ha? Distances further than they look on map. It hot out there and air not good." Niran-

Atid put his hand over his mouth as though to sift his breath.

Spiked high-rise buildings of concrete and glass began to appear. The car nudged its way under the shadows of the skyscrapers where, beneath the thick clouds of pollution, there was a heady mix of chaos and refinement. Frenetic markets next to hushed golden temples, dispiriting zombie-like sex shows, beside almsgiving ceremonies. It was a wonder to see. There was so much colour and contrast.

"You take refuge from your pain in Bangkok, Miss Sarah?" Niran-Atid said breaking the awe-filled silence.

So it was real; she had not misheard, nor was she still dreaming. Just her luck to land a psychic taxi driver! "What do you know of my pain, Mister Niran-Atid?"

Smiling at Sarah in the mirror, Niran-Atid winked. She smiled back. "There is no place in the world that I can take refuge from my pain."

"You are Sarah?"

"Yes, but how do you know that?"

"Sarah is name for a princess, ha."

"Yeah, so they say," Sarah grimaced at the meaning of her name. "But I'm no princess and my life's no fairytale."

"Every life is a story. A story be a fairytale and every fairytale have conflict and pain, and every princess in pain must seek refuge or ending not so happy. Dis Khao San Road, Missy," Niran-Atid announced with barely a pause.

He pulled the car into a heaving and vibrant street lined with colourful ethnic stalls. Guest houses were crammed between dodgy-looking travel agents and Sarah could see between the stalls that it was speckled with tattooists, tailors, massage parlours, hair-braiders, restaurants, pubs and clubs. There was nothing unassuming about Khao San road. The sign pollution was phenomenal, a sea of tat and bootleg tags spilling into the street, which was full of travellers from every ethnic walk of life.

"Goodness … it's so …" Sarah stammered.

"It backpacker world, Miss Sarah." Niran-Atid drove slowly. Sarah's face was pressed to the window, her eyes and ears absorbing the sounds and sights, though her heart was still numb.

"I told you it noisy," Niran-Atid went on.

"It's so colourful; slightly dingy looking," Sarah said, "but it's only a short walk from all the major sights," she reminded herself.

"You pursue your past." It was not a question, it was a statement. Before Sarah could respond, Niran-Atid stopped the car outside a mustard and red building. "Dis … Lek Guest House." He pulled up the hand-brake hard. Sarah took in the building outside. Next door was a seedy-looking bar called 'Silk', white plastic tables and chairs pouring onto the pavement, a few early dreadlock-ridden punters were propping up the bar.

Niran-Atid turned to look at his passenger in the backseat. "You cannot live in shadow of the past. We must all move on. I'm a Buddhist, Miss Sarah, and Buddhists believe we should live the life of harmlessness. Take refuge, Missy … I mean a place of safety. I feel you must protect yourself, for you no go the way of harmlessness. You seek the past and this bring you harm."

Sarah looked from Niran-Atid's glistening and pleading brown eyes to the bedlam outside the car. She understood completely what the ancient Thai Buddhist was saying even though she could not believe he was saying it. She had seen the same look in her mother's eyes before she left

England. A wild bear deep inside Sarah had taken over. When Archie died, part of her had gone with him, she closed off to everyone and yet through closing off and living in her thoughts she felt whole and stronger. She needed to be alone. The path she was on had taken a hairpin bend and the rebel inside her had put her on a perilous self-destructive path. When the news of Archie's death had broken, she had initially felt suicidal, but something deeper had pushed her back and forced her to keep her feet on the ground and air in her lungs. It was her dreams more than anything that kept her alive, the visions of Archie and the gut feeling he was still out there somewhere, searching for her too. She knew it was dangerous to live in her dreams and they frightened her no end, but if he was out there, she had to find him no matter how dangerous the road was.

"And what does the name Niran-Atid mean?" Blinking back tears, Sarah turned to face her driver.

"Eternal Sun," Niran-Atid said.

A flicker of a smile crossed Sarah's face. "It's beautiful." She closed her eyes; a single plump tear fell onto her lap. "No more tears," she said more to herself than to Niran-Atid. "I promised myself, no more tears." Rummaging in her purse for local currency, she handed Niran-Atid 300 Baht. "Keep the change."

"Take refuge," he said, pocketing the money. "Accept what is, Miss Sarah."

She couldn't do this. Acceptance was not an option. It would never be an option. Her mind shot away from any refuge as she grabbed her bag. She supposed he meant well, but the whole weird experience was unnerving. "Thanks," she muttered getting out of the car.

The intense heat hit her again, she felt submerged in hot water. The taxi's air-conditioning had really cooled her. The noise was out of this world. There were so many different languages from so many different voices. People meandered past, sightseeing and shopping, whilst the Thais called out their wares of vivid silks, exquisite handicrafts and counterfeit watches.

"Miss Sarah," Niran-Atid shouted over the noise. Sarah turned back to the car. The taxi driver had wound down the window and leaning over the passenger seat, was passing her a business card. Sarah took it automatically but didn't look at it. "Treat your body with the respect it deserves, ha – quit smoking – there's enough pollution in Bangkok to destroy your lungs. Walking intoxicated around the 'City of Angels' you might just meet one or become one. Take care." He pulled away.

Left alone on the road Sarah looked down at the card in her hand. Eternal Sun Refuge was printed in English and, she presumed, Thai underneath and then a phone number. Taking in a deep breath Sarah shoved it deep into the pocket of her dungarees.

"No more tears," Sarah whispered, making her way up a dingy soi running off Khau San Road to the entrance of Lek Guest House.

CHAPTER FOUR

AUGUST 2003
THE TOIL OF THE MOON

Sarah lay on the bed of her whitewashed room, her eyes closed, balcony doors overlooking the madness of Khao San Road wide open and the ceiling fan brushing a warm breeze over her near naked body. The no option cold shower had washed away the flight and the taxi ride. Commotion from the street below penetrated the room and somewhere in the house a stereo throbbed Beyonce and Jay Z's, Crazy in Love.

Lek Guest House lived up to its promise of being clean and at 250 Baht a night it was the right end of Sarah's budget. The people downstairs who ran the place barely spoke a word of English, but they were very accommodating, with welcoming smiles, mystifying stares and a helpful list of local amenities. However, Niran-Atid had been dead right about the noise factor, the walls were thinner than tissue-paper. Only with sleeping pills, jetlag or a drug-induced coma could anyone sleep in such a place. Sarah's eyes stung with tiredness, it was as though red hot needles were being pierced into the corners of each of them. They did not want to stay open and when she finally gave in and allowed them to close they burned right through to the back of her head. She knew sleep was coming, despite the noise, it would somehow find her again. She knew she would have to lie back and embrace it. She waited a while, felt her consciousness dip and as she had supposed, sleep found her quickly.

It was nearly six o'clock in the evening when Sarah woke. It was dusk outside. She was hot and clammy; mosquitoes swarmed her head, the unbroken racket continued to pierce through the walls and open balcony doors. Swiping at her head at the malicious bugs, Sarah jumped to her feet in irritation and slammed the doors shut. She hated mosquitoes, she always flared up and had to take antihistamines if she got bitten and she hadn't got any on her. Frantically delving in her backpack, she began to throw her neatly packed belongings across the bed. Realising what she wanted was already out, she stretched for the distressed wooden chair at the end of her bed and emptied out the contents of her wash-bag. Retrieving the insect repellent she ripped off the lid and frantically began to squirt the air around her.

"Die, you buggers – you've had your fill here." She moved onto squirting her body, nearly intoxicating herself with the nauseating solution. Next, she viciously began to squash any lingering mosquito, watching the blood splatter white walls. "I don't want Dingy Fever thanks – I've just got here."

Recovering from the massacre, Sarah quickly began to tidy away stray clothes she had pulled out whilst searching for the repellent. Beneath a sarong she found an aged cream envelope still sealed with an unread letter inside.

"Archie's letter," Sarah muttered to herself, as she ran her hand across the air above the seal, almost afraid to touch it. Was now the time to read it? Did she have the strength to read it, more to the point? She had to read it at some time. Archie had been dead a month, so she was entitled to. That was the deal. Only in the event of his death was she to read it, he had said when he gave it to her seven years ago.

Just do it. Sarah's mind implored. Taking a deep breath, filling her lungs, fighting back tears, she tore open the seal, her eyes widening when she saw the date. He must have carried this letter around with him for four years before he gave it to her.

23rd June 1992

Dear Sarah,

I can't believe at fourteen I'm writing you this letter! I hope you stuck to your part of the deal and are reading it after 20th July 2003. You'll probably be twenty-five now. You will be – but I won't.

I haven't gone loopy! What I'm about to tell you may come as a bit of a shock. Try to understand. It's about me - and you in a way - in fact it's about us. We've talked about weird stuff in the past, I know, but this may just blow your mind. Sit down.

Do you remember, at Nanny's house this Easter, (1992 - eleven years ago now, for you) when we played Dead Game? Well something happened. Something I've never told anyone. I think I'm going to die, Sarah. That is, I'm going to die young. I'm not afraid and I don't know how it will happen. I met someone who told me. I'm going to die on 20th July 2003! I know... our birthday. You probably think I'm daft to take any notice of a stranger I met on the mountain, but honest, he was creepy and there was something about him made me believe him.

I want to tell you so much, but I know this isn't what you want to hear, especially when you're tucked away in that private boarding school you detest, so that's why I am writing instead – a letter for your future, so you'll know I am still out there somewhere. Hey - maybe I might even be able to fly. I've always wanted to fly.

Have you ever wondered where we've come from? Why we're here?

There's one more thing and it's important. One day, after I've gone, I need you to tell my story? I'll help you. God, I feel like I'm giving up on life just writing this. I feel like I'm breaking a deal, but at the same time as sealing my fate, I feel oddly like a new journey will begin. You are the one who must narrate my journey, Sarah. It's a massive and bizarre ask I know, but you must remember you'll never be alone. I'll be with you every breath of the way.

Love Archie

PS. How I know all this doesn't matter either, you'll find out soon enough.

Sarah could barely see by the time she got to the final line. "Narrate my journey?" she repeated in a hoarse whisper. "Still out there somewhere?" Sarah's mind reeled. "I know you are, Archie, and I'm trying to find you, but what do you mean; what journey?"

The letter in front of her, written in Archie's adolescent handwriting, confirmed everything she felt inside. She wasn't dwelling in her past, clinging to memories. How she felt was real, he wasn't dead. She was sure of it.

Sarah's thoughts turned abruptly to England. Home; she would have to get up, find a payphone to call her parents and let them know she was safe, they would be worried. A pang of homesickness struck her. Sarah's only delight at that very moment was that her sleep had been dreamless. God knows she had needed a decent sleep and yet, thinking about it, she somehow missed it. She couldn't remember the last time she'd not dreamt. To be without her nightmare made her delight turn to panic. It had become her norm. To be without it meant things were changing. Was she moving on? Terror flared inside her stomach again and loss burned at the hole in her chest. She couldn't be without her nightly reminders of Archie. Sitting, hugging her knees, on a bare mattress in that Thai guest house, high on jungle-strength mosquito repellent, clasping Archie's crumpled note, lost once again in nostalgia, Sarah's floodgates burst. And in a brief moment of weakness she allowed herself to pine, the heat and noise pressing her misery.

"No … no more … come on girl," Sarah scorned herself.

Throwing on a white, mini smock dress, threading her broken St Christopher onto a single piece of cotton from her travel sewing kit and securing it around her neck, she grabbed her room key and wallet and left her room quickly, slamming the door behind her. She would only wallow in self pity if she stayed alone. It would get her nowhere. She had to get out. Storming the corridors, down the stairs and out onto the street she charged like a bull. Catching sight of her reflection in a shop window she saw her face clear of makeup, her eyes shining like sapphires enhanced only by a harsh red rim. Her mousey hair had dried as she had slept and had taken on a crimped, cavewoman style. Her cheeks were flushed and her forehead shone with sweat as she blew into the bar next door.

"Large gin and tonic please," Sarah said to the barwoman.

"Welcome to Silk Bar, Missy. You here first time?" The local woman didn't wait for Sarah to reply. She seemed friendly and her manner was customary Thai, but something startled Sarah at how quickly the foreign woman changed the subject. There was a smirk creeping up at the corner of her mouth and a flash of wilfulness trying to hide behind dark lashes. "You wanna try Thai special drinky missy? It Sang Tip – it very good – cheapa cheapa."

"I'll give it a try," Sarah agreed, her eyes slightly narrowed. She was weary but still willing to try anything with a kick, desperate to kill off her emotions, her head still full of Archie's crazy letter.

"Me Chanthira, dis my Silk Bar." The bartender reached forward placing two drinks, light on ice and coke and shimmering with spirit, on the bar mats in front of her. "It happy hour; two for one. You first punter tonight, it on house missy. Welcome to Thailand." Chanthira looked past Sarah to the open front and empty seats outside. "It get busy later. What your name?" Chanthira looked back to Sarah, her Oriental, almost black eyes glinting.

"Thank you, Chanthira," Sarah said with a genuine smile. "I'm Antoinette, pleased to meet you." Sarah stretched out her hand. She knew the likelihood of meeting this woman again was minimal and she had always loved the name Antoinette, it was a bit of harmless fun she liked to have, occasionally changing her name and re-inventing herself and today she didn't want to be Sarah. Chanthira, who was busying herself with wiping down the bar, suddenly looked at Sarah's hand in disgust, raised an eyebrow and huffed, a smirk, baring small brown stubs for teeth. She did not take Sarah's hand.

"Where you stay? I call you Annie, ok?" Chanthira said Sarah's new name with such distaste it made Sarah well up as she nodded approval. "You stay Khao San Road?" Chanthira asked a smirk still across her face. Withdrawing her hand, Sarah frowned. She had not expected such a beautiful face to hide such dreadful teeth and persona.

"Yeah, just ..." Sarah mustered, unsure she wanted the conversation to continue.

"You fly in today, Annie?" Chanthira interrupted, again haughtily.

"This morning," Sarah replied, taking a small sip of one of her drinks. Her eyes watered but her gaze never left Chanthira's face; she was so alluring. Wincing as the mystery alcohol burned down her throat, Sarah thought, 'It's not bad – it'll certainly do the job.' Inexplicably magnetised by Chanthira's eyes, curious to catch another glimpse of those tombstone teeth, Sarah smiled a wry smile and tried to turn herself away, but she couldn't seem to break the gaze, it was as though she was hypnotised.

Another Western customer joined them at the bar, Chanthira instinctively turned to serve him, cutting the thread that was running between her and Sarah, who immediately took it as her cue to push away from the main bar. Troubled slightly, with her two double Sang Tip and Coke's she quietly sat at the furthest table, out on the pavement, almost on the street.

She felt as if she was sat in the heart of a ghetto. There was so much hustle and bustle. People were pushing around her table to pass by, whilst she sat and watched. She had never before seen a busier street. It was an odd position to be in, having every nationality in the world shuffling around her and yet she felt totally alienated and alone. She barely even noticed when a young man sat down and joined her at the table amongst all the kafuffle.

"Hi," said the man.

Sarah was unaware that someone had spoken to her through the noise. It was the hand waving in her face that grabbed her attention.

"I'm Joe, how are you?" The man nearly shouted.

Sarah just stared at him, wide eyed, whilst he shook her hand, a confused look spreading across her face. What was going on here? Since she had woken up from her jetlag nap everything, especially the last few moments, felt incredibly surreal. It all seemed familiar, like she had met this man and Chanthira before, and yet she knew she had never met either person. Joe's hair and face were dark, he had striking looks, with piercing blue eyes; very unusual, yet oddly handsome. She would have remembered this face. It was as though she were stuck in a rotating moment of déjà vu but didn't have a clue about any of it. Was she losing the plot? Had she gone crazy? Maybe Niran-Atid was right, she needed to seek some sort of refuge.

Somebody bumped past her chair knocking her out of her train of thought. Looking up she saw that the man, Joe, still sat in front of her, waiting for some sort of response. "Hi," Sarah stammered. "I'm ok, thanks."

"It's manic here tonight and it's going to get busier," Joe shouted. "You up for a good night?" He looked fleetingly down at the two drinks sitting in front of Sarah. "Full moon party," he said, moving his eyes to look up at the smog-ridden night sky. "Always a party."

Sarah didn't respond. She just focused on trying to understand what this toff was saying. His plummy accent combined with the music pumping out from the bar behind made it difficult to hear. His accent and character seemed so out of place here.

"In fact," he grinned, "full moon, half moon, quarter moon – there's always a party on Khao San Road."

"What do they do when there's no moon?" Sarah asked. She didn't know where the question came from and Joe just looked at her and frowned. "You know," she added, "when the moon's not there." An insecure feeling crept into Sarah's stomach as she took in this stranger.

"Oh, I know what you mean," Joe said. "When there's no moon," he leaned in towards Sarah slightly, "that's when we all escape." He winked, leaning back, taking a huge lug of his beer.

"Escape?"

"Yeah, you know, everyone has a night off; we go home," Joe explained. "Isn't that why we all come here? To party, lose ourselves and escape?"

"I suppose," Sarah sighed and smiled, taking two big lugs of her own drink. The taste was harsh but drinkable, she winced on the second, gulping it down hard. "Cheers," she said, raising her glass with a grin, deep dimples pronounced on each cheek, her face flushing as the alcohol swirled into her bloodstream. "Here's to the moon," she raised her glass to the heavens and took another gulp. "And here's to partying in Thailand," another slurp, "and here is to us lovely people." She drained her first drink through the ice, which she then began to crunch on. "Good stuff this Snag Tip."

Joe finished his beer encouragingly. "That's strong stuff, riddled with amphetamines. It's what the locals round here drink, but if you're not used to it, it'll knock you sideways. Go easy." Sarah's pert grin faded as soon as the word amphetamines left Joe's mouth. A pulse at the base of her skull and behind her ears began to throb. She drew in a deep breath, blinked hard and fumbled for a fag.

"I'm fine." She finally said, lighting up, forcing another brilliant smile, as smoke billowed out of her nose. "Hmm, do you want this other one? I think I need a glass of water."

"Sure, I'll get you one." Joe stood up taking Sarah's untouched happy hour bonus with him, leaving her alone at the plastic picnic table. The crowds in the street were growing thicker and she had to keep her elbows tucked in for fear of knocking passersby.

She watched Joe for a moment as he manoeuvred his way around the other tables to the bar. There were still no other customers inside so he wouldn't be long. Turning back to the street she tried to focus. Her head was spinning. Across the road neon colours glowed in the dark as an artist painted a human canvas. Her gaze was then swept away by four Thai lady-boy's, who were larger than life, shouting and singing, garnering stares and kisses from confused and inebriated foreigners. Sarah had been told she'd know a 'lady-boy' when she saw one and indeed it was true. Not wanting to gawp at the spectacle of men dressed as women and not wanting to have any attention of that kind drawn on her, she turned back to the bar where Joe and Chanthira appeared to be deep in conversation, staring directly at Sarah. She clocked them instantly. Her heart skipped a beat at the thought of them talking about her. Chanthira gave a gummy smile, then in a swift and guilty movement the pair turned their heads back to one another. Chanthira passed a glass of water with ice and a cocktail stirrer in it to Joe and the thickset, nigh on stranger headed back towards Sarah, gently stirring her drink.

In a moment of panic Sarah found her feet. She had an unbelievable urge to turn and flee from this man. What had come over her? Such a feeling of distrust, why was she taking a drink from a person she had only just met? She never would have back in London. Yet this feeling had merely emerged because of the way he and the bartender had looked at her. For all she knew they were looking beyond at the scene in the street. She was being paranoid. He was just a friendly backpacker like herself enjoying the Thai life.

Joe was back in a split second; even if she'd wanted to flee there was not a moment to run. It was all in his eyes, they were the colour of the sky on a summer's day, yet sunken into such black sockets they pierced through her, like the sun piercing through a black cloud. They were so intense it startled Sarah.

"I'm tired, must be the jetlag. I should go," Sarah stared at the water, not daring to look him in the eye.

"Your water."

Sarah took it automatically. Not meeting his gaze, she too began to stir the ice into the water.

"Hey, I didn't catch your name," he said.

"Annie," Sarah mustered, forced to look into his face.

"Cheers then, er, Annie," Joe raised the Sang Tip and Coke in his hand then clanked Sarah's glass of water. "You'll feel better once you've got some water in you."

Sarah looked into the drink, it seemed slightly murky, or was that her eyes and the bright lights bouncing off the ice? She was desperately thirsty and another sip of that Sang Tip would literally tip her over the edge. She needed water. She moved the glass to her lips and made a point of sniffing it before her mouth gave into its desire to quench her thirst.

CHAPTER FIVE

AUGUST 2003
TRUST YOUR INSTINCTS YOUR MISTAKES
MAY COST YOU DEAR

"Is she out?" Sarah heard a harsh Thai voice snap.

"She's in Alpha, she ain't goin' anywhere."

The toff accent was gone, but Sarah was sure the second voice belonged to the man, Joe. She felt a hand wandering over her body, stroking firmly across her chest, up her neck to her cheek and then an eyelid was lifted and smoothed shut again.

"See ... gone," he said, sniggering.

Barely able to feel her body, it felt so heavy, Sarah attempted to move, but nothing would respond. Struggling, she tried to open her eyes to get her bearings, but they felt as if taped down. All she could see behind her eyelids was black. It was a suffocating feeling being covered in darkness with no way out, trapped. She cursed and loathed the dark so much that even had she been able to she would not have reached out into it.

A door somewhere behind her opened, spirited voices briefly filtered in then the door shut with a bang. Sarah was left alone in silence. Concentrating, she tried hard to remember how she had got into this room and in the state she was in. It was pointless; she couldn't remember a thing, except drinking that water. She had known at the time she was a fool for drinking it, but she had been so very thirsty. Her instincts had told her; why hadn't her head listened? Her suspicions should have been enough to stop her.

As though a switch had been flicked, a shrill ringing pierced her ears, slicing the silence like a knife. Her skin prickled with goose-bumps. The noise faded slightly then a voice, sweeter than music and the very essence of perfection, washed through her head. "Wriggle your fingers, Sarah."

Sarah would have jumped could she have moved. The background ringing turned to a hum, like a fridge-freezer buzzing in the distance. The voice had sounded so close and so real but she must have imagined it. It spoke again. "Focus on your hands, Sarah, wiggle your fingers slowly, it'll help you to come round." The sassy voice was so pronounced it felt part of her.

"Who's there? I can't move," Sarah said, panic overwhelming her. "I can think and hear, but I can't see." Sarah's mind screamed.

"Easy; stay calm," the little voice comforted. "The more you panic the stronger their hold."

"Who are you?" asked Sarah, her eyes still glued shut, yet frantically flickering.

"Your guardian angel it seems," giggled the voice. "Come on now, wiggle those fingers, we've got to get you to come round and get you out of here."

Sarah hadn't the strength to lift one finger, her body felt numb like it didn't exist. Sleep was all she could think of, she was fighting it every second. Maybe this was all a dream and she had already escaped into sleep. Would it all be fixed when she woke?

"I'm so tired ..." Sarah's mind began to swim deeper.

"Sarah, you cannot sleep. You have to try to wake up and get out of here. You're in a room just behind the bar.

All you need to do is stroll out of that door behind you and you're out."

"How? I can't move," Sarah asked. This little voice sounded so familiar. "Do I know you? What's your name?" Sarah asked. Was she already out cold and this voice was in fact a dream poisoning her sleep?

"Sarah," came the whispered reply.

"What? No that's my name." If she was asleep, it was a very baffling dream.

"No, Sarah, I'm you – this is your higher self talking, now wiggle those fingers girl. They'll be back in here any minute."

"I don't understand, how can you converse with me like this? Am I asleep?"

"No, you're not sleeping. It doesn't matter now, if it helps call me Fee. Just wake up and get that heavy, dense body moving."

Sarah's dry, bee-stung lips slowly pressed together. A finger twitched and beneath closed lids her eyes darted. "You're drunk and sedated, it's not going to be easy – come on ... you're running out of time. You're sitting on a chair; feel it."

Concentrating, Sarah felt the hardness of a chair beneath her buttocks. "Good, now lean to one side, roll off the seat," said the voice.

The door flew open and through it came the laughter of punters.

"Oh no you don't!" He was back.

As Sarah's body leant over and began to fall, tough arms wrapped around her and forcefully placed her back on the chair.

"Chanthira," Joe yelled.

"Wha..?" came the reply from beyond the door.

"I'm going upstairs." Joe shouted.

The door of the bar flew open again. "Why?"

"She needs to lie down." An arm remained on Sarah's shoulder holding her firmly on the chair.

"So lay her out on the floor there. Is she waking up?" Chanthira asked.

"Na, but I'll watch her for a while."

"Give her another shot," the Thai's voice sneered.

"She don't need it – we don't wanna kill 'er."

The door slammed and Sarah was slumped onto the ground. It was hard and cool, the fact that she could feel the ground beneath her, gave her hope that the drugs were wearing off. A chair scraped across the floor and it creaked as Joe sat down on it.

"Do not fear him, Sarah," the inner voice whispered.

'He obviously warrants my fear?' Sarah thought, snapping at the voice in her head.

"The more you fear him, the more he has you in his power. Have faith in yourself - have faith in me."

'But I am you. I'm going nuts. I'm talking to myself.'

"You'll block me completely if your fear of him heightens, then where will you be? You'll be alone. Wait a while, lie still, he'll get bored and the drug will wear off."

'Who are they? Why have they drugged me?'

"Who do you think? You must start trusting those gut feelings."

'I do feel like I know them though – I thought that earlier, out there, but how can I? I don't know anyone in Thailand.'

"Those gut feelings are generally based on facts you've filed away in your subconscious."

'You're saying I know these people?'

"You'll never free yourself from the past; your past is part of you, just as your limbs are part of your body. What you should know about your past is that whatever happened, it has all happened to bring you to this very moment. And this is the moment you can choose to make everything different."

Sarah focused hard on her fingers, willing all the blood in her body to rush to them and help them to move; slowly but surely it worked and she was able to clench a fist.

"No chance little lady," Joe's voice drowned out her concentration. Sarah suddenly felt her lips become wet, forcibly parted by rough fingers, liquid squirted into her mouth, her nose pinched. Breathing didn't seem to be an option here, she held her breath and made a spluttering gulp, praying it was enough for Joe to let go. He did. "Just sleep now, it'll be easier in the long run if you're asleep."

It seemed like hours passed, as Sarah lay on the cold stone floor. The combined smell of stale cigarette butts and ale burning her nostrils, she listened to a distant dripping tap and the slow creaking of Joe's chair as he loomed over her. She dared not move. She was chilled to the core, terrified inside. What had he meant, 'It'll be easier in the long run if you're asleep?' What would be easier? The voice in her head had stopped at least. The only thing preventing her from passing out with exhaustion was fear. She knew Joe's feet were only inches away from her head, she could sense them. There were so many questions her jumbled mind was trying to unscramble, but there was no logic, she didn't understand any of it. Did these people have a vendetta against her or had she merely been picked at random? There was no way they could know her, or think she had any amount of money worth taking. If it had been money surely they would have just taken it there and then. No, this was not about money. Was it a set up? What were they going to do with her? The answer to that question didn't bear thinking about, for Sarah knew all too well from horrific news stories broadcast, what was possible.

The door flung open again. Sarah tried hard to lie still, the drugs were wearing off.

"It's dead in there, let's do the transition now and get it over with. Take her back to my place." Chanthira's voice sounded different, crosser and resolute. Joe did as he was told immediately. His chair scraped back. A coarse material was draped over Sarah and wrapped tightly round her. It made her itch, the drugs were definitely wearing off, she could feel her body again, yet she didn't move a muscle. She was then flung over Joe's shoulder and felt herself being carried, heard a door opening. It must lead straight out into the street. His feet squelched on wet ground. It felt cooler, like the humidity had been dampened with rain. In seconds she was thrown down into the back of a car.

"I lock up here; meet you in ten minute, ok?" Chanthira snapped.

"Be quick won't ya, I don't like waitin'," Joe hissed back.

The ignition turned and an ancient engine spluttered into life. The car rolled forward, slowly at first. Sarah could hear multitudes of jolly accents murmuring behind the closed windows of the car. Windscreen wipers squeaked. Moments later the voices faded and the car began to speed up. They must have left Khao San Road.

"Get out ... get out ... get out now, Sarah!" An angst voice rang in Sarah's ear. Her body seemed to be recuperating quickly, the numbness was wearing off considerably but she knew if she tried to make any great shift to escape, it would be in vain.

"Stop being defeatist, Sarah," the voice again. "He's driving. He'll have to stop the car to hinder your getaway. You have to get out of this car now."

'Then what?" Sarah thought. 'Stumble down the road away from him, paralytic? I can't out run him.'

"You'll know what to do, Sarah, just please get out of this car. We do not want to go where he's taking us. I will not be trapped again." Sarah knew that voice. It was the voice she used when she begged; she had used it many a time in her life, pleading for one thing or another. "There's no time to think about failure."

'We? What's this we business?' Sarah asked.

"Stop questioning me and just get out."

'Do you know where he's taking me? Do you?' Sarah could feel her heart starting to pump faster, an adrenalin surge rising. 'Fee? Where is he taking me?'

"The Moon's fury is raging," Fee's voice stuttered. "He's taking us back ... back to a world where it is always night, always dark, you loathe the dark."

'Us? Moon's fury? What are you talking about?'

"You need to move, Sarah, and fast," Fee insisted. "Now is not the time for questions."

Joe braked hard, grinded the gears, he hit the steering wheel and shuffled in his seat.

'Tell me what you are talking about?' Sarah insisted, convinced she was going crazy, talking in thought to a voice in her head. Was she schizophrenic?

"There's no time. I'll explain later, please, for once in your life, just listen to someone, get OUT of the car."

Sarah's awareness had totally returned now, yet she had to resist the urge to budge until she made her ultimate move. Although she was fully conscious the voice still talked on. She wasn't dreaming. As unlikely as it seemed, this was really happening. Or was it?

"Get out of the car."

It was no good discussing this; she knew she had to move. The car had slowed right down and was nudging forward every now and then; traffic. Sarah fluttered her eyes open, she squinted at first, watching the man in the driver's seat in front of her. His thick, tanned arm rested on the gear stick. He stared ahead out of the windscreen. Sarah rested her eyes again.

"Do it!" the voice persisted.

Sarah looked across to the door handle just above her head. She could reach it easily. She clocked the silver button lock, it was open. Would her body be able to move fast enough though, once she'd managed to open the door?

"There's only one way to find out," Fee said.

'I can't,' a wave of nausea rushed through her. 'I don't want to, I want to sleep; this is just a bad dream. I'm jetlagged and drunk. I'll wake up in my room in a minute.'

"Sarah, you're awake and this is all very real – just think what might happen if you close your eyes to it."

Another wave of nausea struck. Sarah felt she may vomit. She forced herself to hold back the urge to gag.

"Now, Sarah."

In one swift movement, Sarah heaved herself to sitting, flicked open the door handle and threw herself out of the moving car. She army rolled three times; her cousin, Archie had once shown her how to fall without hurting herself. A concrete wall impeded her fall. She heard the brakes screech, bringing the car to a sudden halt. A door slammed.

"Get up!" Fee ordered.

On all fours Sarah, took in her surroundings. She had hit her forehead badly, a trickle of blood seeped down her bruised cheek. The road was floodlit. Sarah's eyes blinked hard trying to focus. The traffic was, as ever in Bangkok, heavy. There were huge concrete walls on either side of the road; giant cables hung high above her in the air. She was on a bridge, a suspension bridge.

'You'll know what to do ..." Fee's panic-stricken voice rang in her ears.

Joe stormed towards her across the tarmac, he didn't speak, his arms outstretched ready to grab. Getting onto her feet, Sarah wobbled backwards. Her eyes bulging as this giant beast of a man lunged at her. Without a moment's hesitation, for there was no time to think, Sarah threw herself over the bridge wall. It seemed, at that time, the most logical and sensible escape route, but what with the adrenalin rush and the brief spectacular view of Bangkok at night, the lights bouncing off the river below, in slow motion she realised the error of her reality. The world went momentarily black as she closed her eyes. Legs flailing, her arm was caught before she could descend. She jolted, looked up into Joe's eyes and screamed.

"What are you doing?" Joe yelled down at her. "This is Phra Pin Klao Bridge, one of the busiest and highest bridges in Bangkok. Don't do this. Give me your other hand."

Sarah shrieked, her cry of panic piercing through the air, she automatically reached for Joe's free hand.

"Oh dear God, help me," Sarah wailed. Unable to resist looking down she glimpsed a floating market on the river below, probably selling silks and Thai handicrafts, things that Sarah had longed to see. The caged animals cringing among the pots and pans were not top of her sightseeing list, but she would have given anything to be down there with them now. The Grand Palace was lit up in the distance. Would she miss it all?

'Let go of him Sarah,' Fee whispered in her head.

'Are you mad? What was I thinking to jump over that wall, have you seen the drop? I'll be killed,' Sarah's mind hissed back.

Joe began to drag her back up the wall.

"The wretchedness of where he'll take you will be worse by tenfold. Trust me Sarah. Trust yourself."

Sarah stared up into Joe's sharp blue eyes. Bystanders had gathered to gawp. Dazed, her face was bleeding and flushed, there was a fleeting pause, where everything felt strangely familiar. She knew those eyes, they had watched her before, they were lined with retribution, there was no peace hiding in the corners. She didn't know how she knew them but she did.

"Hold on to me Sarah and listen. Get over this wall and I'll explain everything. You're going to be fine, I'm not going to hurt you," Joe bellowed down at her, his hands slowly pulling her back up, inch by inch moving up her arms towards her shoulders.

'He called me Sarah?' Sarah whispered to herself. 'He should have called me Annie. He knows me!' her mind reeled.

"Don't listen to him, just let go, Sarah, listen to me. This man is a part of your past from long ago. It won't make sense to you now. Trust me. He has more than a grudge against you. You humiliated him – he wants vengeance."

Sarah's heart was in her mouth as her feet tried desperately to scramble back up the wall, her tortured gaze never leaving the man whose hands held her. The rain had ceased but a humid wind picked up cooling her hot face, the smell of the stagnant water wafted from below, Joe's black hair blew wildly around his head. Sarah's hair blew away from her neck and face revealing the St Christopher pendant hanging loosely around her throat from a single thread of white cotton.

'What are you talking about; he's part of my past?' Sarah thought, her fingernails now gripping into Joe's arms in desperation. His hands were nearly to her armpits now, ready to hoist her back. "How do you know my name," Sarah bellowed at him.

"Unseen forces are at work here, Sarah," Fee whispered through the wind. "He is a liar, a danger ... all that is bad. I will help you."

It wasn't what Fee had said; it was how she said it that instigated Sarah to allow her hands to slowly push away from Joe. It was an eerie and horrifying moment. Her instincts were split, one half telling her to get back over the wall and fight for her life, whilst the other half told her to get as far away from this man as possible and drop.

"No! Don't slip, Sarah, hold on to me." Joe grappled to get a grip of her and realising he was losing he snatched at her neck, breaking the one strand of cotton holding Archie's St Christopher in place. He grasped the pendant in his hand.

But it was too late. She fell.

CHAPTER SIX

AUGUST 2003
YIELDING TO AN ANCIENT TIME

The gut churning sensation of falling from that height was irrepressible. Her terrified scream ceased abruptly, her breath taken from her as she dropped. Being way out of control, her stomach left high up where her fall began, it was like one of those terrifying nightmares of falling, where your physical body is trying to shock your dreaming mind into being awake. There was no point in trying to fight it and yet it was impossible not to at least try to oppose it. She chopped though the air, twisting and rolling, the wind thrusting her like a dead leaf in gale-force wind. Her mind did not think to wonder where and when she would hit the water. Instead her thoughts pushed past that reality and searched for any glimmer of light on the purple, smog-ridden horizon. She found one. The sun was rising.

Sarah had half expected to pass-out whilst falling; or at least black out when she hit the river, especially from that height. It did not happen: Chao Phraya River, which breaks up Bangkok City's landscape with its network of canals creeping off the main backbone of water, enfolded Sarah into its body. She didn't smack the water as she had expected, instead, the water was bath-warm, like a heavy wet blanket being wrapped around her. It wasn't shocking or painful in any way. The only fright was the speed at which she was whisked away downriver. She didn't have chance to hit the river bed, the current was so powerful there was no likelihood of stopping. Her dress caught and ripped on jagged boulders beneath her and was gradually tearing from her body. She did not surface.

One question repeated over and over again in Sarah's mind, like a scratched record, as she coiled with the torrents. 'What's my sacrifice for?" For she now believed, with there being no pain, that she was either unconscious or soon to be dead. The river's current seemed to speed up each time she reiterated her question, until it transformed into a rollercoaster, a nightmare. Faster and faster she was swept downstream. She had no control, her arms flailed above her head helplessly and her white smock dress, ripped beyond repair, washed away. Her head, already bleeding, smacked hard against a boulder, bruising and gashing open another wound. She gulped in river water, tried to scream when her hair caught on anchored debris and ripped from her scalp. She was sure she was drowning and her thoughts would cease at any moment.

Then, more abruptly than the impact itself, Sarah hit a rift, where the water flow ended and she was left floating and fizzing like a lost bubble, and like most bubbles she naturally rose up to the surface. It was a long way up, her head was spinning but she soon found she had strength to swim up to meet it. The last shreds of her clothes disintegrated, the water was cool against her skin and with every stroke she became increasingly aware that she was naked. Breaking through the water, she gasped a huge breath of air. She didn't care that she had no clothes, she was awake and alive.

Looking around she was dumbfounded. She must have been washed some way; the city seemed to have vanished completely. There were no skyscrapers or river-markets, no hustle and bustle on the riverbanks or canoes transporting people from one area to another. There was nothing. It was deathly quiet. The water she had broken through didn't even ripple: it was like a mill pond, with not a single swell; it was spine-chillingly sinister. Feeling breathless and uneasy, too distracted to feel pain, Sarah's gaze darted about from one side of the river to the other. There was nothing except dense foliage on both sides. The air felt cooler than before, nowhere near as humid. Maybe it was because she was wet. The sky was not purple any more either, it was bright crimson. The sun was peeping over the horizon. Where was the smog? Bangkok was renowned for its hazy atmosphere. Here, the air was flawless, it tasted deliciously clean. Everything about this place didn't make sense. It still appeared tropical but the comparison from where she had come from was extraordinary. A sudden rush of cold air overtook her from behind, the croak of a frog breaking the eerie silence. Frantically treading water, Sarah watched as an array of lily flowers of every variety emerged from beneath the water, in seconds this floral display unfurled around her to the density that not a single particle of water could be seen between them. The scent was intoxicating. What she was witnessing, of course, was not at all possible, she must be dreaming. The whole thing was a dream. And yet, bleeding, her head pounding, how could she be dreaming? So she must be dead.

"I'm not afraid, I'm not afraid," she whispered to herself. Suddenly something beneath brushed her leg. Immediately and instinctively she drew her knees up to her chest.

'Oh God, he's followed me,' Sarah thought. "Fee? Are you there?" Sarah shouted out loud. There was no reply. "I'm not afraid," she whispered.

Using only her arms to keep her afloat, her legs floating on the surface, so terrified was she to lower them; Sarah started to pull herself through the lilies, cautiously and quickly aiming for the nearest bank. But the sound of a sudden wave behind her forced her to turn sharply. To her astonishment, Sarah nearly bumped into the biggest lily pad she had ever seen in her life. Its curved edges must have been at least the depth of her arm.

"This is not the Chao Phraya River, Sarah," a new voice rang in her head. "This is the River Styx."

She did not have time to question the voice, for she was abruptly yanked under the water by a firm hand pulling on her foot. Her eyes slammed shut. With no chance to scream, only an array of bubbles floated from her mouth, as the air escaped her. The hand moved up her leg as it pulled. Sarah dared not open her eyes for what she might see. She knew it was not a shark or an octopus, as it was without doubt a hand that had hold of her. The hand moved further up her body to her waist, it was gentle and seemed to almost give her a light shake.

"Look at me," another female voice rang in Sarah's ears. It was not Fee. This voice was more intense and quieter. Hesitantly, Sarah opened her eyes. The disturbed water was dense with particles of silt, but through them she saw a girl, who looked no older than she did. The immediate feature that struck Sarah was the flowing black hair, which was longer than she had ever seen before. Then she looked into the girl's eyes and saw, that although she may be no older, she was infinitely wiser.

"I am Lillian. You must come with me." The girl's lips did not move and yet Sarah heard her voice as clearly as if she had spoken aloud. She let go of Sarah's waist and swam away from her, leaving her in mid-water.

Automatically, Sarah shot to the surface, again gasping for air, eyes bulging with shock.

"That's it ..." she spluttered. "Either I'm dying or I'm already dead, oh God!" Before she could panic any further, she was once again dragged beneath the surface. This time the girl did not let go. She kept a firm hold of Sarah and started to pull her effortlessly through the water. The hand was small, cold and slippery, almost fish-like, but strong.

"Please listen to me. You must not surface. Not here," the girl said.

"What's happening to me? I'm drowning, aren't I?"

"The water is your friend. Don't fight it," Lillian replied. "You are not drowning."

Sarah dare not think or speak. She simply shook her head, her eyes pleading for air. Terrified, she thought she was going to explode if she held her breath any longer.

"Perhaps this is what it's like, when you die. I can't believe this is happening. This isn't real. I need to call my parents. They don't know where I am." The collection of thoughts that went through Sarah's head was ridiculous and intense. "Let go of me, please; I need air. Let go!" Sarah fought against Lillian's firm hand, constantly pushing for the surface. Terror had gripped her, she was not listening to Lillian, she couldn't, what she said didn't make any sense. All she was certain of was that she was being zipped away into a vortex of madness. Her natural instincts forcing her to fight, the hand not letting go, Sarah tried to peel the fingers away. Trembling now, frantic for something stable to cling to, preferably her sanity, she desperately wanted to contain some inner mental balance. "Oh let go. Why won't you let go?"

"The water is my sky," the girl whispered into Sarah's mind, her lips again unmoving.

"You're crazy! Let go of me." With a great heave of strength, Sarah tore herself from Lillian's grasp and shot once more for the surface.

Giant lily pads loomed above; their toxic spines sinking down beneath them greeted Sarah, as she rose upwards. She felt their appalling sting, knew in that instant that she didn't stand a chance against them.

***

"We all go naked into the underworld." The voice was just a whisper but it was crystal clear. A light hand lay across her forehead, stroking her soaking hair back off her face. "Your head will heal well, the wound is clean but your shoulder has been poisoned by my lethal friends above and it has penetrated deep. You'll need to rest with me a while. You're very lucky you only got struck once."

It was the most irritating of sounds, a voice you could only just hear. Sarah found herself straining to listen. The hand continued stroking back her hair. "Drink please," the hand gently lifted Sarah's head, tilted it slightly and poured a sweet juice into her mouth. Sarah automatically swallowed.

What had the voice meant, 'We all go naked into the underworld?' Gently, Sarah's head was laid back down. If the pain in her shoulder had not been so excruciating, her body would have trembled harder with the cold, but the pain forced her to control it. It was like the dead of winter biting at her very core. It was dark where she lay, and damp. Her body was numb. The whispering voice echoed as though they were in a deep hole, it was hypnotic and yet, at the same time that voice was the only thing that kept her conscious and seemed to warm her slightly. She felt drawn to it, like it was a magnet she had to connect with. She could feel the girl's breath on her face and the hand laid on her head was a comfort. She knew they were still by water because she could hear it sloshing gently on rocks nearby.

"You are a defiant child. Why must you always refuse acceptance?" The voice whispered on. "The old way is dead and will never return. You cannot change what is written in the stars." Again, the hand gently lifted Sarah's head and made her drink more of the juice.

Sarah's eyes were open, she knew they were, but everything was black. "I can't see!"

"You should never have come back here. You're trapped now. What are we to do with you?" the whisper sighed.

"Come back where?" Sarah spluttered, her throat throbbing as the liquid slipped down. "The voice in my head told me to jump, I didn't want to. Fee. She said her name was Fee." Her head was laid back down.

"Ah, Felicity ... yes, that was the name you liked so much," the voice whispered. "The poison has blinded you, it is temporary. Your system is flushing it through. It may take a day or so. Don't try to move."

"I'm so cold," Sarah cried.

"I am used to it – let me find you something to cover you. I won't be a moment." The breath and the hand moved away, leaving Sarah shivering and colder than ever.

"Come back, please," Sarah's voice was so small she could barely hear it herself.

"I'm not far," the voice whispered back.

Trying to move and sit up, Sarah felt the wet ground beneath her. "Where am I?"

"You're in the safest place in Transit, with me. I am Lillian, the Keeper of Secrets. I know the destiny of every human soul. Well ... I thought I did." Sarah listened intently, as each word was articulated with perfect lucidity. "Please lie back and keep still."

"Transit?"

"It is the world between yours and the next and you should not be here," Lillian snapped. "You have lived only twice on the Earth-plain and yet in both lives you have managed to challenge your providence."

"I don't understand," Sarah croaked, her neck straining and aching.

Lillian's hand returned to Sarah's forehead and laid her back down fully onto the ground. "You will. You must. But first you must rest. There is a long road ahead of you, Sarah. I cannot stress enough how fit and smart you must be to travel it. You have dared to spin your wheel of fortune for a second time." Lillian draped a light material over Sarah's naked body, which eased her instantly, the shivering subsided and her body began finally to relax. "My records show me that you lost your soulmate, Archie Fletcher. You seek him. So now you must be brought face to face with the irrevocability of your loss."

At the mere mention of Archie's name, Sarah grasped at Lillian in the darkness. "Is he here? Is he in Transit?" She knew her blind eyes were bulging, beseeching.

"Even if he were, Sarah, I cannot allow you to enter Transit," firmly Lillian eased Sarah's grip. "There is only one way out of Transit and that is to cross the bridge to the other side of life. But it is not your time. My records never lie and you have much to live for, believe me. If you enter Transit now you will be gambling your soul. The stakes are high, Sarah. Would you wager one moment with Archie for an eternity in exile?" Lillian asked.

"Yes ... yes I would," Sarah insisted.

"You are angry, you must search deeper. Do you think Archie would want you lost in Transit? Do you want to be a slave again? This is exactly where the Moon wants you, so she can snatch you back," Lillian explained.

"I don't know what you're talking about," Sarah cried, her consciousness fading with each word.

"It will come. Rest now ...."

***

When Sarah woke again the only part of her that throbbed was her shoulder. Her sight had returned but it was slightly blurry. Propping herself up on one elbow, she took in the empty and gloomy cave in which she lay. It was bleak, a bit like a tomb, Sarah thought. The material Lillian had laid upon her was still with her, the feeling of warmth it transmitted was phenomenal. Sarah fingered it, questioning how such a thin, chiffon-like garment could possibly give off so much heat. It was the shape of a full-length gown, no detail, just pale pink and sleeveless.

"Lady Sarah Belmont?" Lillian's voice whispered from kneeling behind her. "You are awake," she said, still stroking back Sarah's hair with the greatest of care.

Looking up, Sarah tried to focus on the pixie-looking face that loomed above her. "No, I'm Sarah Walker. I think you have the wrong Sarah." Part of her relaxed at the possibility that their previous conversation, which was fuzzy in her mind but still there, was irrelevant if Lillian was mistaken.

"Oh yes, I know exactly which Sarah you are: born to Jack and Patricia Walker, you have a younger brother Dominic too. Archie was your cousin. Drink ..." Again Lillian placed a cup to Sarah's lips and poured.

Panic flew straight back into Sarah's stomach as she helped steady the cup to her lips. Did Lillian know everything? She said she knew the destiny to every man's soul.

"You're right, Patricia and Jack are my mum and dad," Sarah stammered between sips, suddenly feeling sick. "What is this?" she asked.

"Pomegranate juice, its healing properties are miraculous, its antioxidants have helped flush the poison out; it is the antidote, if you like." Lillian handed Sarah a halved bright red pomegranate the size of her fist. "Eat it, please, you must get well." Hesitatingly Sarah sank her teeth into the fruit, its thousands of tiny seeds twinkled up at her from the pulp.

"So who is Lady Belmont then? I've never heard that name before," Sarah asked, her mouth full.

"You are Lady Belmont, Sarah." Lillian raised her eyebrows and her sombre mouth formed a wry smile. "It is not often necessary for our past lives to be spelt out in such clarity. Sometimes earthlings attend what they call 'Regression Psychics'," Lillian turned her nose up at the name, her eyes briefly closing in disapproval, "and learn snippets of what has occurred in their past lives but on this occasion it is vital that you understand everything. Your life – your soul - depends on it."

"I am a Lady?" Sarah sat up straighter, her mouth full.

"Yes, well, you were, but you don't look much like one now," Lillian whispered as she tiptoed barefoot off the ledge Sarah was lying on and onto a giant green lily pad floating on the surface water in the cave. This was the first time Sarah had seen her properly. Lillian was tiny, a good head shorter than she was herself. She wore a long, smoky white dress; her skin was pure white. Sarah wasn't sure if it was Lillian's hair, long and ebony-black, that made her face look so washed out, but the girl was exactly how Sarah imagined a ghost would look.

"There's not much chance of a tan down here, Sarah," Lillian said in reply to Sarah's thought.

Sarah dismissed the comment, not comprehending what Lillian meant or even realising that Lillian had read her mind.

"You have re-formed to your Transit self," said Lillian, "for indeed, in the land of Transit the soul can choose its happiest form." She sat down and dipped her toes into the icy looking water. Sarah shivered and snuggled deeper beneath her cover. "It seems when you were here last, which was not so long ago now, you were at your most content." Pulling her feet out again, Lillian knelt forward towards Sarah, only a small pool of water separated them. "Take a look at your reflection," Lillian gestured with a lily white hand.

"Why?" Sarah asked, but she didn't wait for the answer. Curious and vexed, she leaned forward to look at her reflection in the water. She gasped. Her once thick, golden hair was cropped to her scalp, parts of it white-blonde and other parts singed black. She had bald patches where a blistered scalp showed through. Her face was somehow different, she still had her deep set dimples and Sarah could see through her blue eyes that it was still her hiding behind them, but the complexion was all wrong, she looked ashen and ailing.

"Who is that? What's happened to me?" Sarah could feel a lump burning in her throat and tears springing into her eyes. The half pomegranate fell from her hands, as they searched for her hair and then down to her face, feeling each feature in turn, smearing red pomegranate juice all down her cheek. Her fingers splayed, searching for something familiar. At her throat where, since Archie's death, St Christopher had hung, there was nothing. "Where's my ..." she stammered, her bottom lip quivering with the sickening feeling of loss. "It's gone!"

"Like I said earlier, we all go naked into the underworld. You are moving from the Earth-plain into the Shadow-land and with every moment you remain here you will continue to slowly transform into your spirit self. Every soul has an inner spirit, it is the voice we talk to when we are alone, some call it our conscience. It will take only a few days and at times it may be painful."

"I don't understand," Sarah cried.

"Not long ago in Transit time, when Archie was crossing over, a part of you found him and helped him. There was an incident with a fierce dragon, you were trying to rescue a friend and you succeeded, but in the process you were burnt. You lost your life and in a great flood you were washed down the river ... to me, my dear Felicity."

Sarah's head snapped upwards, anger flashing across her face as the name Felicity fell from Lillian's lips.

"Such a stubborn soul," Lillian tutted, "I had a feeling you'd try to come back somehow; I just never dreamed you would jeopardise Sarah's chances of a full life."

"What are you talking about?" Sarah said, backing away from the water's edge on all fours, her legs still not strong enough to carry her. "I may not look like Sarah Walker anymore, but I can assure you it is still me inside this skin.

This Felicity, this voice, this inner spirit girl is not in here." Sarah clutched at her chest, felt her heart beating beneath her hand.

Lillian rose to her feet as Sarah's angst intensified. "You must listen to me very carefully now and try not to be alarmed," she soothed.

"Alarmed? More alarmed than I already am? You've just told me my spirit was burnt to a crisp by a dragon. I have sores and burns all over my body. Look at me. I'm naked, my hair is gone and my face is a mess. What the hell is going on?" Sarah's voice was shrill, tears starting to her eyes.

Hurriedly, Lillian continued. "You have lived twice before on the Earth-plain, Sarah. Your first life was centuries ago when you were Lady Sarah Belmont; that is who Felicity is or was. I understand it is not who you are now, but she is still very much a part of you. In one respect, as Lady Belmont you had a contented time, you found your soulmate, a rare occurrence for any human being."

"And in the other respect?" Sarah pushed, her mind in a whirl of utter confusion.

"You were forced to marry another against your will. Your soulmate, the fletcher, died fighting in a war and you took your own life in your misery, desperate to be with him again." Lillian paused, searching Sarah's face for a glimmer of understanding. None came. Sarah looked blank. "Like I said to you before, your soulmate is Archie," Lillian clarified.

Sarah gasped again, backing away further. "What does that mean?" she asked, her breath becoming short with panic.

Hastily, Lillian joined Sarah on the ledge. "Be careful," she whispered moving quickly behind Sarah, stopping her from backing into the cave wall. Sarah turned sharply to look at it, her eyes staring in shock and wonder at an entire wall completely covered in glittering crystal. "It's phantom quartz." Lillian explained. "It won't hurt you," she reassured, responding to Sarah's anxious look. "I told you, I know the destiny to every soul and it is within this crystal library that the records are all stored. It holds the history to the cosmos: all that has occurred in the universe and all that will occur.

Sarah was dumbfounded and simply stared in awe from Lillian back to the wall. "Are you well, Sarah?" Lillian asked, her tiny hand placed lightly on the small of Sarah's back. Sarah still didn't say anything. "I feel you need more rest. It's too much information for you to comprehend. Come, lie back and sleep."

Sarah did not question Lillian, but did as she was told and lay down to sleep. However, the stone floor seemed bumpier than before and she struggled to get comfortable. Initially, it felt as though two giant lumps were protruding into her spine. Wriggling about for a moment, arching her back then lowering her shoulders, she soon found a position she could cope with, exhaustion won swiftly and any irritation dissolved into sleep. And now she really did begin to dream.

CHAPTER SEVEN

AUGUST 1685
EAVESDROPPERS RUN FASTER THAN THE WIND

In an age when the class divide was as far apart as the Earth was from the stars, the poor endured a mortifying existence and wars blazed in faraway lands, it was a dangerous time to be alive. With religious beliefs dictated by the Anglican Church, those whose faith was not fashionable were but a step away from persecution – even the gallows. There was a common belief amongst the intellectual elite that the world was a mystery never to be fathomed by humanity. Most, however, continued to trust in the Church and God's great interventions, believing the world existed solely through the miracle of His love. The young Lady Sarah Belmont was no exception.

In a small village in the heart of Hertfordshire, Sarah lived a privileged and splendid life with her parents at Belmont Hall. She performed her duties to an extent, she was accomplished and well mannered; dressed to please, danced an arming or straight-hey like an angel; embroidered, composed music and agreeably took tea. Conversely, she was strong-minded and obstinate and her days were filled not only with responsibility, but imagination and reverie. Most of all she dared to dream that she would only ever marry for the deepest love. As a child and young adult, her faith in the power of the human spirit rarely wavered, but when it did she would visit Old Nick.

His life was harsh and basic, as any peasant's of that time was. He worked the land hard and was ruled by the seasons. He lived in a two-roomed, whitewashed, thatched stone hut, unmarried and alone, but for his familiar, a tabby cat named Tabitha.

It was chilly and dark inside when Sarah called on him that morning, for the fire had died out overnight and would not be lit again until evening. The sun had not yet risen and there were no panes of glass in the windows, only linen soaked in linseed oil to keep the wind from blowing through. As always, Old Nick had welcomed her and by the light of a solitary candle, they had talked about what was troubling her.

"I talk too much, Miss Sarah. What I have told you, though, is all true. Make of it what you will."

Sarah's eyes were filled with tears, but as usual, Old Nick's soft voice soothed her. "Chin up, Miss Sarah," he said, brushing a tear from her cheek. "That is the future. So now think about the gift of today. You have someone to meet, do you not? Best not have you being late."

"Thank you, Nick," Sarah squeezed the old man tight, her admiration for him heartfelt and strong.

"Remember what I said child," he whispered, as he returned the embrace. "Love is the answer. It is the only answer to our existence. You cannot deny it. Be true to yourself."

Old Nick pulled away, holding Sarah's bare shoulders in his grubby hands. His hazel eyes, twinkling out of a craggy face deeply scored by wrinkles, bored deep into hers, as though he could read her thoughts. She had secretly visited this man for many years and her trust in his knowledge was absolute: he was the wisest and most accurate of all the 'cunning folk'.

"Indeed and thank you again," Sarah said, turning to leave in a rustle of fine, pallid pink silk and lace, her gown a stark contrast to Nick's humble home.

"What was that?" she gasped, startled as someone dressed in grey darted away from the doorway and into the thicket behind the hut. "Who's there?" she shouted, not moving from the entrance.

The old man peered over her shoulder. "Whoever it was, they moved fast. Didn't want to be found out I reckon," he whispered, his face suddenly taut with worry.

"Who do you suppose ...?"

"It could have been anyone." Old Nick's gaze darted from left to right outside his front door. "Lots come to see me, but they don't want it known."

"It might have been my teacher, Mistress Grey. She is up the earliest in our house. What if she's gone to wake me, found me not there and come looking for me?" Sarah exclaimed, suddenly anxious. "What if she overheard what we were saying?"

"Do not let it trouble you, Miss Sarah. We have spoken of nothing but truth and the truth can stand on its own. It's only fibs and hearsay which need support." Nick spoke loudly, as though someone may still be listening.

Sarah could not move. She stood frozen on the doorstep scanning the area outside Nick's front door. The only part of her that moved was her chest as she sucked in the morning chill.

The old man's face creased in the wrinkled semblance of a smile, "I am certain Mistress Grey would not dare come here looking for scandal. I have too much scandal on her for it to be worthwhile."

"What do you mean?" Sarah frowned.

"Never you mind," Old Nick said in a gentle but silencing tone. "Whatever it was they needed to hear, I'm sure they heard it. A scandalous story will run faster than the wind, Miss Sarah, twisted and lengthened before it reaches the intended ear. Regrettably, and it is a fact," Nick philosophised, "the truth will always begin with sacrilege."

Feeling calmer now that the land lay still, Sarah found it in her to cross the threshold.

"Do not allow them to govern you, Sarah."

Nick's warning broke her step. She turned back to look at him.

"If you do," he continued, "your conscience will, in time, overrule; it is a dangerous place to be walking with a tarnished conscience."

Sarah knew he was right. She had lived with a lie between her and her family for over a year now. She knew how they would react to her courting a fletcher's son. It didn't bear thinking of.

"Remember, Miss Sarah, not a word about this to anyone, or I'll face worse than another afternoon catching decomposing vegetables with my face in the stocks." Nick grinned, revealing a gapped row of rotten black teeth. "I never want to meet that Witch Hunter," he hissed.

"A rabbit's foot for luck my old friend," Sarah smiled.

"Not a word," he reiterated with a wink, his fingers pressed to his withered lips.

"I wouldn't dream of it," Sarah chuckled; her eyes now dry, her thoughts focused on meeting her love as she skipped down the two deep steps leading out of the hovel.

She was not far from the cornfields and with every step she took she looked over her shoulder to ensure she was not being followed. The closer she got to the fields, the more her excitement grew. It was dawn: the sun only just edging over the horizon, so she had time; time to enjoy the freedom and the peace.

It was not long, though, before her thoughts began to press her again, anxious not only for her meeting with Archie, but also fearful of snooping eyes. Her parents had grown suspicious of her early morning rambles, when she failed to take breakfast and which recently had begun to encroach into the afternoon. Her tutorials were increasingly disrupted by her late arrivals and it had been noted by Mistress Trinity Grey, her tutor and governess, who in turn had reported Sarah's absences to her already dubious parents.

Sarah, at seventeen years old, was still unmarried. Local gossip whispered this was ludicrous; why, she was close to being an old maid! Her parents would not have it so. They had arranged a marriage months before and had insisted on Sarah meeting Mister Joseph Jackson, whose wealthy, respectable parents owned a large glass house in the remote village of Great Finborough in Suffolk. It was a symbol of their wealth: one of the first of its kind, introducing lead oxide to the glass, which, according to Sarah's father, apparently made both the glass and the nuptials even more brilliant.

Sarah's simple, free-spirited nature was broken, her romantic ideas for her future crushed, as she was forced to make ties with this man whom she barely knew. She had met Mister Jackson three times now and on each occasion their meeting had ended in a quarrel. Her parents were distraught at her behaviour, but Sarah would not conform, not even when they thrashed her.

The moment the fields came into view, Sarah's psyche locked Mister Jackson in a cupboard and threw away the key, for this was Archie's moment. The ground was wet with dew, but the day was already warm. She flurried into the depths of a far field, her hand brushing lightly over the waist-high tips of golden corn as she entered into the sea of yellow, now over a mile away from the village and its prying eyes. As she ambled, a young, athletic man jumped suddenly from his hiding place in the corn, tumbling Sarah over in a burst of pink and giggles as he pulled her down, concealing them both from all but the birds.

"I never knew it was possible to feel like this," Sarah whispered into his ear, her lips gently brushing his earlobe as she spoke. His clothes were mere tatters, his face unwashed, his mousey hair was long and matted, but Archie Fletcher, with his handsome features, beaming smile and merry eyes, was finer than any other young man in that small country village. A breeze blew over them, the corn quietly swaying around them.

"Nor I," Archie agreed. "It is madness and magic combined; you make me feel like this is the first time I've breathed air or seen the sky, and the feel of your lips on my ear is sending shivers tingling down my spine."

Both lay flat on their backs taking in the summer blue above, the sun still rising slowly, a glowing ball of fire, tenderly warming them. Sarah giggled, nuzzling in closer, feeling his arm instinctively wrapping round her shoulder, pulling her in.

"You make me feel more alive than I've ever felt. My life began when I found you," Sarah said, still smiling up at the heavens.

"Yes and what's crazier is, I seem to love you more and more with each passing day." Archie rolled onto his side to look at Sarah. "Yet how can that be possible, for yesterday a thousand hearts could not have held the love I felt for you," he whispered.

Thrilled to hear him say those words, Sarah murmured, "Indeed, I feel the same. The world with you seems perfect, but reality outside these cornfields is quite different." She paused, sighed, still staring upwards.

Archie thought a moment. "My world revolves around you, Sarah, your world outside these cornfields is different. That is your so-called reality." His finger traced her jaw line, turning her face towards him. "You are my reality and with every breath I take I will fight for you. For without you my life is meaningless." Yielding to the truth, he kissed her. "I will not live a day without seeing you," he breathed, not drawing away. "I don't want to live a day where I can't disappear in your kiss." Pulling back, he gazed sincerely into Sarah's eyes, taking in every part of her face. "I love you, Sarah. And no matter what happens, I will continue loving you, with all my heart, until the end of time."

Sarah giggled again, rolling onto her side and propping herself up on one elbow, her head resting in her hand, golden ringlets surrounding her beautiful face, she leaned slightly over Archie, her mouth inches away from his.

"And what if things were different, Archie? What if society won and I married Mister Jackson?" she asked.

"I would rather die than let that happen," Archie said, jealousy flashing in his eyes, "... unless it pleases you?" He drew his head back slightly from Sarah's gaze, his eyebrows raised.

Her mischievous smile continued beaming down at him. She could not contain herself, her laughter spilling out. "No it would not please me. I too would rather die than spend an hour in Mister Jackson's company, let alone marry the fool." She dropped a kiss on Archie's lips. "I love you too, Archie Fletcher, how could I marry another? My heart is consumed with you and only you; there is no space for anyone else."

"He's worth a fortune," Archie reminded her.

"He is devoid of love and you're my soulmate, what are we worth really?" Sarah whispered.

Archie's hand found the back of Sarah's neck and pulled her close, both smiling all the while. "Our souls are two of the same you know and I don't want our love to end," he said, his eyes twinkling with emotion.

"It will never end, Archie, I promise," Sarah said.

"Don't you just wish we could fly to a far away land where nobody knows our names and our ranks in society don't matter: a place where we can be Archie and Sarah, with no rules and regulations hanging over our affection?"

Sarah smiled at the notion. "Is there such a place?"

"Who knows," Archie shrugged. "Oh, Sarah, let's do it, let's run away together ... tonight." Archie sat up abruptly, smiling, screwing up his eyes as he thought. "A fletcher's pay is the same rate as an archer's these days you know, it's a skilled job. I can look after us."

"Tonight?" Sarah smiled at his enthusiasm, her thoughts reeling also.

"Have your parents set a date for the wedding?" Archie asked, his eyes squinting slightly, as though in pain at the thought of Sarah being in the same room as another man, let alone marrying one.

"A week yesterday," Sarah said hastily, "only five nights away. Don't look at me like that, Archie. The arrangements are out of my control."

"I know, but it is sooner than I thought."

Sarah saw the pain in his eyes and the hint of jealousy that devoured him. He couldn't help it; she knew it was only because he loved her so much that his envy overwhelmed him, his inferiority to her position in society a constant burr under his skin.

"Then tomorrow morning we will go," he said. "We shall head southwest for Cornwall and ..."

Just then they heard someone whistling in the distance. Archie stopped speaking abruptly, put his fingers to his lips and silently lay back down. Sarah followed his lead, their gazes locked as the whistling got louder. Neither one of them breathed. They were right in the very heart of the cornfield, so this rambler was nowhere near the perimeter. He was cutting through and all they could do was hope and pray that his path did not cross their patch.

"Thought I might find you two here," a booming voice shouted from only a few feet away.

Sarah thought her heart might burst, as the silhouette of a tall man loomed over them. Archie sat up immediately, Sarah shying behind him.

"What is your business here?" Archie hissed, trying to find his feet.

The man stepped closer revealing himself in dark breeches and a white linen shirt, the neck opened slightly, his tanned face blinded by the sun. "I'm sorry I did not make an appointment," he said with a chortle in his throat. "I came to see old friends, so I thought."

"Oh, it's you!" Revealing himself, Archie relaxed and they both crouched down beneath the corn so they were on Sarah's level.

"Of course it's me," the man laughed.

"Kriss," Sarah yelled, throwing her arms around the visitor's neck. "Oh, my oldest friend, how are you? How long are you home? How on earth did you know where to find us?"

Kriss chuckled at Sarah's hysterical greeting. "I am as well as can be expected, given where I've come from and the things I have seen. I leave this evening, Miss Sarah. A war messenger's relief is never long. There are hundreds of armed men out there fighting and only the dead ones will see the end of it," he smiled. "But I came here now with haste to tell you ..." he paused, frowning.

"Tell us what?" Archie asked, his hand on Kriss's shoulder.

"I called for you, Miss Sarah, at Belmont Hall earlier this morning. Mistress Grey is it?"

"Yes, my tutor," Sarah agreed, nodding her head, imploring him to speak faster. "What about her?"

"She came to greet me and informed me of your absence, then told me that your parents had sent Renshaw, that cranky stable-hand, who spends most evenings boozing in the King's Arms, to look for you. He's been told to find you, Miss Sarah, along with whoever else is with you, and bring you back to Belmont Hall immediately. He's got the hands out searching." Kriss looked from Archie to Sarah.

"Do you know where their search has begun?" Archie asked urgently.

"No, but they have been out looking a good while and the sun is nearly at its summit; you must depart each other's company and hurry or I fear it will go ill for Archie."

CHAPTER EIGHT

AUGUST 2003
ENCOUNTERING YOURSELF AND RECOGNISING YOURSELF ARE POLES APART

The sky was grey with smog. At dawn, Bangkok still slept, but the sun was slowly rising. A lone, three-legged crow circled like a vulture over its prey, its beady eyes fixed on what it saw beneath it: the white and twisted body of a girl, half submerged in thick mud, hidden amid river weeds on a narrow bank. Swooping down, it landed inches from the bruised and sludge-splattered head. Eying the hair matted together with blood, the bird stalked forward, its vicious beak pecking at the ground, only millimetres from the girl's nose. Suddenly, her lips moved, a shallow breath emerging from her body. Startled into flight, the crow soared to the heavens once more.

***

A great sadness filled Sarah as she roused from her dream, the scent of a sun-kissed cornfield lingering in her nostrils. Tears stung her eyes and her chest began to heave. She was face down on the cave floor, her forehead pressing into the ground as she wept, racked by sobs, her shoulders shaking up and down.

A hand on her back startled then warmed her. "It's okay, Sarah. It was only a dream," Lillian's voice whispered into her mind.

Allowing her body to relax, Sarah laid her flushed cheek down onto the damp cave floor and stared out at the giant lily pads bumping together on the water. Lillian was right, it was just a dream, but Sarah knew that, as well as being a dream, it was something far more; it was a memory and strangely, for reasons she could not quite recall, it was a mournful memory. She could not grasp it; like fine sand it slipped through her fingers and was whipped away from her, down an empty passage of time. Although it was a moment impossible to remember and her heart felt heavy and her fear-rate was high, the dream had left her with a sweet taste on her lips and a longing for more.

After a few moments, gathering her thoughts, Sarah pushed herself onto her knees. The cave seemed lighter than before, or maybe it was her body healing and her eyes clearing. Lillian handed her a cup of pomegranate juice. Sarah took it gratefully, so thirsty she drank it down in one. Lillian replenished her cup and Sarah drank for a second time.

"I hate to press you, Sarah, but I am concerned. You should not be here. This has never happened before, even those in a coma never get this far. You must return to the Earth-plain as soon as possible, but how I do not know," Lillian said kneeling beside her.

"Lillian," Sarah cleared her throat, her mind now alive and reeling, "you said you have the destiny to every man's soul in this, er ... library," Sarah looked across to the shimmering wall.

"That's right, you're sitting next to the 'Mind of God'," Lillian smiled. "There's not many who can say they have done that. In fact you are one of only two who have." Together, sitting side by side, they took a moment to look in wonder at the wall.

"No," Sarah said, smiling, her head dipping in awe. "No, I suppose not." Then she looked up at the wall again, "But surely then, you know my fate?"

It was Lillian's turn to fall silent for a moment. She got to her feet, still deep in thought and then, as though reaching a decision, she walked to the wall. Her arms were held above her head, worshipping. She pressed her hands against the crystal and bent her tiny head as though in prayer. Sarah, her legs still weak, could only sit and watch and admire.

Lillian began to shake her head from left to right. She hummed and the muscles in her arms tightened. Her breathing slowed, she seemed to be in a deep meditation, lost to her surroundings. Then, without warning, as though a separate force had vigorously pushed her away from the wall, her head snapped back and her eyes rolled open.

"What were you doing?" Sarah asked? "Were you praying?"

"No, I was not praying, I was listening," Lillian said as she sat back down beside Sarah, taking her hand again. "Being the custodian of the wall's secrets - the guardian of this hidden shadowy realm - has its riches and its benefits too," she whispered, her awareness slowly coming back into the cave. She squeezed Sarah's hand tight and looking down at it, Sarah marvelled at how tiny and white Lillian's hands were in comparison to her own. "But not even I can penetrate its knowledge for you, Sarah," Lillian whispered. "To find the upshot of such a defiant soul, one who has tempted fate more than once, no, I cannot - at least, not without the consent of its ruler."

"God?" Sarah asked.

Lillian smiled, "If that is what you choose to call it." She passed Sarah a whole red pomegranate. "In more ways than one, it is better not to know your path. You always have freewill to do as you choose then."

"But you said I should return to the Earth-plain," Sarah said.

"Yes, you should and you must," Lillian urged, squeezing tighter.

"Did you know that a madman was trying to kidnap me and do God knows what to me on the Earth-plain? It is why I fell from the bridge; Fee helped me."

"I did indeed, Sarah," Lillian replied. "Did you not recognise him?"

"What? No ... and why would I want to go back to that?"

"You must face your fear. Your past will always catch up with you; you would have been far wiser to have turned and faced it, not tried to escape from it. However, you have freewill to do whatever you want, Sarah, I am just advising you to go back to Earth. It is not your time to enter Transit or cross to the other side. You have a life to live. Archie would want you to live it. You must start listening to your heart. Living in despair is so destructive, but whatever you choose to do, I will not hinder you. Maybe this accident of your coming here is somehow a blessing in disguise."

"Is Archie out there?" Sarah cut straight to the point, at the same time wriggling in discomfort. Something right between her shoulder blades was beginning to itch, becoming almost painful. She sat up, straightening her back.

"He is on the other side," Lillian answered with the utmost sincerity. "Sarah, if you were to find him, what would you do? He can't come back with you. He has returned to other loved ones and is safe and happy." Sarah could feel Lillian's eyes pleading with her to listen and take heed.

"He wrote me a letter," Sarah said, her bottom lip quivering, as she tried to scratch the unreachable itch on her back. She was aware that Lillian already knew about the letter, but she needed her to know her reasons. "He asked me to tell his story and I will not let him down, that's why ..."

Cutting across her, Lillian sighed in sympathy and leant forward into Sarah's space, "That's not the reason you want to find him, Sarah."

"It's my reason, it's a good reason. Whatever unconscious reasons this ... this Felicity has ..." Sarah faltered into silence, her tears flowing with frustration as she stared into Lillian's big brown eyes, their noses inches apart.

"Love is everlasting, Sarah, and it has no other objective but to unite itself and become whole. Love will cross eternity to find its destiny. It's like a magnet. Archie has already crossed over. He has gone somewhere you cannot follow."

Unable to speak, Sarah stared hard at Lillian, each word sinking in like liquid into a sponge.

"The choice you make today is the crux of your destiny. Which bridge will you burn and which will you cross? If you enter Transit, from what I know of it, there is only one path out and that takes you to the other side, once that bridge is crossed you can never come back. Your life as you know it will be ended."

"Is it dangerous?" Sarah asked, wiping away her tears, her fear rising.

"Transit?" Lillian asked. Sarah nodded.

"Yes, in many different ways. Far more dangerous than the Earth-plain ever was," Lillian said.

"How can that be? Before I fell, Felicity told me Joe and Chanthira, the two who kidnapped me, would send me somewhere worse by tenfold."

"Indeed, yes, that is true, but who is to say they would have succeeded?" Lillian asked.

That had not occurred to Sarah. Why should it have done? There had been no saviour or shining light, there had been only a voice in her head called 'Fee'.

"Well they didn't succeed did they?" she retorted. "I'm here now, with you." Sarah eyed Lillian for a moment, a question hatching in her mind. "Do you know Joe and Chanthira?"

"Yes, of course I do."

"Well, who are they and why did you ask if I recognised Joe?" Sarah asked impatiently.

"Joe was your husband in a former life. In ancient times he was Joseph Jackson. His soul has been seeking revenge on you and Archie since the day you left him. He has haunted you both and waited patiently for his moment of vengeance. "

Sarah gasped. "I've always despised that name," she murmured, her nose wrinkling.

"And now you know why."

"What about Chanthira?" Sarah asked.

"Chanthira is the Moon incarnate. You amazed me, how you managed to pull away from her glare back in Thailand, in the Silk Bar. Most are hypnotised in seconds. You have shown great strength against her power. Your history with her will have helped."

"History?" Sarah asked, her shivering beyond control. But Lillian did not reply, instead she got to her feet, picking up the pink chiffon material that lay loosely across Sarah's legs and holding it up in front of her. Looking at it more closely, Sarah saw that it was a garment – a gown of sorts. There were two small holes in the back of it, which made Sarah frown, what was the point in them, she wondered.

"Put this on, please," Lillian ordered.

Carefully, Sarah got to her feet and took the garment from Lillian. She pulled it on over her head and allowed it to fall to the ground. It clung to her curves perfectly, but Sarah could feel there was great elasticity in it. The holes in the back were out of sight now and instantly forgotten.

"If Chanthira is the Moon incarnate, how can you say that the Earth-plain is a safer place for me?" Sarah asked, feeling the strength coming back into her legs.

"Her power on Earth is strong, Sarah. She can control the tides and our emotions, yes, but in comparison to her power in Transit ..." Lillian paused, her trembling breath conveying her sincerity, "... it is as nothing. You have placed yourself in untold danger coming here." Still talking, Lillian walked away to the other side of the cave. "I fully understand Felicity's fears. She must have been petrified as soon as your gaze fell upon Chanthira."

"I certainly felt edgy," Sarah said, thinking back. "It was surreal; I thought it was my jetlag to be honest."

"Felicity will do anything not to be captured by the Moon again," Lillian stated, coming back towards Sarah and holding something in her hands.

"I've made up my mind," Sarah said, choosing to ignore Lillian's final comment about the Moon. "I want to find Archie, even if it means facing the dangers of Transit."

Lillian sighed, "I know you have. This path you are on is no doubt part of your journey. The reasons for it will come to light as you move forward. It is your journey and all I can do is advise you and trust in the protection of the cosmos. But here, take this as well." Lillian handed Sarah a flat, deep blue stone veined with gold, it was about the size of jam-jar lid.

Sarah looked down at the cold rock Lillian had placed in her hands. "It is beautiful," she said. "It looks oddly like the night sky, the flecks of gold being the stars."

"Lapis lazuli is a powerful crystal, Sarah. Along with the dress you are wearing, it will help to protect you. Never ever take it off." Lillian fumbled with the corner of the pink gown and tore a thread off the hem. She threaded the stone and held it up to Sarah's throat.

"It'll never hold with that thread," Sarah said, trying to help by pressing the heavy stone to her chest.

"Only you can break this thread and only when you no longer need the stone's protection will it break. Until then no other outside influence will ever sever it. Your destiny is hanging from a thread, Sarah." Lillian gave a half smile, "It is raw irony that this protective stone hangs by one also. This dress is your armour, but this crystal is your sanity. Take care of it."

"I will," Sarah said. "What does it need to protect me from?"

"Your own thoughts. Lapis lazuli will recognise any cruel or cursed attack and has the power to block it and return the negative energy back to its source. It will also ease your sadness and reveal the inner truth deep within you, but you must be careful; the truth won't hold back or compromise. Be prepared for anything out there. You seek the truth, for that is what your deeper subconscious, Felicity, desires you to do. And Sarah, when you find it, whatever it is you find, you must accept what it teaches you, even if it's not what you desire. You must be true to yourself." Lillian stretched out her hand and clasped Sarah's, "You must leave me now."

"Where do I go?" Sarah asked, panic freezing her.

"It is your journey. I can only reiterate what I have said before; take cover from the Moon; do not let her find you."

"No, no I won't," Sarah stammered as Lillian led her to the edge of the ledge and released her. Looking down, Sarah's fears intensified, knowing that her only way forward was through the water, glistening in the darkness of the cave.

"Goodbye, Sarah. Find Archie and appease yourself. I don't know how, but when you do then you must try to get home. Your future is too promising for you to quit now. It is not your time."

As Sarah slowly immersed herself into the chilly water, Lillian bent forward, extending a hand to halt her. "Another thing ... please, you must remember this: Transit is a mighty thought amplifier. Out there," Lillian's gaze darted upwards, "you may find yourself having dreams you can't understand, but every dream is relevant, a piece to the puzzle. More dangerous, though, are your thoughts, be careful what you think, Sarah, for as I've told others before, in Transit, your thoughts will become your reality."

"So if I think of Archie, will he come?"

Lillian smiled, her eyes showing true compassion. "That is not a thought, Sarah, that is wish, a longing ... a want. Transit will not give you what you want, but it will reveal the truth in all its glory." Her smile vanished. "In short, my gifts will make your journey home easier and with a bit of luck on your side possible."

Submerging herself into the water, Lillian took Sarah's hand and gently pulled her under, guiding her to a safe place to enter Transit.

CHAPTER NINE

AUGUST 2003
FOREST OF SEASONS

Incense swelled into the air around Niran-Atid's peaceful mind. He knelt alone on the edge of an abandoned pier on a deserted stretch of the river, searching his thoughts for insights. Attaining wisdom this way was never easy, but he had managed to shut off all hindrances of the outside world. His eyes were gently closed, his concentration was immense and his breathing shallow. Before him, as an offering, were a large ripe peach and a long length of wood from the peach tree.

"Buddha, help her. Ward off the evil," he muttered under his breath, picking up the peach wood, holding it above his head to the sky, then placing it on his forehead before giving it to the river.

"Buddha, may she come back to us." This time his hands found the fuzzy, round peach, he placed it to his lips as though he were going to eat it, but instead of biting into the succulent fruit, he exhaled a long breath onto it then placed that too into the water.

***

Sarah swam with strong strokes; she had always been an able swimmer. Lillian guided her part of the way then signalled for her to ascend. Glancing back, Sarah saw her ghost-girl companion fading into the depths until she was lost from sight.

All alone Sarah entered Transit. But the place where she found herself was not at all what she had imagined. The day before, when she last had a fleeting glimpse from the middle of the river, it had been warm, but she was sure it had not been scorching to the point of not being able to place a foot on the shore. Hauling herself out of the lukewarm river, she sprinted flat out across the pebbly riverbank, each stone equal to a hot coal, her feet blistering as she ran. Her pastel pink dress dried instantly and shimmered brilliantly in the dazzling sunlight. She found shade quickly, only metres from the shoreline, where grew a dense row of sad and dehydrated fir trees. Her fair skin, which was burnt and scarred since entering the underworld, now felt worse than ever and had started to peel in the heat. "This temperature is dangerous," Sarah said to herself.

Taking in the view of Transit from the moderately refreshing shade, she could not understand how everything could be so barren and grey; the land had been baked as though it had not rained in weeks. Sarah's mind started to swim. "It's drier than a desert," she whispered to herself, her bare feet toeing a large crack in the ground.

"Transit is a mighty thought amplifier, Sarah. Be careful what you think. Your thoughts will become your reality," Lillian's voice rang in her ears.

Stunned, Sarah took in a breath of the dry air, her throat burning as the heat scorched its way down to her lungs. It was boiling. Sweat stinging her eyes, dripped from her tiny button nose. "This must be like summer in the Sahara," she said, turning to look into the woods. Away from the sun and the river it looked far cooler beneath the trees, a few deciduous ones were still green, but it was dark and creepy. As soon as she thought that, a shudder of concern crept into her bones and her imagination automatically kicked in.

"Don't think ..." Sarah warned herself as she took a few steps further into the shade, her feet cooling. A twig cracked beneath them and instantly she dropped to the ground, curling herself into a ball, afraid. She waited a moment, then realising she had made the noise herself, she uncurled, regaining her composure. A quiet wood like this was sure to have creatures in it somewhere: woodland creatures or maybe desert animals, given the heat, but nothing sinister. Of course there would be noises. Sarah found she was trying desperately to reassure herself. Still squatting, taking a moment to find her courage, she watched a small army of ants march out of a tiny crack in the ground.

"Don't think," she cautioned again as she watched the ants tramp, one in front of the other out of the crack and up a nearby tree. "How do you not think?" Sarah wondered to herself. "It's impossible, surely?"

Without warning the ground began to shake vigorously. Sarah screamed. Falling sideways, she clung to the bottom of a nearby tree trunk. She stared, her eyes wide and filling fast with tears of fear as she watched the ground split. At exactly the point where she had been watching the tiny crack a vast crater had opened up.

"Oh my! It's an earthquake! What's happening?" Sarah squealed, as the ground continued to vibrate and shudder. The trees above her shook, dropping foliage and leaves on top of her.

The rift that appeared before her was now over three metres wide, yet out of it continued to trudge ants, except they were no longer a normal size. These ants were huge; not even the size of her fingernail, but as big as dogs, with long, jointed skinny legs that had wiry hairs protruding out of them. The rumbling of the quake was augmented by their synchronized stomping as they marched towards her.

Again, Sarah screamed, scrambling around to the other side of the tree as fast as she could. The leading ant, spying her sudden movement, jerked its head round to look with beady black eyes in her direction. Pouring with sweat, Sarah pinned herself to the back of a tree, not daring to look at the giant ants, her knees tucked in tight to her chest.

"Did I just create that? Don't think, Sarah, please just don't think," she panted, knowing full well she had created them. "Breathe," she muttered, taking in a deep breath, closing her eyes and shaking her head. "How do you not think?" Exhaling forcefully, she felt a presence press in front of her. Quickly, she opened her eyes. Inches away from her nose was the leader ant. The one fact Sarah knew about ants - that they can lift twenty times their body weight - raced oddly through her brain. She had nowhere to run. The enormous insect had her up against the tree. "Oh God, that's it," she thought, "I'm going to be destroyed by my own stupid imagination, crushed by an ant."

Suddenly, two giant black feelers lurched forward and started to prod and poke at her fragile face. She could not breathe. The monster jaws in front of her looked like a giant pair of scissors chomping frantically in her face. Was it going to eat her? Panicked, it took all Sarah's strength not to scream, she thought she might burst with the effort. With each antennae stroke her scalp felt cooler, smoother and less tight. Her skin suddenly started to peel rapidly and like a snake shedding its skin, began to fall away. At the same time, the roots of her hair began to tingle wildly.

She could see her own reflection in the creature's black, glassy eyes: blonde hair still cropped short, ugly burnt bald patches strewn throughout, but now with new tufts poking through. It was a fleeting glimpse, but enough to remind her that she was not at all the beautiful, young and carefree Sarah Walker she had once been. She was inside Felicity's broken body and she felt old, older than time, with the world on her shoulders instead of at her feet.

"Your resistance to fear is pathetic," Felicity's impertinent voice chirped in her ear. "Where are your guts...? Use your instincts. Its stroking you now, in fact its healing us, but that ant will eat you for lunch in a split second once it gets the taste of you."

A wrath for Felicity began to rise deep inside Sarah. "You always seem to show up in times of crisis don't you?"

"Always," Felicity replied quirkily.

"I don't know what to do," Sarah whispered back at her inner self. The giant ant's eyes blinked at the sound, its head pulled back slightly and stared at her body, feeling every part of her with its antenna.

"If I were you ... which technically, I am ... and seeing as my wings are burnt to stumps still, I would think with my legs," Felicity advised.

Wings? Sarah caught the word, but had no time to think what it meant. She didn't know where her courage stemmed from or realise just how much she had inside her, but on impulse she ducked in between the ant's front legs and made a dash for it, deeper into the forest.

Although she made her escape boldly and well, her initial sprint sudden enough to perplex the ant leader, Sarah could not maintain the pace. She was a strong, long-distance runner and had stamina, but naturally her speed was slow. The ants would be much faster, she was certain of it, and stronger by far. She had to think. Ants could easily climb trees, so looking for safety above was useless. They had come from beneath the ground, Sarah thought as she pounded through the woods, her breath coming in painful gasps, her bare feet catching and tearing on roots and twigs. Where else was there to hide?

She could hear the ants scuttling in all directions around her. A pulse thumped in her ears, her eyes darting in every direction trying to work out a route or an escape plan of any description. She could see them all moving so fast around her, but none yet moving in for attack. It was as though they were herding her; they had complete authority over this chase. She did not stand a chance.

Through the dense foliage, Sarah could see a clearing in the distance. She upped her pace; a huddle of ants foresaw her move and were on her heels within seconds, swiping long legs at her, attempting to trip or impede her in any way they could. One actually pounced, but missed its target, Sarah's dress, astoundingly, seeming to fend off the outstretched jaws.

"Oh Sarah! Run faster, they are gaining on us," Felicity cried.

"Shut up, okay ... just shut up! I can't cope with you in my head. I can't think straight as it is. Don't you think I'm running as fast as I bloody can," Sarah snapped.

In her fury she tripped, skidding to the floor on her knees and there on the ground lay an abandoned bow, two arrows strewn close by.

"Archie!" Felicity's voice rang in Sarah's head. Ignoring it, she dived for the weapon, grabbed it up and tested the tightness of the string, it was taut. Her head very clear now, she picked up the nearest arrow, placed it in the notch of the bow and aimed. Lining up the jagged flint arrowhead with the closest ant, she fired. It was no accident that her aim was perfect: archery had been one of the more enjoyable pursuits in her wretched existence at boarding school. The arrow flew true, shooting the ant straight in the chest. It fell suddenly, screeching in pain, its fellow ants halting, hesitant and tentative.

"Kill the leader," Felicity urged.

"Go away," Sarah hissed stubbornly. "I don't need your help."

Again she lined up her arrow, there were more than a dozen ants surrounding her, each black and identical. She turned full circle, the arrow poised in the bow, ready, desperately searching for the chief ant as they slowly gained confidence and closed in on her.

"Your target is moving," Felicity squawked, ignoring Sarah's plea for silence.

Taking in all the ants possible in her sight range, Sarah noticed the largest ant as it moved quickly towards her. She had to act immediately.

"Don't miss. Your aim must be perfect," Felicity whispered.

"No pressure then," Sarah thought, horribly aware that she had only the one remaining arrow.

The biggest ant had quickly gained on her; it was nearly on top of her now. Staring deep into its eyes, her hands started to shake; the load just too heavy. Overcome with terror, Sarah shut her eyes and with purpose but no direction she fired. Fear striking her down, she curled to the floor. The ground continued to vibrate with the pounding of feet as the ants stalked her. Then the noise and the shaking softened and finally ceased. She waited, trembling, eyes still tight shut, anticipating a blow or a bite, but nothing came.

Slowly, she sat up and opened her eyes. The ants had gone, but the woods were changing and so was she.

Rapidly, the leaves that were left on the trees turned from green to brown then fell from the branches like a shower of gold. Sarah sat and watched in awe as a gentle wind picked them up and blew them, swirling into a vortex. The temperature dropped and before she knew it, she was sitting in a bed of crisp leaves in a beautiful autumnal paradise. Her hair roots had never stopped tingling from the moment she had set eyes on the giant ants. She had thought initially that it was her body's natural instincts, like a dog's hackles going up, but the feeling had never subsided and continued stronger as she sat watching the world around her change. Fingering her head she could feel that her hair had grown considerably in the past few moments, to a short blonde bob.

"That's unbelievable," Sarah thought to herself as she got to her feet, her fingers still playing with her hair as she watched more red and yellow leaves float to the ground. In the space of less than a minute the season had switched from a blistering summer to a crisp fall. Sarah longed to know if her arrow had struck true and hit the leader ant, or if it had been the sudden climate-change that had caused the ants to flee. Either way, she felt a sense of ease. She looked down at the bow that she still held in her hand. Felicity's last words came back to her.

"Archie," Sarah whispered to herself. Flashes of the dream that had haunted her back in Lillian's cave slipped into her thoughts.

"A fletcher's pay is the same rate as an archer's these days you know, it's a skilled job." They were words she could not quite comprehend fully and they fell away from her thoughts as quickly as they had arrived, leaving her slightly confused.

Taking the bow, she searched around for the two arrows, thinking to retrieve them. There was only one. Of the ant it had killed there was no sign. Picking it up and ignoring her sore, bleeding feet, Sarah kicked her way through the messy mix of russet and auburn leaves, taking in the spectacular mosaic of autumn. Its grace and beauty hid the pathways as she wandered aimlessly, in awe of what she had just witnessed. She had seen many autumns in the past, but none as breathtaking as this. Her eyes still shifted, a little nervously, her gaze flicking between the trees at the mere memory of the giant ants. "Don't think!"

Yet all the while she walked, the land seemed constantly to be changing. A nippy and strong wind picked up and in the white sky above a fluster of swallows headed south. The foliage soon had no freshness to it and Sarah felt as though she had shifted from a delicious late September morning to a dismal early evening in November, again all in only the space of a few minutes. It had even begun to drizzle.

Always vigilant, aware that the ground had become slippery underfoot, her bow and arrow poised and ready, she stopped as soon as she felt uneasy, trying, as Felicity had advised to trust her instincts. Suddenly, once more she became aware of the ground rumbling. Boulders on the forest floor shook and shifted.

"Please, not again," she whispered to herself, but the grumble stopped. Catching her breath, hoping it was just her imagination or fear, she continued on cautiously, only to be halted again by another giant rumble. "That's not my imagination." She stopped, braced and ready. Again it ceased then started again, the sound like a giant's footsteps hitting the ground every few seconds. Her blue eyes widened at the thought; quickly she tried to suppress it – too late.

"My mind's come into it again, hasn't it?" Sarah whispered to Felicity, who she had no doubt was somewhere inside her listening and would emerge in time. It was clear from what direction the foe was coming by the noise and it was not long before the trees began to part as the beast bore closer to where Sarah stood. Her mouth dropped open and every hair on the back of her neck rose. Thrusting towards her was a thirty-foot, bald creature with one giant glaring eye in the centre of his forehead.

Instantly realising her one arrow would be useless, Sarah took hold of a nearby boulder and with all her strength heaved it from the ground and lifted it high above her head. She could not hold it for long. Turning her head away to protect her eyes and face from flying shards of flint, she smashed it down hard on top of a neighbouring, bigger rock. The stone broke up into pieces, leaving a dozen chunks, knife sharp. Grasping hold of one, her whole body shaking with fear, she watched the Cyclops lunge closer.

"Friend or foe Sarah?" Felicity's voice screamed in her head.

"Foe," Sarah replied. "I don't know."

"Did you imagine a one-eyed giant before he appeared, as you did the ants?"

"I don't think so." With a thick, razor-sharp flint poised in her hand, Sarah thought she might faint. Adrenalin and horror drowned her, overriding any flight instinct, she stayed ready to fight, primed to charge.

"Stop! Your only enemy here is your own imagination. If you did not create this Cyclops then maybe he doesn't plan to hurt us," Felicity said.

"It doesn't look friendly," Sarah stammered aloud, the giant closing in. It was so close now she could see its mouth drooling and foaming.

"Let's see if I'm right." Felicity giggled.

"I'd rather not wait and find out to be honest. It looks hungry. I'm not risking it," Sarah insisted, squeezing the blade harder in her hand, a trickle of blood sliding down her wrist.

With a whiff of blood in the air, the Cyclops instantly stopped less than ten metres away from her, its one eye scanning for the source of the smell. Sarah froze; her chest heaving up and down the only movement, her azure eyes glistening with tears of fright, yet glinting with courage.

"If he is a foe, I can't hide now, because he can smell me," Sarah thought to Felicity, looking down briefly at the cut on her hand. "I don't think I can cope with this. I read my classics: didn't Cyclops plan to eat Odysseus as he did his shipmates? What shall I do? I couldn't bear to have my bones crunched by a giant."

"Yes indeed, but you are not Odysseus and did you also know that Cyclops is a skilled blacksmith, he could help you," Felicity's voice sounded in her thoughts.

"You know him, don't you?" Sarah spat. "That's why you're giggling."

"I know that he is no foe, but that cut on your hand will do you no favours in befriending him. He does love the taste of blood."

The giant twitched slightly, causing Sarah to flinch. She frowned hard into the Cyclops's one, ogling, grey eye.

"Friend or foe? Friend or foe? Friend or foe," she repeated over and over in her head. But no answer came to her.

"Use your lapis stone, Sarah. Protect yourself." Felicity suddenly warned.

"How?" Sarah asked, dropping the flint knife and clutching at her neck instead.

"Talk to it, connect with it, ask for its protection." Felicity replied. "Believe in it and it will help you."

"Really? Okay, come on then lapis," Sarah murmured. Her gaze never leaving the staring Cyclops, she curled the fingers of her wounded hand round the pendant that hung heavily on its slender strand of thread. "Protect me, please, or heal my hand. Quickly! Your timing is core." Beneath her hand, Sarah felt the blue crystal heat up rapidly. Astounded she pulled her hand away and looked at her palm where the fresh wound had been. It had scabbed over. "That's not possible!" Sarah spluttered.

"Now wait. He won't hurt you, Sarah," Felicity promised. "Just keep your wits about you and your lapis crystal charged. He's an oaf, I know, but get him on your side, he has skills that will help you."

Sarah did not say a word. All she could think to do was to visualise herself in a safe bubble. The crystal around her neck remained warm on her chest bone. The Cyclops started to walk slowly towards her. It didn't take long, three earthquake strides and he was leering down on her. Petrified, Sarah could smell his foul breath pouring over her and could barely find the courage to look up at him, yet shyly she managed to sneak a peek. She found that she was looking through a pale blue light, almost like a veil, which seemed to envelope her, permeating from her lapis lazuli pendant.

Although gruesome and mammoth in size, the Cyclops did not crush her with his fist, or crunch her bones and eat her as she had anticipated. The more Sarah stared into what she had thought was an evil eye, the more she could see that the beast's single eyeball, the window into its soul, was not only dull grey and mournful, but trustworthy. She exhaled a deep, anxiety-laden breath and felt it carry her fears away.

"Never judge a book by its cover," Felicity piped in quietly, a silent snigger hiding beneath her words.

"No, indeed, but after the ant saga I was on my guard," Sarah hissed back.

The Cyclops did not speak, nor did he enter Sarah's blue bubble of protection; instead he went straight to work on the stone she had shattered. Using forces unseen by Sarah's eyes and with much banging, welding and sparks, which she was sure could only be wrought by magic, in moments he had made a weapon.

Sarah's mouth dropped open as she saw taking shape before her a beautiful slender sword made entirely out of stone, a perfect handle carved at the end. The tip of the leaf-shaped blade provided a lethal looking point, its curved edges sharp enough to slice effortlessly through floating silk. The Cyclops, with the finished weapon in his hands, still did not invade Sarah's space, but laid the sword on the ground in front of her then turned away, stomping his way back through the forest.

"Wow," Sarah whispered to herself. It was all so hard to digest, everything: where she was; what she'd just seen. It was all blowing her mind. "I'm in some warped fairytale, a dream, or is it a nightmare?" She did not budge until the Cyclops had moved on and was completely out of sight. Then slowly, she crouched down and picked up the sword. It was a work of art. Each shard that she had smashed into tiny pieces had been fused together to make this one weapon; she could see the tiny seams where they had been sealed.

"I'd take it with you if I were you ... which I shall remind you, I am," Felicity urged.

Trying to ignore the meddlesome voice, Sarah, feeling a little more relaxed, left the bow and arrow behind and clutching her new weapon, continued to walk through the woods. The healing power of the lapis seemed to have reached her feet, for they no longer felt sore. However, as soon as she picked up pace the world once again began to swirl around her. Leaves were picked up in the gale and filled the air, their colours fading from oranges and reds to brown and black and, in the blink of an eye, they seemed almost transparent or skeletal before they vanished completely.

"Autumn has moved on," Sarah whispered. "Winter's next, and what creatures with it? What is this place? Where's Archie in all of this?" The temperature suddenly plummeted and Sarah's feet were chilled to the bone, the earth hard and colder than stone. In seconds the deciduous trees were bare, the evergreens glistening with frost. All that was left of the landscape was Transit's skeleton.

Searching the barren, silent land, her shallow breath visibly misting the air, Sarah took in the bleakness of Transit's winter. At home she would have loved a day like today, to be all wrapped up in a woolly scarf and thick coat. As unlikely as it seemed, however, her thin, pale pink garment did offer some protection against the cold, so she did not immediately feel the effects of the climate change, but it was not cosy as she desired to be and she longed for a woollen jumper to cover her bare shoulders. She felt the sudden loneliness of the dead of winter, as a sudden gust of wind lifted her gown and cut through to her bare skin. The sword she clutched was frozen and stuck to her fingers and the crystal around her neck hung like a block of ice against her collarbone.

It was all so hard to believe. The silence was eerie and once again she found herself almost waiting for the action to begin. She could feel it building; or was that just her anticipation? She knew she was not alone. Then it started. It started as a low whisper, whistling through the naked trees. It was not plain to see what exactly it was at first, but as the noise level rose from a low gargling to a shrill screeching, Sarah suddenly realised what she was hearing. Birds. Big black birds had begun to fill the heavens, to the point where she could hardly see the white sky above her. They were landing in the trees in their droves, all grinding their serrated bills. Sarah could see they were not normal birds, they were so much bigger and the purple gleam off their jet black feathers, and the metallic glint bouncing off their beaks, told her they were dangerous. Some were bigger than others and a few were gigantic. One of them stood out as even larger than the rest and its feathers did not gleam purple, they blazed bronze.

Sarah had seen crows and birds of the like before, but these, she was sure, were giant ravens, like the ones she had seen on a school trip to the Tower of London years ago, only much, much bigger. Their deep crowing and burnished, gimlet eyes bore down at her intently. Sarah's eyes strained upwards to stare at the trees. Petrified to make any sharp movements she did not move a muscle. She did not need to. The birds had their target in focus, their intentions were obvious. Abruptly, the loud cawing stopped; the freezing wind now the only sound. Then, in the sudden silence, each bird dropped from its perch and swooped towards her.

Curling to the ground, her arms held over her head, her scream echoing through the icy air, Sarah braced for their impact. She had no time to call upon the lapis crystal; the ravens attacked in waves, their outstretched claws reaching for her back, but just as Lillian had promised it would, the pink gown protected her, forcing the birds' wicked beaks to rebound.

Daring to look up to see if she could make a run for it, Sarah's forehead was swiftly pounded with a metallic whack. Her vision blurred and her head spun; already on her knees she sank into unconsciousness.

CHAPTER TEN

AUGUST 1685
LOVERS SPARK MAKES A MIGHTY FIRE

Sarah gazed first at Kriss and then at Archie as they all three knelt on the parched ground, their heads hidden from sight below the level of the corn tips. "What do we do?" she asked, her voice quieter than a whisper, panic underlying every word.

"You stay down,' Archie whispered. "Do not let your head rise above this corn. Kriss and I will go first. Wait until you hear my signal - I'll hoot like an owl - then you must head home as quickly as possible." Archie's voice was intense, his face only inches from hers, his eyes pleading with her to obey.

"To Belmont Hall?" Sarah asked, her sapphire eyes glistening, bulging with tears. "I'm sure someone followed me earlier on my way to Old Nick's and was snooping about. I saw someone pass his door."

"My gut instinct tells me it was M-Mistress G-Grey," Kriss stuttered.

"My governess?" Frowning, Sarah looked up into Kriss's face, wondering what had made him stumble over Mistress Grey's name, almost as if he were afraid of her.

"She looked, er ... how should I say it? Smug ... when I asked where you were this morning," Kriss explained. "Don't trust her, Sarah. I know she's your teacher, but I also know what she's like. Promise me you will be on your guard." His eyes beseeched Sarah, his black, glossy curls blowing gently round his face.

Sarah's frown deepened. "She may be a bit of a bully when it comes to my whereabouts and studies, Kriss, but I always believed her intentions were ..."

Kriss did not let her finish. "Her intentions are twisted, Sarah, believe me. Her attitude toward you is wicked, you must not trust her motives," he implored again, suddenly looking away.

"Of course," Sarah soothed, mystified, but seeing his concern. She turned quickly to Archie and threw him a look. Behind Kriss's back, he gave a shrug in reply, one eyebrow quirked.

"She's not all she proclaims to be," Kriss insisted, looking through the sea of golden corn. "There's an evil streak and ..."

"Evil?" Sarah interrupted, perplexed. "That's a bit harsh, isn't it?"

"Evil, yes, and it comes naturally to her, it's in her veins. It is an evil that comes without any effort at all."

"Kriss, what are you talking about?" Archie cut in.

"Your world has become a far more dangerous place since she has entered it," Kriss announced, staring from one friend to the other. "Had I have been here when she nuzzled her way with her bogus papers into the post of governess, I would have tried to dissuade your father from hiring her."

"I've known her but three months, if that," Sarah said, frowning.

"Indeed. Well I have known her far longer." Kriss turned back to look at her, his face lined with worry.

"How long?" Archie said.

"That's not important ..." Kriss paused then added, "What is important is for you to know she is an escapee from a House of Correction."

"What?" Sarah gasped. "Why was she in such a place?"

"That's another time's story. She has had a hard life without doubt and for that hard life she has become calculated and desperate for a reprisal on the upper crust that put her there."

Sarah wrung her hands, "But how did Father not know?"

"It's not his fault, Sarah. It is merely the mechanics of the fates."

His comment was profound, but Sarah was thinking logically, "Can't we just tell Father?"

"Do you want to be the one to tell Lord Belmont he is wrong?" Kriss said. It was a rhetorical question and all three of them sighed, overcome by the thought of how Sarah's father might react.

"I've seen her papers," Kriss went on. "They are without flaw, every reference is given by a villain who has managed to tiptoe back into society and blend in. Everything looks legitimate, perfectly accountable and acceptable. Even if we did manage to explain, she is untouchable. She's corrupt and her motivations are sealed and deliberate." Again, Kriss paused and took in a deep breath, sweat beading on his top lip. "But at present, we have more pressing and important problems. We'll look at dealing with her later."

"Oh, my! I hope Old Nick ..." Sarah stammered as her eyes finally brimmed and overflowed with tears.

"Nick will be fine, he always is. You just make sure you get yourself back to Belmont Hall as soon as you hear our signal to say the land is clear. Don't move until you hear it," Kriss ordered.

"If they catch you ..." Sarah faltered, stumbling on the words, horrified by the thought as she gazed at Archie.

"They don't know it's me you're spending time with. So long as we don't get caught together I'll be fine," Archie reassured.

Sarah knew he was trying to sound calm for her sake. He knew as well as any of them what the punishment would be if anyone found out he had been courting the squire's daughter.

He took hold of her hands to still them, "Meet me here just before first light tomorrow morning, wear dark clothes, nothing bright, travel light and bring only what you can run with. We'll head south for London on foot; they'll never find us there." Sarah listened carefully, her head pounding and her stomach churning. "We'll be all right, I promise."

"Be careful," she planted a hasty kiss on Archie's cheek.

"Always," Archie smiled.

"I'll look after him," Kriss assured. Sarah knew Kriss would be true to his word. Ever since they were all children he had been their sentinel, silently keeping watch over them, his course, unlike theirs was one of solitude, yet his loyalty was genuine and strong, his aim always the same, to protect and to bring hope in the warped society in which they lived.

With a backward glance and a fleeting smile, Archie was gone, Kriss following his lead. Alone and troubled, Sarah slid from her knees onto her hip. Plucking a long sheath of corn from the ground, slowly she began to peel back ribbons off the stem, as she watched the two young men disappear, then she rolled onto her back, tossing the corn to one side, her blonde ringlets splashing out around her head, as she prepared to wait. The sky was bright blue; birds circled above her, searching for food in the heat.

Closing her eyes with a sigh and a troubled heart, Sarah found herself beginning to pray.

"Dear God, Jesus, Great Spirit, whoever you are, please, please keep my Archie safe; don't let them find us out. Let this plan of his work. I'll do anything. I'll be good ... I am good. I would never mean to hurt anyone. I learn my lessons: I have become a proper lady; you know that, you can see that. Is that what you want of me? Surely you can see that Archie and I are meant to be together? I would do anything to be with him. I cannot possibly marry Mister Jackson. It would be wrong for me to marry Mister Jackson. I do not love him. I could never love him." Tears flooded her face, "Please let us get away from here, to a land where there is liberty, let our freedom and the world broaden our minds and our feelings. Even if it means we brave the seas and cross over to the New England. I would go that far to get away from here. There's so much more to life than this. I can't believe you would create a world where we are here to be judged on all we do, hiding from our true natures, the natures you instilled in us at our very creation. What would be the point in that? You want us to be happy. Surely there are sections of our paths better left to our own instincts. Is there no freewill? Please, I beseech you, keep us together. I don't want to live without him. I cannot live without him."

Sarah's rambling prayers continued inside her head for some while, time slowly creeping by. Close to begging, she stumbled at only one point. "Running away ... daring to challenge my own family?" Her mind reeled with reasons for and against leaving. The grounds for going with Archie were endless, they made perfect sense. There was only one striking reason to stay: "If they catch up with us after we run, Archie is sure to die. Oh, how could I live?" Yet, though it was high above all the others, it seemed ludicrous even to consider this one reason.

Time drew on, as did Sarah's thoughts. She waited but no owl signal came. The sky turned from bright blue to white. Light cloud had drifted in; the day was cooling and the sun beginning to dip. Sarah waited, forcing herself to stay put and keep true to Archie's word she remained where she was lying motionless amongst the corn. It was hard to keep still. Occasionally she found herself sucking in long, deep jittery breaths to control her apprehension, her heart sporadically having minor palpitations. Rolling onto her stomach, she looked along the ground through the stems of corn. It was like looking into another, shadowy world. Baby frogs leapt past on their way to the nearby brook; beetles crawled over her and around her on the dry soil; ladybirds, bumble-bees and butterflies fluttered through; a dormouse teetered halfway up a stem. Sarah saw them all and yet was somewhat oblivious to them. Turning onto her back again, she gazed up at the sky. It seemed to pulsate above her, the day's heat rising up to meet it as she waited. It was a long and agonising wait. Why was it taking so long?

Then something changed in the heavens. The white wispy clouds quite suddenly turned to dense black, the breeze picked up and Sarah felt a few spots of rain. Sitting up she took in more of the sky, a storm was coming, the wind beginning to gust noisily, tossing and bending the corn all around her. She would never hear Archie's and Kriss's signal now. Her senses on high alert she scurried on all fours towards the perimeter of the field. As she crawled, the ground began to dampen with the rain. She wrinkled her nose, the smell of moist earth tickling her nostrils. Then, mixed in with it she detected the distinctive aroma of burning.

Sarah stopped crawling and knelt back on her heels. Indeed, it was without doubt wood burning. She looked up and sure enough, thick black smoke lined the horizon, its origin streaming back to the village. Sarah didn't think, she stood, uncaring of anyone who might be looking; she had to be sure of what she saw.

The church spire piercing through the trees showed Sarah exactly where the fire was coming from, it was somewhere inside the market square near the church. Her eyes scanned the village, which spanned across a small valley. Another fire was billowing in the Nookin where the farm workers lived, as though a house was on fire. Something was far amiss and it made Sarah feel sick to her stomach. Fires on a day as hot as today made no sense at all; surely nobody would start one deliberately, it was much too dangerous. With this wind to spread the flames, the corn might catch and if it did, the harvest, on which the village depended, would be destroyed. Her heart sank: everywhere was too dry; it would take hours of rain to have any effect once the fire took hold. She could see the smoke clouding into the air, waves of smog blackening the view, a dark nightmare now hanging over the village.

Suddenly, the most hideous thought crept into Sarah's mind, "Oh God, no! They wouldn't ..." she broke into a run, her gaze never leaving the skyline, as she made for the field gate, toxic thoughts poisoning her brain. "Don't hurt him! No, please no!"

The rain became heavier. Stumbling towards the road that would take her back into the village, Sarah prayed for a long and heavy downfall. Her mind swam in a sea of confusion and fear. Every step felt like trudging through treacle, bumbling all the way, the wind blowing her ringlets wildly into rats' tails around her head, which was throbbing. She felt as if something inside it may burst at any moment and trickle out of her ears. As she struggled onward, her energy drained, unconscious gasps of disbelief teemed from her mouth and tears streamed down her blotchy face. It was as though her soul ... or was it her fear ... had doomed Archie already.

"Archie," Sarah muttered under her breath, her thoughts always falling back to him, her feet pounding the ground under her heavy silk gown as she ran, desperate to find the fire's source, convinced that Archie was caught up in it. "Please don't hurt him," she gasped. "Please God; please don't let them hurt Archie." Sarah could no longer feel her legs, they were numb with terror. She ran as fast as they would carry her, tripping over the uneven ground, her dress ripping as she charged over stiles and through gates, uncaringly leaving them wide open, anger and fear broiling through her veins. "What have they done to him? What made us think we could ever outwit or outrun them? Run faster, Sarah; Run!" she panted.

Taking the most direct route into the heart of the village, she scrambled to the top of the earth mound that divided the village from the fields at its highest point. Breathless, she dropped to her knees and peeped round the stump of an old oak tree. Below her the villagers were crowded, all focused on the fire raging to the side of the church.

Sarah knew now what was happening. Blood-curdling screams came from deep within the flames, along with the cries and sobs of distressed onlookers. Someone was tied to the stake and burning. The Church said, burning cleansed the soul of those found guilty of practicing witchcraft. Similarly, women who committed crimes against their husbands, and servants who harmed their masters, were accused of petty treason and consigned to death by fire. Sarah's father had once told her, when she was just a little girl, that burning at the stake was the cleanest way to punish traitors, as no blood was ever spilt; they burnt to ashes leaving no trace behind. Coming of age, Sarah knew in her heart that it had nothing to do with cleansing; all it really did was drive fear into the hearts of the people. Appalled, she had been forced to acknowledge that her father was cold-blooded and cruel. It broke her heart, riled beyond belief by his ignorant, inhumane approach to the villagers whom he, as squire, was supposed to protect. In recent days Sarah's mother had pleaded with him to stop the burning of a woman found guilty of murdering her husband, even though everyone knew it had been in self-defence. Lady Belmont, sure the offender would enter the afterlife with no body, which thought she could not abide, had pleaded with her husband to stop the burning. She had pleaded in vain.

"Would you burn me too, Father?" Sarah whispered to herself. "For I have wronged you it would seem, as much as Archie has. If that is him in those flames I want to die with him." Silent sobs rose from within her. She laid her cheek flat onto the wet, muddy ground, the rain still pouring, soaking her through as she listened to the wailing and horror below, the appalling stench of roasting human flesh making her retch. She felt sick as noxious fear grabbed her by the throat. "How could they?" she sobbed. "My own flesh and blood; I don't understand it."

Was that Archie screaming in the flames? She had to find out. Driven by unyielding courage, Sarah picked herself up off the mound and stumbled down the hill into the village, her hair dishevelled; her dress filthy. The state she was in, if someone noticed her, they would think she had been attacked. The horror was still unfolding as she rounded into the market square and stopped in the shadow of a cottage, gasping as she glimpsed through the crowd the limp, blackened carcass of the person still burning at the stake.

She started forward, but without warning and with great deliberation, strong hands suddenly grabbed hold of her and reeled her back just before she came out of the shadows to be seen by the villagers.

"Sarah," Kriss whispered in her ear as he pinned her gently up against the cobbler's cottage, "they know." His words were very clear, his big hands cupping her bare, trembling shoulders.

"How?" Sarah begged, her voice desperate, her eyes closing with exhaustion.

"Old Nick told them."

"No! I do not believe you; Nick would never have betrayed me."

"He was tortured," Kriss said shortly. "I was right about Mistress Grey. She followed you this morning."

"Where's Archie!" Sarah panicked, "Oh God! The fire ..." Trying to break free from Kriss's grasp, her face sheet white and bile rising in her throat, Sarah vomited.

"It's all right, Sarah," Kriss soothed, stroking her back, his grip stopping her from falling.

"Let me go. I cannot bear it. Who are they burning, Kriss? Who was that screaming in agony? Please tell me it's not Archie ... please!"

CHAPTER ELEVEN

AUGUST 2003
THE PATHLESS WOODS HAVE EARS

When Sarah woke the woods were quiet, bar the chirping of birds in the trees, each greeting the sun as it rose beyond the horizon. She had survived an entire night beneath the shelter of the forest. Sitting up she heard the occasional rustle of a woodland creature on the forest floor, maybe they were rabbits or squirrels. Looking around, she could see wild flowers growing in abundance all over the earth: colours and scents that Sarah was sure could only exist in her dreams. There were so many smells: honey-sweet blossom; wild dog roses; spicy herbs, each aroma as pungent as the next. Without doubt this was springtime, her favourite season. She was alert, every one of her senses heightened, and yet she felt calmness flow through her, as much as the sunshine flowed through the trees. A fresh, gentle breeze tugged at her hair as though longing to play with it. Reaching up she ran her hand over her head and was amazed to find her hair had grown back completely and felt even thicker than before. Coiling a strand around her finger she pulled it down and saw that it was a lighter shade of blonde and curlier. She giggled nervously then felt her face, it was not taut or rough anymore, her hands had healed as well. Sarah pulled up the skirt of her dress, searching anxiously for any tiny blemishes, but there were none. It was as though her rapid journey through the seasons had restored her back to full health. Elated and feeling like a child again, she sank her bare feet into the earth, permitting the soil to wriggle between her toes, she loved squelching in mud. Drawing in a fragrant breath of pine, cedar, fir and poplar trees, in that tiny moment Sarah delighted in nature. Only then did she become aware that the birdsong and hum of the forest was accompanied by the rising sound of music, as though somewhere an orchestra was playing. Was her mind playing tricks again? Frowning, Sarah picked up her sword.

"Music?" she whispered to herself confused, looking up to search the canopy of trees, for the sound seemed to be coming from above. Sunlight filtered through the awning of green. The music was so soothing it was hard to be afraid; it appeared to be scaring away all her fears, serenading her into tranquillity. Striations of more vibrant colour drifted through the air with each note. Sarah watched fascinated as colour filled the atmosphere, the musician was not only composing music, but painting a picture of serenity. Clutching her sword at the ready, part of her not sure what to expect, but determined to be vigilant after all Lillian's warnings and the trauma of the last few days, Sarah found that the most part of her was lapping up the colour and the peace.

"Lady Sarah Belmont?" a voice boomed around her. Sarah jumped, although it didn't startle the woodland creatures, not even a bird flew from its branch, it was as though this voice spoke to them all the time. Her grip tightened on the sword as she looked all around, but could see no one. Not sure whether she should answer and unaccustomed to the name, Sarah waited.

"Felicity?" the voice continued. "For that is who you look like, a spritely little star. Or would you rather Sarah Walker? Hope? Or is it Rapunzel today?" Sarah could hear the tenderness in this voice and she could also feel herself blushing; she understood the notion of these questions, given her obsession of changing her name, but recognised none of them. "Maybe you'd rather Genevieve or Annie?"

"Just Sarah, is fine." Her voice trembled slightly as she directed it up into the canopy from where the voice seemed to come.

"Your sorrow is lifting," the voice said. Sarah did not reply. The voice was right to a certain extent; she did feel calmer inside, but she thought maybe it was stemming from the crystal Lillian had given her.

"Who are you?" Sarah asked, forcing herself to be composed.

"I am the Sun. I am the Spirit of Understanding, combined with the Spirit of the Future. You have, wisely, been given great foresight by the Keeper of Secrets, which will stand you in good stead throughout your journey." The voice paused for a moment; a breeze rustled and parted the trees above, allowing more sunlight into the wood. Stunned, Sarah was rendered speechless.

"However, since Archie's passing you have lost both your confidence and the power of action in your life. Both of which are vital attributes to keep." There was a much longer pause and Sarah wondered if she should respond in some way.

"You are lingering in the past; you are seeking out what has gone before and now your past is catching up with you." Sarah wasn't sure she understood fully, but was still too nervous to speak.

"Your history has the power to hound and horrify you if you insist on hunting for it." Another slight pause, as a squirrel scampered past barely a foot away from Sarah and up a nearby tree. "That said, I understand your reasons, just as I understand Felicity's, for of course, she is you and you are she."

Still rooted to the floor, Sarah watched the squirrel as it sprang up the tree, her gaze caught by the entwined foliage above her, parting then merging, the sunlight flashing through, dazzling her.

"I will help dispel any fear, Sarah. My light can help cast away shadows. Shadows of your past, the shadows of the Moon, they are like the nightmares of your childhood when you felt small and unimportant."

Sarah gulped. How could she be having a conversation with the Sun for goodness sake? And how did he know so much about her? It was true; she'd had recurring nightmares as a child and even now as an adult, especially since Archie's passing. Until recently she'd had no idea they had something to do with a distant past. This past life of which Lillian and now the Sun spoke, was, as he said, catching up with her. It was as though he understood and knew everything.

"That is because I do understand, Sarah," the voice boomed.

"How did you know what I was thinking?" Sarah asked, dumbfounded.

"I can read your thoughts, most use telepathy in these parts. You have the power to do this also. I have told you; I am the Spirit of Understanding. You have the inheritance of nobility and your spirit - who I'm sure you are aware of now, is Felicity - has the determination and courage needed to travel this road."

"The road to Archie?" Sarah asked, finally finding her voice again.

"Of course, you are absolutely right, and you must tell Archie's story. You have to find him first, though, which won't be easy. But more importantly, the only way you can tell his story is if you can get yourself back home to tell it and that will be even less easy."

Sarah sighed with relief to hear this voice, this sentinel, agreeing with her; he wanted her to find Archie. He was on her side. She appreciated Lillian's view, she realised the complications she was creating; changing what was written in the stars, what was embedded in Lillian's records. But this guardian, this angel, whatever it was, this embodied Sun, could really see the importance of her quest.

"It is far from a normal occurrence, this being in Transit. No person should linger here. You are attempting to alter your own destiny through the power of your own freewill. A very dangerous and slightly insane mission, but I understand why you are doing it, Sarah, and I will help you."

"Thank you," Sarah mustered.

"I will help you in any way I can, but I cannot walk the journey for you. Every choice you make is yours alone. My mystifying and wicked sister will aim to impede you and pilfer you back into her darkness."

"Your sister?"

"The Moon. As far as she is concerned you belong to her, you were rightly one of her many stars, trapped for centuries in her realm, all because you once denied your soulmate," the Sun explained. "She has the power to twist your thoughts, to delve deep into your memories and slowly dismantle each and every one. No one has ever swindled her the way you did before. If she catches you, your journey will be over and no doubt, she will banish you to a black hole, or worse, set you before the witches who cannot be avoided. Trust me, you must not be captured. If you are, there would be nothing I can do."

Sarah understood: the Sun was just clarifying what Lillian had told her. Before she could say so, the Sun spoke again.

"Ah yes, you must remember what the Keeper of Secrets told you. Your journey is ambitious. Nonetheless, it is also of great importance and if you survive it and progress to actually finding a way home to tell Archie's story, you will restore faith not only in your life's purpose on Earth and revive the desire to continue on to live it, but you will restore faith in the meaning and purpose of every human's journey."

Sarah felt quite blown away by the way the Sun had worded her mission and how he had magnified the enormity of her quest. She had not thought of it in such rarefied terms: searching for Archie was for herself alone, and telling his story, whatever that may be, was because he had asked it of her.

"How do I find Archie?" Sarah asked.

"He has already crossed the bridge. Once a soul has paid his due to Death he can never cross back. Death's law is irreversible."

Sarah's heart sank: did that mean her quest was dead in the water before it had even begun? "So ... what should I do?" she asked.

"Just follow your heart." The Sun's voice seemed to weaken slightly, the orchestra faded out. "I am never far away. I'll be watching. Remember, I am the Spirit of Understanding: nothing in life should be feared, only understood."

In total awe of what had just happened, for a time, Sarah remained perfectly still, but beneath her chiffon pink gown her stomach grumbled. She could not remember when she had last eaten anything more substantial than

Lillian's pomegranate. The Sun had gone, his light still filtered through the trees, but his music had faded completely. Pushing herself up, her eyes instinctively searching for something to eat, Sarah spotted some dew-wet berries hanging in the shadows of a wild bush. She knew better than to eat unfamiliar berries, but she was unbelievably hungry. Grabbing up her sword she allowed her feet to take her there.

Crossing the lush carpet of pine needles that covered the woodland floor, Sarah's feeling of contentment abruptly vanished, as she felt something watching her. The wilderness, with all its dream-like qualities, couldn't hide that feeling. She stopped midway to the berries and searched the area, turning full circle, her stone sword swinging aimlessly as she peered into the shadows.

There was silence, and then came the gentle playing of pan pipes from somewhere not too far away, behind the trees. "Who's there?" Sarah called out, raising her weapon, all ease vanishing and her fear heightening. Whoever watched her made it no secret. A scampering body darted from behind a tree to another. Sarah froze, rooting herself to the spot, only her eyes dared to move. She waited. Again, more pan pipes, then Sarah saw it, this time more clearly: a creature as tall as she, on two legs, scuttling across the forest floor, taking cover behind yet another great pine. Could it possibly be Archie? Sarah knew it was a foolish hope, even before the Sun whispered in her ear: "Once a soul has paid his due to Death he can never cross back. Death's law is irreversible." Crushed, she continued to wait.

The woods lay still for a moment as though even the birds were waiting. Then came the sound of a voice right inside her head. Not Fee, but the curt, gruff voice of a male. “Coming for tea? Coming for tea? Coming for tea?” it repeated over and over again. It sounded as though he was right on top of her. Flinging around, petrified, Sarah ducked to the ground and squeezed her eyes tight shut. The voice continued to chant. “Coming for tea? Coming for tea? Coming for tea?”

“No,” Sarah shouted, dropping her sword and sticking her fingers in her ears. “Go away ... who are you?”

“Sarah and Fee, coming for tea?” the voice chirped on. “Sarah’s coming for tea.”

“No, Sarah is not coming for tea.” Her eyes still closed, Sarah heard heavy footsteps approaching her from the forest. “Oh God; I don’t know if I can open my eyes to see you. I can’t bear it. You’ll be another unearthly creature out to kill me. Or am I already dead? Is that what this is? Have I been dead all along?” Tears squeezed out from Sarah’s tightly shut eyelids, “I’m so afraid,” she whispered.

“Nothing in life is to be feared, only to be understood,” the Sun’s words murmured in her ears.

Before Sarah had chance to open her eyes two strong arms wrapped around her in a colossal, hairy cuddle. The stench from the chest her head was pressed against reminded her of a Billy goat; it was appalling. She attempted to push herself away. “Get off me,” she shouted, her voice muffled by matted fur, but the arms did not release her. Instead they tightened and then began to swing her round and round, like her father had done when she was just a little girl, and all the while the voice continued to sing.

“Sarah and Fee are coming for tea? Sarah and Fee are coming for tea? Sarah and Fee are coming for tea?”

Well at least this uncouth creature appeared to bear her no ill will. It was small comfort. Helpless, Sarah thought maybe it would be easier to wait until he had finished his wacky greeting and got the excitement out of his system. Around and around, up and down she was thrown until finally, like a child who has finished playing with a now unwanted toy, he dropped her to the ground.

"Hey," she wailed as she rolled several feet before coming to a halt. "What are you doing?"

She looked round and got her first proper sight of the ill-mannered beast. Gasping, her gaze travelled from his hooves, up his goat's legs and past his naked torso to his face. "Oh my God!" Finding it hard to look, yet instinctively drawn to the ugliness of every feature, Sarah wanted nothing more than to run; run fast and far away, but the shock had her grounded.

"You be the first to look the Devil in the face. My hug is my handshake," snarled the goat man.

"Some hug, you nearly frightened me to death!" Sarah said, finding her feet and sword, shaking the debris off her dress and staggering back a few feet to keep her distance.

"Most travellers never stay still long enough for me to say hello," explained the creature in a hurt manner.

"What are you?" Sarah asked, her curiosity overcoming her fear. She couldn't believe quite how repulsive he was, his black wiry beard scrawling down to his solar plexus, a bulbous cherry nose, half squashed to the left, as though some brave person had given him a good right hook. His skin looked like leather, with open pores, spider veins covering both cheeks and deep set wrinkles and scars, all blended to create a mesh of rough peel, much like the magnified skin of an orange, only brown. His only redeeming feature was his eyes, which were bright green and sparkling.

"What do you think I am? A satyr, of course: half man and half goat. Some might call me a faun. It depends which books you read." His brashness never failing, he grabbed hold of the short horns on his head and swung his rear end round to swish and show off his pathetic tail.

"Do you have a name?" Sarah asked.

"Anian Pan," replied the satyr. As the name rolled off his tongue, he went into another song and prancing dance, screeching at the top of his gruff voice, "Anian Pan, Anian Pan, Anian, Anian, Anian. My name is Anian Pan, Anian Pan, Anian ... "

"Okay, okay, I've got it, Anian," Sarah shouted over him, hoping to stop him before he drove himself into another frenzy of hugging.

"Sarah and Fee, coming to tea." It wasn't a question this time. Anian took hold of Sarah's hand and began to drag her through the woods, "Sarah's coming to tea in my house."

All the while, Sarah persisted in trying to pull away. "No, Anian, excuse me, but I don't want to go to your house. You're hurting me ... please let go." She waved her sword at him, tempted to use it, yet somehow she felt this uncouth, feral creature did not mean to harm her.

Anian took no notice of her pleas or her sword. His hold was burly and rough and she was powerless. He dragged her with ease, on and on, at least a couple of miles through the dense forest, her bare feet pierced by sticks and stones. Even when she stumbled, he marched on ignoring each cry with every tumble, unhearing and uncaring, until at last they reached a giant, gnarled oak tree with huge spreading branches.

"This is the only oak in the forest," Anian Pan said, dumping her unceremoniously on the ground. Dishevelled, exhausted and hungry, Sarah struggled to her sore feet, dusting off her gown, checking her lapis lazuli pendant, relieved to find it still there.

Singing to himself Anian disappeared, leaping up the tree and out of sight. Sarah could do nothing but gawp in awe at the mighty tree before her. Ten men with their arms outstretched would have struggled to encircle its twisted trunk. The branches were as distorted as the trunk itself and the foliage as thick as any she had seen. To Sarah, looking up and up, the oak seemed to go on forever. It would have fitted perfectly in an enchanted fairytale as a magical gateway, she thought, momentarily forgetting that it was a bad idea to think.

Looking down at her feet, she marvelled at the notion of the oak's roots gripping the ground, spreading through the earth beneath her. She had always held a fascination for trees and nature, but this tree was at the top of the hierarchy, it was awesome and seemed to have a presence and persona all of its own. The bark looked antique, the richness of its leaves were a colour Sarah had never seen before or could never have imagined, not even a paint pallet would have recognised it. Furthermore, its size was remarkable. The trees flanking it were at a respectful distance and looked mere shrubs in comparison. Yet contrary to how much it stood out, the oak looked perfectly at home.

It was mind blowing to think of this titanic tree developing from a tiny acorn. Part way up the tree Sarah could see sections alive with activity, it took a moment to realise exactly what it was, then she heard the buzzing and realised. The tree was alive with beehives, all sectioned throughout the first part of the tree trunk, two hanging visibly from the first great branch.

Bemused, feeling too weary to be afraid, with a big sigh, Sarah laid her sword on the ground and sank down beside it at the base of the tree. It wasn't long before the foliage above her began to rustle, the bees buzzed louder, seeming disturbed. Then Anian reappeared, looking uglier than ever, covered from head to toe in sticky, sweet honey.

"Boo," the satyr shouted, as he dropped to the floor.

Sarah had heard him coming but was still startled, annoyed and irritated by his rudeness. "Don't do that," she insisted, jumping to her feet, sword in hand. "You really frightened me."

"Sarah and Fee coming for tea, up the tree? Oh, that's pretty ..." Anian leapt forward and grasped at Sarah's lapis lazuli. Again the thread was tested, but it held strong.

"Get off!" Sarah stepped back, her hand instinctively protecting her throat.

The satyr cowered apologetically, embarrassment creeping into his eyes. For a moment he looked so pathetic, Sarah almost laughed. "What's for tea?" she asked gently, giving into the invite, in an attempt to soothe the situation and her new acquaintance's shame and at the same time, hoping to sound enthusiastic and not too anxious, though her stomach was in knots.

"Honey, of course, and lots and lots of fruit." The satyr's green eyes sparkling with obvious delight he glanced up the tree. "Honey from my friends," he explained.

Sarah wasn't sure if she could eat beside a creature so ugly, maybe she could if she shut her eyes or tried not to look at him. She started to say "Okay," but before the word had left her mouth, Anian's sticky hand grabbed hers and they were off again, not across the ground this time nor up the oak's trunk as she had half expected, instead he wheeled her round the back of the tree where there was a small opening leading into a giant hollow.

Inside it was dark, but Sarah could make out a rope ladder climbing up the side of the cavity. The buzzing of the bees was amplified by the echo of the giant hole and it made the hairs on the back of her neck prickle, but Anian did not give her a chance to express her woes.

"Come on," he shouted, as he charged up the ladder, causing it to fly away from the tree wall and shake with each leap. Trying to grab hold of it, Sarah looked doubtfully up at the departing satyr, his ungainly form soon lost in the darkness. The last time she had climbed a rope ladder had been as a child in the garden at Archie's house – the home of her Aunty Jo and Uncle Robert, Archie's mum and dad. The memory was like a shard piercing her heart.

"Are you sure it's safe?" she called after the satyr, but he did not reply. Grasping the wobbling ladder with both hands, Sarah tugged on it gently to feel its strength. "Anian?" she shouted again, but there was no sound from above except for the hum of bees. "Oh my! What am I doing? What is this place?" Sarah muttered as she began slowly and carefully to climb.

As she ascended, chinks of daylight filtered through from the beehives, enabling her to see that all were formed within deep holes gouged in the trunk. All were alive with the busy, buzzing insects and Sarah faltered, flinching, expecting at any moment to be stung. Clutching the unstable ladder one-handed, the other reaching for the lapis stone, she continued past the hives. She had no idea what would await her at the top of her climb, but her gut instinct told her that Anian, although desperately rude, did not mean her harm and that the oak tree was indeed a safe place to be. This thought made her feel a little calmer as she advanced, one rung at a time, towards a square of light that she could now see above her.

Poking her head through an open trapdoor, she peered into a sun-filled room. It was made entirely of wood and smelt wonderful. Either Anian's rank goat smell had diminished or she had got used to it! The room had windows with no glass, but beautifully carved wooden shutters. There was a wooden table in one corner and the most unusual looking chairs Sarah had ever seen, both were carved out of wood in the shape of giant cupped hands, the palms forming the seats. A single bed, also made of wood, was in the other corner. Sarah guessed that the tree house rested on huge branches and had been constructed around the giant oak's immensely thick trunk, which rose up through the centre of the room as though it had spiked the house and claimed it as an integral part of itself. There was a quaint arched door set into the trunk, which intrigued Sarah. Turning to the other side of the room, she spotted a spiral staircase leading up to another trapdoor. Behind the stairs were a few cupboards, again beautifully constructed and engraved with the same swirly design as the shutters.

"Maybe that's the kitchen," Sarah thought, her stomach reminding her how hungry she was. Her eyes widened as she saw that to the left of the cupboards was a stone-built fireplace. The fire was lit and had a pile of logs beside it. How dangerous was that inside a house constructed entirely of wood in the middle of a tree! Flames licked up to a large cauldron hanging over them, the smoke rising and dispersing through an open window. The tree house was cosy, yet simple and Sarah could see that a lot of effort had gone into its design. Was it immaculate or bare? She could not decide.

"Come in, come in," Anian chattered, appearing from the trapdoor above and clattering down the spiral stairs. "More honey for our tea, it's the purest and most divine honey you will ever taste. Try it," he held out a carved wooden bowl.

Sarah propped her sword at the hatch entrance, hoisted herself into the main body of the woody- and fruity-smelling room and courteously took the honey from Anian.

"Tell me," Anian asked, "this realm is normally inaccessible. How is it that you are here?"

"I don't know." Her mouth watering, Sarah stared at the golden honeycomb shimmering in the bowl. "From what I understand, the part of me that's Felicity told me to jump off the Phra Pin Klao Bridge," Sarah explained. "So I did."

"Very stupid aren't you." Anian began to rummage in his kitchen cupboards, taking out bottles and jars and then pouring a concoction of ingredients into the big pot over the fire. Sarah remained silent dipping her finger into the honey, tentatively breaking off a piece of comb and popping it into her mouth. As soon as her attention was on the sweet taste Anian moved swiftly across and snatched the bowl away. "Don't eat all of it," he said, proceeding to pour the honey directly into his mouth, the gooey syrup overflowing, dribbling down his hairy chin and through his black beard. The sweet taste on Sarah's lips was indeed divine, she instantly craved more but Anian had already drained the lot.

"It's not very nice to call someone stupid, Anian," Sarah reprimanded.

"But you are. Since when have you listened to voices inside your head? In fact, since when have you listened to anyone, Sarah? You're a law unto yourself," Anian snapped back.

"I've never had voices in my head," Sarah insisted.

"Of course you have. We all have, it's called your conscience."

"Felicity is my conscience?" Sarah asked, baffled.

"No, no, no ... Felicity is you, Sarah, you and she are the same person. Your conscience is totally different. Surely you've had moments in your life when you've known something was wrong with no real explanation? It is your sense of moral awareness or in simple terms, what is right and what is wrong, a voice that says 'don't do that,'" Anian explained, his top lip snarling in disgust.

Confused, and disliking the feeling that this bizarre creature was beginning to lecture her, Sarah turned her back on Anian and wandered over to the open window to gaze unseeing at the thick foliage. "Why is it that the people around here all seem to think they know more about me than I do?"

"Because we do; Lillian especially, she knows it all: your past, your present and ..."

"Yeah, yeah, and my future, I get it," Sarah cut across him. "But I'm defying her records," she retorted and almost smirked, which she knew was wrong as her conscience kicked in, but she just could not help herself.

"Now who's being rude?" Anian snorted, without a hint of aggression in his voice.

Sarah suddenly realised how riled this short conversation was making her. Her anxiety levels were at their maximum and she could feel her body fuming, beads of sweat breaking out on her forehead, too distressed and wound up now to feel hungry - in fact, the thought of food turned her stomach.

Clutching the lapis at her neck in an effort to calm herself down, it dawned on Sarah that as rude as he was, Anian wasn't actually being nasty or lecturing her, he was trying to help her. Why couldn't she accept that? Giving herself a mental shake, she took a deep breath. Not turning to face Anian, she focussed through the oak's canopy to the spectacular view of Transit. She could see over all the treetops of the forest and right across to a river. Jungle and woodland met at the riverbank, as it did on this side, but beyond were mountains; ranges and ranges of mountains, their tips flushing pink as the sun sank towards them.

"I'm sorry Anian," she turned to face him at last. "My head can't remember anything Lillian spoke about concerning my past life. I've tried but I can't. Now I just want to find Archie, that's all. It is the only reason I am here."

"It is not for your head to remember, Sarah; it is for your heart to remember."

"Why must I remember? What's the point?"

"Because that is the story Archie wants you to tell ..." Anian started.

Sarah gasped with sudden excitement, "How do you know what Archie wants? Have you seen him?" she snapped.

The satyr ignored Sarah's questions and continued on with his thread, as though she had not spoken, "To tell in minute detail, with all the feeling and passion you possess. I can come with you to help you find Archie, you should not be alone on your journey, it is dangerous out there. I could be the conscience you are lacking."

"You?" Not troubling to hide her distaste, Sarah went to turn back to the view.

"Don't turn away from me, Sarah. I know what you see. Look at me. I am disgusting aren't I?" Anian's head bowed, his voice trembled. "I often want to cry, you know, but my tears burn like acid and only scar my face more and it hurts.

"No ... I didn't mean ..." Sarah stammered, hopelessly backtracking, shame and compassion, warring inside her.

"I am, though, disgusting. I'm all that is shadowy and shameful, I am chained to Transit by my own panic and self-disgust. I was relegated to the nethermost recesses of this place long ago. It feels like I've been here forever. Let me put it this way: I planted the acorn this tree grew from."

Jaw-dropped, Sarah stared at him. He must be hundreds of years old! "Why Anian? Why are you here? Lillian said any soul trapped in Transit would become a lost soul. Are you lost?"

"Well and truly," he grimaced, "and for a reason too shameful to speak aloud."

It was Anian's turn to move away. He picked up his panpipes and started to play a soothing tune. The soft melody washed over Sarah; it was like a tranquilising medicine soothing her raging mind, rinsing away the dust of her journey to the mighty oak. Leaning against the window frame, she listened, allowing her frustration and disgust to fall away and seeing another side to the satyr, past his ugliness to the sweetness beneath; he was in fact not unkindly.

When he had finished his tune, he laid the pipes down on the wooden table and walked back to her. "I'm sorry, pipe playing is my way of comforting myself," he explained. "I don't mean to be rude."

"It's I who should be sorry. You're right, I don't listen to anyone it seems. Only a little while ago the Sun told me that nothing in life should be feared; only understood. I failed to try and understand you, Anian. I was wrong." Sarah bit her bottom lip to stop it from quivering. "We all have our own stories to tell."

"Indeed that is so, but we are all connected in one way or another," Anian said gently. "I'll forgive you as long as you allow me to come with you on your quest. I need an adventure."

"Of course you can come with me, though I don't know where I'm going. Archie's on the other side, and another thing the Sun said was that once a soul has paid his due to Death he can never cross back. Death's law is irreversible."

"And the Sun is right. In all my time here, I have never seen a soul cross back. But that said," he smiled, "in all that time nor have I seen anyone enter Transit whose time it has not been to cross over. Yet here you are. So anything is possible. Maybe we could send Archie a note, a letter?" Anian suggested.

"We used to write to each other all the time," Sarah said with a sigh, her mind once more filling with nostalgic thoughts.

"We could find the boatman," Anian put forward, his head going through the motions.

"The who?"

"The boatman: I've seen him once, rowing the Styx," Anian explained.

"The river?"

Anian nodded. "We'll have to be careful and move only in daylight, although ..." he paused, his misshapen face deep in thought. "In fact there will be no Moon this evening." His face flashed with delight for a brief moment, as though an idea had struck, then the delight faded and action kicked in. "Come with me. You love to watch the stars at night don't you? Let's go see them now." Anian grabbed Sarah's hand, dragging her to the foot of the stairs.

"I suppose," replied Sarah, realising the last time she had properly sat out and stargazed was years ago with Archie. She had shied away from stargazing ever since – particularly since his death - it reminded her too much of him. She followed Anian up the spiral staircase of his tree house, right to the very top to an uneven decked area open to the sky. It was twilight, the light fading fast. The air was filled with mosquitoes, crickets and hunting bats. Sarah stumbled along behind Anian, tripping over her long flowing gown. He paid her no attention, he simply made himself comfortable lying flat on his back on the decking and stared up into the moonless sky, waiting for the stars to emerge. Getting used to Anian's seemingly uncaring manner, Sarah didn't grumble but quickly followed suit and lay down next to him. The height of the tree seemed to amplify the heavens that domed endlessly above her.

"Close your eyes," Anian grunted.

"What? Why? It's so beautiful."

"You'll see, just do it."

Sarah did as she was told, allowing nightfall to set in without her watching, and at the same time, strangely, having complete trust in this warped creature beside her. Staring at the back of her own eyelids, her mind began to wander. She had to find Archie. He was here somewhere.

She could feel it deep inside. He was close. He was trying to find her too. The hole in her chest didn't burn as it had or maybe that was the power of her lapis lazuli pendant trying to heal her broken heart. She needed to get home afterwards, though ... but how? According to Lillian and the Sun there was no way back.

She was just drifting into a restless doze, when suddenly the satyr spoke. "Right, open your eyes."

Once again, Sarah complied. The moment was powerful. Her head spun and she thanked God that she was laid flat on her back and not standing, or she would have fallen over for sure. It felt as though the stars were all rushing towards her - or as though she had taken flight and was zooming through space. "Oh my!" she gasped.

"Impressive hey?" Anian snorted. Sarah could feel him looking at her, but instead of answering she decided to lie in silence for a while, taking in the celestial star-studded show of shooting stars, watching and listening. She wished Archie could have been beside her instead of this great hairy goat.

Without warning there was a great commotion and a frantic flutter of wings. The oak's branches, which until that moment had been still and peaceful, were disturbed by a giant bird. It swooped in and settled on a bough a short distance from them.

"Bran?" Anian sat up fast. Sarah copied, shocked by the disturbance. "Shoo, shoo, go away!" Anian got to his feet shouting; clip clopping his hooves all over the decking in an angry dance to startle the bird. "Go on ... away with you ... shoo."

"It's just a bird, Anian," Sarah whispered in an attempt to calm him.

"That's no bird. That's Bran."

"Who's Bran?" Sarah asked.

"Raven," Anian spat, still stamping.

"I can see that, Anian, but ..."

"Chief Raven," Anian added quickly, cutting Sarah off.

"Why don't you want him here?" Sarah asked, holding onto the decking as it shook under the satyr's beating hooves.

"There aren't many nights we tree-folk are allowed to sit out and enjoy the stars. In fact, out of thirty nights there is only one night when we can. I don't want that fluttery, black feathered fiend spoiling our moment." Anian spoke gruffly, still trotting about, waving his arms attempting to spook the giant bird. "I'll stuff you when I get my hands on you, Bran." Anian thumped his hoof down so hard that Sarah quickly lay down again, flat on her stomach, for fear of falling off the decking. The bird squawked fiercely at Anian then flew away, seemingly unperturbed by the satyr's song and dance.

Anian half-heartedly chased after the bird, shaking his fist then satisfied Bran was gone he turned back to Sarah with an anxious look. "Humph, I didn't want to say, er ..." He looked awkward, his grotesque face frowning into a screwed up mess, yet his big green eyes glinted through the repulsiveness and Sarah saw in them only warmth.

"Didn't want to frighten you," he said, "but Bran is also a man-eating bird with a beak of bronze and lethally sharp, metallic feathers. You don't often see him, but when you do it means ... well, that he'll be back. Especially now he knows you're here."

Speechless, Sarah stared in shock at Anian, her eyes bulging.

"I loathe him," the Satyr bleated. "He is my greatest enemy. I live off the fruits of the forest and he and his flock eat most of it before I get a chance to harvest it. He'd see me starve for sure. He does it to spite me; bet he wishes I would just cross over, but I can't, not yet ... not until he's a useless ornament. One day I'll get him."

Getting to her feet slowly, now that the satyr had stopped moving and seemed to have calmed down, Sarah brushed herself off, her head so full of questions she hardly knew which to ask first. "What do you mean Anian, now he knows I'm here?"

"Well, he'll report it straight to his mistress, the Moon, of course," Anian explained.

"The Moon again," Sarah sighed, her voice small.

"You don't stand a hope coming face to face with her, Sarah. Remember never to be caught out, find shelter before dusk, you'll be dead if you don't," Anian insisted.

"So people keep telling me," Sarah said. "What about you?"

"She won't bother with the likes of me, so long as I abide by her rules and don't show my disgusting face at night, how do you think I ended up looking like this? She'll hex anyone she gets her hands on."

"The Moon made you look like that?" Sarah asked her voice full of pity.

Anian nodded, his head drooping with shame. "A long time ago, yes. It was my fault for getting caught. I chose to remain in Transit; it was only a matter of time before she found me. She has the power to winkle out the insecurity and fear you hold deep inside and bring it to fruition and light. She is the invincible queen and the ruler of this realm, even the Sun cannot override her, though he'd never have the horror of ever facing her. He is gone from the sky before she rises."

Anian started for the trapdoor. "We should go back downstairs; it's too risky being up here. I can't believe how stupid I was," he muttered, slapping himself hard on his hairy flanks and trotting to the stairs. Glancing nervously over her shoulder, Sarah followed, hot on his heels.

"Why? You said earlier, the Moon is not out this evening, we will be fine," Sarah said as they re-entered the tree-house. "Now the Moon knows you're with me though, won't you be in trouble?"

"Don't worry about me," Anian said, stoking his fire. "All I wanted to do was show you the stars. I've shown you them now, so that's done. It'll be the only time you see them here in Transit."

"It was awesome," said Sarah, remembering the rush she had got when she opened her eyes.

"They certainly are and you were once one of them, owned by the Moon," Anian said, still focusing on the fire and filling his cauldron with different sorts of fruit, the delicious jammy smell filling the room.

"What?" Sarah exclaimed at the ridiculousness of Anian's statement. The Sun had mentioned she had been a star and the Moon's property too, but she had not comprehended it.

"YOU WERE A STAR," Anian shouted in a mocking voice, turning to face her.

"There's no need to shout, I heard you. I just don't understand what you mean. How could I have been a star?" A slight smirk caught on Sarah's face. Almost she laughed; the idea was so blatantly ridiculous. "It doesn't make any sense to me."

"Do I make any sense to you? I'm half goat!" Anian laughed. "Does anything that has happened to you in the last few days make any sense?" His point made, he ushered Sarah over to the bed in the corner.

Crestfallen she sat on it, suddenly aware of just how tired she was, her eyelids drooping as she watched the satyr stirring the concoction in the cauldron. Her eyes must have closed, for moments later he was standing over her, shaking her shoulder and holding out a bowl of honey and cherry soup. The steam rose deliciously into her nostrils making her mouth water.

As she took the bowl and lifted it to her mouth, Anian smiled then trotted over to the table with its hand-shaped chairs. Pulling out a hidden drawer, he retrieved a scrap of tatty parchment and a handmade pencil and waved them at her.

"You have a letter to write, Missus. But first you must sleep, it will help your troubled mind, I promise."

CHAPTER TWELVE

AUGUST 1685
WITH EACH DYING EMBER HIS SPIRIT TWISTED UPON ETERNITY

The timber door was brutally smashed in. This type did not knock to enter. The old man inside was heaved from his humble home just before it was torched and went up in flames.

"Petty Treason!" the stout Parish Constable yelled at the top of his voice for all the villagers to hear, the scroll in his hand evidence for his arrest, forcing the elderly man onto his knees to watch his abode and all his meagre belongings burn. "You, sir, have committed an offence under the common law of England," the Constable announced.

"W-w-what offence w-w-would that be?" the man stammered, his head down in blind panic and shame as his neighbours scattered from their homes to see what the commotion was all about. Old Nick was once again being forcefully removed from his home by the Constable and two of Lord Belmont's ruffians, however this time things had gone one step further, the severity plainly evident as thick, black smoke swelled into the skies.

"You are a servant of this land, are you not?" the Constable shouted, antagonism lining his brow, his plump crimson face inches away from Nick's as he dragged him to his feet by the scruff of his neck and started to haul him down the dusty road.

"I am, and I work hard on the land for my lord every day," Nick insisted, his eyes still down, as he was dragged and yanked to the centre of the market square just outside the church.

"Well, it seems Lord Belmont would disagree," one of the enforcing ruffians spat in his ear. Old Nick knew him well, as did most; he was Renshaw, Lord Belmont's most unforgiving and loyal stable-hand. "Furthermore," Renshaw continued, "Lord Belmont does not like his daughter keeping company with dirty old fools like you," he sneered, shouting louder, ensuring everyone could hear. "Especially since she is now betrothed to Mister Jackson of Great Finborough. You have connived at bringing Lady Sarah into disrepute and thereby caused your master harm."

Nick lifted his head, his eyes swivelling, his gaze darting from the pristine, fat Constable, to the lout, Renshaw, then to the other thug, whose shirt hung open, his unshaven face streaming with sweat. These brutes meant every word of what they accused him of, there was no doubt in Nick's mind. It hardly constituted Petty Treason; he had done Lord Belmont no physical harm, but neither the squire nor his bullies would consider such niceties. His measured gaze moved to his lifelong friends and co-workers, all of whom stood frozen to the spot. The market had come to a standstill, even the stray chickens seemed lost for something to peck; all were motionless, staring with dread at the old man.

Nobody really knew how old he was – at least seventy-two years, some said. Born and bred in the village, Nick had been part of the community for longer than most of them could remember. An only child, his parents had passed on decades before, but like his cat, Nick seemed to have lived nine lives, playing 'catch me if you can' with the law. He was not a bad man; he was no criminal. He did not have a malicious bone in his body. He was healthy, wise and kind; honest and true as the day was long, but he had a secret, a big secret, which he closeted and guarded more vigilantly than the king did his jewels. He had a gift, which very few knew about and those who did were entrusted purely because they had Nick's complete confidence. He was a warlock; a warlock with the gift of longevity.

"Who told you Miss Sarah came here?" Nick spat under his breath.

"So you don't deny it?" the Constable asked. Nick did not reply. "Who informed us of Lady Belmont's whereabouts this morning is no concern of yours old man. At this present moment you stand to have committed adultery with your master's daughter."

There were smothered guffaws in the crowd as this preposterous accusation was heard by those nearest and passed back.

"Adultery?" Nick's jaw dropped, stupefied. "Don't be ridiculous," he hollered, his wizened face reddening. "That's sordid and blatantly untrue. I'm old enough to be her grandfather! She's but a child and a friend."

"Denying it now are we? Speaking out about it? Oh this is just the start, you dithering old fool," the Constable said. "Seems you've been around a few too many years and have one too many enemies in high places, Old Nick. That's what you're called around here, isn't it?" the Constable leered, his rant nowhere near its end.

"By my friends," Nick replied shortly, his mind reeling as he filtered through all his associates who might have spun tales about him. He could think of none.

"It has also been reported," the Constable started to circle his victim closely, causing Nick to feel dizzy and disorientated, "that you bear the mark of the Devil."

Horrified gasps rose from the audience. Again Nick shot Renshaw and his mate a glance then stared round in terror at the villagers.

"And we all know what happens to those who worship him," the Constable grinned.

"I worship no Devil, you imbeciles," Nick hissed, his panic intensifying.

"No one can live as long as you have Old Nick, not without some sort of magic mischief," the quieter brute snarled. "And how else could you ensnare a beautiful young woman unless by wizardry, eh? Let's take a look then," the thug leaned forward to grasp Nick's collar, "where's your mark?"

"Don't touch me you rat," Nick said, lashing out as the oaf grabbed at his already tattered shirt ripping it from the shoulder seam. Fraught, but in a state of hopelessness, Nick allowed the man to remove his shirt. The humiliation was insufferable. Of all the times he had spent in the stocks, this moment creamed the lot. Sure enough, on the side of his stomach was a raised and prominent strawberry birthmark, just what they were looking for.

"Ladies, gentleman," the Constable roared, using a cane to point at the blotch. "See here, it is true. Old Nick has the mark of the Devil."

"It's a birthmark, they are more common than you think," Nick said in an attempt to defend himself. His body was shaking now, his heart pounding in his ears.

"That your cat?" Renshaw asked, not really interested in an answer. Brutally he kicked the tabby cat that had quietly followed and now started winding itself around

Nick's legs. Nick knew exactly what they were insinuating and if the truth be known, Tabitha was indeed his familiar. She had been with him for twenty-three years. Again, Nick tried to stay silent, knowing his pleas would fall on deaf ears and would only cause him more harm.

Renshaw had picked the creature up by the tail and was violently swinging it, like the sails of a windmill, laughing as it yowled in terror. Nick scowled with distress for his old friend as she was cruelly bullied before him. It was only a matter of time and one cat scream too many, before he could bite his tongue no longer.

"You torture my cat in jest, but if she dies in earnest she will live beyond in rapture," Nick hissed, his broiling fury plain for all to see.

"You'll be next if you don't reel yourself in old man," Renshaw jeered, still swirling Tabitha back and forth, coldheartedly ignoring her wails then tossing her aside where she lay motionless, blood dribbling from her mouth.

"It's like a sport to you, this, isn't it? You are ruthless, heartless with no sense of right or wrong," Nick could not help himself; his rage consumed him and the only weapon he had left to him, his tongue, took over and ran away with him. "I pity you, for you are nothing more than bullies under someone else's command. Until you stop harming living beings, no matter what it is, cat, caterpillar or person, you are all just vile savages. I curse you and all your kind."

A deathly silence loomed over the market square for no more that a second, but to Nick it felt like an eternity. Too late he realised what he had said. He had lost control and there was nothing he could do to unsay his words. All eyes and hearts transfixed, every breath held. The Constable continued to march around Nick, eyeing him with distaste tinged with fear. Then he halted abruptly.

"Curse me, do you? String him up," the Constable ordered.

"NO!" The shouted cry came simultaneously from several onlookers, but as the villagers stirred and voiced their protest, Renshaw and his mate seized Nick by either arm and towed him relentlessly towards the west wing of the church, where punishment and sentences were carried out and where the vicar was waiting.

"There will be no trial or acquittal," the Constable shouted to the spectators as they shadowed Nick's unwilling tracks. "Upon this day, Thursday, the eighteenth day of August, at two hours into the afternoon, in this place ..."

"Don't do this!" screamed one terrified woman in the crowd, quickly silenced by her husband.

The Constable glared in her direction and ignoring all pleas for mercy continued, "Old Nick here shall be tied to a stake and cleansed by fire until he is dead and thereafter until his body is burnt to ashes," he concluded, stopping beside bundles of faggots piled high around the stake, prepared and waiting.

"What is my crime? Tell me?" Nick hollered struggling against the brutes in panic then turning his pleading eyes to the vicar, an old friend, who stood by as a witness. "Don't let them do this," he begged, but the vicar just shook his head, refusing to meet Nick's gaze.

Renshaw and his companion forcefully hoisted the old man onto the sticks and tied him by the neck to the stake in the centre.

"What's my crime, I beg you?" Nick cried again.

"Petty Treason," Renshaw shouted out for the benefit of the crowd then turning nose to nose with Nick, his arms wrapped tight around him as he ensured the rigid rope was secure around the old man's neck and fragile wrists, he whispered, "I'm sure all this smoke and this whole to-do will bring Miss Sarah and her real lover out of the fields with some haste, don't you?"

Nick stared at Renshaw, hate burning through his eyes. "So you know," he spat, his nostrils flaring, unable to move his head.

"Know what, old man?"

"About Lady Sarah and Archie Fletch ..." too late, Nick realised he had been tricked.

Renshaw guffawed. "I do now, and so do you, which makes you an accomplice in the affair," he smirked. "Lord Belmont does not like those who help plot his daughter's life, for he has it all planned out for her, whether she likes it or not. I expect you can imagine what he will do to Archie Fletcher when I tell him that's who's been playing fast and loose with his precious offspring."

Nick groaned, "Love is the answer, Renshaw. It is the only answer to our existence. Why do you want to destroy the lives of those two young people? What's it to you?"

"Humph, you old fool. Isn't it clear to you? It's nothing to me. The law will always win," Renshaw coughed. "We've built the firewood up high so your friends won't see you suffer. Couple of minutes is all it takes 'till you're forced to breathe in the flames." He stepped back with a sneer, leaving Nick, half naked, tears of fear trickling down the runnels of his face, lashed to a wooden stake surrounded by bone dry kindling.

"Any last words?" the Constable called up.

With an obvious effort, Old Nick straightened his body to look down at the hushed crowd. "I will have no trial because you know I have done no wrong. Everyone here witnessing this can see that what you do is not ridding the world of another rascal. You know full well that your accusation is false. Lord Belmont uses you as his tool to once again force others to deny their true nature and conform. Why can we not be who we are and love who we want? Answer me that."

"It is the law," the Constable shouted. "You consort with the Devil and must be cleansed."

"What you do here today has nothing to do with the law, Constable. I will be murdered here by you and your bullyboys, but I will have a clear conscience. You will not. And I swear to you, I shall wait for you in the beyond to take my vengeance."

"A clean conscience? Why the tears then, old man?" smirked Renshaw, lunging forward and jumping up to pluck a fat tear off Nick's chin.

"There are certain times in life when fear cannot be controlled," Nick said sadly. "I do not mean to weep; I wish I could forbid myself to shed another tear until my vengeance on you is complete."

"Your tears will soon dry up once this pit gets burning, then let's see your tears; they'll melt into your face for eternity."

"You have no shame do you Renshaw? You are nothing but an ignorant fool."

"And you are a damned dissenter, a witch and an inferior," Renshaw retaliated.

"I am a man," Nick hollered, his voice cracking under the pressure, he had gone past caring, he knew his fate and he knew he could not be saved. "An old man at that, but I am just a man. No different from you or the next man." Tears began to flood down Nick's scarred and wrinkled face. "You curse me as the Devil because I choose to worship in the old way and because I have a blemish, no more distinct than the mole on your neck. No, it is not because of what I believe that you have strung me up. Even our vicar has become a Vicar of Bray because Lord Belmont has forced him to change his principles and his religious beliefs, but I don't suppose you've ever heard of him, have you Renshaw?" Nick spat. "It's impossible for anyone around here to really comply with these ridiculous and constant ecclesiastical changes, this so called 'Act of Uniformity', and I don't believe anyone in their heart of hearts ever really will change what they believe. They say they do because they are scared." He stared hard at the vicar, whose face tinged pink with shame. Nick drew in a short breath, gaining strength to continue.

"Enough!" Renshaw called.

"No," Nick continued. "It is not because of what I believe that I am here today it is because you choose to defy love. Miss Sarah, as everyone knows, does not love Mister Jackson, she loves another. And in your refusal to accept it, you forget one thing: true love is wild, a thing of raw nature, you cannot tame or control it; it is as free as an eagle soaring in the sky, but no matter how beautiful that may sound, love will still draw blood when challenged. Sarah's and Archie's story is not just a love story, it is priceless knowledge, an education; we must all learn from. Let us love who our hearts desire. Their story must not be lost to the world."

"Ah yes, Archie Fletcher," Renshaw smiled as the Constable handed him a flaming torch. "He will be next. Thank you, Old Nick, you've been very, er ... amenable." He placed the torch to the kindling, which caught instantly and began to crackle and hiss. The crowd moaned, a woman screamed. The vicar's lips moved in a soundless prayer.

"Oh, Miss Sarah, forgive me. Like I told you, I talk too much," Nick cried as the flames leapt about him, the heavens opened and it began to pour with rain.

CHAPTER THIRTEEN

AUGUST 2003
POWER COMES FROM THE SPIRIT, NOBODY GIVES IT TO YOU

The Buddhist monk's prayer was a form of meditation, slowly converting his confusion into clarity. Niran-Atid glanced up to the firmament. He asked for no favours for his own personal gain, or for any favours at the expense of others, as this would crush the power of his prayer. Devoid of any self-centeredness and calculations, relying solely on compassion, he called quietly to the heavens from where he sat, in a small long-tail boat in the middle of the Chao Phraya River. The cosmos seemed to answer his prayer directly and he beamed at the sky a toothless grin.

"The greatest action, Miss Sarah, is not conforming with the world's ways."

***

Sarah, her head still fuzzy with dreaming about an old man tied to a burning stake, laid down the pencil and sighing, read what she had written.

Archie,

I'm trapped here in Transit looking for you. It was an accident.
Joseph and Chanthira the Moon tried to kidnap me.
Please help.

I miss you.

Love, Sarah

PS I finally read your letter

"Is that it?" Anian said gawking over Sarah's shoulder. She sighed and laid her head on the table next to the note. "I don't know what to write. After all, what do you write to your dead cousin who has turned out to be your soulmate, when you've found yourself trapped in a dreamlike world full of otherworldly creatures, where the Sun talks and the Moon hexes? It's all too complicated Anian."

"He'll understand," Anian soothed. "Remember he's been here too."

"Anian ... how come you're trapped here?" Sarah asked. She had asked once before and hit a wall, but she was intrigued now, he seemed so familiar and she felt so comfortable in his presence, which given their first meeting was extraordinary. She didn't want to push him, but maybe he needed her help too. What was Anian's story?

"Even if I told you, Sarah, you would never recognise me, it is best you don't ask," Anian said walking away from the table, retrieving a large bowl of cherries off the kitchen shelf and instantly guzzling the fruit, pips and all.

"I know you, don't I?" Sarah asked, her mind reeling, lucid dreams becoming clearer. "I mean, I knew you ...."

"It doesn't matter," Anian insisted, red cherry juice seeping out of the sides of his mouth. "What matters is getting you to Archie as quickly as possible." He offered the cherry bowl to Sarah. A few lonesome overripe cherries remained in the bottom.

"No thanks," she grimaced.

"Cherries are so good for you, along with my honey they have kept me alive. They are a natural pain reliever, so I've learnt and even better than that, they help you to regulate sleep. Oh, there have been times when the Moon's ravens have been out, screeching and screaming through the skies all night long, I could have shot them had I a gun. I've been desperate for sleep and even in quieter times my body has refused point blank to find it, memories drown me, they haunt me Sarah, but cherries help."

"What memories?" Sarah asked, her eyes widening at Anian's obvious distress.

His face changed rapidly from a deep, concerned trance to an open and ugly cherry-red grin. "You really want to know my story?"

"Of course I really want to know," Sarah insisted.

"Well then ... I have a letter for you to read," he announced, rummaging in the table drawer. "It was written a long time ago; you must read it."

"Who is it from?" Sarah sat up with a grin.

"Just read it please," the satyr whispered, handing her a screwed up note and turning away to busy himself with his cooking pot.

Intrigued, Sarah took the crumpled note and smoothed it out on the table.

Dear Miss Sarah,

For your sake I must write this letter. I need to tell you a story. It is my story and it is on this page I must pen my final confession.

A long time ago there lived a man whose name was Nicholas. He had no family, orphaned as a young child, but he lived a life of love, he was happy working the fields, living in nature. To the outside world he was never ageing, never changing. Most people adored him, he was wise and as constant as the stars above, but some thought him to be the Devil. To them he was breaking the law. His potions and intuitions frightened them and because he did not worship God in the way they wanted him to, he was called a Dissenter and was disgraced. Their ruling saw fire as a way to wash away his crimes and cleanse his soul.

Years ago, he was your friend, he had your absolute trust, you were like the daughter he never had. He did not mean to betray you, but I confess he talked too much. It was he who leaked Archie's name. If it had not been for him your escape from the village could have been accomplished. It all went wrong because of him. You could have lived the life you dreamed of together. He told them when he was strapped to a stake and he could not save you. How could he? He is worse than the Devil they claimed he was.

Even now he still lives under their watch, the Moon and her ravens. Every day, for hundreds of years, he is reminded of what he did and the reprisal he would take on those who chose to judge him and burn him. Now like you, he waits, but not for love: he waits for vengeance. Nothing changes, nothing ever will. He is still the same: just a man, only trapped in Transit with the humiliation of having the legs and tail of a goat, unable to shed tears of regret.

It is me, Anian. I am so sorry. If there is a God, let it forgive me.

Sarah pulled the letter into her chest, tears bubbling in her eyes, her recent dream coming back to her in all its vivid, horrifying detail. Anian had come to sit with her at the table while she had finished reading.

"I understand, Anian, and I at least forgive you," she said, her heart pouring out to her new and old friend. "You've lived with this shame for so long. Please don't feel guilty any more. The world back then was so different. It wasn't your fault." Sarah thought a moment. The strange dreams she had been having and the people in it slowly clicking into place. It was like a missing link or finding a missing jigsaw piece, her dreams were all slowly beginning to make sense.

"Life on Earth today is very changed," she said. "Materialistically we're more advanced, we have more technology now, but our ideas and arguments about God go on. I don't expect they will ever stop. I wish they would. The world would be a far nicer place if they did. Ridiculously, people are still losing their lives because of their beliefs. Archie would never have been sent to war if ..." Her voice trailed away. Always it came back to Archie.

"Thank you, Miss Sarah," Anian grunted, his head still down in shame.

"Please ... look at me," Sarah said warmly, gently putting her hand on his shoulder. Anian looked up; his big green eyes were full of tears he was afraid to spill.

"What happens now then?" Sarah asked. She frowned. She had thought it was becoming clearer, but now the pieces of jigsaw jumbled in her mind. In her dream she and Archie had been going to run away together; she had been waiting in a cornfield ... had seen Old Nick burning and thought it was Archie, but that was in another life – a life that was centuries ago. What had it to do with this life –

that is, the life she'd had before she'd jumped over the bridge? Archie was dead, killed in a plane crash just a month or so ago - and he had died without really knowing that she loved him. And then there was Felicity; who was she? It was all very complicated and she couldn't get her head around any of it.

"I don't know," Anian shrugged, staring hard at Sarah. "I've been trapped here for such a long time, living in my own self pity and gloom. I never fooled myself that I would ever be forgiven for betraying you and Archie. What happens beyond being excused, I never thought."

"Well, you are excused and you've got me here now to help you work out what to do, for you and for me," Sarah insisted, her hand not leaving his shoulder.

"Where am I going to now, Miss Sarah? What should I do?" Anian implored. "Life here has been so long and lonely."

"I can only imagine, but you must stop worrying about that. You're not alone anymore. What do you want to do?" Sarah asked.

"Cross the bridge I suppose, and follow where all the other souls go," Anian said.

"That's it. Why don't you do that then? Let's get you across. You should be elated. Shouting from the top of your tree, 'Hallelujah, I'm free from guilt!" Sarah said, jumping up from the hand-shaped chair.

"Do you really think so? But there's one thing I need to do before I go. I told you in my note."

"What's that?"

"Revenge, Miss Sarah! The ravens... Bran ..." Anian, his eyes wide, stared at Sarah. "I've been hoping that your dreams and your reality would merge into clarity. Everyone takes a different form here in Transit, but their underlying character remains the same. Don't you know who Bran is?

"Renshaw?" Sarah said hesitantly, her eyes squinting slightly with uncertainty.

"Yes, they are one and the same," Anian's oozing blistered mouth formed a delighted smile.

"Oh... I see." Sarah said, nodding.

"He set fire to my stake all those years ago and I have waited all this time to take my vengeance, but it seems all the time I have waited, he has been with me hovering close by. Merely a pawn the Moon plays with, but still an evil rogue who will not leave me alone."

"Why did you wait here in Transit, why didn't you just cross the bridge and be rid of him forever?" Sarah asked.

"My own self-disgust has kept me here; my guilt about what I did ... and the way I look now." Anian stared hard at Sarah. "Look at me! I'm a monster. Even my own mother, if she could see me, would run a thousand miles away in fright. I have become the Moon's amusement and the uglier she made me, the more uncouth and odd I have become. My confidence and self-esteem are shattered. They took away my dignity when they torched me and then the Moon changed me into what you see. My bees and the animals in the forest have been my only friends all these years, I have become so uncivilised, I am not worthy of crossing over into that blessed place. Why would they want me? It's no use, Miss Sarah. I am destined to be lost here forever."

"Well you've a friend in me too now, so please drop the 'Miss' and just call me 'Sarah'," she smiled. "I won't hear any more of your guilt; it is forgotten in my mind. Start accepting who you are and what you look like. Free yourself from this torture you're putting yourself through.

Beneath all these scars and deformities you are no different from me, I promise you. It is what you are on the inside that counts. How you are feeling is natural and I suppose, I would feel the same if I were you." Sarah took a deep breath hoping she had not offended or spoken out of turn.

"Well ..." Anian said his face suddenly mighty serious. "Maybe, just maybe there is a God above us." The satyr's eyes filled with tears again. "He brought you to me, for that I will say hallelujah. HALLELUJAH!" he hollered at the top of his voice. Yet through his smiles of joy, tears uncontrollably began to overflow and tumble from his eyes.

"Ahh ...." he screamed with pain, thrusting up his hands to cover his face.

"Anian, what's happening?" Sarah shouted gazing at the satyr, for as the tears of happiness seared down his buckled features, wisps of smoke gusted from behind the hands that cupped his face, the smell of burning flesh filling the air.

"Anian, are you okay?" Sarah cried in alarm, pulling down his hands to reveal fresh wounds tearing down his face. She gasped in horror and pity at the mess of his face, which in places resembled the melted wax of a candle.

"I told you, I am unable to cry," he whispered. "It is the Moon's little joke. It'll be all right again now. Come, we should go."

"Where?" Sarah asked, taken aback.

"Down to the river, the faster you get that letter to Archie, the faster you can get home. I'm not crossing any bridge or getting in any boat until I know you're home safe and sound. Getting you back will be my vengeance on Renshaw and the Moon, and then I will cross. It's not good for you being trapped in Transit with Anian. You should not be here. Come, let's go," he said, trotting towards the tree house exit.

"Wait, Anian, tell me ..." Sarah grabbed her stone sword, which was propped up by the hatchway. "What other memories do you have?" She ran after him, totally in awe and fascinated by their past life together, wanting to fill in the gaps.

"The last thing I can remember when I was on the Earth-plain was seeing my local vicar praying for me," Anian said, as he scrambled hand over hoof down the dodgy rope ladder, through the centre of the hollow tree.

"Surely that's a good thing?" Sarah said, starting after him.

Anian huffed and said no more on the subject. "Remember, control your thoughts," he reminded instead. "You must keep them tamed or we could be in grave danger."

"I will, I know. After the ant attack yesterday, I promise I will think of nothing except getting my note over to Archie. How exactly are we going to do that?"

"Like I said, the boatman."

"Boatman?" Sarah asked, baffled. He did not respond. They were out of the hollow trunk now and on firm ground. It was still springtime outside, the weather was warm and the sun was shining. Sarah held her sword at the ready, whilst Anian looked about.

"Follow me," he whispered. His eyes constantly searching the treetops, as though he thought he was being watched, Anian darted between the trees. Sarah was worried that if she blinked she might lose him, he was so fast. With great effort she managed to keep close to his hooves. It was a struggle at times, running barefoot over the woodland floor. Exhausted, she wondered about later trying some of Anian's cherries, so she could have a dreamless sleep. 'Not until Archie has my note, then I'll rest,' she thought to herself.

Eventually, after what seemed miles, they arrived at the riverbank. The river was high and flowing fast when they found it, the water churned up and murky. Sarah had not realised how wide it was. From her glimpse on top of the oak tree it had seemed not much more than a stream. Up close, the other side seemed such a distance away and was blurred by mist.

"Where's the boatman then?" Sarah panted, catching up. Anian halted abruptly at the river edge looking it up and down. "Don't we need to pay him or something?" Sarah asked.

"We're not crossing, Sarah. You only need to pay him if you want to travel in the boat. We're just passing on a message,"

"Do you think he'll take it for free?" Sarah asked from a few metres back. "Will he be able to bring a reply?"

"I don't know. I've only ever seen the boatman once." Anian said.

"When was that?" Sarah's said, falling in beside him.

"A long time ago, when I was supposed to cross over," Anian explained. "It's been a long time, but I don't think he'd have forgotten me, the palaver I made refusing his lift."

"I wonder if Archie crossed over with him."

"I doubt it. The boatman only takes those who are ready to cross. All adventurers with lessons to learn must find the bridge and ..." Anian started. He stopped speaking abruptly, "Prepare yourself!" he shouted.

"W-what? W-why?" Sarah stammered, looking around fearfully.

"Here he comes."

A long, narrow gondola pulled towards them through the mist rising off the river. It seemed to materialise out of nowhere and appeared to be made from all different kinds of wood patterned in a mosaic of red, black and honey-gold. Propelling it with a long oar was a tall, dark figure, draped in a brownish, grubby looking cloak. The hood was down revealing the boatman's bald head. Everything about him looked weathered; he had haggard cheeks and an unkempt beard. He was slightly hunched, as he drew his oar out of the water, but the nearer he got, Sarah could see he was not at all old or stooped. In fact he was a tall, able man, but his eyes were so frightening that she had to glance away: they burned bright red. His boat hit the beach gently and stopped, motionless as though anchored. The boatman did not get out of his boat; his piercing red eyes stared at Anian in silence, and Anian stared back. Moments passed.

Unsure of what was happening, Sarah became restless. "Are you going to ask him then, Anian?" she asked, giving Anian a soft nudge. The satyr did not reply, he just continued to stare at the boatman. It was as though they were already communicating and Sarah couldn't hear them.

"What's going on?" she tried again.

"He wants me to go with him," Anian replied. "I've told him again that I won't."

"When exactly did he say that then?" Sarah asked.

"Telepathically, from his mind to mine," Anian explained.

"Oh yes, of course," Sarah breathed, remembering what the Sun had told her.

"He won't talk to you because it is not your time to cross."

"Charming," Sarah said aloud. "What about the note? Will he take it?"

"He said I must deliver it to Archie personally," Anian said, shaking his head regretfully.

"What does that mean, you have to take the note, cross over and never return?" Sarah asked, frustrated to be a third party to the whole conversation. She stood in the river, the water lapping at her ankles, the hem of her dress soaked as she jiggled up and down in annoyance. She wanted to reach out and grab the boat and pop her letter in, but she knew it had to be delivered by someone. It would never find Archie if the boatman or Anian didn't agree to take it.

"Yes, he wants me to go with him in the boat and cross over and deliver it to Archie," Anian clarified.

"Can you come back?" Sarah asked.

"Of course not, once a soul crosses the river he can never come back," Anian reminded.

The boatman began to push away.

"Where's he going?" Sarah exclaimed, stepping forward with outstretched arms.

"He's angry. Even if you can't read his mind, he can read yours, Sarah. Did you think about throwing the note into his boat?"

"Yes, briefly," Sarah admitted. "Why can't I hear him like you do?"

"Because you are not really here; not yet – or at least, not all of you is. Anyway, now you've made him angry and so have I, by refusing to go a second time," Anian explained.

"But what about my note?" Sarah cried, wading into the river after the boat.

"We'll have to find another way. Sarah, get out of the water."

"What other way is there?" she replied going in further. The boat was only metres away; she could reach out and grab it if she dared.

"Sarah, that is not the way. Come back," Anian hollered.

But Sarah, once again, was not listening; she was neck deep now, nearly swimming after the boatman, her toes only just touching the pebbly riverbed.

"Come back," she cried at the boat. It was no use; no matter how much she willed herself to grab the side of the boat it was always just out of her reach. Water splashed around her face as the river became choppier the further out she swam. The boat began to break away from her. Propelling herself on, she started a strong front crawl stroke, her stubborn streak taking the lead, determined to catch up with it.

"Sarah ...!" She could hear Anian calling from the shore, demanding she swim back.

"I can't go back," she puffed to herself. "I'll swim to the other side if I have to," but her endurance began to drop when she looked up at the distance between her and the other side. It never seemed to get any nearer. The water was becoming rougher and the current stronger. She would never make it. The boatman, from a distance, slowed the boat and stared hard at Sarah, his disrespectful crimson eyes boring into her. Frantically treading water, from which the morning vapour was still lifting, Sarah felt a sudden chill run up her spine. She began to back pedal to Anian as fast as she could, her dress getting caught between her legs with every stroke. Above her she could hear the squawk of a bird – a raven? Finding it easier to swim on her back, she rolled over and floated, looking up into the sky. Soaring high, Sarah saw the giant raven, possibly the one she had seen in Anian's oak or the one that had attacked her in the woods. Were they one and the same? Was it Bran? It was surrounded by smaller birds, they too were black and could well be ravens, but she couldn't be sure from that distance. All she knew was that they were circling her and making such a row and then the largest bird leading the others, began to dive.

"SWIM, Sarah," Anian hollered. 'Didn't want to frighten you, but Bran is also a man-eating bird with a beak of bronze and lethally sharp metallic feathers,' the satyr's voice rang in her head.

Not wanting to take chances and turn her back on the swooping bird, Sarah started to backstroke as fast as she could. Her legs kicked and pounded through the water with such speed, propelling herself to the water's edge. Bran swooped down on her just as she felt the pebbles beneath her feet again. She ducked under the water. Bran followed her under, along with a dozen other ravens. Why had she dropped her sword on the beach? Beaks pecked and snatched at her, but none could penetrate through her dress. Only her shoulders and her face were in any real danger and she got a nasty gash on her cheek from one serrated bill. She could feel the blood pouring into the river. Continuing to push towards the shore under the water, Sarah battered and grabbed and yanked at the birds, pulling them off her. As she rose from the river, she was covered, head to foot, in birds, trying to attack her.

"CATCH!" Anian cried, throwing the stone sword. She caught it and her body took over, fighting off the ravens, instinctively wielding the blade with sweeping, skilful strokes. Anian waded in to help with a battered stick he had found strewn on the ground.

Very conscious of what she was doing, but oblivious to how or where the talent was coming from, Sarah ducked and jabbed. It was as though a dust cover had been pulled off her mind and information of old was jumping to the forefront. If she had stopped to think about it, she would have been lost. Ripping through feathers, black down, blood and fluff flew everywhere. Like an enraged warrior, Sarah continued to slaughter, pierce, stamp and roar at the birds; dot to dot, cryptic messages coming through in her mind of how to sword fight. She must have been taught in a former life. It was the strangest and most exhilarating feeling she had experienced.

Bran held back, watching the massacre. When Sarah paused and took breath, she noticed he was hesitant and inspecting her. She stepped forward fiercely and Bran flapped away; in seconds he was out of sight.

"He's a coward, that bird," Anian said. Sarah was unable to speak. She stepped out of the river, dropped her sword and threw herself to the ground. She was soaking wet and her cheek was gushing blood.

"What did you think you were doing, swimming out like that after the boatman?" Anian hollered in despair. "Don't you know you might have been caught? Where's the letter?"

Sarah shrugged and began to wash her facial wound with the river water, her hand clamped over the top of her cheek to help stem the flow of blood.

"I've got some cranberries back at the tree house that will stop that bleeding. Amazing little tart berries with extraordinary medicinal properties," Anian twittered on, picking up the sword and pulling Sarah to her feet.

"Come," he said, heading her back into the woods. "They are my best discovery so far. Smear cranberries on your wound, they act like a bandage to contract the damaged tissues and believe me, I've had a few wounds living here in Transit. Just think what my face would have looked like if I didn't have cranberries. They are amazing, not only do they help stop the bleeding, but the best bit is, they have a numbing effect so the pain is eased as well."

"Anian," Sarah said quietly, pain clearly in her voice.

"Yes?"

"You talk too much," Sarah whispered from behind her hands, blood still seeping down her cheek to her chin.

"I know, I can't help it."

"I dropped the letter," Sarah said. "It's probably disintegrated in the water by now; the paper was falling apart anyway."

"Indeed," Anian said. "I shall have to make some more. My last batch wasn't very good."

Together they walked calmly back through the woods, Anian, carrying the sword under one arm, the other wrapped caringly around Sarah's waist, helping and guiding her. By some strange alchemy the giant oak seemed much nearer than before, the journey taking only a few minutes. Sarah had begun to realise that in Transit, nothing was as it seemed. As they neared the tree, both of them noticed Bran waiting for them. He was on a lower branch of the oak with a small scrap of yellowish paper in his mouth.

"He's got my note!" Sarah exclaimed.

"Don't move your hands, Sarah," Anian warned. "That bird loves the smell of blood." But Bran was not there to attack, he was there to taunt. He began to peck his razor sharp beak deep into one of the bee hives nestled in a knot in the tree. The bees naturally got angry and began to buzz uncontrollably. Then, when satisfied he had caused enough disruption amongst the bees, he flew off with Sarah's note still held in his beak.

"He's riled my bees now. We'll have to leave them a while to calm down," Anian said looking at Sarah. Her hand still pressed hard to her face, her brow furrowed. "Come, the day is still young, I know a crop of cranberry bushes where we can go to patch you up and then we'll rest and you can sleep."

"But I'm afraid of what I might dream."

"Don't be. Your dreams cannot hurt you, only help you to understand."

CHAPTER FOURTEEN

AUGUST 1685
SOMETIMES RUNNING AWAY CAN BE BRAVE

"No," Kris murmured in Sarah's ear, "it is not Archie, it is Old Nick. There is nothing you can do for him. It was his time and he is beyond pain now." Pulling her away from the market square, Kriss spoke in urgent whispers. "Come, we must hurry. Go home now and behave as if nothing has happened. Act the penitent; tell them you felt unwell and lost track of the time. Do everything you can to allay their suspicions, go straight to bed and avoid Mistress Grey. Archie is in hiding waiting for you. You have to get away before your father learns from Renshaw what Nick said before he died. I will do what I can to delay him. This is the plan ..."

Devastated by what she had seen, feeling numb, Sarah tried to listen carefully to what Kriss was saying, allowing the big man to help her home. Scraps of what he said sank in, but some went completely over her head, particularly the part about her father's circumstances being much changed, his estate financially distressed. Whatever was Kriss talking about? Her father was as rich as Croesus! Shaking her head, thinking she must have misunderstood, Sarah clung onto the big man's hand and concentrated on putting one foot in front of the other. At the front gate he left her, vanishing into the shadows. Her knees were wobbling, her mind in a whirl, but somehow she managed to follow Kriss's instructions.

***

Well before dawn, Sarah was woken from a fitful sleep by her new timepiece, a gift from her betrothed for her seventeenth birthday. In the shape of a lantern, it was made of brass inlaid with ebony and had an alarm bell on top. Afraid that she would oversleep she had set it the night before, placing it under a cushion to muffle the sound. To save time when she woke, she had slept in her mourning dress, one she had never yet worn, but the darkest she possessed, just as Kriss had advised. Tossing and turning in her elaborately carved four-poster bed, Sarah waited for the faint light that heralds the dawn to come stealing through the gap she had left in the drawn valance. She strained to listen, but all she could hear was the lattice window, which she had left slightly ajar, banging in the wind. Her tomb-like room was freezing. It did not matter: nothing mattered, for today she was to embark on the biggest adventure of her life.

Unable to wait any longer, she threw back her satin quilt. As the heavy, rich material slid through her fingers she thought of all she was leaving behind and knew she would not miss a single part of it. She would take nothing, for there was nothing here of importance. Even had there been, she would not be travelling in the accustomed luxury of a coach, so luggage was out of the question. Today she would elude any status and on foot, with Archie, run as fast as she could, away from the misery of the life her parents planned for her. She had appeased them well into the evening, telling them she would do what they wanted and marry Mister Jackson. Her mother had been tearful, begging her to conform, 'for the sake of your family' she had said, and Sarah had agreed, while wondering why it mattered so much to her family that she should. Yet despite her apparent submission, they had still forbidden her to leave her room and instructed her maid, Katie, to sleep in a truckle bed outside her bedroom door. Her father had seemed preoccupied and bothered, his normally callous manner overlaid by a strangely quiet and troubled approach, which puzzled Sarah, but any fleeting concern she had for him was quickly quashed by what had happened to her dear old friend, Nick, which her father could have stopped and hadn't. Reaching the quiet of her room at last, thoughts of what she was about to do had swept everything else from her mind.

Shivering, Sarah pulled back the heavy velvet valance that hung around her bed. Slipping on her boots, positioned ready to step into, she hurriedly laced them, all fingers and thumbs in her haste. She tiptoed over to the open window. Her bedroom curtains were of the same magnificent, rich material as the valance, patterned green and ochre, fit for a princess. She peered through them relieved to see that it was not raining. The moon was setting, casting an eerie light over the land and so quiet, as though everything held its breath waiting for the dawn.

Then, away in the distance she heard the long quavering note of a tawny owl. Three times it sounded, shivering over the still air. It was time to go.

From behind the door little snores told her Katie slept soundly. Even had she woken, she was a loyal friend and would turn a blind eye as she had done so often in the past. Grabbing up her dark, woollen cloak and black bonnet, and lighting no candle to guide her way, Sarah slipped silently, like a shadow, out of her bedroom along the corridor and down the dramatically sweeping staircase, heading straight for the front-door. Ancestral portraits seemed to watch, as she paused on the bottom step to check no one was lurking in the darkness behind her. Two suits of medieval armour cast long shadows in the moonlit hall. Passing them, she pulled on her bonnet and tied it beneath her chin. Taking a deep breath she slowly pulled back the bolts on the front door. It opened noiselessly; she slid through and closed it gently behind her. Freedom!

Stealing down the stone steps as lightly as a ballerina, Sarah decided to stay tight to the house. Her heart was pounding, but not a bead of sweat formed on her brow, it was too cold. Like a mouse, she tiptoed around the outskirts of the main building and past the stables, hearing the horses snorting and hoofing the ground within. She knew them well, having ridden them since early childhood and for a fleeting moment was tempted to take one with her, but it was too much of a risk. The stable boy slept in the loft above and Renshaw may well be sleeping only yards away in his quarters, or possibly he was still out hunting for Archie. The thought frightened Sarah out of her wits.

Picking up her pace and praying with every step she took that Archie was safe, Sarah crept on down the long, stony driveway, dodging and weaving her way through the trees that lined the road and out of the west entrance of Belmont Hall. She did not once look back.

***

"Did anyone see you?" Archie asked.

"I don't think so," Sarah whispered back.

They were in the middle of the cornfield where they had made their pact, a good mile out of the village, but still Sarah felt they should keep their voices low. "You never know who lurks about after dark. It'll only take one drunken lout to spot us and give the game away and our plan could all go horribly wrong," she insisted. "Where did you sleep last night? Renshaw was out looking for you, he won't give up you know. He's like a dog with a bone, he won't be outwitted."

Ignoring Sarah's concern, Archie pulled her close. "I slept up a tree in the woods," he whispered in her ear, "having first waded down the stream then doubled back, so the hounds did not pick up my scent. They'll be out hunting again at first light. Are you ready?" His hand brushed her unpinned hair curling beneath her bonnet.

Sarah smiled up at him, understanding Archie's wish not to discuss the remorseless Renshaw. "You got about as much sleep as I did then! Yes, I'm ready. Let's go."

With one arm around Sarah's slender shoulders, Archie took hold of her hand and gently squeezed it. "Are you really sure you want to do this? You may never see your family again."

"I've never been surer about anything in my life." They both smiled at one another in the gloom. Sarah's thoughts went fleetingly to her parents, the unfamiliar expression of worry etched on her father's face flashed into her mind's eye. She dismissed it, as Archie placed a firm kiss on her forehead.

"Come then," he said. "We have maybe a couple of hours before sunrise. We must go quickly. Kriss is watching our backs and will lay a false trail."

They picked up speed and keeping away from the road and main tracks, ran through woods and across fields. Sarah felt as if each step was taking her away from her prison, away from her suppressers. She was walking to her freedom and she could feel it, as if the morning dew was washing away all that had passed.

First light found them in a wood. A single blackbird trilled his paean to the dawn and instantly the wood was filled with birdsong. Sarah had never been this far on foot before and had no idea where she was. She was gripped by a surge of excitement and fear, as the sun began to raise, the world coming into view along with the reality of their actions. Pausing to catch her breath, aching with tiredness, Sarah gazed at Archie. He looked as exhausted as she felt. It came home to her that today was the day she would become a missing bride and he a hunted outlaw, whose only fate if captured was to burn at the stake.

"Do you think they know I'm gone yet?" she panted. "Katie comes in to light the fire and help me dress about now, but she doesn't always open the valance until the fire is roaring," Sarah whispered. "It won't be long before they start searching."

"They may think you have gone rambling again and wait to see if you return after lunch," Archie said positively, pulling her along, his stride still wide and his pace still fast. Sarah could feel his anxiety; she had to jog to keep up with him.

"No such luck today, Arch, not after yesterday. Renshaw will tell Father all about us, in fact, after the way Father was acting last night, I'm sure he has already," Sarah said.

"Why do you say that?"

"He was vexed, Archie, to the point of silence. I've never seen him like it before; it was strange, almost like he was worried about something. And when they can't find you in the village and I've disappeared too, they will know we are together and try to track us. What about your father?" Sarah asked. The old man had been close friends with Old Nick, losing his son and best friend within a few days of each other was sure to be a great blow.

"I told him nothing, that way he has nothing to tell. He's the only arrowsmith in the village now I've gone, they won't harm him," Archie insisted. From the sound of his voice Sarah knew he was trying to reassure himself and assuage his guilt.

"Arch, I have to stop ... just for a minute," Sarah puffed. "My legs are shaking and I need to catch my breath." She pulled her hand away from Archie's, and he stopped and turned to look at her.

"Are you all right? You look so pale," he whispered, "and why are you crying? He grasped her shoulders and stared into her tear-filled eyes. "What is it? What's wrong?"

"I think I can hear the dogs ... they are coming for us, aren't they?"

Quickly, looking over Sarah's shoulder, Archie's tired eyes scanned the woods behind them. He looked back at Sarah and nodded, both their fears expressed in one anxious glance. "Yes, I'm afraid you're right. We need to hide," Archie said. "Quickly!"

"Where?" Sarah asked fraught with fear.

Frowning, Archie turned full circle. "The trees," he whispered. He looked Sarah up and down and a broad, cheeky grin crossed his unshaven stubbly face. "You're dressed perfectly for tree climbing!"

"How can you jest at such a time?" Sarah said as Archie began to drag her towards a giant oak. "I can't climb that," she gasped, panic seizing her. She turned to look behind, she couldn't see them yet, but the baying was closer now and she knew the hounds were closing in. They were her father's dogs, uncontrollable and aggressive, bred purely for hunting and putting the fear of God into those they hunted.

"Yes you can, I'll help you." It took Archie seconds to haul himself onto the first branch, using the knots protruding from the trunk. Sarah fidgeted at the bottom of the tree, watching him and continuously turning to look behind, expecting the dogs and their handlers to appear. "Give me your hand," Archie said, reaching down to her.

"I feel unwell, Archie, I'm no good with heights," Sarah said, her voice shrill, her hand outstretched, but not quite enough for Archie to grasp it.

"Today is the day to overcome that fear, Sarah. Come on, stretch up a bit further, hurry," Archie begged. Her hands were clammy and slippery and she wiped them down her dress. She planted her foot on a knot high on the trunk and extended her hand up to Archie's.

"When all this is over, Archie, please let me change my name, I can't bear the name Sarah ..." Her other foot left the ground and found the second knot further up the tree.

"That's it, I've got you. I think it would be quite sensible given our circumstances to change both our names," Archie's voice was strained as he heaved on Sarah's hand.

"I like the name Felic ..."

A roar emerged from the trees. Renshaw, running ahead of the slavering hounds like a crazed madman, lunged at Sarah's half elevated body, tackling her to the woodland floor. She screamed, banging her head as she fell. The snarling dogs, tongues lolling, foam dripping from their jaws, reached them in seconds, their handlers struggling to pull them back by their leashes.

"Daddy's missing you," Renshaw snarled as he pulled Sarah to her feet, "and so is Lord Jackson." One of the hounds tore at her mourning dress, ripping it through to her petticoats beneath, her face flushed with confusion.

"Lord...?" she muttered to herself then terror took over. "Run, Archie, run!" Sarah screamed up at her lover, as she kicked out at the dogs and Renshaw's shins. Archie was nowhere to be seen, lost in the topmost branches of the great oak and hidden in its foliage.

Throwing Sarah to one of the five thugs that accompanied him, Renshaw hollered up the tree. "Archie Fletcher?" The oak was completely surrounded now by half a dozen big hounds. Lifting their noses they continued baying, their claws scrabbling at the trunk eager to get at the victim they had run to ground. Sarah was hauled out of the way. The man holding her slapped his hand over her mouth to muffle her screams.

"Quiet!" Renshaw kicked out at one of the dogs, which yelped and dropped to the ground. The others whined and fell silent. "Son of Gabriel Fletcher of Belmont, you will come down here right now, before I order my men to fell this tree. Make no mistake, Fletcher, I will cut it down, I promise you that," Renshaw hollered, the veins in his neck protruding and corded. "These dogs 'aven't eaten in over a week," he spat, a gleeful smile spreading across his sweaty face.

Still struggling, Sarah could feel rather than see Archie's gaze on her and knew that fury would be burning in his heart; that he would be blaming himself for letting go of her. Yet this was all her fault. If Archie had gone in the night instead of waiting for her, he would be well away by now. It was hopeless; they should never have tried to escape together. Renshaw had been hot on their trail from the very beginning of their flight. Whatever Kriss had hoped to do to help them, he had failed. 'Archie,' she pleaded in her mind, 'please leave me. Escape! Run; it is your only chance.'

"Sarah's going home now, Fletcher," Renshaw yelled, "to Lord Jackson, you going to come down and say goodbye?"

Archie made no reply, but Sarah bit hard on the lout's hand that smothered her. He swore at her and as he raised it to his lips to suck at the welling blood, she screamed out, "NO! Archie, don't come down! Renshaw, have this man unhand me at once; how dare you treat me in this way – and what are you talking about? Joseph Jackson is no lord!"

Her voice was quickly stifled as the lout holding her struck her across the mouth, the filthy hand pressed once more to her face. Sarah sobbed uncontrollably. Never before had she believed she could truly hate a person as much as she hated Renshaw at that moment. She wanted to spit in his face she was so riled by him.

Renshaw marched towards her, staring her straight in the eye. "There you are wrong, Miss Sarah, have you not heard?" His eyebrows rose as he lowered his voice slightly, though everyone and everything in the woods hushed to listen. "Your Mister Jackson has but recently come into an earldom. He's even been summoned to the House of Lords. His father's cousin was the Duke of Suffolk. The two cousins haven't spoken in years, some adolescent argument over a woman no doubt. Then less than a week ago, Jackson's father received word that his cousin the Duke had drowned, brother-less and childless, passing all honours to the Jackson family. Mister Jackson's father has naturally taken the title of Duke and credited his only son the title of Earl of Suffolk, making your husband to be, without doubt, a lord. A perfect title for that of a lady, I think you'll agree. Your father's arrangement with the Jacksons has somewhat intensified in the last few days." Renshaw stepped back from Sarah and shouted at his men. "Keep the girl quiet, can't you?"

"The whore bit me," the lout complained.

"I'll do more than bite you," Renshaw threatened. He beckoned two of his grinning men forward, each clutched a large axe. "Cut it down," he ordered, pointing at the tree. "And you lot," he glared at the dog handlers, "get those brutes away from the base."

Swinging their axes, the two men laid into the trunk.

"STOP!" called a voice behind them. It was quieter and calmer than all others, yet holding such authority it caused everyone to stop in mid-motion. Even the hounds stopped their whining and lay prone, tails wagging.

Renshaw spun round, fists clenched, but when he saw the huge man before him his courage apparently failed him. Draped in a hooded red cape that reached to the ground, one great fist holding a long, walking staff, the man eyed him sadly. "What's going on here?"

"It's no concern of yours," Renshaw stammered, embarrassment creeping into his tone.

"Really?" the large man seemed unperturbed. "Tell me, what creature is so terrifying it takes a dozen dogs and five men armed with staves and axes to attack it?" He looked up into the foliage in exaggerated wonder as though expecting to see a fearsome ogre.

"A man, sir ... an outlaw and a kidnapper," Renshaw explained quickly.

"A man you say? Where?" He continued to stare up into the oak tree.

"In the tree, at the very top, hiding like a coward."

Sarah, still dumbfounded by what Renshaw had revealed to her, knew the red-caped man instantly from his deep, commanding voice, and yet he had never seemed so tall and he looked somehow older, even more authoritative than usual. It startled her to realise that Renshaw and his thugs were afraid of him, though, of course, his station in life was far above theirs and they would never dare to touch him.

Just then she caught sight of Archie's face peeping from behind a thick upper branch. He was gazing down at the tall man and even from this distance she could see them exchange a look of warmth and respect. Then Archie lifted his head. His gaze met hers and Sarah gasped at the sorrow and love she read in his eyes.

***

Archie, instead of feeling salvaged by this unexpected turn of events felt a deep sense of loss. He knew this was the end ... the end of his adventure with Sarah. He should never have imagined they could make a life together. She was a lady and he a humble fletcher. What chance had they really stood? Now they had been caught red-handed trying to escape. There was no way out, surely?

"Ah yes, I see him," the tall man said, turning to Renshaw. "He doesn't look fearsome to me. So what has he done exactly?"

"Taken Lord Belmont's already betrothed daughter and corrupted her," Renshaw stated, nodding towards Sarah, who continued to struggle between the two men now holding her. "He will be charged with petty treason. Lord Belmont will decide his fate," he grinned, "but we all know what that will be, don't we."

The big man swung round to Sarah, "Let her speak," he ordered.

As soon as the hand dropped from her mouth Sarah shouted, "Lies! It is all lies. Renshaw, you oaf. Why can't you just leave us alone?"

Seeing the tears pouring down her face, Archie's heart ached for her. "Oh God, Sarah, what have I done to you?" he whispered.

"Lies is it? That's not what Old Nick told me," Renshaw sneered.

The man in the red cape stepped forward and pushed back his hood. "You do know who I am, don't you Renshaw?"

"I do. We don't see you around here often these days, but I've not forgotten that we played together as children. This is no business of yours, Kriss. Fact is, I do not know what your business is here at all," Renshaw snapped.

Archie listened intently from the branches above. He too had played as a child with both Renshaw and Kriss; children cared little for the status of other children, even Sarah had been allowed to engage with them from time to time, until her parents judged it unsuitable and forbade her to associate with them. By then Sarah had grown into a beauty and had always been a favourite topic of the growing boys' conversations. As time drew on, age had parted the three of them - as had society - and they had gone their separate ways. Renshaw had taken the back door into Belmont House, ingratiating himself with Sarah's father. Kriss and Archie stayed remote but true friends, though Renshaw would not be aware of that, both following the legacy they had been given by their parents: Archie becoming an arrowsmith and Kriss, a court messenger, so trusted that he was now a 'Silver Greyhound', as the King's messengers were known.

"I am sent to recruit volunteers for the alliance of the Holy League to help defeat the Ottoman Empire. Many European powers are involved now," Kriss explained in a clear, calm voice.

"What's that to me?" Renshaw snarled.

"Volunteers to serve in foreign lands are hard to come by. I am authorised to recruit criminals awaiting trial in our gaols and as you will know, they are full of the Duke of Monmouth's rebels just now. This man you are attempting to capture is an outlaw, you say. Is he employed?"

Archie, perched high above, lingered on every word. He swallowed hard, his heart pounding, knees trembling. He knew what Kriss was trying to do. Would he succeed? 'And if he does, what then will be my fate?' Archie thought. Whatever it was, it had to be better than being burned at the stake. He would be alive and if Sarah waited for him, maybe one day ...

"He's a fletcher's son, an unemployed apprentice," Renshaw informed, distaste smearing across his rugged face. "I don't suppose you remember him?"

Kriss ignored the implied question. "A fletcher? Then he would be extremely useful. Unmarried? I can only enlist single men," he explained.

"Yes, of course he's unmarried, but ..." Renshaw stuttered to a halt, obviously unsure of what Kriss was getting at.

"Good, good. Well, I think I may well be able to take this lawbreaker off your hands and save you and Lord Belmont a lot of trouble. I'm sure after yesterday's spectacle and the villagers now close to rebellion, he will be only too pleased. I just need one witnessed signature," Kriss pulled out a scroll of parchment from beneath his cape, reaching into his scrip for a stick of graphite and holding it out.

Renshaw looked from the parchment to the graphite, to Kriss, his face a picture of confusion.

"You can sign on Lord Belmont's behalf, can you not? One of your men can make his mark as witness. Or do I mistake your authority, Renshaw? In which case, forgive me. Naturally, if Lord Belmont does not trust you ..." Kriss started to roll up the parchment.

"Of course he trusts me. I have authority to act on his behalf, Renshaw spluttered, eyeing his eagerly listening henchmen, his face flushing a dull red.

Archie knew he had no such authority, the man was arrogant and stupid and Kriss was playing his pride like a fiddle. Renshaw would be in terrible trouble if he let this go on, but the man deserved everything that was coming to him and Archie felt no sympathy. He glanced down at Sarah and saw the hope shining through her tears as she realised what Kriss was doing. She must know they would be forced to part, but the chance that he might live after all, even if it meant going to war, had brought a flush to her pale, bruised cheeks.

"I am sure Lord Belmont will be delighted to have this matter put to rest quietly and this vagrant disposed of and at the same time put to good use ... for King and Country," Kriss added, sketching a little bow in respect of the throne he served.

"That's as maybe, but I think Lord Belmont should ..." Renshaw was clearly having second thoughts, but he didn't have the chance to go on.

"I'm leaving today," Kriss interrupted sharply, his eyebrows raised. "In fact I am on my way to London right now with my list of new recruits and cannot delay. We are really struggling for the necessary measure. Large numbers of troops are required and at the moment the Holy League is enlisting everyone and anyone willing, as well as unwilling; unemployed vagrants and even, dare I say it, capital offenders like this fellow here. It is now the King's alternative to the gallows. Between you and me, Renshaw," Kriss tapped the side of his nose, "the banks of the River Danube are a death sentence, if you know what I mean. At least as horrifying as the gallows," he winked.

Silence filled the air. Renshaw searched the faces of each of his men. All looked dumbstruck. Then he smiled a slow, leering smile, "Well, if that's the case ...," he took the parchment and stick of graphite and signed the document without troubling to read it, then stood over one of his henchmen, who marked an 'X' as witness, pressing so hard he broke the graphite. With an apologetic glance at Kriss, Renshaw handed it back then gazed up into the oak tree.

"Get down, Fletcher. I'll spare you from the hounds tearing you limb from limb. I will even spare you the gallows and the stake, but I have condemned you to war, a war from which you will never return. But hear this: if by some miracle you do, I will be waiting."

Archie could hardly believe his reprieve. He swung down through the branches, stopping out of reach to peer down at the ring of tense faces looking up at him. As he moved, the dogs alerted by the rustling foliage started baying again, growing wilder as they caught sight of their quarry, their jaws snapping and snarling.

"Call the dogs off!" Kriss demanded.

Complying, the dog handlers took control of the hounds, pulling them right back, away from the base of the tree. Archie dropped to the ground beside Kriss, keeping his head down, not looking anyone in the eye. Kriss, propping his stave against the tree, pulled a coil of rope from inside his cape and quickly took hold of Archie. Under Renshaw's satisfied gaze, he bound the prisoner's wrists tightly behind his back then pushed him roughly forward.

Archie cast a glance at Sarah and sent her a warm smile that said 'All will be well my darling, have courage.' He knew that she understood, for she smiled back at him as the louts pulled her to her feet and dragged her slowly away through the woods.

CHAPTER FIFTEEN

AUGUST 2003
WIND BY ITS VERY NATURE IS CHAOTIC

A taxi was parked up alongside the Phra Pin Klao Bridge. Beside it on the pavement a Buddhist monk sat cross-legged, his bare feet placed on opposing thighs. Passersby most likely did not notice Niran-Atid deep in meditation on one of the busiest streets in Bangkok, their busy lives causing them to completely pass him by. His lotus position was perfect, his back was straight but not tense, his head was tilted slightly forward with his chin tucked in, so his eyes, which weren't quite closed, were cast downwards looking straight down his nose. The moist air picked up around him and flurried his hair while he pondered. His breathing was shallow but whilst he deliberated, a question muttered from his lips. "What colour will the wind be for you today Miss Sarah?"

***

Sarah woke as the light was fading. Anian snored loudly beside her. Her cheek was sticky, the wound inflicted by the raven still numbed by the crushed cranberries the satyr had plastered on it.

"Anian," Sarah whispered, shaking his shoulder. "Anian, the sun's going down. We should go back now." He did not wake. Instead, his heavy body rolled away with a deep snort.

Getting to her feet, leaving her sword where she had slept, Sarah circled the cranberry bush, picking and eating the fruit as she walked. Looking through the trees she caught sight of the forest edge and beyond she saw vast rolling fields. Intrigued, but not stupid, she slipped back to Anian and quietly retrieved her sword. She would take a short walk and see what lay beyond the river and the trees and leave the satyr to sleep a little longer. She wouldn't be long.

Sarah jogged to the boundary of the forest and stepped out from the shelter of the trees into the vast space before her, it was a world beyond her imagination. To her right were rolling green hills, her only memory she could compare it to, would be the hills surrounding Nanny's house back in Wales, where she used to stay as a little girl. Each rounded hill was so perfect and had such grace, full of meadow flowers, bull thistles, poppies and buttercups. The place had a familiar, fresh smell too, it was the meadowsweet. She would know that scent anywhere. To her left, in contrast was a barren looking wasteland, with burnt shrubbery and crisscrossing pathways cutting through the undergrowth. Past the land, in the distance was the sea and sinking into it, the setting sun, a blazing semicircle all that was left on the horizon. Sarah caught her breath; it was so beautiful.

With a little smile on her face and a hand on her wounded cheek, Sarah lost herself in memories of her childhood with Archie in Wales. Many-a-time in their early teens they had watched the sun go down, telescope at the ready, waiting for the first star of the night to appear. It all seemed like such a long time ago. The time that had come between them seemed to surpass eternity. His face was so clear in her mind it was almost as if he was there, yet from the picture she conjured up, she was sure he looked slightly different. He looked wiser than she remembered. Or was that her mind putting him on a pedestal because he was no longer with her? The more she thought about Archie, the more she found herself talking to him in her head.

"Where are you, Arch? I'm trying to find you? Here ... in this place," she whispered. "Where am I? Where are you?"

The sun's last splinters of light bled across the land and in the final striations a silhouette appeared. Sarah gasped. Gradually, as the night set in, the figure walked towards her. Sarah could see clearly who it was, but dared not believe what she was seeing. "You're dead," she whispered bluntly, tears springing into her eyes, a hard lump rising in her throat. It was all she could muster, for shock had set in and her body had frozen.

"I thought you were looking for me?" his voice called to her, a hand outstretched. "You've found me," he said with a smile. "Come with me."

As he came closer, Sarah too stretched out her hand ready to meet his. His clothes looked odd; they weren't what he would normally have worn, he looked almost like a prehistoric caveman, scruffy and unshaven, not clean cut and tidy as she remembered. Everything about him looked slightly off kilter. It was Archie, she was sure of it, but he had changed.

"Is this a dream?" she asked, their fingertips were millimetres apart; she could feel the heat from him penetrating her. A broad smile spread across both their faces. "It can't be. I'm awake ... I know I am. It is you, isn't it. This is real." Her heart hammering, she reached for him anticipating the warm clasp of his hand. It never came.

"What ya doin'?" screamed a crazed voice from behind her. Anian came charging through and knocked her sideways, pushing her back into the trees. She fell with a hard bump, but was unharmed. "Run, Sarah, back to the oak. Quickly!"

From the ground, Sarah looked up at Anian, a hot flash of anger overriding her disappointment. "No, Anian, wait. I've found him," she insisted, her eyes glassy and unfocussed.

"That's not Archie, Sarah. The sun has set. It's the Moon's trickery. Trust me," the satyr pleaded.

"No really, it is Archie, I've seen him, he's over there, look ..." Tears flooding down her face, Sarah was entranced, her gaze fixed on the figure that remained just beyond the boundary of the woodland, but Anian continued to push her back deeper into the forest.

"I know you can see him, but it's not him, I promise you. What did you do, wake up and think 'I'll go looking for trouble'? Why didn't you wake me up?" Anian demanded.

Grasping her by the shoulders, the satyr shook her. Sarah was dimly aware of him, but her trance was not broken. She was awake and could hear everything Anian was saying, but she was hypnotised by the now distant figure of Archie, his arms still outstretched.

"Sarah!" Anian began to click his fingers in front of her dazed face. "Sarah, snap out of it." He grabbed her sword and poked her with it.

"Ouch!" Sarah screeched. "What did you do that for?"

"Are you coming?" Anian asked. "The Moon will turn you mad. You must come with me NOW!"

"No, I can't leave him. Look, Anian, he's there, I've found him," Sarah said, her mind focused solely on one thing.

Giving up trying to reason with her, the satyr grabbed hold of Sarah's arm and began to drag her kicking and screaming back in the direction of his tree. His strength and speed were extraordinary. As he had done before, Anian whisked Sarah off her feet, dragging her with no concern for her physical hurts at all. Her screams only made him run faster, his hooves bullishly thumping across the forest floor, stamping through bushes and over fallen trunks. He was taking the shortest route home.

Once inside the hollow of the oak, Anian did not ascend. He lunged at a pile of rotting fruit and salvaged a festering lemon. Breaking it open with his hands, he squirted the bitter lemon juice into Sarah's face.

Sarah screamed. Clawing at her stinging eyes, she tried to rub the juice out of them. She attempted to back away from the satyr, but Anian held onto her arm and squirted the lemon again, this time in her open mouth. "What are you doing?" she screamed again, her face screwing up as the acid taste hit her tongue.

"So sorry, Sarah, but I need you awake and not under the Moon's spell if we're to get out of this mess." Suddenly he released her, placing his fingers on his lips to silence her and listened.

Sarah's senses were now on full alert; the lemon had certainly woken her from any trance. The night had set in around them and she could see Anian's hair standing up, like a dog about to attack. He hardly seemed to be breathing, his head on one side, listening. Above them there was a mighty ruckus. Screeching and squawking, crashing and banging, ripping and flapping.

"The ravens! That's Bran," Anian whispered grabbing hold of Sarah again.

"What are they doing up there in your home?" Sarah asked.

"Shhh. Listen to me, Sarah. I need you to awaken your natural instincts and powers."

"Powers?" Sarah frowned. "Now who's gone mad?" she muttered.

"The power that is within us all," Anian explained. "The Earth-plain deadens it, but it is inside you. I know it is."

Sarah stared at Anian convinced he was loopy, her eyes still stinging from the lemon juice. "What are you on about Anian?" She asked pouting and licking the bitter acid taste off her lips.

"I am not loopy," Anian whispered harshly, obviously distressed.

"I know you're not," Sarah replied quietly as it dawned on her that the satyr had read her thoughts. "You're overreacting; it's just that I don't know what you're asking me to do."

"It was a taboo subject when I was alive. They called me loopy back then too. I don't know if I can say it plainly to you. Remember, I was labelled a crank and the Devil for it, I died for it." Anian said his voice low.

"If I remember rightly from the dreams I've been having lately, you were also labelled a very wise man," Sarah reminded him, for she now had no difficulty in recognising Anian as the old man of her dreams. He had been her friend ... and there was something else, something dreadful, but she couldn't remember what.

"Indeed. By some, but ..." a sudden surge in the noise above silenced the satyr, who turned to look up the ladder leading into his home.

"Anian," Sarah said, breaking through the commotion. "What do you want me to do? I'll do it if it'll help. At least I'll try."

The satyr looked back at her, his face lined with concern. "Magic," he hissed quieter than a whisper.

Sarah nodded. Somehow she had known he would say that.

"Our spirits, our minds, our bodies are all linked, just as we are all linked with nature," Anian said. "It is only nature we have to work with, it is part of us. You've lost that connection but you can find it again. You must find it now," Anian pleaded.

"How?" Sarah asked. Her angst heightening she looked up the ladder then out of the entrance. It was full dark now; she could barely see the trees outside.

"Harness the life force that runs though you, it lies latent within you, Sarah. Employ the power of your mind, I promise it's all there, an ancient wisdom. If you would rather understand it as saying a prayer, that's grand. The power of prayer and thought is the same as what I am going to do," Anian said.

"What are you going to do?" Sarah asked.

"I'm going to cast a spell," Anian explained, "and I need you to hold my hands and try to join in if you can. The more energy I can get behind the spell the stronger it will be." Anian took hold of Sarah's hands, their eyes locked. Above them the brawl rose to a crescendo.

"Strong winds rise and flow from the East," Anian called, his eyes closed. "Scream through the trees like a roaring beast. On this oak's branches shall you feast.

Only on our command shall you cease." Anian paused, opened his eyes and nodded at Sarah.

"Strong winds rise and flow from the East," she said, her voice low, but she repeated the satyr's words, bringing her mind to bear on what he had said. "Scream through the trees like a roaring beast. On this oak's branches shall you feast. Only on our command shall you cease."

Outside a wind began to pick up. Sarah could hear it shushing through the trees. With a feeling of awe she realised they were summoning the wind! "Strong winds rise and flow from the East," Anian shouted. Sarah joined in with the volume and the tempo and they repeated the spell. The ravens were screeching and flapping, the disorder in the tree-house intensifying. Anian's rhythm quickened, his voice rising above it. The wind had become a gale: branches were cracking and snapping under its force and tumbling to the ground. Bushes and debris hurtled past the oak opening, yet inside the air was still.

"That should do it," Anian said with a cheeky wink. "Well done. Don't let go of my hands. On the count of three I want you to say 'cease'." Sarah nodded. She was still in awe and shock at what they had just achieved. Only in her dreams had she thought such things were possible. "One," the satyr intoned. The screeching above was slowly dying. "Two." There were a few bumps and the rustling of the leaves. "Three." In perfect unison Anian and Sarah said the word 'cease' and instantly the wind dropped. Above them was silence.

Relaxing and letting go of Sarah's hands, Anian turned and immediately started to climb the insecure ladder up to the remains of his tree house. Sarah went to follow, but just as she grabbed hold of the ladder, a movement outside caught her eye. She peered towards the doorway and saw the shape of a figure standing in the shadowy moonlight beside a tree. It was Archie! He had followed her. A huge grin spread across Sarah's face. She let go of the ladder and dashed to the entrance.

Then stopped short. In the light of the Moon, before her eyes, Archie's body drastically malformed. It eluded definition to start off with and then morphed into that of a woman. Sarah, transfixed by what she was seeing, could hardly take it in and at one point was ambivalent as to whether the woman was there at all; the figure was insubstantial, like a hologram. Sarah stared harder. Now she saw the woman was old and draped in grey, with not a hand or a foot showing, as though she were floating just off the ground. Then her face seemed to change from that of an old hag to a middle-aged, motherly-looking woman. Even as Sarah watched, the figure changed again, now to a young lady not much older than she was herself. For a fleeting moment Sarah thought she recognised the younger face, but it happened so quickly, it was all such a haze and a blur. It was as though the face was ageing through the main phases of life in an unremitting cycle.

Too frightened to cry out, Sarah saw beside the figure three large and fierce-looking dogs and then they too seemed to change, merging with one another to become another creature entirely: black and feathered. Within seconds, Bran appeared and flapped onto the woman's shoulder, ruffled but very much alive. Only then did Sarah realise who and what she was looking at: it was the Moon incarnate.

Her stomach churned as terror pulsed through her veins. The wind picked up again outside and Sarah felt the desperate urge to turn and flee after Anian, but she could not move. She was paralysed to the spot. Her legs were like dead weights, her heart thumping in her chest like a jungle drum. The woman, whose face had once more changed into that of an old hag, smiled revealing tombstone rotten teeth. Sarah recognised her immediately. "Chanthira," she whispered.

The woman's dark eyes glinted in confirmation and the smile vanished. A voice cackled in her ear. Sarah went cold to her core. She wanted to scream, but no sound came out.

"That goat creature has no power here. If he wants a storm I'll give him a storm." The woman lifted her arms high into the air, throwing Bran off her shoulder as she sang out in a high, keening voice, "Wind so strong and cold, strengthen and hold."

Grey light streamed like smoke from her fingertips, twisting upwards into the night sky and forming a dense black cloud above the trees. Any starlight that may have been illuminating the forest was put out instantly. "Blow from me; breathe from me," she hissed, drawing in a deep breath and slowly releasing it, to gush through the trees and into the swirling thundercloud building above. The elements obeyed her every command: "Thunder growl, wind howl, lightning strike, storm prowl."

As the words rolled from the hag's mouth, sheets of torrential rain began to slice across the forest, Sarah could hardly see as she clung onto the rough trunk of the oak. Again a violent amount of energy flooded out of the Moon's hands and pulsed up into the air. "Louder storm, louder I say! I call to thee. Show the Devil and his nymph friend here exactly how I take back what belongs to me." The voice was so shrill that Sarah thought her ears might bleed.

"You see, Felicity? Had you forgotten my power?" the Moon said. Unmoving in the wild hurricane she had created, neither her robe nor her streaked grey hair moved, as though she were immune from the currents of air swirling about her. The Moon turned her focus back on Sarah. "You cannot hide from me, Felicity." Slowly the Moon stepped closer and as she did her face changed again from the haggard crone, to a middle-aged woman, to an adolescent girl.

Frozen and pale, Sarah could not move, her eyes glued open yet desperate to close. Almost fainting, somehow she clung onto consciousness weeping silent tears of terror.

"I rule the skies!" Obvious rage began to fill the Moon's voice, her face continuously morphing through the ages of a woman's life. "And I rule the seas. Transit is my kingdom. All the elements in it and all of nature are in my power. You thought you could defy me, trick me and leave me. Well, you were wrong, for even death will not part us." The Moon smiled, a cold, humourless smile and said in a more hushed tone, "I say when it is time to leave and when it is time to stay. Not you." Her voice rose again to a crazed, frenzied shriek and she paced forward towards the oak. "I was given the key to your destiny when you defied your heart and took your life. You cannot turn back time to fix it and you cannot have the key back. You're too late. Archie is gone and you are and will remain mine."

The world around them spun into a cyclone. The ground shook, as large and established trees were ripped from their roots and sucked up into the air. Even the mighty oak against which Sarah cowered, began to sway. Beyond terror, she opened her mouth in a silent scream. Thunder roared and lightning flashed, then as suddenly as it had started, it stopped and only the wind remained, gusting through the battered trees. Above the sound, the Moon's keening voice continued to taunt.

"You only know a fraction of the truth, Sarah Walker. By entering Transit you have perceived a totally new dimension of life. The world you came from is but a minute proportion of what life is really about. Your little brain will see only what your mind wills it to see. And today you see me in all my glory." The Moon howled with maniacal laughter and continued to torment Sarah, creeping ever closer. "Felicity is indeed the root of your trouble, but in truth you are the same soul. How dare you take it upon yourself to change your destiny! You are my slave, like all the rest of those pathetic little stars up there."

The Moon lifted her gaze to the sky and in that moment, Sarah felt a tiny surge of feeling in her limbs. Forcing herself to move, she dropped further back into the hollow oak, crouching down by the pile of festering fruit.

"Anian," she mouthed, the sound no louder than a sigh. Terrified, her body trembling, tears still flooding down her face, she noticed her sword lying beside her. Anian must have dropped it as he came in. She grabbed it with both hands, hugging it close to her, almost hiding behind it.

"My friend Cyclops only makes weapons for those who know how to use them and win. We took on the ravens and won didn't we?" Fee's voice whispered in Sarah's head. "Do not fear her Sarah. I won't allow you to. She's won if you do. You are protected. Our spirit must be very powerful or she wouldn't want us back so desperately." As much as Sarah didn't want to admit it, Felicity's words were a comfort and calmed her.

But the voice of the Moon, taunted on. "The moment you step out of that hole, Sarah Walker, you are mine. Day or night."

"That's a lie, Sarah. She has no power in the day. Don't listen to her."

Sarah dared not look up. She knew the voice was close, just outside the opening. She didn't understand why the Moon didn't just reach in and take her, what was to stop her?

Shivering behind her sword, Sarah remained cowering on the ground, but just then Anian bounded down the ladder. Without a word, he scooped Sarah up, flung her over his shoulder and began to carry her up the ladder. The Moon did not utter another word, but Sarah glimpsed her silhouette still hovering outside the cavity below and suddenly beside her, the dogs were back and with them a dark-haired man, even taller than the Moon.

"Don't look at them, Sarah," the satyr puffed, heaving her up through the hatch. "My oak stands for values beyond her black magic and as long it remains standing she won't enter. You are safe here."

From his shoulder, Sarah looked around fearfully. Part of the roof was missing and the table and chairs had been broken into pieces. In fact most of Anian's furniture had been destroyed; even the fireplace had been demolished and the wind, which had not let up and was still very much under the control of the Moon below, continued to charge through the walls of the tree house. "She'll send Bran in to spy on us but that's as close as she gets."

"What do you mean about the oak standing for values beyond her black magic?" Sarah shouted in Anian's ear.

"My home denotes the truth," he replied, raising his voice over the howling wind. "The Moon talks of the truth as if she cares, but she doesn't care about anything except how bright her stars shine around her. She calls them her children, but they are not her children, merely slaves – lost souls, most of them. She said you know only a fraction of the truth, which is true, we all know only a fraction of what is happening, we are merely able to interpret and try to understand what is real and what is right. In truth we are all blind. This oak is my bubble of fidelity. It represents my longevity, it's the oldest tree in the forest and it symbolises my loyalty. I don't think the Moon has ever been loyal to a single star, well not in my lifetime anyway. I've been loyal and beholden to you and Archie infinitely, which drives her wild."

Anian laid Sarah down on the mattress, which was now spread on the floor, ripped to shreds in the ravens' brawl. He knelt beside her. "The Moon will be loyal and true to one thing and one thing only."

"What's that? Sarah asked.

"The three Fates." Sarah frowned, not really understanding.

"Are you all right?" Anian asked, placing a hairy hand on her forehead.

"I think so." She sat up, still clutching her sword, staring at the wild weather hurtling through the open windows and demolished side wall. "There was a man out there, Anian."

"Archie again; I told you ..." Anian began.

"No Anian, it wasn't Archie," Sarah insisted. "Oh, look at your home. I'm so sorry, this is all my fault."

"Nothing that can't be fixed," the satyr said in an unbothered tone, yet looking about with a wince. "If this storm takes anymore off the side and roof, though, we could be in serious trouble."

No sooner had the words left Anian's mouth than the front section of the tree-house shuddered violently, then strip by strip the wooden boards slowly began to ping away from the structure as though someone was aggressively ripping them off. Bran returned, fluttering in across the exposed branches, and beyond him in the branches of a neighbouring tree perched the Moon.

"Sometimes the journey beats the destination, don't you think?" the Moon cackled into their minds. "You have nowhere to run Miss Sarah," she taunted. "It's not like you can get back to the Earth-plain now you're here. No one ever has. There's no way back to your old world."

Trembling with fear Sarah squirmed her face into Anian's hairy chest, her heart pounding.

The Moon laughed. "It's only a matter of time before my gale rips that goat's tree from its roots, then you're all mine and you can come home, with me. I've someone waiting who'll be thrilled to see you again."

"You're used to this kind of trouble aren't you Sarah?" Anian whispered, shaking with fear at the sight of the Moon in person.

"N-n-no," Sarah stammered, her eyes squeezed shut.

"Well Felicity certainly was used to it. It's beyond me, I'm sorry."

They clung together, Anian cowering over Sarah, trying to shelter and protect her from the elements, hiding his face from the unremitting light of the Moon.

In a moment of innocence and blindness, lost behind closed lids, Sarah could almost have imagined, all that was occurring, was just a nightmare. Confined in Anian's hairy embrace, her ears plugged to the tattered mattress, the gale was only a muffled moan. She could easily have been at home in her bedroom hiding beneath the covers.

"It is not a dream, Sarah. Don't for a second be complacent where you are. It's too dangerous," Fee's sassy voice twittered in her ear. "I will not go back to her world. I don't like the dark."

Finding and accepting this fleeting moment of refuge, Sarah ignored Felicity. In that moment she recalled her conversation with Lillian, the Keeper of Secrets. "Lapis lazuli will recognise any cruel or cursed attack and has the power to block it and return the negative energy back to its source." Of course! How could she have forgotten?

With all her might, Sarah concentrated on the stone at her throat, projecting her lapis lazuli, pushing, with all the force she could muster, every ounce of energy she possessed, she expelled it outwards from her heart and her chest, with all the oomph of her inner power. The force pushed through the pendant and a deep blue aura enveloped them.

The Moon cackled louder. "Lillian's little gifts have no power against me, Sarah," she hissed, "just as I have no power in her domain. That bubble you've created is as easy for me to pop, as a pathetic soap bubble."

"Don't listen to her Sarah," Anian whispered. "You are protected, I promise you that. Lillian would not lie to you. Your energy and the power of your crystal are strong and worthy. The Moon only says such things to frighten and lull you into forgetting that. She is wicked and will trick you into thinking anything, and the moment you believe in what she says, is the moment that what she says will happen. Remember your thoughts will become your reality. Believe in yourself." Anian whispered in her ear, unmoving.

Sarah did not reply. She did however continue to project her aura and use the power of the lapis stone. The shield around them expanded outwards engulfing parts of the tree house and the oak itself, and inside that deep blue bubble the wind ceased to blow.

"You're doing it, Sarah, you're using the power that lies within you," Anian applauded, holding her close.

"I don't think I'm doing it on my own," Sarah's whisper could barely be heard muted through the foam mattress. "Felicity's helping me."

"Wherever the power and knowledge is coming from, it's part of you. Don't stop. Keep propelling it."

It demanded all her concentration and she was oh, so tired, but Sarah kept projecting the power of the blue crystal. Then the ravens returned, flocking in, swooping and diving, battering at the shield with their beaks, trying to break through. The dogs below, which had been standing calmly beside the Moon now turned savage and wild, howling and snarling, their claws scrabbling against the tree trunk as they leapt up at it.

Sarah felt her resistance begin to weaken. "I don't think I can do it for much longer, Anian," she hollered.

CHAPTER SIXTEEN

AUGUST 2003
A RAINBOW APOLOGISES FOR FRENZIED SKIES

"Is she alive?" Niran-Atid whispered to himself. "Twenty-three, twenty-three ... why do I keep coming back to the number twenty-three?"

The weather had turned in Bangkok, from heavy smog and drizzle to blistering heat but the temperature seemed to have no effect on Niran-Atid, even as he bustled across a heaving floating market. His thoughts were so focused inward that he overlooked the colourfully clad merchants, their canoes laden with fresh fruit and vegetables in the lively paddle-along bazaar.

"It a special number, it add up to five. Hmm... Us human's have twenty-three sex chromosomes ... I feel it must be fortunate number; it be the number of life? If she's meant to survive she must have protection from them in high places ... take care Miss Sarah."

***

A splinter of the sun's rays seeped over the horizon, flooding the battered tree-house with warmth and light, Sarah began to stir. The sunlight did not last and in moments was gone and she could hear rain now pummelling the thirsty trees and ground, yet not penetrating the thick foliage of the oak above her. The air grew cold, but was bracing and delicious. Feeling weak and slightly pummelled herself, nonetheless with a strong urge to get up and move, Sarah sat up, arching her back, her mouth stretching in a wide yawn. She had a lot to do before night fell again and she had no desire to waste a single minute.

Anian had slept right beside her, his heavy arm protectively draped across her chest. It was odd, but she no longer thought of him as half goat, even though his strong shaggy legs and black hooves were plainly in view, they no longer seemed abnormal. He was just a person to her now. It was the same with his horrendously scarred, deformed face: she saw past it, to the gentle wisdom that shone from his startling eyes, which were now closed, a snore whistling softly from his slightly open mouth.

Easing herself away from him, she stared around at his beautiful tree house. It had been almost completely demolished during the Moon's storm, but they had survived - if only just - thanks to the combined powers of Anian's oak tree, the lapis lazuli crystal and a willpower Sarah had not known she possessed. With the coming of dawn, the Moon and her ravens had gone. Fingering the pendant, Sarah got to her feet and rummaged quietly through the debris, finding one of Anian's old pencils inside the table drawer that lay on its side by the hatchway. The only piece of parchment she could find was the letter Anian had written to her; the one telling her all about Nicholas - or 'Old Nick', as she now knew the satyr to have been in a former life. Reluctantly, on the reverse side of the letter she scribbled another note to Archie. Folding it, she grabbed her sword and headed for the rope ladder down into the hollow. To her dismay she found it gone, the storm must have ripped the ladder from its holding. Composed and determined, with no time to stop and ponder, Sarah dropped her sword down the hollow trunk. It fell to the ground with a thud. She followed it, the parchment clutched between her teeth as she climbed down, using the tree notches as handholds, her experience of rock climbing on holidays in Wales coming to her aid. Tree climbing, however, with her feet bare and hampered by her flimsy pink gown, seemed harder, but she made it to the ground safely, retrieved her sword and drawing a deep breath ran silently through the rain, towards the river.

She knew Anian would be angry with her for heading out alone again. She had been unwise and careless last time, but it was daylight this time and once Archie's letter was safely to the other side, she could quickly return to the oak, maybe even before Anian woke up. She felt just a little guilty, but he would only try to stop her from talking to the boatman; he'd tell her it wasn't her time or something like that. She was without doubt being foolhardy, but she was on a mission and the faster she got the letter to Archie the faster this nightmare could end. Justifying her actions in her head, she increased her pace, desperately praying that the boatman would be slightly more forthcoming than the last time they had met. She would reason with him, she wasn't sure how, but she would have to try. It was the only way to get word to Archie that she was here.

The rain kept on seeping through the trees, sometimes in big spills and at other times the foliage was so thick it didn't seem like it was raining at all. The river was in full force when she approached it. Swelling with rapids, it did not look like the kind of water you wanted to be on in a gondola! Surely it would be swept downstream in such torrents? She couldn't see it. Perhaps the boatman wouldn't come, which would be a sure way for him not to communicate with her. Maybe he would only come if someone who was ready to cross was waiting. She had been with Anian last time and the boatman was determined he should cross.

"Ah," Sarah sighed, "I should have brought Anian after all." Feeling frustrated and getting soaked, for out on the open riverbank the rain was heavy, she looked up at the sky and could not see a break in the dense, black thundercloud.

"Hello!" she shouted with no fear of feeling foolish. She was desperate. "Come on boatman, give me a break, I don't want to cross, I just want to give you a note. Please," she called.

Pacing up and down the river, she could see clearly for miles in both directions. The water was rough and there were no vessels on it anywhere. "Oh, this is useless, how am I supposed to ... I could try swimming it again ... no, not a good idea. Should I try finding the bridge?"

Sarah battled with herself and pondered out loud, walking for some time, until, drenched through, she sat down at the foot of a nearby conifer, irritated, kicking out with her bare feet like a grumpy child. She thought about going back to the oak and talking to Anian: two minds were better than one and oddly, given all his quirks and uncouthness, he did seem a little saner than she was just now, what with her hallucinating and completely irrational behaviour.

The rain seemed to be easing, the sky lightening and Sarah, her eyes closed, her head pressed to the tree behind her, felt warmth on her face that grew in intensity: the warmth of the Sun? Hadn't he said he would help her? Taking a deep breath, she smiled, anticipating that the Sun's orchestra was about to fire up and welcome words of wisdom come into her head. But nothing happened. Had that been a hallucination too? "Come on Mister Sun, where are you? You said you would help me." After a moment, beginning to feel slightly uneasy she opened her eyes, squinting into the brightness.

Before her in a haze of moisture was a dreamlike veil of every colour in every shade imaginable. Sarah had never seen anything like it in her life; it was as though she were sitting inside the end of a rainbow. It was all around her, streaming from the sky through the drizzle. She could not see any arch, only an abundance of magical and intense colour that seemed to consume her. Too awestruck to be frightened, she saw in the mist a silhouette materialising and within moments a beautiful woman stood before her in a shimmering gown. She was tall; long black hair fell to her shoulders and curled on down like a waterfall to the small of her back. She carried two large jugs in either hand, water cascading from both.

The woman was dazzlingly bright and so lovely it took Sarah's breath away. Screwing up her eyes she raised her hand to shield them, almost shying away from the light and wishing she had sunglasses.

The apparition moved slowly towards her. "I am Grace, Angel of the Rainbow. You must go back. You should not be here." The angel's lips were unmoving, her eyes saying everything, the soft voice entering Sarah's mind.

"I'm not going back until I've found Archie," Sarah responded automatically through her thoughts, barely aware that she had communicated them telepathically. "Anyway, I can't go back, there's no way back. Everyone I have met has said that. Finding Archie is the only way forward."

"I should not be here talking to you. If Death sees me ..." the angel started to say, glancing over her shoulder.

"Death?" Sarah questioned, now speaking aloud, her eyebrows rising as she squinted up at the angel.

"Give me the letter, Sarah. I will give it to Archie," Grace whispered, laying down a jug and stretching out her hand.

Sarah smiled with delight. "Really? You'd do that for me?"

"I will give Archie your letter, Sarah, but in return, you must do something for me."

"Of course, anything," Sarah said without thinking. "What would you have me do?"

"Help Nicholas – or Anian as he now calls himself. This moment in time is his only chance. There has been no other for the hundreds of years he has been trapped here in Transit. He must seize this opportunity right now, for the chances of another soul like you coming here in the near or far future are remote. The boatman is riled," Grace explained, her eyes still shifting uneasily as she glanced up and down the river.

Sarah nodded and passed the note to Grace. As she did so, her hand brushed the angel's fingertips and she felt a rush of peacefulness and calm pulse through her.

"You must persuade Anian to cross the river," Grace continued, taking the note. "He has resisted every opportunity. Never before have I known someone so wilful." She paused, looking Sarah up and down. "Well, saying that, you could be on a par with him!" Her comment was not in any way impolite, it was said with a sublime smile, filled with compassion and concern. "Anian has become a lost soul, but he can be saved. He is punishing himself for ..."

"I know," Sarah interrupted. "He is punishing himself for something that happened hundreds of years ago, but it wasn't his fault. I don't blame him and I'm sure Archie doesn't either, but Anian will not cross until he has helped me find Archie and got me safely home. He's already told me that. No matter what I say to him. Like you said, he's as stubborn as I am. I promise you, I've tried," Sarah explained.

"Then you must go back home and quickly, Sarah, for Anian's sake as well as your own," Grace insisted.

"What about Archie?" Sarah said, searching the distant riverbank behind the angel. "He has asked me to do something for him and for that I need to see him. When you give him that note he'll ..."

Grace cut across her, "Both Lillian and the Sun, and now I have told you, it is not possible. Archie has crossed the bridge. He cannot come back," she said, her tone sharpening.

"I understand that he's gone, but all I want is to talk to him ... just one more time," Sarah whispered, looking down at her hands, knowing she was being reprimanded.

"You cannot," Grace reiterated.

"I need to talk to him," Sarah begged.

"Why?" Grace asked. "Because of the letter he wrote you when he was fourteen?"

"How d-d-did you ..." Sarah stammered.

"I know a lot of things, Sarah, and you now know everything you need to know to tell Archie's story. Your research here has been done. He has told you everything through your dreams. You do not need to see him."

"I do," Sarah insisted.

"No one has ever come back from across the river, Sarah. Grace stared deep into Sarah's eyes, empathy pouring out of her. "I would like for it to be possible, particularly for you and Archie. I have never seen a love so raw, but I'm afraid it cannot be."

Sarah pushed herself up onto her feet and stood there feeling like a lost lamb whose mother has vanished, her mouth curled down and her bottom lip quivering. Grace leaned in close to her face and she thought for a moment that the angel was going to kiss her, but instead Grace's lips parted and in a soft musical voice she whispered, "I should not be telling you this, but sometimes, in moments of extreme stress or when a loved one has been placed in acute danger before it is their time to cross, a spirit can come back and intervene to help them. People on the Earth-plain think it is an illusion, but it is not. It can happen, but only rarely and never without Death's consent. Archie would have a lot of persuading to do beforehand if he did decide to cross back, and you would have to be in mortal peril for Death to even consider it."

Sarah caught her breath, "You talk of Death as though it were a real person."

"He is," Grace smiled slightly, pulling back, her lips firmly sealed again. "I must go," she said telepathically. Searching the riverbank with worried eyes, she tucked the letter in her gown, picked up her stray jug and began to move backwards into the river.

"Wait! Please ... you said I must go home. Is there a way back for me? The Moon said ... she said ..." Sarah cried out, faltering as it suddenly struck her that she had not really considered the implications of not returning to Earth. Her only thought had been to find Archie, but what of her family? Her lack of forethought filled her with shame and yet she had not planned any of what was happening to her. It all seemed to be the domino effect of circumstance that had brought her to this place, right from when she booked her flight to Thailand. Maybe even before then. So was it fate that she should be here?

Grace nodded. “She said you could never go back, I know. The Moon said that to frighten you, Sarah, and because she doesn’t want to lose you again. Indeed, there is a way back, but it is difficult and has never happened before. You must listen carefully to what I now tell you and do exactly as I say.”

Grace spoke with haste and Sarah listened intently, hearing the soft voice in her head, her eyes watching the angel’s unmoving lips. They were so full and pink. She was so beautiful. Sarah stood awestruck as a waterfall of colour enveloped her, intensifying the moment as though a deep, unspoken mystery were about to be revealed.

“Go deep into Transit,” Grace said, “find the cliff caves and from there follow the cliff path. It leads to a hidden beach ... you will know it when you find it; most souls who have a lesson to learn before they cross over enter Transit via this beach. It is deserted and will be a struggle to get onto, but if you will it, you will succeed. On the beach you will find a tree. It is the Tree of Life, Sarah. It can give you life again. The tree is a portal that connects Transit and Earth, but only you will be able to see it, for you are the only one who needs it in order to live. Do you understand?”

Sarah nodded, straining to hear the angel’s words.

“On the tree, if your timing is right, there will be an apple. That apple is yours and nobody else’s.”

“My timing?” Sarah asked.

“Yes, you are a soul who has found yourself in Transit when it is not your time to cross over. You must not stay in Transit for any longer than five days. If you do, Death will take you and hand you over to the Moon; then you will become a star again. Every second you stay here the apple is ripening and soon it will be inedible. Once that happens, the portal will close. You must find it before your time runs out and the apple rots and falls from the tree. Five days is all you had," Grace explained.

"Had?" Sarah questioned, her heart pumping loudly, banging against her chest.

"You have already been here four nights, Sarah. Today is your fifth day and your time is running out. By sundown tonight you must be gone," Grace clarified, her warm eyes comforting Sarah as she broke the urgent news.

"Today? What do I do when I've found the apple?" Sarah asked.

"Pick it off the tree and eat it, one bite is all it takes. Then submerge yourself in the waters of the ocean and like the waters of the womb, it will give you life again. You must go back; the jeopardy that awaits you here is beyond your nightmares."

"What about Archie? Will he come?" Despite everything the angel was saying, Sarah's obstinacy came to the fore. She stared at Grace seeking an inkling of hope, the faintest chance of her reuniting with Archie once again.

Grace turned away with a look of resignation, a look that said, 'Have you heard a single word I have said? Or are you just so persistent in getting what you want you have chosen to ignore me.' Sarah blushed, not sure what to say.

"I will pass him your note, Sarah. But he has crossed over, he cannot come back. Only in the event of your death will you see him again." Grace began to walk away, fading into her rainbow.

"Wait! I cannot beat the Moon, Grace," Sarah called out. "She's a sorcerer, a witch; she has the gift of magic."

Hesitating, Grace turned back and whispered. "I would gift you with a protective aura, but I am not permitted, Sarah. I can give you no greater power than you already have. It is more than you know. You have come a long way simply by using your heart as a guide. I believe you can do this by yourself. May good luck be with you. Hurry back to Anian and let him help you find the secret beach ... I must go ..."

The skies grew dark and Grace evaporated. The rainbow had gone, leaving Sarah in a chillingly dark dawn. The waters before her suddenly began to broil and churn, with no light shining on them the river looked black. With every second that passed the waters grew rougher. A gale seemed to blow from nowhere and Sarah stared in awe as rapids appeared in the river. Then, before her, a good twenty metres away, there emerged what appeared to be a giant triangular rock. It was quite far out in the middle of the river so it was hard to see clearly, but it was certainly there, not a smooth rock but bumpy and dappled. It did not rise far above the surface and the water continued to gush over the top of it, seeming to drown it at times and Sarah wondered if it was actually there at all. After a moment or two, it submerged and disappeared from view completely, leaving Sarah baffled and on edge.

"Whatever that was ... it's alive," Sarah said to herself, "unless I imagined it, but I doubt that." She looked up at the skies. It had started to rain heavily again and giant raindrops dashed into the river making it bubble and gurgle, like soup in a witch's giant cauldron. The gale turned into a squall; it was hard now to make out the bank on the other side of the river, yet Sarah could plainly see the water undulating in front of her. It was rising and falling as though something was twisting beneath it. Should she stay to find out what? She didn't think so.

The moment she thought about moving was the moment the swelling waters exploded and a wicked snake the size of a dinosaur reared into the air, its body thicker than Anian's oak trunk. Sarah could not imagine how long it was, nor did she want to.

Gasping with fear and shock, she fell back into the woods, stumbling and hiding, clinging to trees for any sort of protection. Glancing behind, she noted the snake was green with large round markings on it, a Boa maybe? It must be well over a hundred feet long, perhaps even two hundred, she thought. It was like imagined pictures of the Loch Ness monster!

"My God!" Sarah stammered to herself, her chest heaving. "Lapis lazuli protect me please ... I've never seen anything like ... it's monstrous ..." A blue aura enveloped her instantly as she called upon the power of Lillian's crystal.

The head of the snake held erect, twenty metres above the water, turned and looked directly at Sarah, its piercing green eyes locked straight into hers through the indigo shield.

"Don't look at it!" Sarah told herself, but as she tore her gaze away, she saw another snake's head emerging, peering at her from the waves, its long neck rising up beside the other.

"Oh my God, there are two of them! Lapis, protect me ... please!"

There was no way to distinguish between the two heads. They were identical in every way. Sarah knew she had to face this adversity; she could not shun these creatures and turn her back on them. To do so would surely be suicide. "Jeez," she whispered, for it was all she could muster as the Jurassic creatures began to edge out of the river.

Eyeing her closely, the snakes' necks were never far apart from one another, they swayed from side to side, moving in perfect synch and then, as though their inspection of the river bank and Sarah was done, they slowly began to follow her. She cowered in the thicket, her fragile body trembling. She was desperate to close her eyes and block out the beasts from her sight, but it was as though her eyes were glued open.

"This is just my imagination," Sarah reminded herself. "Oh help, I'm sure it's not. I didn't think of a snake, I know I didn't. I thought it was a rock. I can't linger here or I'll be slaughtered and eaten for breakfast! Think of a way to help yourself, think ... think ... think."

Sarah had no doubt that she would not be spared by these beasts. Every emotion surged through her as she cowered, frozen to the spot by fear, convinced the blue aura would not be enough to protect her. In one hand she held the sword; it looked too puny to be of any use against these enormous creatures. With menacing grace, they slithered closer and closer to the riverbank, their bodies symmetrical, never moving more than a few metres apart from one another. Then, as more and more of their bodies were revealed, Sarah suddenly twigged that they were not two separate snakes, but one giant, dual-headed serpent.

"It's connected," Sarah mumbled. "Oh help me! Someone, please help me !"

"Run..." hissed Felicity's voice in Sarah's head.

"I c-c-can't move," Sarah stuttered, rooted to the spot.

"Run, Sarah!" Felicity cried again. "Get up! Move!"

"There's no point, if I run it will catch up with me. I don't stand a chance. I need help," Sarah bellowed, the blue aura beginning to wobble as her concentration wavered.

"Who can help? For God's sake Sarah, get up and run NOW! Get me away from that thing!" Felicity hollered, horror saturating her voice.

Tearing her gaze away, Sarah finally did as she was told. Scrambling to her feet she turned away from the river. Head down, she leapt out of the bushes ... and smacked headlong into Anian's solid, hairy body as he came charging towards the shoreline. Sarah screamed, realised who it was and grasped hold of him in panic.

"Anian, help!" she cried, burying her head in his chest.

Holding her tightly in his arms, the satyr pulled her behind a stand of sturdy conifer trees. "Concentrate on your lapis crystal, Sarah," he gasped, looking up at the monster towering above them.

"Lapis, protect us, lapis protect us," Sarah intoned as a mantra, forcing herself to concentrate. Within seconds, the aura strengthened, blue light streaming around them.

"What have you done?" Anian whispered, his eyes widening as the creature's body undulated out of the water and slithered up the bank towards them, both great jaws snapping in unison.

"Done? I did nothing," Sarah gabbled, "I came down here to ..."

"Save your reasons," Anian interrupted. "Come." Roughly he grasped hold of her arm and began to drag her backwards at speed, deeper into the forest, muttering all the time.

"It is the Moon. I told you she'll stop at nothing now she knows where you are. All she wants is to get you back. You are driving her wild with frustration. No star has ever escaped her before. Even during the day you are not safe now. The beasts of the sea or the earth will turn on you at her command. She can manipulate anything in Transit if she so wishes. Why did you go out alone?"

"I just wanted to get my letter to Archie and I knew you would stop me."

"And now you know why!"

"There was a lady," Sarah tried to explain as Anian dragged her along behind him, her sword clutched in her nerveless fingers, catching on the bushes.

"What lady?" Anian stopped abruptly.

"A lady in a rainbow," she panted.

"Grace?" Anian turned to face Sarah, his eyes widening. Over her shoulder he sighted the serpent closing in on them and started on his hasty retreat again. Sarah, who in only the few days she had known him, had become used to his curt manner and rough strength, allowed him to haul her away from the danger.

"Yes, her name was Grace," Sarah's voice shook as she was dragged this way and that, over the rough terrain.

"Did she speak to you?" Anian puffed, out of breath.

"Yes, she told me to find a tree on a deserted beach."

"What tree?" Anian stopped again.

"An apple tree; she called it the Tree of Life. It's a portal; a way for me to get home. She said I have to leave right now or Death will take me," Sarah explained.

"Oh dear me ... what has Grace done?" Anian's eyebrows furrowed inwards with a deep frown. "Death will be riled now that she has spoken with you. She has broken the law." He looked at Sarah, then turned and ran on again, towing her behind him.

"What do you mean? What law?" she gasped.

"No deity can talk to a soul who is not due to cross. Not the boatman, not Grace," Anian grunted.

"What about Lillian? I spoke to her?"

"She is the only link between this world and Earth; she never comes up here and usually nobody ever goes down to her. Lillian's different. She can enter the unconscious mind; she is not ruled by Death."

"Grace was only trying to help," Sarah, her breath coming in short gasps, tugged at Anian's hand to slow him down. "She said she had never seen a love like mine and Archie's."

"That may be so. Grace's heart is huge; her feeling for what is right is strong. I do not doubt what you are saying is true, Sarah. She was trying to help. But I've learnt a few things living here in Transit for as long as I have and by Death's law, nobody should talk to you, not even me," Anian said. "Quite simply, you should not be here."

"Why are you talking to me then? Why are you helping me?"

"Because ... let's just say I'm helping an old friend," he puffed. "Anyway, I am just me. Death doesn't care about me. I am a nobody, a lost soul, what do I matter? Anian Pan, a nobody; nobody that anyone would recognise. I have been lost too long. I matter to no one," Anian whispered, muttering as he ran.

"Anian, please ... stop." Sarah pulled away from the satyr with all her might, releasing his grip on her arm. He had bruised her where he had been holding on so tight, but she ignored the pain. "What do you mean you do not matter? Everyone matters. Of course you matter. You matter a very great deal to me. You're my friend and you were my friend a long time ago. Where would I be without you?"

"Well, there are a few possibilities, but I'd rather not go into them right at this moment if you don't mind, Sarah. Please come. I don't much fancy being eaten for breakfast!" Anian smiled at her and held out a dirty hand, a gesture he had never shown before.

Sarah smiled back, looking up into his deformed face and placing her hand in his, "Thank you," she whispered. Then she heard the rustling, crunching and cracking of undergrowth behind them and gasped. "Oh God! We need to run faster, it's gaining on us."

Squeezing her hand, Anian set off again. They ran with all their might back towards the remains of the giant oak. Thoughts and questions pounded through Sarah's head with every stride. What should she do? Should she continue her search for Archie or do as Grace had told her and go on a new search for this life tree that was a portal home? She didn't want to give up on Archie, but what if Grace was right and she only had today left? She needed to live, everyone had told her that. She wanted to be with Archie, but she also wanted to live. Had she learnt all she needed to know through her dreams? She had been dreaming constantly since she had arrived here in Transit and each dream seemed to link into the next as though they were telling a story. Was that the story Archie wanted her to tell? Were all these lives connected? Was it real or was it only her fevered imagination making up stories as she slept? If these dreams were really part of her past life and Anian was too, why could she not remember it? She had often wondered about reincarnation; she knew it was what Buddhists believed. Was it possible to remember what happened to you in past lives, hundreds of years ago? Was it necessary? The Sarah from all that time ago had loved Archie in a very different way from the way she did now. Did that moment in time need to be found and rectified? What had happened to make it so imperative? How had she become a slave of the Moon? None of it made any sense to Sarah. It was like some weird fantasy; a nightmare from which she was unable to wake. She still desperately wanted to find Archie and see him face to face. More than anything she wanted to be able to touch and hug him, skin to skin; to know that he wasn't gone completely and that one day she would be with him again. Maybe even ask him the universal questions on every human's lips: 'What happens next and why are we here?' Maybe he would know or maybe he wouldn't. Maybe he was still trying to work it all out too.

Lost in her thoughts and focused on putting one foot in front of the other, without falling over or stumbling on any of the exposed tree roots, Sarah was startled when suddenly the ground beneath her feet began to quiver. Anian tugged at her hand and pulled her down with him onto all fours. Like a pulse the quivering happened again, the ground, rocks and trees all vibrating. Sarah turned to the satyr, "What ...?

He looked back at her, his brow furrowed. "Cyclops is moving."

"Coming here?" Sarah whispered, trying to steady herself as the ground shook. The tremors became stronger and with them a low rumble, like distant thunder.

Anian nodded, "He's in a hurry too."

"Is that good?" She looked behind her to see where the giant, dual-headed serpent was. It was terrifyingly close, its forked tongues flicking out from between its rubbery lips.

"Get up," Anian shouted. "Move!"

It was too late. As they had lingered to talk, the serpent had gained on them to the point where its long, tapering tail could circle around and above them. In a trice they were surrounded. They got up to run, diving for a gap, but were abruptly pushed back into the giant coil of the snake. Both hissing heads reared up, viciously snapping double danger from every angle. Sarah's sword was poised ready to attack, Anian beside her hopped from one hoof to the other, thumping his feet violently on the ground as though he was about to charge. All their defences were up.

"It's useless, it's all around us," Sarah cried, turning full circle.

"Remember how you used that sword before, against the ravens; use it better than that now," Anian suggested, his eyes bulging with fear.

"Right," Sarah gasped, giving a firm nod, her mouth bone dry, aware she could not recall exactly how she had fought the ravens. Hoping that by some miracle it would come back to her, she raised the weapon holding it in both hands. The ground trembled violently. Sweat beaded on Sarah's forehead and top lip as she battled to stay on her feet.

The serpent drew back; hesitated, each head poised to strike. Five more mini-earthquakes shook the ground. Five giant strides as Cyclops bashed his way through the forest, pushing trees over in his great stomp. Then the great, one-eyed colossus was there before them, taller than a tree, and was lunging at the Moon's creature.

Distracted from its prey, the snake's heads whirled round to defend itself, but Cyclops was ready, his enormous hand grabbing at one of the snapping heads.

"RUN!" Anian screamed.

Seizing the moment, Sarah and the satyr charged under the arched coil of the snake's neck as it struggled against the giant's grip on one of its heads. They dived between Cyclops' legs and were away. "Don't look back," Anian urged. "Just keep running until you get to the other side of the forest." His flying hooves were all Sarah could focus on. He could run a lot faster than she and he didn't have hold of her this time, so she started to fall behind.

A giant roar bellowed from somewhere behind them. A howl of pain filled the air; it was so harsh it halted Sarah briefly in her tracks. Anian charged onwards and as the howl faded, Sarah followed, but was now more than twenty paces behind. She could hear movement close by. The ground did not quake, so she knew it was not Cyclops stalking her.

"Keep running, don't look back," Sarah panted to herself, her lungs burning. "Just keep running."

She tripped; face planting into the leafy ground, her sword flying from her hand. Dirt shot into her eyes, pain blasted through her nose, she could feel blood trickle down her throat as she skidded across the woodland floor. In seconds a pressure seemed to sweep over the top of her. Not massively to the point of being crushed, but enough for her to know that the serpent was preparing its prey. Grasping outwards blindly for her sword, her hand thrashing about in the earth, searching, she found the handle, got a good strong grip and stabbed the weapon with all her force deep into the area where she could feel the serpent's presence. It was a lucky strike. The creature wailed, enraged. Still blind, Sarah knew she had struck true. She ripped the stone blade back out immediately, wanting to go in for a second strike, but the ground suddenly began to tremble again.

"Has Cyclops found his feet?" Sarah wondered. As the thought ran through her mind, the snake collapsed with full force on top of her tiny frame, squashing her into the earth, the sword dropping from her hand.

Crushed, unable to breathe, Sarah struggled and fought against the dead weight on top of her, although something told her the creature was not dead, not hurt at all in fact, it was merely covering her until it could manoeuvre her down one of its throats. Anian, where are you? She thought, her mind battling to find a resolution, a saviour. Felicity, help me!

A low humming noise caused her to focus. It was a bizarre sound, fizzing through to her beneath the snake. Suddenly the weight lifted. Sarah sat up immediately, gasping in air, spitting dirt out of her mouth, shooting mud out of her bloody nose and brushing debris from her face, her hand feeling for the sword and finding it. The humming noise intensified. Grasping at her eyes, rubbing and blinking, she tried to open them to see. Falling back onto her elbows in a giant's shadow, her heartbeat thumped into frenzy. Towering above her stood Cyclops and held above his head with both hands was the serpent, thrashing and coiling, both heads snapping at the giant and the air around them. Furious bees swarmed everywhere.

Sarah could see that Cyclops would not be able to hold the serpent for long. He wasn't being stung all over, as was the thick-skinned serpent, but the snake was huge, even to Cyclops and he was hurt; beneath the fringe of his ragged tunic, she could see an oozing gash on his naked thigh, he had been bitten badly. Anxious for the amiable giant, Sarah back-peddled fast on all fours, just as Anian's hand seized her bruised upper arm and pulled her to her feet, dragging her further back from the battle now taking place.

"You all right, Sarah?" Anian gasped.

"Yes, I'm ok." Sarah replied, her gaze never leaving Cyclops and the serpent.

"I called my bees," the satyr smiled, nodding his head towards the swarms of flying insects. "Come on." He took hold of Sarah's hand and once again they began to run.

Another roar erupted from behind them. "Oh, Anian, don't let go of me this time," Sarah pleaded as they ran. She could feel her feet starting to drag, beginning to stumble.

"I've got you. I won't let go," Anian replied. "Cyclops won't last long with that bite on his leg."

"What do you mean? I thought it was a boa ... a constrictor? Is it venomous?" Sarah panted, as she lunged over thick tree roots and around various berry bushes.

"Anything sent by the Moon is toxic," Anian explained. "The bite is on Cyclops's leg, so it may take some time, especially given his size, but once that venom takes hold and works its way up to his heart ..."

"What?" Sarah said, nipping the end of her tongue as she ran, tears springing into her eyes.

Anian turned his head to look at her, his eyes sombre. Glancing behind he grimaced, "It's all over for him, I'm afraid."

Sarah stopped abruptly and turned to look. Cyclops had crashed to the ground like a felled tree and was now swaying on his knees. Hunting them once again, the serpent was moving rapidly in their wake. Sad for the giant who had tried to help them, Sarah was overwhelmed by fear and panic. The feeling of vertigo whirled around her head and she wanted to be sick. The trees and shrubs merged into a blur of multi-hued colour. All she could think was that her death was imminent. "I'm going to die," she whispered as she ran. "The Moon will enslave me as a star forever."

"No, no, no, Sarah," the satyr ordered, "don't even go there. Block that thought. You are not going to die. I will die before I let anything happen to you. Now run!"

Sarah gulped as the image of her own imminent death was overlaid by the thought of Anian's looming end. The world continued to blur in front of her, her legs went heavy and numb, she felt as though she were running in slow motion through treacle, making no progress at all.

The dual-headed serpent closed the gap in a trice and struck again, lunging out to trip its prey with one swift flick of its divided neck.

Sarah recalled with precise and vivid detail the moment of falling: Anian's voice could be heard above all else. His scream of anger, pain and terror split the air around her. She felt as if daggers were piercing her eardrums, making her forehead throb. The gigantic reptile's spotted skin filled her mind. She could hear it hissing and gnawing, and other terrifying sounds of cracking and ripping. A scarlet splash of blood crossed Sarah's vision and she felt something warm and wet splatter on her face. This then was the end. She closed her eyes, her heart hammering as she felt sticky liquid drip down her chin and onto her chest. She did not know what was happening, it was all too fast for her to take in and yet each moment seemed to last an eternity, everything misted in an indistinguishable blur. Her feet didn't seem to be on the ground. Was it her blood on her face, seeping down onto her rose-tinted dress? Surely she would be screaming in agony if it was, yet she could feel no pain at all. Where were the serpent's heads?

Then suddenly she saw Anian's bent and broken body go flying past her, and as though someone had hit the fast forward button, she was winded by an unseen force and whipped away in the opposite direction.

"This is it," Fee whispered, terror distorting her voice.

"I'm going to die," Sarah replied to herself.

There was no pain; she did not scream, it was almost akin to sinking slowly into a giant bundle of hay. Fresh and bright images flew into her mind of spring days and cornfields. Over Anian's cry, she could hear ravens squawking in the distance. The pounding in Sarah's head suddenly washed away and she could no longer see the forest; the terrain of Transit. She felt herself crumbling, as though she were somehow being reduced to her core, and at the same time being pushed through a thick spectrum of colour into a different stratosphere.

Then very suddenly ... everything went black.

CHAPTER SEVENTEEN

AUGUST 1685
UNTIL DEATH DO US PART

Overcome with gratitude towards Renshaw for tracking Sarah and bringing her home safely, her parents did not even question the whereabouts of Fletcher, the scoundrel who had, according to Renshaw, abducted and attempted to corrupt their daughter and who, having eluded his pursuers, had mysteriously disappeared from the village. Renshaw, seeing how distracted they were and afraid for his job should the truth come out about what he had done in Lord Belmont's name, spun a pack of lies and Sarah, listening, was too exhausted to care. She was summarily given into the care of her maid, bathed and salved and put to bed, where she fell into a troubled sleep. It was not until the following morning that she learned from Katie - who delighted in listening to gossip - what was actually going on with her father and why he had been acting so strangely.

Sarah was horrified. It transpired that Lord Belmont had entered into a business venture, investing everything he had in a new development in London. Ever since the Great Fire of '66 had necessitated rebuilding houses for the suddenly homeless population, the capital had been expanding rapidly, way beyond its original boundaries. Moorfields, an area of drained marshland outside the city walls, had seemed a racing certainty for profitable enterprise and Sarah's father had sunk every last penny into it. Indeed, there would have been great fruits to be harvested had the project been successful. But it wasn't. It went catastrophically wrong. Lord Belmont had lost everything and now, heavily in debt, was likely to lose his entire estate. The imminent nuptials of their daughter to a wealthy, new-made earl no less, had come as a godsend. As the bride price, Joseph Jackson had agreed to pay off his father-in-law's debts and Sarah's tearful protests fell on deaf ears. "You must do your duty," her mother said and oft repeated during the run up to the wedding.

Right up until the moment Sarah walked down the aisle and was standing at the altar she had been kept to her room under close guard, seeing no one but her maid, her mother and Mistress Grey. On the morning of her wedding, Katie came bustling into her bedroom with a broad smile on her face.

"I have something for you, Miss Sarah," she said, passing over a note in a cream-coloured envelope.

Sarah recognised the seal immediately. "How did you...?" Taking the note from Katie, she brushed the seal with her thumb, "Did anyone see you?"

"Nobody. Mister Kriss passed it to me at first light on my way back from the church. There wasn't a soul about." Sarah glanced at Katie with a quizzical look. "Your mama asked me to go down and check if the flowers were arranged ready for ..." The maid faltered and flushing pink looked down at her hands. "They were beautiful," she added.

Wide-eyed, Sarah stumbled backwards and sat down on her bed staring at the note clutched in her fingers.

"Are you going to open it?" Katie asked. "I thought it would have been ripped to pieces by now."

Sarah smiled slightly and nodded. Seconds passed and still the note lay unopened.

"Would you like me to read it?" Katie asked.

"Can you?"

"Yes, Miss Sarah, my father was a good man. He had me schooled along with my brothers, said it would always come in useful."

Looking up at her maid and seeing her with new eyes, Sarah nodded. "Thank you, Katie, if you would."

Quickly, Katie took the note and broke the seal, sitting down beside Sarah on the bed she cleared her throat and read out loud: "Dearest Sarah, All is well. Archie is safe. Meet me at nine o'clock this morning, by the black pit down on the south side of Belmont, where we used to play and swim as children. I will take you to him. I am forever at your service, Kriss."

Sarah burst into tears, "Oh Katie, what am I to do? Even if I could get away, I cannot go to him," she cried, feeling her maid's caring hand resting lightly on her shoulder. "I cannot see my parents impoverished. I must do my duty by them. I have no choice, not now."

She plucked a handkerchief from the pocket of her nightgown and dabbed at her eyes. "It's not just my family and our name," she sobbed, "there are so many other lives at stake. Yours, for one," she glanced at Katie, who stared back with big brown eyes. "All the household staff, Mistress Grey, Cook, the parlour maids, stable hands and labourers, even the villagers, for what will happen to them if Belmont is seized by the Crown prosecutors? Everyone will be out of work, homeless and destitute. I cannot see that happen, always knowing I could have prevented it."

Katie did not respond, her hand slipped from Sarah's shoulder to her back and began to rub soothingly. Her kind effort was wasted. Sarah stood up and strode to her bureau, snatching a quill and parchment. Dripping ink all over the page she hurriedly wrote a note, blew on the ink and folding the parchment, handed it to Katie.

"Take this to Kriss, now, quickly before I change my mind," Sarah whispered. Katie nodded taking the note, turning for the door.

"Katie," Sarah called after her.

"Yes, Miss Sarah?"

"Will God forgive me for not following my heart?"

***

"Dearly beloved, we are gathered together here in the sight of God, and in the face of this congregation, to join together this man and this woman in holy matrimony," the vicar's voice trembled as he recited the words, his anxious gaze darting continually from Sarah to her father, on whom his living depended. The book in his hand quivered and his forehead gleamed with perspiration. The church was hot, the sun blazing through the window casting patterns on the stone floor.

Standing before him, Sarah was motionless in her ornate satin wedding dress adorned with silk taffeta ribbons, which her mother had insisted on. The corset was so tight she could scarcely breathe. Layer upon layer of ivory satin and gold brocade had been piled onto the hoop beneath. It was heavy and suffocating. The long, slashed sleeves at her wrists merged into lace cuffs that draped down to her finger tips, and an elaborate gold-coloured train, embroidered with beading, spread out behind her. Her hair was up and off her shoulders in an elegant pleat.

At the altar, she stood side-by-side with the darkly handsome Lord Joseph Jackson, whose attire was bedecked with as many ruffles as her own. Behind them waited every member of the local community who had been able to squeeze into the little church, all wanting to bear witness to this day, some maybe secretly disbelieving and waiting for something or someone to impede its happening.

"If any man can show any just cause why they may not lawfully be joined together, let him now speak, or else hereafter forever hold his peace," the vicar intoned.

He waited, glancing up at the congregation. Nobody betrayed the silence that fell upon the church at that moment, a silence in which Sarah could have heard a pin drop and it broke her heart, for despite her resolve, she had hoped against hope that somehow this nightmare would be stopped. The vicar turned back to the couple and looked deep into Sarah's face. His grey eyes said it all: 'You are about to become the wife of a man you do not love.'

Silent tears streamed down her cheeks as she accepted the inevitable. Sarah knew she must become Lady Jackson, purely for her family's sake. With all their questionable ethics and ridiculous faults, she could never see her mother and father rendered homeless, mocked, maybe even imprisoned for debt. Nor, as she had said to Katie, could she grasp her own happiness at the expense of all those who depended on them. And yet still she hoped. Unbelieving, Sarah glanced round to look, but no one in the congregation moved. She glimpsed Renshaw's sardonic features, his lips lifted in a knowing leer as he met her gaze. How could this be happening? Sarah's head started to spin and her ears to ring. What had she done? Not far away from here, the man she loved with her whole being lay waiting, risking his life. Had he yet received her note? Would he understand why she had done what she had done or would he feel betrayed?

The silence lay thick across the room and seemed to go on and on, as though even the vicar did not believe it, but even a clap of thunder would not have dared break that moment. Sarah looked fleetingly at her parents, her mother's face was forlorn and tired; her father, as always, looked stern and forbidding. They had pleaded with her to do as they had asked and save the family's reputation and fortune; the pressure on her shoulders today was immense. Then she glimpsed her governess, Mistress Grey, who stood directly behind her parents and whose face was intent and devoid of emotion.

Turning back to face the altar, Sarah was conscious that the man at her side was fidgeting. She could feel his body heat, so close to her that she shuddered with revulsion, aware of what was to come. Trapped in her own thoughts she wondered how anyone here, lifelong friends and family, could pronounce this situation as right. Surely there was another way. She begged with all her soul for Archie to rescue her, but she knew he would not. Her note to him had put an end to any rescue. She had made sure he would not come running to risk his life and face the gallows. It was all she could do for him. 'This is what I want ...' she had written. 'God, forgive me this lie,' she prayed silently. Yet even if he had ignored her note and come, would she have run into his arms? She knew she could not go with him, her allegiance, as she had heard so many times in previous days, lay with her family and she could not condemn them. The presence of her father looming over her stressed and obligated her. He was indeed the keeper of her destiny, had been since the day she was born. Why had she ever believed it could have been different? And now here he was, passing her over like a parcel of his belongings for another to use and dominate.

Her teeth gritted behind a false smile, she nodded at the vicar, who drew in a deep breath and with a sigh continued with the service. "I require and charge you both, as ye will answer at the dreadful day of judgment when the secrets of all hearts shall be disclosed, that if either of you know any impediment, why ye may not be lawfully joined together in holy matrimony, ye do now confess it." He nodded gently at Sarah, with a worried smile.

Sarah felt her father's hand in the small of her back, always reminding her that he was there and that there were to be no outbursts of denial. His lectures and wrath over the past weeks told Sarah all she needed to know: he was a broken man and only she could fix him. She stared with glistening eyes up at the vicar. He had listened to her lengthy confession and kept it to himself, for what could he do to help her? Hers was not the first arranged marriage to take place against the wishes of the helpless bride. She knew that. It did not stop her from thinking how wrong it all was.

"Lord Joseph Jackson, Earl of Suffolk," the vicar said, turning to address the groom. "Wilt thou have this woman to thy wedded wife, to live together after God's ordinance in the holy estate of matrimony? Wilt thou love her, comfort her, honour, and keep her in sickness and in health; and forsaking all others, keep thee only unto her so long as ye both shall live?"

"I will," sneered Joseph, ogling Sarah with intent.

"Lady Sarah Belmont," the vicar's voice softened considerably, his fear clearly seen by all those standing near. Would she throw a spectacular tantrum as unwilling brides so often did? Not in public surely. Everyone waited with bated breath, some eager, some fearful.

"Wilt thou have this man to thy wedded husband, to live together after God's ordinance in the holy estate of matrimony?" The vicar's voice sped up, his anxiety making him almost gabble out the words. "Wilt thou obey him, and serve him, love, honour, and keep him in sickness and in health; and forsaking all others keep thee only unto him so long as ye both shall live?"

This time, another type of silence filled the church. It was a silence that would pass into legend, so tense and long. Sarah could feel every set of eyes boring into her back. Not a cough nor a sigh rose from the onlookers as they waited for her response. Could she rest her head on the same pillow as this man? She would be his trophy, nothing more, something beautiful to drape on his arm. Would he look after her? Not likely. She had so much love to give, but not to this man. There were no feelings of affection or even friendship between them. They knew little about each other, although she was fairly certain Joseph knew about Archie and it must be obvious to him that she did not want this marriage, which set a negative start to any possible bond. Her prayers had not been answered. It seemed today that even God had abandoned her. For Sarah, this ceremony was the beginning of her mourning for Archie; it was far from a celebration that a marriage should be. She had so much anger and pain broiling inside her; so much resentment and bitterness towards her parents for forcing her into this situation. Tradition and standing were not a good enough reason for her; where was the love in this life. The circumstance was desperate, as was the lingering silence.

"Lady Sarah," the vicar prompted.

"I will… not obey," Sarah whispered to the ground.

"What did she say?" an old lady in the front row asked, as those around her gasped.

"Lady Sarah?" the vicar asked again.

"I will not obey," she repeated, loudly and sourly, looking up into the vicar's face. "I will marry Lord Jackson only because I have no other choice, but I will not obey him."

"Sarah!" her mother shrieked.

Not once did Sarah acknowledge the man she was about to marry as she spoke. She looked only at the vicar. His grey eyes looked imploringly back at her, but Sarah refused to give an inch. On this matter she would stand. She had known the vicar all her life; he knew she was a free-spirited girl, who had always thrown caution to the wind and done as she pleased one way or another. If he forced her on this, she would mutiny and he knew it. She would not agree to be treated like a dog, obeying her new husband's every command. She glared at the vicar, willing him to understand that the freedom to decide had always been hers.

Her father coughed, "Yes, she will obey," he said from directly behind her, pushing his way further forward and in that moment removing that precious freedom to decide that she had always taken for granted. "Please carry on Vicar," he ordered. "My daughter clearly said 'I will', so get on with it, man."

"But I do not love him, Father," Sarah hissed, "why would I obey a man I do not love?"

"Continue," Lord Belmont snapped, throwing the vicar a hard look.

"Who giveth this woman to be married to this man?" the vicar continued weakly.

"I do," Lord Belmont said, passing her hand into that of the furious man at her side.

Sarah's head dipped further whilst the rituals continued around her. No matter what she said, it was clear her father did not care. She had never thought him capable of wishing unhappiness on her; in her heart-of-hearts she had always felt he was not entirely merciless. It had only been recently, since her betrothal to Lord Jackson, that his attitude towards her had changed. Maybe that was when his troubles had started down in London. Sarah tried to find excuses for him, but it was hard. Since she was a little girl he had always been strict, yet fair, not affectionate, but showering her with gifts to show he cared. Today, nothing seemed fair: 'What crime have I committed to be forced into a life of misery?' she thought, railing against her fate. Sarah knew her father would never willingly have let her marry a common arrowsmith, but could he not have let her live out her life a spinster? Would he have done so had he not lost his fortune? She would never know.

Sarah listened to the harsh voice of the groom, angered and rushing through his vows with no care or meaning. Her father stayed close to hand and just before Sarah's turn to speak, he stooped to whisper in her ear. His words made her sway on her feet, bile raced up her throat and she swallowed hard, then, with no alternative, in a broken voice she spoke the fateful words, "I, Sarah Belmont take thee, Joseph Jackson, to my wedded husband," she whispered. Sarah's breathing was laboured, her frame of mind seemed to shift as she started speaking her vows; it was as though she were outside herself, looking at herself through a mirror. It was a cold and dark vision. It was not her, but someone else. Involuntarily she paused, her hesitation lost in the emptiness of the moment. Her father again leaned forward and whispered into her ear. The words echoed in her mind, the horror of what he threatened, driving her once more into terrified submission.

"Speak up child," her father commanded loudly, pulling away from her with a nervous grin towards the frowning congregation. "The people at the back can't hear you!"

"To have and to hold from this day forward," the vicar intoned. Automatically, her mind dulled, Sarah repeated his words. "For better, for worse … in sickness and in health, to love, cherish, and to obey, till death do us part …."

There; it was done. Completely detached, Sarah held her head high, boldly moving herself away from her father's touch. She was no longer his. He would keep his estate and his debts would be paid, but she had another to deal with now. She felt as if she had left her body, that her spirit had taken flight away from the danger. Like a winged fairy she seemed to float up to the ceiling of the church and look down on the couple at the altar. A rush of wings seemed to beat in her ears, as below her she heard the vicar say, "I now pronounce that they be man and wife together, in the name of the Father, and of the Son, and of the Holy Ghost. Amen. Let us pray."

Sarah was dimly aware that she had collapsed and was lying on the cold stone floor; heard her father say with a nervous laugh, "Such joy! She is quite overcome." She knew the vicar and Katie had rushed to her side, patting her hands. Someone was offering her water. Her eyes were wide open and from where she lay she could see what she thought was a ray of sunlight dancing on the beautiful ceiling. A moment ago she was sure she had been up there too. A strange and shrill laugh seemed to bounce into her mind, as though from another world. The harder she stared at the dazzling light the more it changed, dancing now on the walls, changing shape. A sick feeling rose in her belly as a face appeared through the beam. Was it a ghost? It was the middle of the day, surely not a time for ghosts and haunting? The church was full. Could anyone else see it? She could not move or speak to question them. She did not feel afraid; it was more like a fairytale. The face was so pure and beautiful, like an angel, so bright and vivid that it was difficult to divert her eyes. Sarah knew deep in her soul that this vision had not come to frighten her; it came to help and comfort her.

"Have hope," a voice rang in Sarah's mind.

"Hope? Where is hope in this church?" Sarah's mind whispered back.

"I am here… I am with you and always will be, I am part of you," the voice sang in her head. 'There is always hope.'

"No, you are wrong, even in the house of God, there is no hope here, convention has won," Sarah mumbled. "If I had been gifted with poverty I would be with Archie. I want only to be with him. I do not want to live this life ordained for me."

"Archie is alive; he is well," the voice offered.

"And when he is not alive and well, then what should I do?"

"You will know what to do, Sarah. I promise you that."

"My future is destroyed," Sarah whimpered aloud for all in the church to hear, squeezing her eyes shut.

"She is coming round," the vicar said. "Stand back, give her air."

"I will help you," Katie breathed softly in Sarah's ear, her head only millimetres away.

Sarah's eyes opened at the sudden change of voice. The atmosphere and congregation returned to her. A hand stroked back her hair gently and Sarah's wide, terrified gaze found her maid. "It is all right, Miss Sarah, I am here," Katie assured her, helping her to her feet.

White-faced, Sarah turned to face her new husband. Looking down his nose at her, Lord Jackson lifted his arm. She took it reluctantly, her head still pounding, her face tear-soaked. She did not have the strength to walk unaided; if she could have, she would have run. Katie gently took hold of Sarah's other arm, and Mistress Grey, who stood just behind Katie, placed her hand gently between Sarah's shoulder-blades, almost propping her up and aiming her down the aisle. It would have been frowned upon if they did not leave the church together and she had caused enough of a commotion by falling over at the altar. The walk back down the aisle felt like an eternity: her legs felt heavy as lead and her chest as though a weight was pressed against it. The faces that stared back at her with puzzled looks swam in front of her eyes in a blur.

Out of the corner of her eye she spied a familiar figure. He was inconspicuously huddled in the corner of the church near a side entrance, dressed in his hooded, dark red cape, his face hidden from the congregation. Sarah, completely losing herself, all inhibitions gone, lunged towards him, leaving her husband, mouth agape, standing rooted to the spot in the middle of the aisle.

"Take care of him, Kriss, please," she begged.

Kriss grasped Sarah as she fell into him. "I will do what I can, Lady Jackson," he said.

Sarah stared at him, eyes brimming with fresh tears. "Don't ever call me that; call me anything but that."

"Yes, Miss Sarah," Kriss murmured, placing her firmly back on her feet.

"My father says he knows where he is, he has threatened to ... to ..." She broke into wild sobs. The congregation gasped.

"Have courage, my friend, have courage," Kriss said softly. "He is safe; it was an empty threat. Your father said it only to force you to say your vows."

"Kriss, please, look at me," Sarah whispered, forcing Kriss to raise his head. "You're my friend; you've always been there for me, always."

"What is this?" Joseph Jackson jeered. He had finally moved and was waiting impatiently by the arched exit. "Wife, get over here. Leave that poor man alone and stop making an exhibition of yourself!" Sarah turned to look at her new husband, sunlight from the open doorway dazzled her and blotted out Joseph's features then she turned back to Kriss.

He smiled at her, "I must leave now, Miss Sarah. I have to go away from here. I came to say goodbye and to give you this." He pushed a scrap of parchment into Sarah's hand. "I may never see you again."

Pressing her finger to his lips, Sarah said urgently, "Of course you will, don't say such a thing. Just promise me one thing, Kriss. Promise me and keep that promise for eternity."

"You must leave me now, Miss Sarah. I shouldn't have come. Everyone is listening. Go back to your husband, quickly."

"Not until you promise."

"I promise," Kriss agreed hastily.

"Promise to watch him, protect him and one day, when it is safe, bring him home," Sarah begged in an undertone.

"I promise to try," Kriss nodded.

"With all your heart," Sarah pleaded, feeling Lord Jackson's firm hand pulling roughly at her arm.

"Go now, Miss Sarah, I promise with all my heart to do exactly as you wish."

"Oh, for the love of God," hollered Lord Jackson, "would you please come on woman." Another spray of gasps rose through the congregation as he dragged his new bride away from the king's messenger and out of the church into the brilliant sunlight. Villagers had gathered to throw rice and flowers on the newlyweds, clapping and cheering as they trotted through a tunnel of arms, everyone gossiping at what had just taken place within the church.

As they continued to move through the arc of people and out the other end, Sarah swung round to look behind her and caught the glimpse of a red cloak disappearing round the side of the church. Her husband clamped his fingers on her arm, "Smile for the people," he hissed, "And now come and let me introduce you as my wife to my parents. You will do as I say and behave yourself or it will be the worse for you!" He strode ahead to where his parents waited to congratulate the happy couple.

Behind his back Sarah un-crumpled the note in her hand and discreetly bent her head to read it.

I will miss you, more dearly than these written words can say.

Arch

CHAPTER EIGHTEEN

AUGUST 2003
THE SEVERED THREAD OF HUMAN LIFE

The Buddhist prayer was a form of meditation slowly converting his confusion into clarity. Niran-Atid glanced up to the firmament. He asked for no favours for his own personal gain or for any favours at the expense of others, as this would crush the power of his prayer. Devoid of any self-centeredness and calculation, relying solely on compassion, he called quietly to the heavens from where he sat in a small long-tail boat in the middle of the Chao Phraya River. The cosmos seemed to answer his prayer directly, a small black crow circled above him and Niran-Atid beamed a toothless grin at the sky.

"The greatest action, Miss Sarah, is not conforming to the world's ways."

***

Sarah woke to the ear-piercing grind of metal on metal, it was worse than someone scraping their fingernails down a blackboard. Something was turning; maybe it was a bicycle wheel that desperately needed oiling, or it could have been an old swing rocking back and forth; whatever it was, the noise went straight through her, forcing her to suck her cheeks in and cling onto her teeth. Her body, which felt numb with cold, oddly also felt weightless; she could hardly make out her head from her elbow. She could hear movement, she was sure she was not alone; a clear rustling somewhere above her confirmed her notion.

"She's met with the Keeper of Secrets," a voice whispered, a cold finger traced across her throat.

"Lapis lazuli's power is strong, the thread will never break; its resilience is countless."

"No curses dear sisters. Lillian's guard will only be wasted," another voice crowed.

"She wakes," a third voice, which was far more fragile, spoke; a gaggle of gasps rose above her. The finger circling the pendant on her chest was persistent.

"Where am I?" Sarah whispered, trying to open her eyes and raising her hand to brush away whoever was touching her.

"In the throes of space and time," hissed an ancient and frail voice.

"The ravens ... that snake thing, it was chasing me ..." Sarah stammered, remembering her flight, torpidly rubbing her eyes.

"Yes, yes, all in the past now. All sent by Mother to bring you here, to us. Our mother always gets us what we want," said a different voice, even more croaky than the last.

"Your mother?" Sarah squeezed her eyes shut then forced them open, a blur of three stark white faces glared down at her. Her heart skipped a beat. Terrified, she struggled with a feeling of paralysis, desperate to retreat but with nowhere to hide. She stared back at the three haggard old crones above her, their eyes were as black as midnight, their skin as thin as tissue and so white, as though like deep sea urchins that had never risen from the depths, they had never seen the sun.

"Indeed, we three are the Moon's daughters, the Children of Night," the second woman heckled, reading Sarah's thoughts.

Sarah's stare shifted from face to face, they were nearly identical, only age distinguished them. Their pale faces were long and oval and their long hair, in varying shades of black and grey, was draped to their knees. The sharp grinding of something turning in the distance continued to stab like a knife through her ears. The woman that claimed them as the 'Children of the Night' looked slightly less haggard than the first one who had spoken; maybe she was marginally younger, but only just. They had to be witches, Sarah decided; they looked just like the hags in Shakespeare's Macbeth. Each one had a long hooked nose, but this particular hag had a large wart protruding through her left eyebrow.

"You don't look like a child," Sarah stammered as the faces loomed closer.

"Ahhh!" screamed the older hag angrily. "I am old, yes, older than my sisters, but I am wiser and far more powerful." From beneath her black robes, she drew out a pair of enormous scissors and snipped them under Sarah's nose.

Wincing back to avoid the snipping blades, she cried out, "Stop that! What are you doing?" She tried to sit up, gritting her teeth at the scraping of the wheel in the background, which made her toes curl.

The old hag cackled with laughter, but withdrew the scissors a few inches enabling Sarah to take in the third woman, who had barely spoken. She was undeniably younger than the other two but just as chilling. It was hard to see what they were wearing other than shapeless black robes, they merged with their surroundings, only their faces were prominent.

"You don't like our spinning wheel?" The youngest whispered, hardly moving her lips, her voice was softer and reminded Sarah slightly of Lillian's.

"What is that?" Sarah asked, twisting herself round to take a closer look at the source of the intense scraping sound. Behind the three crones she could see a giant wooden wheel slowly turning. It was taller than a house, draped in cobwebs and ancient beyond belief. In front of it a flight of steps led to the centre of the wheel and up from there to its pinnacle. It reminded Sarah of a vast watermill wheel, but without the water.

"This is where all lives are sewn and all fates are determined," the youngest woman whispered through the darkness, tickling Sarah's ear with a stray wispy lip hair. She had not realised the hag was so close and it caught her by surprise. She yelped in shock; these women seemed able to move around her without her noticing, almost as if they were floating. This was worse than her worst nightmares: why couldn't she wake up?

"What is this place? What do you mean, where fates are determined? This is a dream, a bad dream. I need to get out. P-p-please let me out, I'm c-c-claustrophobic," Sarah stammered, searching for light in the darkness. There was nothing except the three women and the wheel, everything else around them was a black abyss. There was no door that she could see; no floor or ceiling, so it seemed. No way out. She was entombed and beginning to shake with suffocating panic. Maybe she really was, like they had said, lost in time and space, but how could that be?

"No, this is not a dream, Sarah," whispered the youngest. "This is now your own reality. We are the Three Fates and I am called 'Spinner'. I weave the life of every man and woman from my distaff onto my spindle." Her jet black eyes glimmered like buttons in her stark, white face. "I spun yours," she said with a slight grin.

"I am called 'Measure'," crowed the hag with the wart, revealing a metre rule from beneath her robes. "She may weave the thread, but I determine its length."

"And I'm 'Cutter'," the oldest sister cackled, snipping her scissors, so large they were more like shears, under Sarah's nose again. "I cut the thread of life. I determine when and how life ends."

"Please let me go. Oh God, Sarah, wake up! I want to go home. To the home I know... with my brother Dominic and Mum and Dad. I'm dreaming again, I must be. Things like this don't happen." Sarah pulled and pinched at her skin, crying out, frantically trying to wake herself.

"No, it's true, not often, but they do happen, Sarah, and they are happening to you right now. Don't worry it's not your turn yet," crowed Cutter, abruptly snipping her scissors shut. "But you are contrary and you have tested your providence one too many times, you've tried your luck and now your luck has run out."

"I don't understand. What does that mean? These things don't happen - they can't happen. You're not real. Real, is a house, bricks and mortar, my house ... my flat ... London ... that's real," Sarah rambled, still searching the void for anything at all that would give her some comfort, but finding nothing.

"Of course we're real. We are made of solid mass like you. Seeing is believing and we are here," said Spinner, her arms outstretched.

"You're a nightmare, a really bad nightmare. I'll wake up soon, I'll wake up and I'll be ... where will I be? I'll be back in England, not in some godforsaken time I can't remember. I'll be back in London ... no wait, I'll be back in Wales, at Nanny's house. That's what I understand, that's where I make sense and I refuse to allow you to make me think you are real," Sarah said obstinately, scrambling for answers in her mind, but nothing would compute. A pulse thumped in her ears, proving she was indeed alive even as her head began to spin in disbelief, the wheel's screeching making it almost impossible to think. Transit and her dreaming had been one thing to accept, but this was quite different. She wasn't sure why, but it seemed even more ridiculous and far-fetched than a friend who was half a goat and a duel-headed, giant-eating serpent - and yet she was here. She had never been in a situation anywhere near as frightening as this. Even the snake and Moon's fight combined didn't touch on the fear that bubbled inside her now and nothing these women said made any sense to her.

"Come, come. We sisters can't be all that bad, we've an old friend to reunite you with. You will not be here in this hole alone," Cutter remarked.

"Take me back," Sarah pleaded her head down, shaking, refusing to look at their shrivelled faces.

"Back? Back where, Sarah?" croaked Cutter.

"I told you ... I want to go back to Nanny's house in Wales." A hand took hold of Sarah's chin and tilted it upwards forcing her to look up. She squeezed her eyes shut.

"And I'm telling you, you cannot travel back in time to hide from your true destiny. It is impossible. Besides, it would be rude not at least to say hello to your old spouse. He's searched and waited for such a long time to see you," Measure said.

"Let me go, you old hag, take me back to Transit then; to Anian; to the oak tree. Take me back to Bangkok ... to London ... please," Sarah sobbed. "Anywhere but here, I don't care where, but I don't want to meet any old spouse. I want to go back to Earth. I want to go home to my family. I don't belong here. This is not my fate. I want Archie, I want my mum and I want my nanny. I don't believe in you, so just GO AWAY," Sarah begged, desperate for the excruciating grinding to stop. "How can you live with that dreadful noise?" she wailed, her hands pressed hard on her ears, her eyes tight shut.

"Oh, you can't go back anywhere, not from our black hole, we are in the very core and centre of the Universe now, Sarah, the deepest and biggest black hole you could ever imagine. Once inside there is no return," Measure continued. "No one can find you here. It is just you, Joseph Jackson and us. It is fate," she smiled.

"Black hole?" Sarah knew what a black hole was. "You mean I'm in a region of space-time from which nothing, not even light, can escape? But how did I get here. I don't understand," she whispered.

"You are right. There is no light here, only us and the wheel and there is no escape," Spinner answered. "Our mother brought you to us. Only if you were to travel back in time could you alter this ending and we all know that is impossible, don't we sisters." She giggled, her voice echoing in the darkness, bouncing off invisible walls that were probably not even there. "This hole is our home; it is where we Children of Night were born and where we and you shall remain for eternity with the wheel and your espoused." Spinner looked up at the giant wheel slowly grinding round its course. "Say hello, Sarah, be nice to him, he's waited so long."

Out of the corner of her eye Sarah saw a figure on the steps move forward. She turned her head away quickly, refusing to look up.

"You were naughty, Sarah," Spinner wheedled. "Mother can't trust you out there in the big wide world anymore. You should have stayed where you belonged and served her, but you bent the rules and escaped. Reprimanding you would do no good because you are naturally so defiant, we had to take action and detain you before you not only resist your true destiny, but damage the rules of Death in the process; rules which have been in place since the beginning of time and which you have already threatened."

"Here for eternity? No, I don't believe you. I will not believe you," Sarah remarked, digging her fingernails into the palms of her hands, bending all her will to resisting the hopelessness and terror that was rising up to engulf her. "This awful place is like a tomb," she retorted. "It is nothingness and you do not exist."

"Ahhhh!" The eldest sister screeched in anger. "We were born here; it is our womb and our tomb. Do not insult us or our home, you wicked child."

Sarah swallowed hard and retreated into herself slightly, wary and afraid of what these creatures of the night might do to her, squeezing her eyes tight shut so she did not have to see them.

"We were born here to ensure no man deceives our mother or their own fate," Cutter said, snipping her scissors again. It is only when things go beyond our mother's power that she calls on us to help. You, Sarah Walker, have challenged your fate. In all the history of time no being has done this before, all have accepted their fates gracefully, which means you have now challenged us," she roared.

"We do not like arrogance, Sarah," whispered Measure.

"Arrogance?" Sarah's eyes shot open at the word. She had never in all her life been called arrogant before. "Why do you say that? I never meant to be arrogant. I was just doing what feels natural, following my instincts ... following my heart. Archie was such a massive part of my life ... I ..."

"Where has following your heart ever got you in the past? There are some things you can never change. Your fate is one of them," whispered Spinner, the youngest hag. She was quieter than the other two, less riled, but there was something menacing about the way she eyed Sarah up and down.

Sarah's bottom lip began to tremble. She didn't know if it was because she was so terrified or if it was the cold, or just the youngest hag's whisper, but it was involuntary. She felt completely empty and as her lip quivered so her tears tumbled. "P-p-please let me go back," she sobbed. I need to go home. I need to tell my parents I'm safe. I need to help Anian; I need to f-f-fix where I went wrong and where he went wrong. There are so many things I need to do. Surely whatever course I take is naturally my fate, maybe even this is my fate. I don't understand; can someone defy fate? If I have, it was not done on purpose. I didn't mean to, I promise. I didn't even realise it was possible to do so. I'm sorry," Sarah gabbled, desperate to pacify the creatures before her, for she finally understood that her life depended on it and unless she could persuade them to let her go, she faced this living death for all eternity.

"You have had two chances already, Sarah and you stole the second, which you were not entitled to. You gave your soul to the Moon the day you took your own life," Cutter said.

"But that wasn't me," Sarah cried. "I don't remember that! That was a long, long time ago. A hundred lives ago. I'm not that Sarah you see before you now. I come from a different time: the twenty-first century. I have a mum and a dad and a brother called Dom," she pleaded.

"Whatever time you think you come from, you and Felicity or Hope, or whatever that other Sarah likes to call herself, are of the same soul," Cutter said, turning away and looking towards the giant wheel. "Don't blame us, it's not our fault. Blame him," she pointed.

Sarah turned her head and saw coming towards her the man who in her dream she had been forced to marry. He approached Cutter, respectfully bowing his head and taking her hand. Stunned, Sarah stared hard, her eyes still blurry. Joseph Jackson smiled up at her from a distance, holding onto the witch's hand, his bright blue eyes flashing in the dark. She knew those eyes. She knew them from more recently than three hundred odd years ago, but when and where? She thought it strange that she could see them at all when there was no light to reflect from their surface, but nothing in this godforsaken abyss was as it should be. Sarah looked away quickly, her gaze sliding to the wheel behind him. "Why don't you oil that damned wheel? That grinding noise is agony," she said softly, almost to herself, wondering if she had in fact descended into madness.

"What did she say?" questioned Measure to her younger sister.

"She told us to ..." Spinner started.

"She told us? She told us? How dare she? Such conceit!" screeched Cutter.

Joseph gave a mocking laugh and all three witches turned their furious black eyes to Sarah, moving in rapidly, encroaching and rising above her.

"I'm s-s-sorry ... it just m-m-makes such an awful n-n-noise," Sarah stammered. The noise of the wheel intensified and it began to spin faster, as the Fates floating above her got angrier.

"Silence!" Cutter screamed suddenly, her focus turned from Sarah to the wheel, where Joseph lingered awkwardly, turning too to look behind him. The wheel slowed and the grinding ceased for a moment.

"Look sisters, look quickly! Look at the wheel!" The three hags moved instantly to the steps, to the core of the wheel. Cutter's hands were raised above her head as though she were worshiping the controls. "There is another ... another who challenges his fate!" she cried.

"Anian..?" Sarah whispered.

"But he is surely dead, the snake killed him," Felicity whispered in her head.

"Felicity? I thought you had gone."

"How could I have gone? I am you!"

"But Anian can't be dead ... he can't be." Sarah cried aloud. "Archie, then? Is it Archie? But how?"

"He challenges us, challenges the Fates!" Cutter screeched. "We are the power behind all gods. No one has ever challenged us before you." The hags twisted from the wheel again and stared back at Sarah, "And now here we have another: two challenging us in one day!"

"Don't let your fear grow bigger than your faith, Sarah," Felicity's pert voice chirped in Sarah's ear.

"It's okay for you to say that, tucked away in my head, just popping up when you fancy. Exactly what is it you want me to do, Fee?" Sarah spat back at her, for she knew instinctively that the Fates could not hear her. She guessed it was because of the way she and Fee were inextricably entwined that their telepathic conversations were private, even from witches.

"Just don't panic and just so you know, I am always with you. Like I have told you time and time again, I am part of you. We're in this together. So please stop panicking," Felicity advised. "This is not as bad as it seems."

"Wait ... in Transit thoughts become reality don't they?" Sarah remembered.

"Yes they do. But you are not in Transit anymore."

"Right - I'm in a black hole cast in the centre of the Universe. Okay, so what do I do?" Sarah asked her spirit self.

"I don't know. All I know is you cannot let fear consume you or the Fates will have won," Felicity hissed.

"I've gone mad haven't I?" Sarah whimpered; panic slowly eating away at her. The hags drew away from the wheel and nearer to her, still looming above her.

"No, you are not mad. You don't need your head examining, you need your heart examining." Felicity's tone was curt and cut Sarah's trail of panic short.

"What the hell does that mean? Why does everyone I meet talk in riddles? How is listening to my heart going to get me out of a black hole lodged in the centre of the Universe? I need a logical answer; I can't cope with anymore heartfelt emotion," Sarah blurted out loud.

"Shhh, not so loud. Get a grip. I'm trying to help you. Examining your heart might just redeem you."

"These three Fates are telling me not to follow my heart and to, I presume, go with my head - where you seem to live and won't stop talking - and you're asking me to ignore what my head is saying and listen to my heart. Fee, this is ridiculous. I need thoughts and action NOW. There's no such thing as a logical emotion, my heart works on impulse, it can't help me. It only ever gets me into trouble," Sarah begged the fairy in her head.

"Remember what the Fates just said, there's another who is challenging them, making their wheel slow down. Someone's trying to help us. I understand this is a very tense situation and I'm uncertain how it will pan out, but part of me has no doubt this is a real turning point for us," Felicity said calmly.

"Exactly what part of you?" Sarah screamed back at the insistent voice in her head.

"Sarah, with us, drama has always followed drama. There has never been any calm. We spring from one problematic episode to the next. There is never any logic to the order we do anything. We have always lived by our gut instincts, done as we've pleased. We've been privileged in many respects, but taken it for granted and always rebelled against our fortune in the lives we have lived. I had my go at life, you've had yours. Maybe these hags are forcing us to cross old ground for a reason; maybe to face our past and look at things differently."

Screwing up her face, Sarah tried to follow what Felicity had just said, but Spinner was talking over her, "This wheel turns according to our yarn. We spun your life, Sarah," the hag whispered, her breath bouncing of Sarah's nose. She winced, desperately trying to ignore her and focus on the familiar voice of Fee in her head, for now Felicity was her only comfort and she longed to be comforted. But it was no use, the crone continued speaking, destroying her concentration. "Once the destiny of an individual is woven it is irrevocable and cannot be altered. The wheel of time might slow down, but it cannot run in reverse. The length of life and the time of death are part and parcel. Nothing can be changed."

Any saving grace that had sifted through Sarah's mind leaked away in seconds and judging by Felicity's silence she was having the same problem. Unable to look at the hags' faces, Sarah kept her eyes on the jagged, flyaway ends of their hair. She knew her thoughts were not safe here, these witches would see through them at once. She quickly decided that her only form of defence in this situation was to attack and attack she did ... with questions.

"So the wheel can't go backwards?"

Spinner hissed at Sarah, her fingers clawed like a cat about to pounce, showing off curled black fingernails. Her face screwed into a mass of wrinkles and she grinned, baring stained brown teeth. Sarah drew back panicked.

"Of course the wheel can't go backwards; time can't go backwards, it never has," said Measure.

"It has never been done," Spinner whispered, echoing her sister's view with a quizzical look.

"Time creeps forward, never back," Cutter snapped.

"Never," her sisters echoed in protest as three sets of black button eyes stared at Sarah. She could see she had hit a nerve, but why? Fiction and science fiction stories were the only places for time travel, weren't they? Time had fascinated humans ever since it was invented and would continue to do so no doubt until the end of time itself. Trying desperately to hide her thoughts, Sarah's mind spun rapidly as she sifted through what she knew of time. She had watched many television programmes with her parents and brother on the physics of the Universe. Her dad, being a pilot, loved everything to do with the skies, from meteorology to the 'Big Bang' and the 'Big Crunch', and if there was ever a documentary about quantum physics on TV the family would be watching. She knew that scholars and scientists had long studied and experimented with the hands of time. Then she remembered a news flash she had seen just recently. Way beneath the earth in Switzerland scientists had done experiments in nuclear physics and the results had indicated that in theory, time travel was possible. Yes!

Gazing through the darkness at the giant wheel, another thought flew into Sarah's head, so crystal clear it could not have been coincidence: there was time dilation and the curvature of space time ... so if time curved and the curve was big enough and bent into a full circle ... her mind pounded. Was she staring at the biggest clock cog of all time? Was this more like a key than a wheel? Was it possible that somehow she could do exactly what the hags had said could never be done and ...

Her thoughts were crudely interrupted by Joseph Jackson, who stepped in front of her and stared straight into her face, his nose only inches away from hers. "'Ello again," he jeered, his hands reaching out to grip her around the waist, pulling her roughly closer to him, his sunken blue eyes boring into hers. Her mind flashed away from physics and back to falling from the Phra Pin Klao Bridge in Thailand. That is where she had seen those eyes before: Joe's face had been the last thing she had seen before she fell. This man's face was slightly different, but their eyes were identical and she knew now that Joe and Joseph

Jackson were the same soul, as were she and Felicity. She glanced in panic at the three witches hoping they would come to her aid, but as she might have guessed, they simply looked on with satisfied smiles then turned away as Joseph pressed her against him and bent to kiss her.

"This was where you wanted me ... wasn't it?" Sarah gasped. Her head was spinning and the wheel was turning, and she was falling, falling into blackness, her mind forcing itself to whirl away from this alien nightmare that she did not understand. Trying desperately to safeguard her sanity and memory, which she could feel waning, she forced her mind to go blank. The world in front of her began to dissolve. Losing consciousness, she felt herself fall against Joseph and tried to push herself away and then, as though answering her pleas and prayers, her mind began to draw her back to a safe time; a time where she longed to be; a time she understood and knew so very well.

It wasn't so long ago: a strong and lasting memory.... and with it came drifting the scent of Nanny Fletcher's perfume.

CHAPTER NINETEEN

OCTOBER, 1995
THE SECRET TO LIFE IS TO HAVE NO FEAR

Sarah waited in the drizzle under the shelter of a weeping willow tree at the bottom of Hope Hall's driveway, her trunk and tuck-box packed ready for the holidays and full of all her worldly belongings, a well used lacrosse stick in her hand. It was first thing in the morning, the light only just breaking. Most of the other girls had been picked up by their parents the day before and the boarding school was empty, aside from a few overseas students, who loitered in the library and the dinner hall with nothing to do but wait for the half term holiday to pass. Sarah didn't envy them. Hope Hall was a lonely place at the best of times, but when it was emptied of students it became hell on earth! She had never understood why she hated it so much. It was an odd feeling which made her sick to her stomach and the thought of running from it, down the drive into the village, was at times overwhelming. She just felt desperate to get away. Yesterday, the last two hours of having everyone in the main school had been pandemonium, everyone readying themselves and excited about the holidays. Sarah had snuck off without anyone noticing, she had always been good at disappearing and she was fed up with her class mates asking where her own parents were, especially when everyone knew they were still sunning themselves in Barbados. It was typical, she thought, as she waited in the rain for her ride, getting wetter by the minute. I'm the girl who has everything: wealthy parents, lovely home, first-class education in an exclusive school - and yet I really don't: Mum and Dad know I hate it here, but they never listen and I'm hardly ever at home. Sarah kicked at the exposed root of the willow beneath her foot. What she would not give to have an inch of freedom; what she would not pay to go to an ordinary school where she could go home and sleep on her own bed at night, instead of a lumpy old mattress that a thousand other girls had slept on before her. It was so regimented here, with so many rules and regulations, bells and schedules, day and night. She longed for a kinder routine, to be free to eat her meals and do her homework when she pleased; to see her real friends and go to youth group like all the other teenagers she hung out with in the summer. She wanted to spend time with her parents, instead of being fobbed off with her brother Dominic on yet another au pair, forced to learn to speak French in the holidays, instead of going to camp with her mates. Yet none of that really explained why she loathed Hope Hall as much as she did or why being in its grounds gave her this feeling of sick foreboding.

In a fever of impatience, Sarah bent her head to listen for Archie's car. If he could have picked her up yesterday he would have done so. He knew how she hated it here, but he had school too and his dad, her Uncle Robert, had to work, so they couldn't come until today. It was her uncle who had told her parents that her last day at school coincided with the tail end of their annual holiday to the Caribbean, Sarah had overheard him grumbling to himself that his sister and brother-in-law, Patricia and Jack, her mum and dad, were being selfish as usual. He had arranged to pick up Sarah himself, as he and his wife

Joanna so often did. In fact she saw more of the Fletcher family than she did her own, spending most exeat weekends with them in their modest London home, while her parents gallivanted around the country from one society 'do' to another, always too busy to pay her any attention.

Sarah heard Archie's car before she saw it. He had promised to be at Hope Hall before eight o'clock and true to his word here he was. The windscreen-wipers on his rusty white Fiesta squeaked, working fifteen to the dozen, making barely any difference to the windscreen drowned in rain as he turned up the drive. He had written to Sarah, delighted that he had managed to persuade his dad to come with him to pick her up from school in his 'new' banger - his first car - which had been christened with L-plates only weeks before and of which he was very proud. It was a long drive down from London to the Surry-Hampton boarder, having to avoid the motorways, but it was great practice for him and Sarah knew he would be only too delighted to stretch his new wheels. They had an even longer drive from her school to Nanny Fletcher's house in Llangernyw in North Wales, where they were all going for the October half term.

Sarah and Archie had both turned seventeen in the summer holidays, their birthdays on the same day. Her parents had for once offered to take her for afternoon tea at the Ritz in London, but for the first time in Sarah's life she had put her foot down, opting to celebrate in style with a glass of ice-cream soda and a Chinese takeaway on the floor in the Fletchers' living room, her favourite place in the world. "Very well, dear, if that's what you want," her mother had said dismissively, already thinking of something else. Her dad had looked disappointed, but he would never gainsay her mum. They had given her a Tiffany locket and a stack of A-level study books for her birthday. Her lucky cousin had received his white Fiesta from his mum and dad. It had been waiting in their driveway when he woke up on the morning of his birthday. Sarah sighed, kicking again at the tree; her independence was not on her parents' agenda. So long as she was locked away in her boarding school she wouldn't need to learn to drive. Not that she had anywhere to go, other than to Archie's house.

She peered out from under the tree as the Fiesta drew to a halt beside her trunk. "You're soaked," Archie said as he jumped out the car, wrapped his arms around his twin-cousin and planted a giant kiss on her wet cheek, squeezing her until she could barely breathe. She drank in the sight of him in his faded black jeans and black trainers, and nothing but a plain white T-shirt on top, despite the cold and wet. Uncle Robert, looking slightly more portly than usual, emerged from the car with a brolly and sheltered them while they both fought with her clumsy school trunk and tuck box, forcing them into the tiny boot.

"Good term?" Robert asked, falling back into the passenger seat.

"It was okay," Sarah replied wiping her brow with her blazer and throwing her satchel onto the car floor as she bounced into the back seat, her lacrosse stick across her knees.

Archie eyed it, "Sorry I couldn't make the game last Saturday. Cadets had me camping and helping out with the new recruits," he explained, slamming the driver's door shut, an apologetic glance catching Sarah's eye, as he settled into his seat and released the handbrake.

"Seat belt, Buster ... how many times?" Robert said exasperated, his bulbous nostrils flaring as he shook his head. Archie pulled up the brake and put on his belt, rolling his eyes at Sarah in the rear view mirror.

"It's fine, Arch, we won anyway," Sarah smiled.

"Knock 'em dead did you. I wouldn't like to be on the receiving end of one of your tackles," he teased. "It's a wonder you don't knock your opponent's block off half the time with those sticks. I'm sure the game should have helmets or be illegal. It's lethal," Archie stated. "I mean, Dad, what kind of game doesn't have pitch boundaries?"

Sarah felt her anxiety gradually sink away, as Archie drove the car away from Hope Hall. Taking the main route west, the three of them chatted conservatively at first, Sarah's guard not fully down, part of her head still in school mode, asking the usual pleasantries about Auntie Joanna and Archie's younger brother and sister, Stewart and Helena.

Being in boarding school, Sarah often felt like she was the last to hear anything that was going on in the outside world and in the next two minutes she learnt she was absolutely right. She had not known her parents were also going to Nanny Fletcher's house as soon as they got back from Barbados. This came as a good surprise, yet still riled her somewhat. Archie and Uncle Robert went on to tell her that the entire family were driving from far and wide to Llangernyw for half term. Joanna, Helena and Stewart had gone on ahead yesterday. Even Auntie Frances and Uncle Tom, who had been posted out to Cyprus with the Royal Air Force for the past few months, had taken leave and flown back with their girls, Gillian and Sally, so they could all congregate as a family once more.

Sarah's heart lurched. Apart from the brief time at Archie's and her joint birthday party in the summer, she had hardly seen or spoken to her cousins since last Easter, which as usual the family had spent with Nanny Fletcher, but her joy at seeing them again was buried beneath a weight of fear and grief. It was in the Easter holidays that they had all been told the devastating news that Nanny had terminal cancer. She had refused treatment and wanted to stay at home. Robert had tried to persuade her to go into a hospice, but Nanny had been adamant that she would not leave the home she loved.

"How's Nanny doing?" Sarah finally found the courage to ask. "Have you seen her?"

"She's doing okay, sweetheart," Uncle Robert said, glancing out of the front window with a worried stare and fumbling in his pocket for his inhaler. There was an awkward silence as he puffed and wheezed, seemingly searching his thoughts for the right words. "She's lost weight," he announced with a small cough. "I just want to prepare you. You'll find her quite changed. But for the Lord's sake don't tell her that! She doesn't want to be reminded of her cancer at all whilst we are there. She's insisted that no one is to fuss or utter a word about it. She just wants us to enjoy ourselves like we always do."

Sarah could see in her uncle's face that he was deeply concerned. He didn't need to say any more, it was obvious to her and must also be to Archie, who stared mute out of the front windscreen, that this could well be the last time they would all be together as a whole family.

"Yes," Sarah whispered. "Of course ... I can't remember there ever being a dull moment or not enjoying myself and Nanny's," she sighed, trying to hold back her tears and looked out of the window, the rain on the glass blurring her vision.

"We've got a lot to be thankful for," Robert said.

"And a lot of awesome memories to look back on," Archie added. "I lived half my childhood in Nanny's house, playing in the woods behind it and up on the mountain. They were the best memories a kid could ask for." Sarah nodded, but didn't trust herself to speak.

There was no more talk of Nanny until they reached the Welsh border, guided by Uncle Robert's knowledgeable navigation. These days he was employed as an executive chauffeur driving all around the country and Sarah was sure he had the entire Great British Road Atlas laid out in his head! They took the scenic roads the whole way to Wales – as a learner, Archie was not allowed to drive on the motorways - but Sarah much preferred the minor roads anyway, even though it took longer. The pretty country villages they drove through stirred up great memories of past road trips and the holidays they had shared. After about an hour the rain, taking pity on the little white Fiesta and its novice driver it seemed, finally stopped and for a while the sun shone, lighting up the reds and gold's of autumn in a breathtaking panoply of colour. But it soon hid its face as they pulled into the Welsh valley and by the time they turned into Nanny Fletcher's driveway, it was raining again.

Nanny waited to greet them in the drizzle at the top of Woods Eves drive, standing by the coal shed as she had always done. Peering out from under a large, brightly coloured umbrella she looked immaculate as usual, in a mauve tea dress and matching cardigan, a string of pearls at her neck. The woods behind her were bare, the Welsh mists and blustery weather having stripped them of leaves, and the garden to the left of the drive looked bleak and wet; even the bird-table was deserted.

"Remember what I said guys, not a word," Robert reiterated as putting on a cheery grin he waved at his mother. Archie parked the Fiesta up next to Robert's battered blue Volvo, which Joanna had driven up the day before.

"What is she doing waiting for us outside in the rain?" Sarah remarked, horrified at the amount of weight Nanny had lost since Easter, tears springing into her eyes. It was a real shock and she didn't know if she could handle getting out of the car.

"And let's have none of that," Robert said, reaching over the seat to place a firm hand on her knee and giving it a squeeze, "definitely no tears, sweetheart."

Sarah drew in a deep breath and composed herself, brushing stray strands of her mousey blonde hair from her face. Her grandmother was the most constant part of her life and she adored every moment she spent with her, she didn't want this time to be any different.

"Are you okay?" Robert asked.

Sarah nodded. "I'm fine," she said, clearing her throat.

In typical Archie style her cousin flew from the car. Sarah knew he would be feeling the same way as she did inside, but he controlled his emotions much better.

"Don't hug her too tight," Robert called after him.

They watched as Nanny's face broke into an elated smile, her eyes twinkling in the rain as her eldest grandson, now towering over her, wrapped his arms around her tiny frame and lifted her up, the umbrella slipping to the side. Placing her gently back on her feet he gave her a smacking kiss.

"Come on little lady, let's go," Robert said, his car door ajar, feet reaching for the drive as he pushed himself out of his seat. Pausing, he turned and looked at Sarah, who had not moved. "You okay, sweetheart?" he asked again.

Sarah's eyes found her uncle's through the gaps in the headrest. "She's really sick isn't she?"

"She is, yes."

"Mummy never said it was this bad. I'm not a child anymore, Uncle Robert, tell me. I'm seventeen, old enough to know the truth. How long ...?"

"Your mother probably didn't want to worry you, but there's nothing anyone can do." Uncle Robert's eyes said all Sarah need to know. "I'm not going to lie to you, Sarah ..."

She knew that; he never had. "But she was fine in the spring," she frowned, a plump tear finding its way down her cheek.

"Hey… she's still with us now, so we have to be jolly and make memories to cherish when she's gone," Robert said, "so keep your chin up, little lady. No doubt, Uncle Tom will bring his guitar and we'll have a good old singsong tonight after dinner ... all of us … like we used to and we'll be trick-or-treating tomorrow night," he reminded with a gentle smile.

Sarah dashed the tear away, gave a small scowl at the thought of doing something quite so juvenile as trick-or-treat then gave a reluctant nod, knowing she would have to go along with it, for the sake of her younger cousins and brother.

"Okay." She pulled the pillow out from under her, threw it into the boot, arched her back and gave a yawn. Grabbing her satchel and lacrosse stick, she flicked the door lock and whispered groggily, "Let's do it."

"Atta girl," Robert said with a wink, heaving himself out of the car.

***

An hour after their arrival, Robert went to pick up his sister Frances and her family from the Royal Air Force Valley Airport in Holyhead. He was still gone when Sarah's mum and dad arrived, having managed to pick up her brother from his boarding school – she could not help a twinge of resentment, glad as she was to see Dom. In a waft of expensive perfume, her mum showered her with apologies for not attending her final lacrosse tournament and speech day, and for not being back in time to pick her up from Hope Hall yesterday.

"We can't be in two places at once you know, dear, and your school was a little awkward breaking up a day earlier than your brother's."

She spoke as though it was Sarah's fault that her school finished early. When had her mother ever been there for her? Sarah thought. It was on the tip of her tongue to say that she wasn't responsible for choosing what day the school ended, but instead she gritted her teeth and smiled, as she always did. "No harm done, Mummy, of course I understand," she lied.

Leaving the acne-ridden, Stewart and Dominic to build a Lego fort, something it seemed Stewart would never grow out of, Helena, Archie and Sarah disappeared into the annex where they customarily slept; a separate section of the house just off the back door. They went to wait for their other two cousins to arrive, Gillian and Sally.

"It's quite a journey to Holyhead from here. They won't be back until after lunch," Joanna shouted from the kitchen at the other end of the corridor that connected the annex to the main house.

"Nanny looks sick doesn't she?" Archie stated quietly, throwing his backpack into his bedroom and heading for the girls' room.

"I don't want to talk about it," Helena snapped, plopping down onto her bed.

The annex, with no central heating, was bitterly cold come autumn and winter, with ice on the insides of the windows on occasion. It was divided up into two bedrooms, with a bathroom in-between and Nanny Fletcher's grandchildren had recently been given the privilege of claiming it as their own whenever they came to stay.

"Don't state the obvious, Archie," Sarah muttered, pulling back the throw of her bed, checking to see how many blankets were on it and if they were even made up. "How does she manage here on her own?" she asked, looking around the room. Their grandfather had been gone a good ten years and Nanny Fletcher had rattled about in Woods Eves, their old, six-bedroom Tudor manor house, ever since. "I mean look at this place, it's not spotless, but she's doubled up the blankets and the sheets are clean … for all of us. That's us six kids and with the six olds … that's twelve beds she's had to make up, guys."

"I bet they're damp and cold by bed time, though," Helena said with a shiver.

"She won't ever stop doing and giving, Sarah," Archie said with a smile, "that's just what she does. She loves it when we come to stay. I expect Mum helped her yesterday, anyway."

"I suppose," Sarah said, neatly smoothing back the covers of her bed.

"Mummy said quite definitely not to talk about Nanny," Helena said, "so will you please both stop talking about it or I'm going to tell …"

"Oh give it a rest Hels," Archie snapped, stealing his little sister's lip balm off the end of her bed and puckering up to smoother his lips in cherry-flavoured grease. In a flash of her white-blonde hair, Helena jumped up and snatched it off him and threw it back into her wash bag.

"What do you think about tomorrow night?" Archie asked, hands on hips, looking at Sarah and totally ignoring his little sister, who was sticking her tongue into her bottom lip and pulling faces.

"Halloween?" Sarah remarked.

"Yeah. Dad reckons we're going trick-or-treating in the village."

"Humph, not many houses there, you'll be done by eight," Helena barked in a riled tone. She was used to being snubbed by her brother, but she clearly hated it when anyone else was there to see.

"Hey, we could go to St Digains and see …" Archie started. Sarah stared at him curious as to why he had paused. It was as though an unpleasant thought had popped into his head.

"What for?" Helena asked, looking up from her unpacking, her bed now strewn with all sorts of toiletries, brushes and inhalers.

"See who?" Sarah prompted.

"Well, according to local legend," Archie said, still blanking his sister who was listening intently, "the churchyard is inhabited by an ancient and slightly dangerous spirit called Angelystor," he exaggerated a shaky edge to his voice.

"You've made that up," Helena cut him off, her face creased with laughter. "You and your ghost stories Archie; when are you going to give it up?" Smearing high-strength hydrocortisone cream all over her eczema-ridden shins, she added, "You're just trying to freak us out before Halloween."

"No, seriously, it's true," Archie insisted, still not looking at Helena. "Angelystor has the power to curse and every Halloween his voice can be heard booming through the church foretelling the names of all the parishioners who are going to die in the next year. You must have heard about it?" he asked.

Sarah shrugged her shoulders. "It rings a bell. But it's just a myth, Arch," she said from the dressing table, plucking at her perfectly arched eyebrows with a lethal looking pair of tweezers. The story did stir a distant memory in Sarah's head; maybe Nanny or even Granddad had told it to her when she was small. Was Archie really trying to frighten them? Or did he genuinely believe the story? Surely not? Sarah had seen the look that glinted in Archie's eyes before, it meant trouble was ahead. He looked strangely focused like he had made his mind up about something and the slight squint in his eyes told Sarah there was a lot more to be said about it. He was hiding something and she knew it.

"Seriously, it's true," Archie repeated.

"Who told you that?" Helena asked.

"The vicar, actually," Archie answered, finally looking at his sister and throwing himself down onto Gillian's bed, his arms stretched up behind his head, "a long time ago now."

"St Digain's vicar, Reverend Nevett?" Sarah asked, swivelling round on the dressing table stool.

"Yep, that very man!" Archie confirmed, with a grin. "He's a vicar and he wouldn't lie … would he Helena?"

What was he up to? Sarah thought to herself as she eyed her cousin. Archie's face flushed as Sarah stared at him quizzically. He knew she knew he was up to something. The two of them had always known what the other was thinking. Archie turned onto his side and faced the bedroom wall with an almost panicked look. What is wrong with him? He's behaving very strangely, Sarah thought. He's never been overly superstitious or mentioned Angelystor before, and since when did he chat with Reverend Nevett about the village folklore? He told Sarah everything, or she had thought he did, but he was most certainly hiding something big from her now and she was determined to find out what.

"You know he died?" Helena suddenly announced to Archie's back. "... about a month ago. He was very ill apparently, had been for quite a while."

Archie swung round to face the room again, his face beetroot red; his eyes enormous and glassy. Helena stared at her brother in shock.

"What?" Helena said. "Why are you staring at me like that?"

Archie said nothing initially, his eyes bulging with horror, gawping at his sister. "He knew …" he stuttered.

"Knew what?" Sarah asked, watching Archie with intrigue and concern.

"He knew ..." Archie repeated.

"Are you okay, Archie?" Helena asked. Archie continued to stare from his sister to his cousin.

"What was wrong with him?" Sarah finally asked, in an effort to detract from Archie's weird behaviour. She would question him later when she had him on his own.

"Emphysema I think … is that how you say it?" Helena replied, easily distracted.

"Yes, where you can't breathe properly," Sarah confirmed spinning round on her stool again.

"Yeah, but anyway," Helena continued, both her brother and now her cousin staring at her in disbelief, "he didn't die of that. Apparently he had an accident on his horse. He had gone out at night for a ride, same as he always did and the horse spooked at something and threw him. Curtains for Reverend Nevett and the horse," Helena said matter-of-factly, her hand slicing across her throat.

"Oh, how awful," Sarah squealed, pulling her knees up to her chest and balancing on the dressing table stool.

"How did you know about that and we didn't?" Archie asked sitting up, his face taut, as though he was trying desperately to suppress his emotion. In fact, he looked close to tears, Sarah thought.

"I don't know," Helen shrugged. "Sarah's at boarding school, it's a wonder to me she knows anything at all about what goes on in this family, but I'm surprised you hadn't heard, Arch. He was Nanny's friend; she must've been terribly upset."

"I never know anything unless Archie writes to me," Sarah confirmed, from behind her knees.

"Well, how come I didn't know about the vicar dying ... or being killed, whichever," Archie mumbled.

"You're usually out BMX-ing or at cadets, Arch. It's me who hears what the olds' have to say," Helena said, pulling her jeans over her shins and picking up her hairbrush.

"Meaning, you earwig on their private conversations," Archie said, directing a forced grin at his sister.

"Maybe so, but I still know more than you about what goes on around here and in our family," she said. "Anyway, what did you mean when you said 'He knew'? Knew what?"

"He told me," Archie looked his sister in the eye, "Reverend Nevett that is. A few years ago ... we talked. He told me he was sick and that he didn't have long. Fact is, he seemed to know exactly when he would die and ..." Archie's eyes swivelled to look at Sarah. "Maybe Angelystor told him."

"Are you okay, Arch," Sarah asked, with real concern. "It was probably just coincidence. I'm sure Angelystor's just a myth; you're frightening yourself, as well as me!"

"Arch is fine, Sarah," Helena informed. "He's a great actor you know, he'll keep on and on about this so-called ghost until he gets us down there at midnight tomorrow, to scare the bejesus out of us."

Archie, however, looked totally bewildered, still staring into Sarah's face. "Which means that maybe he's right about …" he stopped abruptly, his face now a delicate shade of green, as if he was about to throw up.

"About what?" Sarah probed, adding, "You look like you're going to puke."

"Nothing. It doesn't matter," Archie shrugged and rolled off the bed, "I'm glad of it Hels, you and your earwigging or we'd never know what the hell was going on, though it sounds a bit like doom and gloom to me," he retorted heading for the door.

Sarah and Helena exchanged glances, baffled by his strange behaviour.

"I'm going for a walk," he announced. "Need some fresh air. Anyone want to come?"

"No thanks," said Helena, forcing a brush through her incredibly thick hair. "I'm waiting for Gillian and Sally and unpacking, it's freezing out there."

"I'm in," Sarah said, jumping up and grabbing her duffle coat. Her twin-cousin had something to spill and she was going to find out what it was if her life depended on it.

***

Half-an-hour later, their feet dangling side by side from a branch of the churchyard yew, they peered down through the beautiful dark green foliage. Drooping over the uneven gravestones, the tree's branches, of deep red bark, were incredibly thick and small red autumn buds, ready to burst, were strewn all over their needle-like leaves. The trunk was immense and quite easy to climb, though Sarah felt uncomfortable even at this height.

"I wonder who looks after the church now?" she said, peering through the leaves and past the moss-covered statues to the beautiful cruciform, whitewashed, medieval church.

Not listening, Archie's rubbed his forehead as though in pain, then seeing his cousin frown at him, he rubbed his hand along the knobbly bark of the yew. "Do you think this tree is really over four thousand years old?"

"I don't know," Sarah said. "I guess … if that's what they say."

"Really? That means it must have taken root in the Bronze Age," Archie remarked, looking at Sarah, with doubt in his big blue eyes.

"Mm," Sarah nodded. "It's not very tall is it? I mean, for four thousand years."

"Yew's don't grow tall, they grow wide," Archie said. "I've seen quite a few in graveyards. Must be some religious thing," he pondered.

"What's going on Arch?" Sarah asked, giving up on being patient and waiting on the right moment to question her cousin.

"Nothing," Archie insisted. "Why?"

"Don't lie, I can tell something's up. You were trembling back at Nanny's. Something really freaked you out, didn't it?"

"Yeah … must be that religious thing, that's why they plant yews in graveyards," Archie said with a grin, avoiding eye contact and blatantly ignoring her inquisition. Riled that he was keeping something from her, Sarah sighed deeply.

"Rebirth and immortality," a mature female voice suddenly called from below. "She's beautiful isn't she … simply majestic."

Momentarily shocked, both Archie and Sarah stared down onto the top of a grey-haired woman. The face turned up to look at them and a broad smile grew on the aged features. "Hi up there, I'm Connie. I come from the Hall, down the lane; Hafodunos Hall. It's an old people's home. It used to be the girls' school."

"Wish it still was. Mum could have sent me there instead of Hope Hall, at least I'd be right by Nanny," Sarah whispered to Archie, nudging his knee with hers.

"I'm looking after the church until they find a replacement vicar," Connie explained. "Dreadful tragedy what happened to Reverend Nevett. He was such a good man." The old lady moved swiftly to the core of the tree and raised her leg as though she meant to climb into the branches, but stopped, knee bent, foot pressed against the trunk. "This tree is a real landmark for our village. It's got great wisdom in its branches. Would you like me to show you around?"

"Around the tree?" Archie said, obviously confused. He and Sarah stared down at her, both mystified not only by her presence, but by her apparent knowledge.

"...Around the tree, the church and the graveyard? You two didn't just come here to sit in this old tree did you? I mean, I know she's beautiful and there's a lot to say about her - trees have influenced religion and mysticism for more than any of us ever dare imagine, that's probably why St Digain's was built around her - but you two really want to go inside don't you?"

"Well, er ..." Sarah murmured, uncomfortable about airing their real reasons for being in the churchyard.

"It's Halloween tomorrow," the old woman continued. "The one day of the year when the two worlds draw closer and ancient myths may be proven to be true. Even Archangel Michael over there can't protect our ears from Angelystor."

A shiver ran down Sarah's spine at mention of the ghost.

"Then it's true!" Archie yelled, his face suddenly ghastly white. "What Reverend Nevett told me about Angelystor? Which means that …" his voice faltered.

Shocked, Sarah stared at him. Rarely had she heard Archie raise his voice like that.

"Of course it's true," Connie interrupted with a grin, seemingly unaware of Archie's sudden tension. "Come with me." She lowered herself down from the tree with grace and ease.

Sarah turned to Archie. "What is wrong with you?" she snapped, fractious that her cousin was keeping something from her and that it was causing him so much stress.

"Nothing," Archie said, his smile obviously forced.

"You're lying," Sarah accused. "Why won't you tell me?"

"Nothing to tell," he shrugged.

"Are you two coming?" Connie called up to them.

Smiling down at the old lady, Sarah jumped out of the tree. If Archie wasn't going to tell her what was going on in his head, she would leave him to fight it out for himself. It was a first and it made her really cross that he was keeping something secret from her, they had always told each other everything before, but she knew he would come clean in the end. She just needed to ask the right questions, that was all.

A meaty grin spread across his face as he looked down at her. "Honest, it's nothing. I'm twisting things in my head, that's all; confused about what was said. It was a few years ago now. I was just a kid. Really I'm fine. You guys carry on. I'll catch you up in a sec."

Reluctantly, Sarah accepted Archie's choice to stay silent. Maybe he was embarrassed to talk in front of this stranger. Or maybe he had no intention of telling her at all. Either way, she had not finished prying yet, but she would let it lie for the moment. She followed Connie along the path leading around the perimeter of the church and gazed at the various fascinating features the old lady pointed out as they meandered through the tombstones, talking about them all, reading out the names. Connie was a fountain of knowledge when it came to the locals and the history of the village; she seemed to know everything and everyone. There was something about her that invited confidence and before they had been inside the church ten minutes, Sarah found herself venting her anxiety on this woman she barely knew.

"I don't know what's wrong with my cousin," she said grumpily, as though she had known the old lady all her life – which, in a strange way she felt as if she had. "I don't understand why he can't tell me what's wrong," she continued, as they came out of the church and into the persistent drizzle. "He's always told me everything, even the most embarrassing things; he knows I won't tell anyone. But now it's like he's scared of something." She leant up against an ancient looking standing stone close to the church wall.

"When someone we love doesn't want to share something, it often means they are trying to protect us," Connie said. "Your thirst for what he knows could be dangerous," she smiled, "as indeed could your leaning on that standing stone."

"Sorry?" Sarah pulled away from the wall and looked down at the unmarked grave beside her. "Did you say what I thought you said?"

Connie nodded. "Dangerous, yes. These standing stones are said to be portals of sorts, which may or may not be true, but it's probably best not to lean on them."

"Portals? Whatever do you mean?" Sarah asked, taken aback, brushing her hands down her back as though she had been contaminated by touching the stone.

A car horn beeping merrily lifted them from their conversation. Sarah's head jerked up and she saw Uncle Robert's car crawl past on the road beside the churchyard. She turned back to Connie, "Portals?" she asked again, aware that her uncle had stopped and was calling out, "Archie? Sarah? Gillian and Sally are here!"

"You'll see," Connie smiled enigmatically. "There's a time and a place for everything, Sarah, remember that. You must go now and so must I."

Mystified, Sarah thanked Connie for showing her around, then leaving the old lady standing by the church door, skipped over the path to the yew and stared up at Archie from the foot of the tree. "Did you hear your dad? Gillian and Sally have arrived, come on."

"Yeah, I heard." Archie peered through the branches at the battered old Volvo disappearing up the lane to Wood Eves then he turned to look down at her.

"You okay, Arch?" Sarah asked. "I'm getting really worried about you."

"You up for it then?" he said, ignoring her comment and giving her a Cheshire cat grin.

"Up for what?" Sarah knew that grin; it was one her twin-cousin always used when he was trying to conceal his emotions.

"Tomorrow night, coming down to the church?" Archie winked.

"Are you serious?"

"Never been more serious in my life."

"I'm not sure ... I'd be worried Angelystor would call out my name? What if he did? It would be awful," Sarah grimaced.

"Or mine, so we'll both be worried, but there's really only one name he should call out if what they say is true, and that's …"

"Oh Archie, don't say it," Sarah cried.

"But it's true, you know it is. The doctors have told us Nanny won't make Christmas. If we come down tomorrow night then that's what we should hear ... and that way I'll also know if …" Archie hesitated, staring at

Sarah. Was he about to tell her? She smiled encouragingly at her cousin.

"If what?" she prodded after a moment's silence.

Archie looked at her intently. The words were there, Sarah was sure of it, right on the tip of his tongue, but instead of saying them he broke eye contact and looked away to the road. "Doesn't matter," he said quietly.

CHAPTER TWENTY

AUGUST 2003
THE DUNGEONS OF TIME

Sarah's beautiful and innocent memory dissolved. Abruptly, a rush of déjà vu devoured every part of her. She stood in comparative darkness, face-to-face with a tall, dark-haired man whom she barely knew, yet knew she loathed. It was as though Felicity had forced open a valve inside her head. Realisation and understanding of what had happened to her came flooding back: a feeling of dread slowly sinking to her core and choking her, her throat closing up with panic. An eternity with him? Buried deep in her brain a distant dream stirred into life. He despised her, just as much as she despised him. He had tortured her mentally and bullied her physically. She had to get away from him.

"I can't ... I don't ..." Sarah stammered.

"Wha'? You can't wha'? Believe it?" Joe sniggered. "It's been a long while, Sarah, so make it worth the wait." He pulled her closer to him, pressing his body against hers, in a way that made her shudder with revulsion.

"I'm not that Sarah anymore, though," Sarah appeased, trying to wriggle free. "I have to get out of here. We have to get out of here. Don't you get it? We're here for eternity, is this what you really want? Surely you can't?"

"Oh, but I do, Sarah. I've been searching a long, long time for you and oh yes, you are that very same Sarah I knew back then, the Fates would not lie to me. Your genetics may have altered, but your soul is the same and that soul is mine. You made a vow," he jeered, drooling over her, attempting to pull her back into his arms.

"No, wait!" Sarah cried, pushing herself away from him, jumbled thoughts and images messing with her head. "I remember you. I married you and when I did ..." she faltered, stared into his face then turned her head away. "There was another man," she whispered.

"Oh 'ere we go! Well you can forget about that peasant, he's gone," Joe spat, pulling her in again.

"No, it wasn't Archie, there was another man there ... his name was ... I can't remember, but I know he was trying to help me," Sarah said, pushing Joe away, as though he were an annoying insect that was irritating her.

"'ow many men did you 'ave? Ya hussy," he retorted crossly.

"Kriss! His name was Kriss, I remember it now," Sarah cried, ignoring the insult.

"That fool got in everyone's way, particularly mine," Joe spat. "No chance of that this time though," he chortled tapping his trouser pocket.

Sarah frowned, glanced down at his hand. "What do you mean? What's that in your pocket?"

"Somethin' of yours, but never you mind. That pretty little 'ead of yours don't need to be worryin' or thinkin' about anythin' anymore. Your days of thinkin' are over," Joe hissed.

Another fresh memory charged through Sarah's head, of falling from the Phra Pin Klao Bridge only a few days ago back in Thailand. Joe's face had been the last thing she had seen; he had snatched at her throat and taken Archie's St Christopher.

"Yessss..." Felicity cried in her head. The sudden intrusion of her fairy friend made Sarah flinch. "Hold that thought Sarah. Tell him you know, don't let him boss you about like he used to. He's nothing but an illiterate, common scamp." Sarah smiled at Fee's comment and lowered her eyes, slightly worried that Joe would think she was laughing at him and get even more riled. There was indeed no point in cowering. If she was to be here for eternity, what was the worst that could happen? She had to fight; it was her only form of defence.

"You've got my St Christopher in your pocket, haven't you?" Sarah accused calmly and loudly. "You ripped it from my neck when I fell."

The reaction did not come from where she expected.

"Noooo," screeched the hags in unison from behind her on the steps of the wheel. "Nooo, don't say you have brought him here," one squealed. Sarah could not tell which one was talking, as they all rushed towards her at such pace, screeching and shouting, arms flailing above their heads in horror and blatant anger. Joe stepped forward, grabbing Sarah firmly around the waist again, pulling her away from the wild women. She realised, astonished, that his move was not to protect her, rather it was to protect himself. But why did that surprise her? Typical of all bullies, he was a coward. Capable of behaving big, but when it came to facing his fate, he had to hide.

"Don't spoil this reunion, Sarah," he pleaded, ignoring the frenzied hags. "Stop pushing me away and let me hold you."

"No; get off me." Sarah shoved against his chest. "What's wrong with them?" she yelled, protecting herself, as the witches reached around her to claw at Joe's pocket. "They want the pendant," she cried as they pushed and pulled Sarah out of the way.

"You've dared bring a fiend to our equation! He is uninvited," screeched Cutter, her face seething with rage.

"It's just a piece of metal, you stupid hags," shouted Joe roughly, thrusting the fragile and supernatural beings away from him.

Horrified, Cutter drew her hand back and slapped him, her claw-like nails scoring marks down his face. "You know neither what you say, nor what you do, Joseph Jackson. You have been brought here not for your own pleasure and fulfilment but to appease us, our mother and Death. Now give me that pendant!"

"It's only a cheap St Christopher," Joe retorted, clearly stunned by the power of the blow to his face. "Why all the fuss?" Rubbing at the rapidly swelling bruise he delved into his pocket to retrieve the medallion.

"The mere mention of his name will make the amulet's energy stronger," hissed Measure to her younger sister.

"Start up the cauldron, sisters; we will liquidise him until he's silver juice and no talisman at all. The universe can then take him back," Cutter cried. Her sisters immediately lurched into action, dragging a giant black pot into view from behind the steps, streams of steam already broiling from the rim.

"Be careful ... be careful," Spinner whispered. "Don't rattle him."

"Wha'? Don't rattle him?" Joe squawked, still rubbing his cheek, shaking his head in disbelief. "It's not a him; it's a trinket. You're insane, the three of you."

"You know nothing, Mister Jackson. We do not want a transfiguration. His etheric body is only a thought away," explained Measure.

"And the etheric body has far more energy than the astral," added Spinner.

"Remember him Sarah, remember Kriss, summon him, bring him here," Felicity pleaded inside Sarah's head, whilst Sarah stared dumfounded at the cooking pot before her.

"What?" Sarah whispered with a frown.

"You heard what Measure just said, the mere mention of his name will make St Christopher stronger. Say his name Sarah ... call him ... ask for his help."

Sarah nodded to herself, as Joe handed over the small pendant to Cutter, who stood with her hand outstretched, waiting.

"Wha' d'ya mean, etheric astral body? Wha's all tha' nonsense about?" Joe slowly turned his hand upside down with the pendant on it. As it dropped into Cutter's palm he snatched his hand away as though he feared he might catch something if he touched her.

"The damage this has done to our plan," said Cutter, her fingers closing around the St Christopher.

The crones huddled together, their grey, coarse hair merging as their heads gathered ever closer. Muttering to one another they shuffled towards the pot and the wheel, which continued to grind excruciatingly.

"Again and again our minds have warned us of this, why did we not listen?"

"So that's what slowed the wheel. I didn't think it was possible," mumbled Spinner.

"Nor I," agreed Measure.

"Anything is possible it now seems," Cutter snapped, glaring back at Sarah. "This is all her fault."

"What should we do?" asked Measure.

"He could take form as a physical body, which interpenetrates with Transit and here," Spinner whispered.

"Don't be ridiculous, that's completely unfeasible," Cutter said curtly.

"I have spun the thread of man for millions of years and to this day there has never been another being like Saint Christopher, sister," Spinner said. "Anything with him is feasible. You saw what lengths he went to helping Archie Fletcher. With his ancient wisdom he is able to transmute to any form. He has defied our mother countless times. We must not let this happen!"

"Find him Sarah, quickly," Felicity said. Frantically filtering through her recent dreams, Sarah tried to put a face to the man she recalled as Kriss. "Just say his name," Felicity insisted, "it'll help, I promise."

"The girl's thoughts are reeling, can you not hear them? She is searching for him!" Cutter exclaimed.

"Shhhh! Don't keep on, just throw him in," Measure hissed.

"Not until the water is boiling," said Spinner. "It must be liquidised in a matter of seconds or ..."

"He is her guardian as much as he was Archie Fetcher's," Cutter interrupted.

"And she has been in many altered states of consciousness since her arrival in Transit; she will be able to interpret many things," said Cutter.

"What are you waiting for? Just say his name," Felicity's voice sounded urgently in Sarah's head.

"Saint Christopher?" Sarah called out. "Saint Christopher," she cried again, her eyes tightly closed.

"Relax Sarah, you'll never find him if you tense up like that," Felicity said.

"Relax? To be honest, given the circumstances, it's fairly tough to relax," Sarah thought crossly.

"Well try! Open your eyes," Felicity urged.

Sarah shivered and opened her eyes again. Around her whirled a white mist, like snowflakes dancing in a blizzard. "Saint Christopher; Saint Christopher," Sarah chanted his name like a mantra trying to conjure Kriss's face from her dream. She could hear a great roar of commotion going on behind the white veil, the giant wheel seemed to grind even louder and the crones squealed and cursed. Behind her, she could feel Joe's grasping hands reaching out to grab her once more. Sarah was terrified, but she did not stop chanting. It was that or succumb to an eternity here, a living death in this nightmare. She had to overcome her fear. "Saint Christopher; Saint Christopher ..."

The stream of white billowed up around her and took on the shape of a figure with no features. Was it an angel she wondered? There were no wings.

"You know my purpose here," rang a voice in her head. It was a male voice and vaguely familiar. In seconds the featureless body took form and before her stood a tall, hooded man draped in a red cloak. Dark eyes gazed out from beneath a long curtain of black curls that fringed his olive-skinned, classical features.

"You!" Joe spat.

"Kriss!" Sarah ran up and flung her arms around him, but he didn't move. He was like a stone statue and felt as cold as a block of sculpted ice, but beneath her hands she could feel he was thawing. To Sarah, now that she saw him again, the events of her dream felt like only yesterday. "What's wrong, Kriss?" she cried. "It's me, Sarah, don't you remember me?"

On either side of his prominent Grecian nose Kriss's eyes came to life, swivelling in their sockets as he regarded her. Then they twinkled, letting her know he knew exactly who she was, and where he was and why.

"A sight for sore eyes if ever I saw one," Felicity shouted jubilantly in Sarah's head.

Kriss's mouth moved and he spoke one word: "Felicity."

"Do you know her?" Sarah asked, somewhat startled. She became aware that the crones were closing in on them, arms outstretched, clawed fingers reaching forward, still intent on wresting the now human form of Saint Christopher into the bubbling cauldron.

"There's no time to explain," Kriss said. Disdainfully he eyed Joe up and down then turned back to Sarah. Flinging open his cape to reveal a long wooden staff, he said, "Stand directly behind me and follow where I go." Then turning on his heel he faced the three Fates with a threatening stare. He didn't vacillate, he moved fast, gripping his staff in both hands.

A defensive roar rose up from the witches, like wild women they threw themselves at Kriss, reaching out with clawed hands to scratch out his eyes. Shielding himself he raised his stick, tossing each crone aside as she flew at him, his eyes focused, heading straight for the wheel. Sarah did exactly as she was told and followed directly in his wake, scampering up the creaky wooden steps to the topmost level.

"Get offffff!" Cutter screamed, distraught, her pain and anger clear to see as she streaked up the steps after them. She looked so ancient and frail that Sarah could hardly believe the speed at which she moved, leaping up two steps at a time and trying to grab hold of Sarah. Kriss had stopped and with both hands was grasping the turning wheel, digging his heels hard into the wooden framework in an attempt to impede the wheel's rotation or maybe even bring it to a standstill. Sarah could not move forward and in seconds, Cutter was upon her. She whacked Sarah with phenomenal strength, hard across the bottom of her legs, knocking Sarah sideways off the steps and throwing her to the ground. Spinner and Measure were close behind their big sister, chasing after Kriss.

From flat on her back Sarah looked up at the scene playing out above her. Kriss had stopped trying to obstruct the wheel, but was now riding on it, away from the Fates, who had clambered onto it, as though onto a giant Ferris Wheel.

"You will leave this place right now, Saint Christopher; this is not your realm. You are not welcome here. We three are the power behind the gods, you are nobody here, you have no power against us," Cutter shrieked, her tone levelling from a feral scream to a shakier but calmer manner.

"Get off the wheel!" Spinner squealed, even more wild than her sister.

Kriss's feet found the ground as the wheel turned, leaving the sisters high above him at the top of the thirty-foot contraption. Once more he dug his heels into the wooden structure, hooking his feet firmly under the base and holding onto the giant spokes, his muscles straining and bulging. He was on a mission to stop this wheel, Sarah thought, finding her feet and rushing to help him. She grabbed hold of his body and pulled him downwards. Reaching for a protruding arm of the cog, she too clung on, marginally slowing the wheel's course.

The crones were at the bottom of the wheel in a flash. Sarah wasn't sure if their move had been magic or speed but they were on them in a split second.

"Hold onto me," Kriss called to Sarah. With no time to think, Sarah once again did as Kriss had asked and pushing herself up, grasped hold of him around the neck. Kriss released his feet and allowed the still turning wheel to take them upwards again.

"Back," screeched Measure, turning on her sisters who were hot on her heels. "Go back!" They all turned in haste and charged back up the steps, moving so fast they were a black blur.

"Pull harder, Sarah," Kriss hollered.

"It's nearly stopped," Sarah shouted back, watching the fast approaching hags.

"We don't want it to stop, we want it to turn backwards," Kriss shouted.

The crones, hearing this, screamed and crowed at the top of their lungs. But once again Kriss was marginally faster; he hauled Sarah onto his back and using the giant cog handles as steps he threw himself down to the ground again, immediately grinding the wheel almost to a halt. He shrugged Sarah off his back and turned to face her. "Sarah, you can't be holding onto the wheel when this happens. Stand back," Kriss shouted, pushing her away with force.

"When what happens? What are you going to do?" Sarah cried over the cacophony of the screeching sisters, uncomfortably aware that Joe was directly behind her, gormlessly gawping up at the crones who were inanely and furiously pushing at the wheel, attempting to make it turn at its original speed. They were fighting a losing battle as Kriss, his eyes popping with effort and the veins corded in his flushed neck, slowed it right down.

"I'm going to rewind time, Sarah. It is the only way to get you out of here and back on the right road. I can't go with you, I have to stay here," Kriss tried to explain, speaking hurriedly, his voice strained with pulling.

"Rewind time?" Sarah threw him a quizzical look, suddenly very frightened.

"There's no time to explain ... this is how it's meant to be," Kriss hollered.

"But what about you?" she cried. "You can't stay here, with them. They'll eat you alive!"

"I'll be all right. They're no match for me," Kriss gave a wry grin. "But I am going to have to keep them at bay while you get out of Transit, which isn't going to be easy. You won't last long if I come with you, particularly if these three are let loose with their spinning wheel. Just make sure you get out, Sarah. You have to go back ... you're running out of time. Please run all the way if you have to. Archie will help you."

"Archie? Is he in Transit?" Sarah asked, her ears pricking.

"As soon as you re-enter Transit, I will have to put the wheel back on its track, moving forwards," Kriss shouted, not answering her question, his gaze never leaving the sisters above, who were straining to move the wheel as he was straining to bring it to a standstill. "You must make sure the serpent doesn't win, Sarah."

"How?" she whimpered, petrified.

"Use your imagination. Yes, it can conjure up obstacles, but it can just as easily conjure up remedies," Kriss shouted. "You have more power than you know. Use it to your advantage."

"Kriss, wait! Anian ... the serpent, it killed Anian, make sure you rewind far enough back to help him," Sarah pleaded.

"I will try," Kriss said glancing upwards.

The hags above him were clinging tightly to their precious wheel screaming and screeching profanities all the while, desperate to hinder Kriss, but his strength was way beyond theirs, even with the three of them put together. With one almighty heave and the glint of a smile in his eyes, Kriss, dragged the wheel backwards. It didn't want to go at first and in that moment it stopped completely.

Like a waxwork model, Sarah seemed to freeze, but although she could not move her limbs her mind was fully alert and she could see everything that was happening. Suddenly, the wheel started to scrape reluctantly backwards and as it did, Sarah's thoughts started to rewind in her mind's eye, everything that had just past beginning to replay like an old movie on rewind in her head. She felt very strange and insecure: it was as though her life was flashing before her eyes, yet it was happening far too slowly. She saw the moment when with a shock of recognition she had seen Joe coming down the steps towards her and had realised he was Joseph Jackson, her husband in another life. The wheel started to rotate more quickly and the images in her mind speeded up. It moved on quicker still, to when she had woken and found herself with the three Fates in the black hole. The world around her was still all completely black. Until, little by little, light began to filter in from somewhere, as though it had started to snow. She had not been conscious when she arrived in the black hole, so she didn't remember any of her transition, but now she was seeing what happened her insides started to writhe, it made her feel quite sick, it was as though she was riding a roller coaster in reverse. With each second that ticked backwards the speckled lights grew stronger and larger, stinging her eyes at first because she had become so accustomed to the blackness. Soon she was back in brilliant daylight, the serpent lurching towards her throat, then falling away from her; Anian's body spooling through the air in a flash of red.

Dimly, Sarah heard Kriss give a great shout, "Get ready, Sarah! I can't take it back much further."

Sarah knew that any moment now the wheel of time would stop going backwards and everything would start to play again for real. She had to prepare herself, stay focused and think about what to do or she would simply end up back in the hags' clutches all over again.

"What will help me? Who can help me?" her mind pounded.

And then it went blank and she was falling ... falling. ...

CHAPTER TWENTY ONE

OCTOBER, 1992
FATHER, SON AND HOLY GHOST

Persuading Archie to come down from the yew tree, Sarah grasped his hand and the two of them ran helter skelter, through the drizzle, back to Wood Eves. She had looked back to wave goodbye to Connie, but the old lady had disappeared as mysteriously as she had arrived, so there was no opportunity to ask what she had meant about the standing stones and by the time they got home, it had slipped to the back of Sarah's mind.

The next twenty-four hours were not as sombre as everyone had anticipated. Nanny kept in good spirits and had only once retreated to her room for a nap and a break from the mayhem. Early on the eve of Halloween, the children were part way dressed up, having a ball; a premade dinner was being prepped again. Uncle Tom had brought his guitar and although it was only six o'clock in the afternoon, morale was high and a different type of atmosphere reigned amongst the olds. Sarah could see from their faces that tears had been shed and brave faces put on as soon as she, Dom and her cousins came in to show off their costumes and make up. There was a lot of love flowing through the house. Anyone could feel it; it was a fuzzy feeling, surreal, as though a celebration was taking place, yet they all knew it wasn't. The mutual support and acceptance seemed to twist into one hazy feeling that could only be love.

Sarah's mum, or 'Auntie Patricia' as everyone else called her, was creatively trying to organize the light tea, premade by Joanna for the children, and was bustling in and out of the kitchen laying the table. Sarah had never seen her so relaxed about preparing food and put it down to the gin and tonic – two or three by the look of things and judging by her shiny red nose. Auntie Frances was hopelessly trying to persuade Uncle Tom to play another song on his acoustic guitar so she could sing along again. Gillian, Sally and Helena, dressed as three witches, were sitting in the inglenook, by a roaring open fire, playing Gin Rummy. Stewart, a spider, and Dominic, a zombie, had given up on the Lego fort and found one of Nanny's two-thousand piece jigsaws, which they had laid out on her bridge table by the grand piano nestling in the corner of the old, beamed living room. Everyone was busy except Nanny, who watched from her high-backed armchair by the fire, her lips lifted in a contented smile. Sarah looked around at everyone and wanted to hold the moment like a photograph in her mind, to stay with her and look back on all her life.

Outside it was cold and very dark; a mist of condensation had formed on the inside of the windows. Sarah stood with Archie in the doorway, both clad in toilet roll and fake blood. All she could see of him were his blue eyes through his mask; eyes that were identical in colour to her own.

"Midnight, I double dare you," Archie whispered, as they propped up the doorframe, looking in on their family.

"You're on," Sarah whispered back. Both strode into the room, Archie popped a kiss on Nanny's cheek and went and helped his brother and Dominic to sort out the edges of the puzzle, while Sarah went over to the inglenook and budged Sally along, peeking at her cards to see if she could help.

"Come on, children, time for tea," Patricia called them to the table. They picked half-heartedly at their cauliflower cheese and baked beans, helped down by the bottles of lemonade and cola, brought by Robert and Joanna for the children's indulgence. Then it was time for the singsong.

"A long, long time ago," Uncle Tom began to sing in a warm and soft tone. It was one of Don McLean's classics and a great family favourite, which they all knew word for word. "I can still remember how that music used to make me smile, and I knew if I had my chance that I could make those people dance, and maybe they'd be happy for a while," he warbled.

Joanna threw herself on the floor at Tom's feet, glass of red in hand, smiling and tapping her thigh to the rhythm. Tom sang the first two verses as a duet with his wife, Frances, but the choruses were heartily crooned by everyone in the room, even the children. Robert, shaking his head at his wife's tone deafness, ensured that everyone's glasses, including Nanny's, were replenished after every sip.

The last verse, always sung as a round robin affair, was started by Uncle Tom. "I met a girl who sang the blues," he sang then pointed at Joanna with a grin, continuing to strum the tune on his guitar.

"And I asked her for some happy news," Joanna sang, giggling, then pointed at Sarah.

"But she just smiled and turned away," Sarah sang shyly, passing the song onto Robert. The verse went round the family, Nanny included, until it came back to Tom, who ultimately the most confident and tuneful singer carried it on.

"And the three men I admire most, the Father, Son and the Holy Ghost, they caught the last train for the coast, the day the music died. And they were singin' ... EVERYBODY," Tom shouted.

Almost in perfect unison, the family belted out the chorus, some who found the atmosphere they had created too much simply hummed along, rocking to the tune. "Bye-bye, Miss American Pie, drove my Chevy to the levy, but the levy was dry; them good old boys were drinking whiskey and rye, singing this'll be the day that I die ..."

Sarah glanced at Nanny and then at Archie and pulled a face, attempting to swallow the lump that had lodged in her throat.

He grinned at her, "It's only a song," he whispered. "Come on, we need to prep."

***

Sarah and Archie, their faces still drenched in white paint and fake blood, though now dressed in day clothes and coats with pyjamas underneath, hid trembling in the shadows and ever-present drizzle just beside the whitewashed inn, the Old Stag, down in Llangernyw village. It was eleven forty-five and their cousins and Nanny had been asleep for hours. Jack, Sarah's dad, was the only grown-up still awake, or half awake, slumped in Nanny's chair with a nightcap in hand, but he never came to check up on the youngsters. They had been peeped in on by Patricia twice and Auntie Joanna once, which was more than sufficient to appease any disquiet. Archie had set his digital alarm watch for eleven-thirty; it had taken only fifteen minutes to wake Sarah, dress, climb out of the annex bathroom window into the woods and run down to the village.

A streetlight beam shone yellow, in a pool of welcoming light, just in front of the inn's entrance. Peeping in at the window, they could see the laughing, red-faced punters, basking in the glow of an open fire. Low, oak-beamed ceilings adorned with weird and ancient-looking artefacts were enticing and alluring.

"This is ridiculous, what are we doing?" Sarah whispered. "I can't believe you talked me into this."

"Look, if it all goes wrong, all you need to do is run through that old oak door right over there and into the Old Stag, where you'll be safe," Archie nodded to the pub window. "It's twenty metres away from the church... and see," he pointed, "Connie's in there."

Sarah had noticed the old lady propping up the bar from a tall stool right in front of the hearth. She was deep in conversation with the barman, what looked like a long glass of lime-soda in her hand and a packet of peanuts on the bar in front of her. Sarah turned to Archie then looked across to St Digain's and the yew tree. It was foggy, the Elwy Valley mists had set in early and if the church had not been white it would have been lost in the night.

"Anyway, nothing's going to go wrong. We know what's expected to happen, so let's go and see it happen. We should be more afraid of the living than we are of the dead, surely?" Archie said.

"Connie said nobody has dared to visit the church on Halloween in years. Are we mad?" Sarah whispered, huddling into her cousin, trying to protect herself from the rain.

"Yep, but all the best people are," Archie grinned. "Come on."

He took hold of Sarah's hand and swiftly they moved from the streetlight and into the darkness, like two lost shadows. They crossed the road and slid through the small wrought-iron gate into the churchyard.

"Do you know the history to this place then?" Archie asked.

"Not all of it, but Connie told me a little yesterday, while you were sulking in the yew."

Archie jabbed Sarah playfully in the ribs. "I wasn't sulking … I was thinking," he retorted, rain dripping down his nose.

"Whatever," Sarah said, unmoved. "It's an ancient place ..."

"Yeah, well I can see that," Archie joked, running his free hand across the top of a weathered grave stone close to the path.

"Pagans came here to make sacrifices. See those stones," Sarah pointed to two large, moss covered, standing stones in the churchyard positioned up against the church itself. "She said they are portals."

"What? Like a magical gateway?" Archie stopped to peer at Sarah and then at the standing stones.

"I suppose," Sarah whispered with a shrug. She didn't have a clue really; she was merely reciting what Connie had told her yesterday.

They continued on along the side of the church, looking for the side door. It was very dark, there were no security lights or street lights to help guide their way.

"The moon's low tonight isn't it," Sarah remarked, glancing up at the full, pink, harvest moon hanging in the mist above them, its light casting shadows around the graves.

"Full moon on Halloween! Now that is a bit spooky, don't you think?" Archie said in a soft, quavering voice – the tone he always used when he was about to embark on one of his ghost stories.

"Stop it," Sarah shivered.

"Only joking," Archie gave her hand a tight squeeze.

Foliage rustled in the light autumn wind, the pitter-patter of rain drops splashed into the puddles on the pathway, the only sound other than this was their own footsteps, until Archie's watch beeped twice pronouncing midnight.

Fear started to eat away at Sarah's insides, but there was no way she was going to display it to Archie. Her cousin was always so calm and collected about even the scariest of adventures and they had shared many in their lifetime, there was no way she was going to miss this and forever be dubbed a wuss by Archie.

They had found the side entrance into the church and Archie's hand was on the handle, ready to open the door, but unexpectedly another sound filled the air. "What's that noise?" he asked quizzically and yet true to his nature, calmly. He pulled his hand away from the knob, turning on his heel to look in the direction of a strange scraping sound that had risen above all else from behind them, back along the path.

"What noise?" Sarah gasped, frantically spinning round.

"The stones," Archie whispered. "Look at the stones!"

What they saw made their blood run cold. The hairs on the back of Sarah's neck lifted and she could feel goose bumps prickling on her arms. "Oh my," Sarah whispered with an overwhelming feeling of terror, her breath misting on the cold night air.

A long black shape, maybe fifteen feet tall, rose out from between the two standing stones, which stood between them and the churchyard gate. It had no physical features or limbs at all. Hovering a good foot above the ground, like a vulture intent on its prey, it loomed over them. The featureless head of the shape turned and twisted, as though it was looking about. Then it seemed to stop and stare right at them. Archie and Sarah remained frozen; their heads bowed slightly, hardly daring to breathe. As though satisfied it was alone, the shape floated silently, black and mist-like, across the churchyard and straight through the wall of the ancient church.

"Did you see that?" Sarah squeaked.

"Did it see us?" Archie stared at the church wall where the apparition had vanished.

"How should I know?" Sarah wailed, hugging herself in an effort to stop trembling. "I'm not some Angelystor guru you know."

"Do you think that was it? Do you think that was Angelystor?" Archie asked, a strange smile lifting the corner of his mouth as he looked at Sarah.

"It's midnight on the 31st October, what else is it going to be? Are you not even slightly scared?" Sarah asked, gazing wide-eyed at her cousin.

"I'm terrified! It's real, isn't it? We just saw that ... didn't we?" Archie was still smiling, but Sarah could hear his teeth chattering and he sounded nervous and strangely deflated.

"I know what I saw and it was certainly real," she said. "Do we really need to go in and listen to what it has to say?"

"Of course we do," Archie insisted, inching his hand back to the door handle.

"Is it really necessary? We know it's real, we've just seen it. Must we torture ourselves?" Sarah begged, like a small child pulling on the bottom of Archie's coat.

"I need to hear it." He took her hand and gave it a quick squeeze. "It's not going to hurt us, Sarah, it's going to say some names ... that's all."

"I know, but why? Why do you need to hear it, Arch?"

"It may not say the name we think it's going to say. Let's just see shall we?" Archie croaked, wiping the rain from the side of his nose.

"But why is it so important to you? I don't understand. Please tell me what's going on with you," Sarah begged, but as before, Archie ignored the question.

"What's the worst that can happen? Let's see, come on," Archie said in a voice just above a whisper, tugging at her hand.

Never able to refuse him anything, all Sarah could do was watch as her cousin opened the church door. It creaked open. The air within seemed colder than the air outside. They did not go in ... they did not need to. A deep unearthly voice was already booming around the hall inside.

"Bydd y rhai a fydd wyf yn awry n enw cyn bo hir fod yn farw," it said.

"What does that mean, Sarah? You speak Welsh," Archie nudged her, not forcing her inside, both feeling a touch safer staying in the doorway.

"I don't want to go in, Arch," Sarah hissed, shuffling backwards slightly.

"I see that, but we don't have to, we can hear it," Archie whispered, pulling her back into the doorway. "So what's it saying? Translate."

Sarah, her mouth dry, drew in a breath, her brain decoding the words Angelystor had spoken. "Those I will now name shall soon be dead …."

"Wow! This is it," Archie breathed, "So it's true; he is actually going to say the names."

Sarah retreated quickly. "I'm sorry, Arch, I can't listen. I don't want to. I want to go back to Nanny's. Please come away now," she implored, tears filling her eyes as she reversed onto the pathway, backing away from the door. Archie did not move. He did not even look back at Sarah. Instead he took a broad step into the church, leaving her outside in the dark on her own. Hesitating for a moment, wondering if she could pluck up the courage to go after him, Sarah took a step forward.

Suddenly, a hand caught hold of her arm and pulled her back. Almost jumping out of her skin, Sarah spun round, saw who it was and nearly collapsed with relief. "Connie!"

"You don't need to go in there, Sarah. Archie has his own reasons for wanting to validate Angelystor's existence," the old lady said softly.

"And you know what those reasons are don't you, Connie? I don't understand how you know, but please tell me what they are."

"His reasons are his own, Sarah. You are an intuitive girl and you care deeply about your cousin. You are also an inquisitive child and that's why you're here, but you are right to be nervous," Connie tilted her head, her gaze on the shadowed path.

"Why? Is Archie in danger?" Sarah cried, pulling away, starting for the door where her cousin had disappeared, her fear for him overcoming her terror.

"He will be fine, Sarah, I promise. I would not have let him go in if I thought any harm would come to him," Connie called after her.

"You were watching us?" Sarah questioned.

"I knew you would try to go in after the conversation we had earlier," Connie said with a small smile. "Your fear got the better of you, didn't it? Archie is no less afraid, but he has succumbed to temptation and now he has to prove something to himself - which he will, but it will not appease him in any way."

"I don't understand what you mean. Who has tempted him?" Sarah demanded, bewildered.

"Someone he trusted. Someone with the power to influence him has lured him into believing a prophesy. What he finds out from Angelystor tonight may put his future - or how he thinks about his future - in peril. Our duty now, once he has satisfied himself, is to calm him, try to tame him in any way we can and try to keep him with us, here. His future is too important to be lost. For his sake, you must be strong."

Sarah stared at the old woman, horrified.

CHAPTER TWENTY-TWO

AUGUST 2003
A POTHOLED QUEST

Feeling the intensity of his reality heighten Niran-Atid parked up in a lay-by. Once more using meditation as a guide on his journey, he sat quietly in his taxi and focused on the lotus flower dangling motionless in front of him. Nothing in the car stirred. Not even the cars that clogged the smog-ridden Bangkok street outside impinged on his consciousness. His mind was completely still and clear. However, it was not his thoughts deepening that took him to the place where he could watch Sarah fighting for her life in Transit; it was his heart.

"Fight harder, Miss Sarah ... what would your culture say?" A Christian Bible lay on his lap, picking it up, he flicked through.

"Genesis twenty-three, The Death of Sarah," he read aloud. "No... no!" He snapped the Bible shut, frustrated and sucked in a deep breath. After a moment, he let the book fall open a second time. "Genesis again ... verse twenty-tree ... hmm, this is complicated." This time he read on further. "Let the waters bring forth abundantly the moving creature that hath life, and fowl that may fly above the earth in the open firmament of heaven."

Again Niran-Atid snapped the book shut. "So be it."

***

A hand reached out and snatched Sarah mid-fall. She squeezed her eyes shut as her stomach did a double flip.

"Open your eyes Sarah! Quickly! You won't regret it," Felicity whispered, but Sarah could hear panic in the voice of her alter ego trembling inside her head.

She opened one eye and at that moment was yanked with force out of the way of a serpent's gnashing jaws, its sharp teeth dripping with saliva as it bent to devour her.

Sarah screamed at the top of her lungs as she was tossed into a pair of arms that closed around her, hugging her tight, the unmistakeable stench of goat making her senses real. She knew she was screaming in fear for her life, but another part of her knew she was screaming in disbelief, for the person who had saved her was none other than Archie! Archie; wearing nothing but a matted animal hide, his mousey hair much longer than the picture she kept of him in her head, his skin tanned and his body far brawnier than she remembered, thrusting her out of the serpent's jaws and into the arms of a severely injured Anian.

"Quickly, come away," the satyr urged. "Leave it to Archie."

Allowing herself to be used as a crutch, Sarah staggered backwards with Anian into the woods, all the while looking over her shoulder to watch the battle raging in the clearing at her back.

With Sarah's sword held in both hands outstretched in front of him, Archie had thrown himself headlong at the serpent. Cutting and slicing the air, he twisted and turned, beating the monstrous creature away, slashing and hacking at its necks. He fought well and the snake was scored and scratched a number of times.

Hardly able to breathe from fear for him, Sarah kept telling herself that he could not possibly be in any danger since he was already dead. And yet it did not help. She watched him, bewildered; she just couldn't believe it was him. Her Archie was fighting the dual-headed monster right here in front of her. Or was she dreaming? She no longer had a handle on what was real.

And there beside him was another man. Sarah blinked. Why was he here? He was attacking the serpent with his bare hands, seizing stones from the ground and using them to batter at the creature's scaled body as it writhed over Archie.

Sarah gaped; she had clean forgotten about Joseph Jackson until she saw him there, battling for his life under the giant serpent's challenge. But he had not been there before, she was certain of it, so how had he got there now? Had he somehow escaped the black hole by hanging onto her? It was beyond her understanding. She looked away from him to focus once more on Archie. Was he real or was it just wishful thinking – an illusion? She had so longed to see him, but how was it possible? Then Grace's words came back to her: "... sometimes, in moments of extreme stress or when a loved one has been placed in acute danger before it is their time to cross, a spirit can come back and intervene to help them."

"No, this is not an illusion," Anian croaked in her ear, reading her thoughts. "That is indeed your Archie. I remember him well. He would do anything for you, in this life and in your past life."

"My Archie?" Sarah whispered, her gaze never leaving Archie's frame. "He came back for me. He got Death's consent and he crossed back over to help me. Grace must have given him my note. But oh, Anian, suppose he gets hurt, I can't bear it."

"He won't get hurt, just look at the way he's fighting. This is a man who has killed a lion with his bare hands, outwitted the Moon and defeated a fire-breathing dragon. Death is going to be more of a problem than a mere serpent, however. I sincerely hope Archie got his consent to cross over, because that young man is going to be in an awful lot of trouble if he didn't!" Anian said, sounding grumpy.

Supporting the satyr's weight, Sarah helped him to walk between the trees, wanting to put as much distance between them and the serpent as possible, her ears straining for what was happening in the clearing, the sounds growing distant as they moved further away.

"Ouch!" Anian's face turned purple and he moaned, "Oh, Sarah, please lay me down here. I can't go on. I need ... oh darn, I can't ..." he dropped to his knees behind a large fern, desperately clinging to his side, sweat pouring down his disfigured face scorching it all the more.

For the first time Sarah took in the extent of his injuries and saw how appalling they were. "Oh, my friend," she said, her eyes filling with tears. "No, Anian you can't stop here, we have to get you away," she panted, trying to pull the satyr to his hooves again, but to no avail.

"There's no way, Sarah, I'm so sorry. My injuries are too severe." Anian lifted his arm to survey the damage beneath, revealing a deep slash dripping with blood and blue venom. "It bit me. It's the kiss of death."

"Kriss didn't get us back far enough," Sarah whispered, "and now he is stuck with the Fates forever." She felt overwhelmed with despair: Archie was battling a vicious, toxic serpent and she could do nothing to help him; Anian looked as though he were about to die at any moment; Kriss was trapped in a timeless hellhole with three screeching hags, and to cap it all, Joseph Jackson had come back to haunt her. It was all too much. 'I can't cope,' she said to herself, feeling the weight of the world on her shoulders.

"Yes you can," snapped Fee in her head.

"What?" Anian asked, his eyes imploring Sarah for help.

"Nothing," she said. "It really doesn't matter. You're in a lot of pain aren't you? What can I do to help? You must have some fruity remedy? What should I find? Quickly, tell me, I'll find it. You know this forest inside out; point me in the right direction."

"I know of nothing, Sarah, there is no antidote to the Moon's malice." The satyr's eyes began to droop and roll in their sockets.

"No! Anian, don't go, you can't," Sarah cried, shaking her friend trying to rouse him. His body had grown limp and his head tilted to one side, a white film crusting around his dry mouth.

"This Kriss you speak of is your friend, I know that, and he has helped you greatly. He must come and help you again," Anian whispered.

"Sadly, I don't see how he can. He's trapped, fighting the hags of doom on my behalf. But he is helping me ... right now, as we sit here, he's stopping the Moon's daughters from spinning their evil thread. He's buying me time," Sarah tried to explain.

"Good," Anian murmured, pressing on his wound, a harsh grimace on his ruined face. "Someday, Sarah, may there be peace within you, I know it's hard to find sometimes, but trust me. All that has occurred has happened for a reason, even me being trapped here for so long had a purpose. It was to find and help you again and set right my wrongdoing."

Tears flooded down Sarah's face. "No Anian, you did nothing wrong, please don't say that."

"Shh," Anian hushed, the effort of speaking making his voice sound harsh, the deepened colour of his face beginning to pale. "Don't cry for me, you will only make me weep as well and in doing that I will only be in more pain."

"I'm sorry," Sarah said clearing her throat, dashing away her tears. "The Fates said that ..."

"Don't worry about what anyone else has said, Fates or not, great deities or not, I don't care who they are. Don't you listen to them. Trust me; you're exactly where you are meant to be, Sarah. You and you alone have the power to control your destiny, nobody else. You were meant to take this journey just as I was. Infinite possibilities are born if you have faith in yourself."

"Have faith in myself?" Sarah said, as though the thought had never occurred to her.

"Let my words of knowledge settle into your bones and allow your soul the freedom to sing again ... to love again. Do you remember what I told you all those years ago in my cottage?"

"You said love is the answer," Sarah nodded, remembering what Old Nick had said in her dream.

"Yes indeed, it is the only answer to our existence, otherwise what on earth is the point? Quite literally, living a life without love is like living under a rock in the cold, it is meaningless. We live every day waiting and delighting in those great moments of love and excitement. You must always follow your heart and don't let anyone else make you think otherwise," Anian said, his voice growing weaker.

"But those hags told me..." Sarah started again.

"Do you delight in torturing me? Do not allow anyone to govern you," Anian reiterated, cutting her off. "Don't lie to yourself. Remember ... it is a dangerous business to be walking with a tarnished conscience. Believe me I know."

"You waited here in Transit for me all these years just to make sure you could remind me of this didn't you," Sarah whimpered, her throat aching with suppressed tears. She pressed her lips tightly together to stop them from trembling.

"Like I said, there are reasons for everything. My lesson here has been learnt, well and truly. I have been faithful and loyal to my friends and to myself. I could never have crossed peacefully knowing the anguish my words caused back then," Anian panted.

"It was an accident, Anian. When you were Old Nick you didn't mean to say Archie's name. You slipped up, these things happen, anyone could have ... it wasn't your fault."

"But don't you see, Sarah, in my slipping up at the crucial hour, your life changed. I destroyed your chance of happiness at that very moment, albeit accidently. It was a truth that should never have been said aloud. You should both have been given the chance to be together, to be free. By stating your names to Renshaw I took that chance away and as a consequence Archie was killed, and you out of pure misery took your own life. That should never have happened. You knew; your soul knew; everyone in that congregation knew that on the day you married Joseph Jackson, one way or another you were doomed."

"Archie was killed and I took my own life ...?" Sarah's face paled. She had not known that.

"You see now why I had to wait for this very opportunity to right my wrongdoing?" With an obvious effort Anian lifted his head to look into Sarah's eyes. "But we're straight now, aren't we?" His words slurred, barely coherent, his head flopping back to rest on the ground.

"Of course, Anian, please don't think of it anymore," Sarah sobbed no longer able to hold back her emotions.

"Forgive me, I talk too much," Anian wheezed. "Find the Tree of Life, Sarah," he breathed, a rattle prominent in his throat, his eyes barely open. "Archie will help you. Find the tree and go home." He tried to lift a hand, which Sarah grasped and squeezed tenderly, her other hand automatically going to his forehead to brush his wispy hair out of his yellowing eyes. "My time here is done."

"No, don't say that," Sarah wept, crouching down in front of her friend, trying desperately to protect him, though from what she was not sure.

"I can move on now, Sarah, and hopefully I can now find the man who wronged me," Anian whispered.

"Renshaw? You mean Bran?" Sarah asked.

"No, I have no time left to me now for birds trapped in Transit. I cannot avenge myself against the likes of Renshaw. He is nothing more than a puppet with the Moon pulling his strings; he has no feeling or soul. No, no ... there is another," Anian sighed. "A good man who lived in fear ... and at the final test he let fear win."

"Who?"

"I will find him," Anian whispered, his voice fading. "Thank you for everything: for caring, for not minding how I look, for letting me share your dreams. It's been a real adventure. I needed an adventure. I've not seen so much action in centuries. You've not only found me, you've saved me; saved me from crossing over. Now I can move onto the next level of this game and hopefully find the man who wronged me – and forgive him."

"Game? Next level? What man?" Sarah slumped down next to Anian, her arm draped across his wounded body. But he did not reply, his eyes had closed and his last breath died away. "A rabbit's foot for luck my old friend?" Sarah smiled sadly, gently pressing her forehead to her dead friend's wrinkled brow, remembering again her recent dreams and the dreadful pain this man had suffered in a former life. At least he was released from it now.

Tears of sorrow and frustration tumbled down her cheeks as she felt Anian's body turn cold under her hand. Why, when she needed him most, did he have to die? She had only just rediscovered him and now he was gone. She did not understand what he meant by her saving him and being able to move onto the next level. Was this really all just a game, a game of questions with no answers, with winners and losers and no graceful compromise?

'All games are surely just battles,' Sarah thought. 'Even if Anian is moving onto the next stage of this so called 'game' we are playing, it cannot merely be a sport at the hands of some god. Anian's right, it is up to me what I make of it, how I spend my time, who I choose to be with. It is all up to me.'

She was not sure how long she sat there pondering and grieving, her body convulsed with giant sobs, her Lapis lazuli stone pulsing on her chest as she wept. It must have been a fair while, for her buttocks had gone numb and she had agonizing pins and needles shooting down one side of her body. She became aware that the distant sounds of battle had ceased and was then rigid with fear that Archie had been harmed after all, or had gone back to where he'd come from and now, without either him or Anian, she was entirely alone in this alien land called Transit, where nothing was as it seemed.

She felt a hand gently grasp her shoulder and a voice said, "Sarah." She knew his voice instantly and froze. Part of her was desperate to turn around and throw herself straight into his arms, but another part was still too disbelieving and in too much shock to react so impetuously.

"Hello Arch," she whispered, not turning to face him, her eyes red from weeping, staring down at Anian's limp and lifeless body. The hand did not move, it squeezed harder, almost massaging her shoulder in comfort. "I think part of me is afraid to turn round," Sarah whispered.

"Why," Archie asked.

"I don't know, maybe because I'm afraid you're an illusion and you'll just disappear on me again." Sarah took a deep breath, her heart racing as she tried desperately to control herself.

"I am no illusion, Sarah. You can feel my hand on your shoulder, can't you?"

"Of course, but this is a strange place, Arch. Lots of weird things have been happening," Sarah said. "Things I don't understand."

To her surprise, her twin-cousin gave a deep laugh. "Yeah, tell me about it! You should have heard the conversation I just had with Death, not to mention the battle I've had to duel with some freaky two-headed snake, alongside some insane bloke claiming he hated my guts and that once he was finished stoning the snake, I was next. A nutter, I tell you."

Sarah smiled; she even almost chuckled under her breath, for now she knew the man behind her was indeed her Archie. Only he could remark on events the way he did. "That was Joe, er ... Joseph. What's happened to him? What's happened to the serpent?" Sarah asked.

"The man hightailed it back towards the river with the snake on his heels. A stone the idiot threw by chance got the creature right in one of its four eyes, which seemed to rile it somewhat and it took off after him, so I got off lightly, well ... without being killed again, at least. The serpent is not dead, though, Sarah; it could be coming back this way at any moment. You're its prime target. We should move quickly."

"Where to? Do you know this place?" Sarah still did not turn to look at Archie. She listened to what he said intently, but she couldn't bring herself to move. His hand on her shoulder felt incredibly warm and comforting and she was so desperately afraid that if she moved he would disappear.

"I do," Archie said. "Grace told me, when she gave me your note, that I must take you back to the beach. It is the one I arrived on when I first came here after my plane went down. It'll take us a while to get there and who knows what we'll encounter on the way. Please come quickly, we are running out of time."

Sarah felt Archie's hand leave her shoulder and knew he was moving round to face her. As he did so she swivelled away from him, still afraid to look.

"Look at me Sarah! For God's sake, this isn't helping."

"If I look at you, you don't think I'll pass out, do you? Or freak out. This isn't me going nuts, is it? This isn't my imagination ... I mean, I know I've always had a wild imagination, but you are dead and I've never been able to see dead people before, I don't think so anyway," Sarah gabbled, staring straight at Anian's corpse. "Except when we went to St Digain's church and saw that Angelystor, do you remember that? My God, that was a scary night. Arch, I don't think I could bear it if you just disappeared on me again. Do you think my brain and heart can cope with me looking at you? Or worse ... what if I wake up? What if this is all a dream?" Sarah squirmed at the thought.

"I don't think this is your imagination, truly ... it's really me. You're not going nuts, Sarah," Archie laughed.

"Okay ... er ... and what exactly are you wearing? Just so I can visualise," Sarah found that despite her anxiety she was laughing too.

"I'm not sure you'd want to know, you being a vegetarian," Archie coughed.

"I thought it looked like some sort of animal hide," Sarah said, sneaking a glimpse of his bare feet, his toes, strong and brown, planted in the soft earth.

"Yeah, it's a lion's hide, if you must know the details. From a lion that I hunted, slaughtered and skinned. I used its bladder to make my drinking bottles, its ligaments as thread," Archie explained.

"Oh my God, Archie, too much information, that's gross!" Sarah shouted, spinning round to come face to face with her feral-looking cousin. Scrambling to her feet, Sarah stood wide-eyed, staring at him for a moment, half expecting him to fizzle out to nothing. But he didn't. She blinked hard, testing her eyes. Archie remained where he was, larger than life. There was no hug or kiss as she would have anticipated; it was almost as though there was an invisible fence between them – a necessary barrier to stop them from getting too close. Sarah felt sure that if she had wanted to lean forward and hold him it would have been possible, but she did not want to push it. Just looking at him was enough for her and she didn't want to stop feasting her eyes on the sight of him laughing at her in the way he always had.

"Wow! You look just like Felicity," Archie exclaimed.

"Oh, not you as well," Sarah sighed with grin. "That girl has been inside my head since before I got here. She's driving me insane."

"Or keeping you sane," Felicity piped up.

"You look beautiful," Archie said coyly, handing her back her sword.

"Thanks," Sarah blushed, breaking eye contact, feeling suddenly awkward. She had not seen what she looked like since catching sight of her reflection in the water in Lillian's cave, and she hadn't liked what she had seen back then. She knew her hair had grown and her wounds had healed, but guessed she was a long way from being beautiful.

"According to the folk who live here, we all go naked into the underworld," Archie quickly changed the subject. "I wasn't quite as lucky as you were," he said, a huge grin on his face revealing the chipped front tooth that Sarah had noticed in her past visions.

"What do you mean?" Sarah asked, beaming from ear to ear, delighting in the familiarity of his features.

"I didn't get swept straight to Lillian's cave to be washed, cared for and clothed. I had to fight for this fetching outfit," Archie laughed, doing a turn.

"How did you know I washed?" Sarah gasped.

"I've watched your entire journey, from start to finish. I've been persuading Death since you arrived to let me come back and help you home. I can watch all of you on Earth as well," Archie explained.

Sarah released a deep sigh. She felt as though a dislodged part of her had suddenly clicked into place. Archie too, seemed more relaxed. "So you're not going to disappear on me?"

"Nope ... I'm not sure how I'd do that. I'm dead, not a magician," he grinned.

"Okay then." Wanting suddenly to break the physical barrier between them, Sarah reached out to touch his arm, shyly changing the gesture into a playful cuff and for a moment it was as if they were kids again, teasing each other.

"Right then," Archie smiled, gently returning the cuff. "Can we go now? I'm getting slightly concerned that we have a tight agenda and a lethal venomous serpent in pursuit of us. I need to get you to that beach before sundown and judging by the sky, we don't have a lot of time."

They both looked up through the overhanging branches to see the sun was already on its way to the horizon, the edges of the clouds tinged pink and orange in an otherwise clear sky.

"What about Anian?" Sarah said. "I can't just leave him here, Archie. The least I can do is take him back to his oak tree."

"I really don't think we've got time, Sarah. He'd understand."

"I'm not leaving him," she said matter-of-factly. Sarah knew Anian would have been fine about it, but after everything he had sacrificed for her it was a matter of principle. She simply couldn't just leave him here to rot. "If you knew what this man went through for me ... and for you too, for that matter - for us - you wouldn't leave him here either," she said.

"Actually, I have a rough idea from this," Archie handed her the note she had asked Grace to pass on to him.

Unfolding it, Sarah saw her own handwriting and on the reverse the confession Anian had written to her. "It was all I could find to write on," she explained, a pang of sorrow for her dead friend bringing a fresh tear to her eye.

"Don't cry. Do you know where his tree is?"

Grateful that she didn't have to delve into the complexity of Anian's story, since it was all there in his note and Archie had obviously read it, she nodded. He took back the tattered parchment and pushed it inside his tunic. "You'll have to fill me in. I know snippets, but not all of what's gone on." He bent down and heaved the dead weight of the satyr off the woodland floor and over his shoulder. "We'll have to walk and talk, we can't stay here for much longer or the ravens will spy us and the serpent will come back. Bring that fairy in your head too; I'd like to talk to her again."

"I can't not; we're the same person," she retorted.

Carrying the sword, Sarah led Archie in the direction of Anian's oak. The forest was quiet as they trudged along the woodland paths, their conversation muted, both listening for sounds of pursuit. Reaching the tree at last, Archie gently lowered the satyr's body to the ground and between them they manoeuvred him into the hollow trunk of the oak. Timidly reciting a brief prayer, Sarah said goodbye to the half-man, half-goat, who had looked after her in Transit and was her friend from long, long ago.

"I'm sorry to rush you, Sarah, but we really need to get out of here," Archie said.

She didn't argue. Anian's bees had been disturbed by the noise and were beginning to buzz loudly, some swarming out of their nests to take a look at what was happening below. Not wanting to get stung, Sarah took the lead, hurrying towards the setting sun and out of the shelter of the forest.

When the trees began to thin, she stopped, "Which way's the beach?" she asked, gazing out at the rough terrain in front of her and the river running through it.

"That way," Archie said, pointing in the one direction Sarah had hoped he wouldn't. Shadowy rocks and boulders tumbled beside a small fork in the river, where a tributary shot downwards in foaming rapids. It looked cold and dark that way. In the opposite direction were beautiful rolling fields full of long meadow grasses that rippled gently in the breeze.

"What's that way then?" Sarah pointed to the more inviting landscape, now drenched in deepening gold as the giant sun sank to the distant horizon.

"The bridge over the river to ... well, to 'the other side'," Archie explained. "The terrain started off hard for me and became a little easier the closer I got to the bridge, though that's not saying the journey was ever very easy. I had to face challenges before I was able to cross."

"Just my luck," Sarah sighed. "So this journey is only going to get harder?"

"The terrain maybe, but you can't look at it as an obstacle," Archie said, giving her an earnest sideways glance. "We need to move fast; we're running out of time. When we get out into the open, don't look back, just run and for pity's sake, don't you dare think!"

"Don't worry, I know what thinking does here," Sarah gasped with a slight chuckle.

"Do you see that willow?" Archie pointed.

"Where?" Sarah tilted her head, her eyes straining to see.

"Over there, see? Right in the distance, leaning over the river," Archie reached out and gently held Sarah's head, turning it in the right direction.

A faint pinprick of ruffling shades of green bowing over the ribbon of gleaming water caught Sarah's eye. "Got it," she confirmed.

"We'll make for that tree. Just follow me and don't look back, okay? Promise me. Not until we get inside the shelter of the willow."

"I promise."

"Okay then, run," Archie said, starting off at speed.

Sarah followed directly behind him, aiming to stay on his heels, trying to keep her mind blank as, like a champion hurdler, her cousin hurdled and bounded over every obstacle in his path, taking boulders and giant tree-stumps in his stride. She could not help but smile as déjà vu swept over her and for a moment she was lost in a memory of when they were children, jumping the chain-link fences in Archie's back garden in the dead of night. Looking at him now, Sarah could see he had not changed so much, he was indeed still as gutsy and wild as he had been back then and she still felt the great and uncontrollable urge to follow him anywhere.

They had been running for a short time when Sarah heard the rush of wings above them. Glancing up she saw the ravens had taken to the skies and were shadowing their every move. Tracking or preparing to attack? Sarah wasn't sure. Too frightened to provoke them in any way, she refused to look at them, keeping her gaze fixed on Archie's back. Her heart was hammering like a drum in her chest; her face streamed with sweat, which ran into her eyes, stinging them and blurring her sight. Archie's stride was long and he was yards ahead of her now, yet the willow tree didn't seem any closer.

Sarah's knees, which always played her up, were beginning to give way by the time she reached the foaming tributary of the main river and followed Archie, who was running alongside it. Here on the bank, the ground was rockier and harder than ever. Twice she tripped, going over on her left ankle, but got back on her feet and stumbled on. With every stride she could feel her joints beginning to seize up, yet her cousin ran on like a gazelle.

Forced to slow to a jog, the space between Archie and herself began to widen. Sarah's mental stamina was immense and she kept telling herself to keep going. "One foot in front of the other," she panted, "just keep running, ignore the pain and just keep going." Her body, on the other hand, had different ideas and every old injury she had ever experienced – most of them on the lacrosse field - seemed to be hurting all over again.

Picking herself up from yet another stumble, Sarah suddenly became aware that someone was behind her. It was just a feeling of a presence at first, but then she heard panting and distinct footsteps, the ground crunching as feet jogged closer. Determined to do as Archie had said, she did not look back. Ignoring the pain she forced herself to run faster and taking a deep breath found her voice. "ARCHIE," she screamed, praying the wind would take her call the distance between them and not whip it away in another direction.

Archie continued to run, but turned when she called. Running backwards he stumbled slightly, dust filling the air as he screeched to a halt then started to sprint full pelt back towards her.

"S-A-R-A-H!" Two voices shouted out her name simultaneously, one from behind and the other from Archie. Still running towards him, at last she turned to look over her shoulder and saw Joe, battered and bleeding, hurtling in her direction, his arms reaching out to grab her.

In seconds the two men were on her. Not knowing which way to turn she ducked to the ground and rolled away from the men's feet as they leapt at each other, snarling like giant cats with their claws out, clashing together above her head, grappling and punching, wrestling each other to the ground. Sarah had never found herself in such a frightening and bizarre predicament where two men, one dead and one conceivably alive, were fighting solely over her. It was too weird to comprehend or analyse. All she could do was watch, but at the same time she was wildly distracted by a severe burning sensation in the centre of her back. Attempting to soothe the hurt she rubbed at it, but the source of the pain eluded her questing fingers.

Meanwhile, Archie was using his powerful legs to throw Joseph away from him in an Action Man style flick. As Joseph tumbled through the air to land in a motionless heap a short distance away, Archie leapt up and dashed to Sarah, seizing her hand to pull her to her feet beside the tumbling waters of the tributary. "You okay?" he asked, blood trickling from his nose.

"I'm fine," Sarah lied, "what about you?" The pain was still throbbing in the middle of her back as though the bones in her shoulder blades were going to break through her skin at any moment. Forcing herself to ignore the hurt, she began automatically to dab at Archie's bloody nose, using the long sleeve of her dress.

"Grand," Archie winked, dropping his guard for a split second. "That guy's a nutter and a half. How the hell did he shake off that giant snake, is what I want to know." Suddenly his eyes focused on Sarah's back and his face transformed from staring at her with a look of concern to one of astonishment, his lips curving in a wide smirk.

"What?" Sarah asked, desperate to look behind her.

"This place never ceases to amaze me. Are they what I think they are?"

"Look out, Arch, here he comes again!" Sarah screamed.

She was too late. Joseph had already dived towards them. In the blink of an eye he had grabbed her by the waist and was throwing himself and Sarah into the river. As they were swept away on the dangerously fast flowing water, she glimpsed Archie standing gobsmacked and alone on the riverbank.

And then everything went black.

CHAPTER TWENTY THREE

AUGUST 1685
BITTER TEARS OVER LOST ACTION

The light had faded and the sky was turning purple, waiting for the moon to emerge. It was the evening of her wedding day, but now Sarah wore very different attire. Back in the mourning dress and cloak she had worn in her abortive attempt to escape with Archie, she stood facing out at the cornfields where they had last met. Joseph, their families and friends, probably relieved that the marriage had been accomplished, despite her obvious unwillingness, had been celebrating all afternoon. They were all too drunk to notice when she slipped away to change out of her wedding dress then made her way out to the fields.

Her thoughts were turbulent, but she had come here, not to say goodbye to Archie, for that she could never do, but to say goodbye to her friend, Old Nick, a man who had been more of a father to her then her own father had ever been.

"I took your ashes from the fire," Sarah whispered. "I've left my husband at Belmont with my parents. They are no doubt still congratulating one another on their triumphant day and drinking themselves insensible – except Mother, who's probably gone to bed already. I've been so used to sneaking out, but now I've no one to sneak out to. Oh Nick, how I wish we could spend just one more night talking the way we used to, with you treating me like any other person and offering me your homemade mead." She drew in a deep breath, reminiscing. "For a brief time I was able to forget I was Lord Belmont's daughter. Now I have to be Lady Jackson and go away to Great Finborough. It is so remote and I'll know nobody. I feel so alone, Nick."

Sarah took the pouch of ashes out of her dress pocket and held it close to her chest. "Enough about me," she sobbed, tears tracing the tracks on her cheeks of those she had shed earlier. "I've come here because they burnt your cottage down and I didn't know where else to go. You were more a part of nature than any person I've ever met, so here is best I think, out in the fields you once tended. I hope it is acceptable?"

"I'm sure he would find it most fitting, Lady Sarah. He was a pagan after all," said a soft voice.

Sarah gasped. She had not heard the woman come to stand beside her, also draped in a black mourning cloak. A white face peered at her from beneath the velvet hood and Sarah's jaw dropped open. "M-m-my Lady Arley!" Sarah stuttered, dumbfounded.

"Constance is my name, Sarah, please use it," the old lady smiled gently, fine lines creasing around her small, warm eyes.

"Constance," Sarah repeated tentatively, "why are you ...?"

"Here? The same reason as you, my dear; to say goodbye to an old friend." She retrieved an almost identical pouch from her cloak pocket, "Old Nick had many admirers who shared his mead. However, no one back at the Hall or the Manor must know I was here tonight, please do not mention it to a soul."

"Of course I won't, but does not even your husband know? My Father would not approve," Sarah said with a grimace.

"Nobody knows, Sarah, especially not my husband!" The old lady's green eyes flashed in the dying rays of the setting sun. "It has been mine and Nicholas's secret for many years."

"Then why didn't you do something to stop what happened to him," Sarah burst out. "You have more power than anyone ..."

"Alas, I had travelled to London Town on that fateful day. Had I known what was to happen, of course I would have tried. Yet I think there would have been nothing I could have done. Once those men get the bit between their teeth ..." she shook her head, her eyes closing for a moment, before fluttering open to stare deep into Sarah's. "I'm so sorry my dear. I feel his loss too." She laid a gentle hand on Sarah's shoulder.

Other than trivial small talk, Sarah had never really spoken with Constance in the past and yet this elderly lady, a countess in her own right and revered wife of Lord Arley, who happened to be her father's oldest friend, seemed now to invite her confidence. "Where has our friend gone, Constance?" Sarah asked shakily, her bottom lip quivering again, as she sucked in a sharp breath in an attempt to stifle her emotion. It was a question she had never dared voice before, though was one she had often thought about, but ordered from the pulpit to accept its answer as gospel, she had been forced to keep her blasphemous thoughts to herself.

"I believe he has gone to a silent land, my dear. He was a good man and I cannot believe he must burn for eternity, whatever the priests tell us. What you believe, I suppose, is up to you. Come, let us say goodbye."

Together they untied and opened their small purses and offered the ashes to the wind. The breeze took them greedily and pulled the dust from the bags, twisting and coiling Old Nick's remains up into the air and out over the cornfield.

"Do you want to say a few words, Sarah?" Constance bowed her head.

"Yes ... I do," Sarah replied, looking up at the sky, awed by the display of colour and the small cloud of ash that flew up to meet it. "Dear Old Nick, I fear the luxury of mourning publicly is not mine, I must do it hushed and in hiding. You will never have a burial site, nor a gravestone inscribed with your name on it. But I do not need a memorial to remember you, for you are in here," Sarah tapped the side of her head, "in my mind, for you are my conscience, always reminding me to follow my heart. Like dust flying silent into the sky, you have gone to the silent land of which Constance speaks." Sarah paused for a moment, gathering her thoughts whilst she looked out over the darkening cornfield. "The sun has set on us here for another day and on you, Old Nick, for another life. You were a good man, a strong and true friend. I will continue to talk to you in my thoughts, just as once we talked in secret. I truly believe you will hear me. Why should you be out of my mind, just because you are out of my sight?" Sarah closed her eyes, unsure of how the Countess would react to her eulogy's end. "Do we really negotiate our death before we are born like you always told me? Or does God have a hand in this somewhere? Your death was no accident and it most certainly was not a natural passing. I do not believe any god would be so merciless as to see this happen. No, your terrible death was at the hand of another man. I beg you - I implore you - to wait for me in your silent land, so that together we can somehow put right this wicked wrong. Keep a vigil, dear friend. I will come, you have my word. Amen."

"And I will help her," Constance echoed. "Amen."

Sarah smiled under her cape. "Thank you," she said turning to face the old lady. "I must go back to the Hall. Do you return to Arley Manor?"

"Not yet. Come with me, my dear. I believe that Nancy has stock of some of Old Nick's mead and is waiting for us with a few other people from the village who wish to mark our old friend's passing."

"Nancy? The thatcher's daughter? You know her?" Sarah was amazed. Her opinion of Lady Arley had transformed dramatically in the past fifteen minutes and it seemed it was about to change further as she allowed Constance to take her arm and walk her down into the Nookin.

"I do, she's the only person I know who always has a stock of nightshade when everyone else has run out. Even the vicar finds it hard to get hold of it and if you've been into his kitchen of late you would think he had every herb known to man. Venice Turpentine and fern roots by the bucket load," she grinned, raising her eyebrows. "I think he fancies himself as an apothecary!"

It was a very short walk and Sarah could not quite believe the number of torches that lit their way to the thatcher's cottage. She recognised faces from the villages all around as well as those she had known from childhood, for nearly everyone was there. They stood in silence, lining the path with a flame, every face weary and sombre with grief. It was plain to Sarah that Old Nick's death had devastated all these people who had known and depended on him to lighten their hard lives in his unorthodox way. They too needed to say goodbye. As Constance had gently reminded her, she was not the only admirer of that sweet old man.

When they reached the cottage, Nancy and her father were at the front door to greet them. Whilst they were making hushed pleasantries, a figure adorned in a brown hempen cloak slipped in through the crowd. He stood before them and removed his hood. Sarah knew him immediately.

"Reverend Nevett!"

"Miss Sarah, please, I must speak with you." Everyone fell silent and turned to look at him.

"Alone if you please," begged the vicar, his eyes were lined with dark rings, tired, as though he had not slept in days.

"Reverend Nevett," Constance piped in firmly, "whatever you have to say to Miss Sarah you must say in front of everyone here present. For I am sure they too would like an explanation for your actions."

Sarah looked from one to the other, straightened her shoulders, raised her eyebrows and reiterated what the Countess had said. "Indeed, My Lady, I too think that every villager here deserves the right to know why you, Reverend Nevett, allowed this assassination of the oldest and most truthful member of your parish to take place."

"I am so sorry, Your Ladyship, please forgive me." Fumbling with his dirt-encrusted hands, the vicar looked Sarah straight in the eye, his agony evident. "I was frightened. All of you here know what those brutal men would have done to me had I not sanctioned ..." he faltered, tears coursing down his cheeks.

"We can't let them get away with this, My Lady," Sarah interrupted. "Look at him ... he's a wreck, forced to sanction a blatant murder in the name of God!" Sarah blurted out. "This is ridiculous, my world has gone mad!"

"Sarah, please," Constance calmed, then turned to the vicar. "Reverend Nevett, we are all dreadfully saddened and emotional. We understand it was not your fault. I appreciate that you were in a very difficult position and I apologise if I seem unreasonable. In truth, I am sure you had little alternative," Constance soothed, comforting the old man, whilst looking at Sarah. "Reverend Nevett was a dear friend to Old Nick for many years," she explained, "but when your father branded Old Nick a vagabond and traitor, their friendship was forcibly severed. I fear that even our vicar is not safe from the likes of Renshaw and his thugs. The world has changed and not for the good, as I see it. Not that I have taken the time until now to see it from your side," she said, looking at the vicar and then out at all the villagers. "Or any of your sides for that matter. There is no compassion or freedom in your lives, every one of you is forced to be someone you are not. What kind of world is it we live in where we cannot be who we truly are?"

"Do you really think that, My Lady? God help me, I shall be damned from the gates of Heaven for what I have done," the vicar cried.

"You must pray, Reverend Nevett," Sarah whispered, unsmiling.

"I can't," he sobbed, shaking his head. "My dear friend is gone and I was the last being he looked at. I saw his eyes staring at me in agony through the flames, his face blackening as he burned ... and I did nothing."

Sarah bowed her head and swallowed hard. What the vicar had seen would have been tenfold to what she had seen. It was hard to recollect the moment at all; she had been too far away to see Old Nick's face, thank goodness.

Clearing her throat slightly, the Countess offered, "If there is a God surely he understands our prayers and hears our confessions, even when we cannot find the words to say them out loud. Come now, dear Emrys, let your tears come, it is natural and it is good for you to weep, but let them come over Old Nick's finest mead, with us, together. He would want it."

There were murmurs of agreement and they all piled into the thatcher's humble cottage, but before the mead could start to flow, another robed stranger arrived. Everyone inside turned to look. Throwing back her hood, Sarah's governess, Mistress Grey, revealed herself. She stood squarely in the doorway, a scowl strewn across her cruel-looking face.

"Lady Sarah Jackson, home now," she ordered. "You have led me a merry dance looking for you this past hour!"

Flushing with embarrassment, Sarah broke reluctantly away from Constance and hanging her head in shame, squeezed through the crowd to the door. Mistress Grey, ignoring the presence of the Countess, turned to the rest of the gathering and snapped, "You should all be ashamed of yourselves." Then, catching sight of the vicar, she gasped, her eyes widening and a crooked smile curling her narrow lips. "Reverend Nevett! How could you? It will be easier for a bull to pass through the eye of a needle than for a traitorous vicar such as yourself to enter the kingdom of God. Come, Sarah," with spiteful fingers she grasped Sarah's arm, "home to your husband. Lord Jackson is waiting for you and has run out of patience!"

CHAPTER TWENTY FOUR

AUGUST 2003
DO YOU BELIEVE IN FAIRIES?

Sarah had seen Joseph coming and had inhaled a deep breath, prepared for impact and submerging. Luckily, the river was shallow in places and it wasn't long before her feet found the riverbed and she could propel herself to the surface so she could breathe again. Struggling to keep her head above water, she caught a fleeting glimpse of Archie diving in after them.

"Phew, thank goodness for that," Felicity piped up inside Sarah's head. "I was beginning to think he was just going to let you free-flow down to the eighty-foot waterfall."

"Waterfall?" Immediately Sarah began to panic, kicking and fighting against Joseph, who had grabbed her again and was pulling her down, preventing her from holding on to any rock or driftwood that hurtled past them in the flood. The water was cold and the boulders she could feel beneath her feet were slippery and slimy. The channel of water twisted and bubbled into rapids; white water foamed into Sarah's face, filling her mouth and nose. Coughing and spluttering, barely able to breathe or see, she yanked and shoved at her captor's unrelenting hands. Occasionally she thought she saw Archie, a limb maybe, or his head, and knew he was also bobbing up and down in the chaos.

"Sarah, you have to get away from Joseph. The falls are near; you'll be killed!" Felicity screeched again.

Frustrated and unable to reply in word or thought, with water fizzing around her head, Sarah pushed and kicked at the man holding her. Yet even as she struggled her gaze was drawn by the grandeur of the river. Catching the fading beams of sunlight the spray looked like golden rain. Again Joseph pulled her beneath the water. Her feet scraped against the bottom. The riverbed seemed to be vibrating vigorously; it felt like a giant washing machine on spin cycle.

"The seas are alive down there Sarah; stay afloat, you don't want to drop," Felicity cried. "The falls alone will kill you if the sea life doesn't. You don't know what terror lives down there, but I promise it will be far worse than double-headed snakes!"

Coughing and spluttering, Sarah thrust her knees into Joseph's stomach, Felicity's words ringing in her mind. He did not let her go, but forced them back up to the surface, his teeth gritted with effort, his face white and tense. She took a great gulp of air and again tried to push his hands away, but the two of them were being carried along by the riptide and it was useless trying to fight against it. Sarah knew she would have stood more chance of defeating Cyclops singlehandedly and with no sword. They tumbled on towards the rapids, being sucked under at times then re-emerging, succumbing to the water's force until they reached the deep, calm section of the river where the water pooled before it slid inexorably towards the falls. Glancing around, Sarah saw Joseph grinning at her, his expression grotesquely triumphant. She looked over her shoulder scanning the river downstream, but Archie was nowhere to be seen. Twisting back round, she looked upstream to where the current was dragging them. Only yards ahead huge rapids broiled and frothed where giant boulders bubbled up out of the water. Sarah had never seen or heard anything like it before: monster torrents roared, frolicked and splashed, sending spray high above the river to create a thick, opaque mist of water vapour shot through with rainbows.

"It's a waterfall ..." Sarah choked, her gaze flitting back to Joseph. "It's a WATERFALL you idiot. Let go of me. We have to get out of here!"

As she screamed at him, a fist came pummelling out of the water and in an abrupt, terrifyingly swift upper cut, struck Joseph's jaw with a crack. His teeth crunched together as his head was jolted backwards, his tight grip on Sarah's waist loosened and at last he let her go.

"Archie!" Sarah gasped, struggling against the river that was dragging her forcefully towards the falls.

Again she felt hands seizing her, but this time they were Archie's. He was pushing her slightly upstream and in the direction of the nearest bank. Sarah kicked and heaved, but the current was too strong, they were still travelling backwards. Her feet searched frantically for the riverbed, a boulder, something, anything to grip on to, or push off from, but her feet found nothing. Relentlessly they were drawn to where the water thundered over the rocky lip of the waterfall.

"It's no use, Archie, we're going over!" Sarah screamed, spying Joseph also battling with the current, even closer to the edge than they were. "This is the end!"

"No, hold on ... Felicity, look at me," Archie shouted.

"Don't call me that, I'm Sarah!"

"No you're not, don't you see, with every day you have been here you've become more and more like Fee," Archie gasped, swallowing a huge gulp of water, spitting half of it out down his nose. He hauled and yanked at Sarah's arm, trying desperately to keep her head above water and pull her away from the torrents. "You will become Fee again the longer you're here. She's your spirit, your inner self, your only hope."

He was shouting above the noise of the falls, but Sarah could not make out his words. "I can't hear you," she cried, "what are you saying?"

"Sarah, you have WINGS," Archie yelled.

"What?"

"Wings, you know ... like a bird or a butterfly," Archie shouted, his words snatched away by the thunder of cascading water, but the word 'wings' found Sarah's ears. It was as though a switch had been flicked on inside her. Immediately the weird and sometimes extremely painful burning sensation she had felt between her shoulder blades and tried in vain to reach and rub began to make sense. She could feel something pulling on her back, dragging in the water.

"Wings? I have wings?" Sarah screeched, attempting to twist her neck to look round at her back, but seeing nothing except Joseph clambering around on a wet boulder and clinging on for dear life, water gushing over the top of him.

"Yes, fragile ones at that, I'm not sure how useful they are when they're wet," Archie shouted with a sly grin, water streaming down his face. Gradually he yielded to the deluge, relaxing slightly, allowing them to be dragged like debris towards the rapids. Horrified, Sarah screamed, grabbing hold of Archie's shoulder.

"What are you doing?" she wailed.

"Just let yourself go; we're going over."

"Are you insane? We'll be killed!"

"Well, I'm already dead, remember. For you, death is seconds away unless you let that fairy inside you fly," Archie said calmly. "Do you want to live? To go home and see your family again; live out your life on Earth as Sarah Walker? It is not your time to die, but you will unless you help yourself."

In that moment, something occurred to Sarah: she was hearing Archie's voice inside her head just as she had heard Lillian and Grace; he was speaking to her telepathically.

Her senses reeling, she wailed, "But I can't, I don't know how."

"You can, if you say you can. Sarah, you're lost between worlds. You can do anything you want to right now," Archie spoke into her mind, as their bodies weaved together and slowly, inexorably, they began to slip over the edge. In the last moments, Sarah caught sight of Joseph staring at them, his mouth hanging open, just as a giant wave knocked him off his rock throwing him backwards. His head hit the side of another boulder and he flopped into the water as though unconscious.

"Do not let go of my hand," Archie said as they toppled over the brink. "You're the star, not me. I'm just a dead man."

Sarah's thoughts were such a mixed up mess, all she could muster was to cling to Archie and scream at the top of her lungs as she, Archie and a short way behind them, Joseph Jackson, toppled over the edge and headed straight down the mighty waterfall.

"FLY," Archie hollered at her.

Déjà vu of her fall from the Phra Pin Klao Bridge devoured Sarah, along with another deadly fall that she couldn't quite remember, yet knew she had experienced. The irrepressible gut-churning sensation of falling swelled inside her once more, her terrified scream ceasing abruptly as her breath was taken from her.

"Fly!" Archie hollered again.

They dropped like stones, way out of control and Sarah, feeling as if she had left her stomach high up where their fall began, couldn't even think, let alone fly. It was like a terrifying nightmare, one where your physical body is trying to shock your dreaming mind into being awake. There was no point in attempting to fight it and yet it was impossible not to at least try to oppose it. Still clinging to one another, twisting and rolling, she and Archie were thrust like dead leaves in a gale-force wind into the force of the waterfall.

"Fly, Sarah, fly," Archie repeated over and over in her head.

"How do I fly?"

"Come on, Sarah, let me out," Felicity screeched. "No matter where you go or what you do, I'll always be with you, I'm part of you. You can't get rid of me. Unless you release me and let me use our wings, I'll die with you and then we will be slaves to the Moon for eternity."

Looking down, past her flailing bare feet, Sarah could see threatening fins and shadows in the fast approaching waters that broiled white beneath the falls. "I can't," she said, feeling helpless and lost, warm tears flooding her cold, wet cheeks. "I don't know how."

"I'm trying to help. Please don't live your entire life within the limitations of your imagination never expanding your awareness of what's possible. I am here ... I am a possibility. Do you know how frustrating it is to sit in the back seat and let you do all the driving? Do something extraordinary: just for once believe in yourself."

"Fly Sarah, for the love of God please fly," Archie continued to chant.

Sarah could feel her heart pounding somewhere in her throat.

"You're still ignoring me," Felicity cried. "You MUST believe in me!"

"Sarah, Felicity, please fly," Archie hollered into her head, his voice now wavering with panic, just as it had when they were children and he thought she was badly hurt, falling out of a tree, or another time that she couldn't quite remember, when she had fallen out of the sky and he thought she was dead. It was like a kaleidoscope of splintered images all mixed up in her head, but the sound of her twin-cousin's anxious cry released something inside Sarah: love for him flickered up through her body from the tips of her toes to the top of her head until it consumed her. She seemed to hear Anian's voice saying 'Love is the answer', and in that moment, letting go of all doubt and using pure imagination, she unfurled her wings.

"Help me Felicity. Help me to fly!" she whispered. "I believe in you, Fee, I believe in angels. Be my angel, help me to live again."

The set of wings that spread out behind her were each as large as she was, transparent as gossamer with veins running through them as in a leaf. Like a giant white butterfly, as though she were stretching forgotten limbs after a long sleep, Sarah found her wings. She felt their strength and beat them hard, holding tight to Archie as their fall began to slow. Then she lifted them both out of the water and they were flying.

"Ah ha ... you DID it!" Archie's elated scream sounded over the roaring waterfall as they hovered only metres above it, both grinning like Cheshire cats.

Looking down, Sarah's grin faded, as in the deepening shadows she saw Joseph, unconscious to his fate, plummeting to his death. She could see sharks, Great White and Tiger, rising up out of the depths and leaping, like trout in springtime, fighting over their dinner. Retreating higher, away from the danger of the snapping jaws that lay in wait just below the surface, Sarah quickly shut her eyes not wanting to see the gory end to a man she had really only just met, whatever they had been to each other in an earlier life. Then a wave of relief washed over her, for it was he who had tried to kidnap her. He had been the one to push her over the edge and force her into Transit. He had shoved her into the river without a care for her wellbeing. He had bargained with the Moon. Now that Joseph was gone, surely her journey home would be easier? "Okay, so where now?" she asked Archie.

"To the beach. Follow the cliffs round," he pointed with his free hand. "It should be there, inside the cove. Do you remember the last time we did this?"

Sarah frowned, "No!"

"Well I do," said a small voice inside her head, and Archie laughed.

The sun had almost set and in the afterglow it was hard to see anything clearly. Sarah paused for a moment, her wings beating as though treading water in the air. Then, concentrating hard on where Archie was pointing and where she wanted to go, she propelled them around the steep, overhanging cliffs and down onto a paradise beach of glowing white sand and indigo seas, completely cut off by the sheer rock face that reared eighty-foot high behind it.

"There, look!" Sarah cried as they landed with a bump on the warm sand. Scrambling to her feet, she grabbed

Archie's hand, pulling him up the beach. "Is that the tree?"

"Where?" Archie scanned the bay.

"Right there in the middle of the beach. It's huge; you'd have to be blind to miss it," Sarah exclaimed, looking quizzically at Archie, as she continued to drag him towards it.

"I was here before and never saw a tree. Maybe I'm not meant to see it?" Archie shrugged. Point me in the right direction," he cried. She did so and he began to run, almost carrying Sarah with him, flicking sand out behind him, his bare feet leaving footprints on the wet beach.

They were under the tree in seconds, a giant apple tree, though not like any that Sarah had even seen before. It reminded her of the yew in St Digain's churchyard and looked just as old, its trunk gnarled and covered in lichen, with thick branches that spread up and out and foliage thick enough to keep anyone hidden. "We're here, it's just in front of us," Sarah said, looking up nervously, but if Archie couldn't see it then surely no one else could?

"Climb, quickly," Archie ordered. "Fly up that tree and find the apple. The sun has gone and the Moon will be rising any minute now, but she won't see you; you'll be invisible in the branches."

"What about you?" Sarah whimpered, as fluttering her wings she flew into the security of the tree, landing gently on a bough a quarter of the way up.

"What use am I to her? She wants you, Sarah. How many times do I have to tell you? I am dead, both to your world and this transitional world. I moved on. I'm not supposed to be here," he called up to her. "I have to go back."

"You're not dead to me ... you'll never be dead to me," Sarah cried. "Please, I don't want to be alone up here." She gazed down at Archie, her lapis lazuli pendant swinging freely away from her neck. He was staring upwards, frowning, looking all around as though searching for her. "I'm just here," she shouted, "can't you see me at all?"

"No, you're gone. Only those who are alive can see the tree and you while you are in its branches. I can't come up, Sarah, even if I wanted to, I'm not allowed. This is the Tree of Life; it's not for the dead."

"Archie, I'm scared. I don't know if I want to go back without you ... please. I'm not ready," Sarah cried, glancing about the branches. "If I stay, I will die and then I can come with you."

"No, Sarah. It is not your time. You would be a lost soul and the Moon would take you, as she did when you ended your life before, hundreds of years ago. It's where all your troubles started. Live out your present lifespan; be happy. One day, when your time comes, you will cross-over and then we will see each other again. "Now find and eat that apple!"

A few metres above her Sarah could see a large apple hanging on a flimsy branch. It was already beginning to go brown and looked as though it might fall at any moment, it would be awkward to get her hands around it without knocking it off its twig. No sooner had she seen the apple, than her head began to spin. Terrified that the end was near, she began to retreat back down the tree towards Archie, when suddenly something happened that stopped her: the thread stringing her lapis pendant broke. The blue stone fell to the ground, landing with a thud at Archie's feet.

"What's ...?" Archie picked it up, glancing vacantly towards her, like a blind man not sure where to look.

"It's my lapis lazuli," Sarah clutched at her neck and felt the thread that still hung broken around her throat. "Lillian gave it to me. She said the thread would break when I no longer needed the crystal's protection," she explained, remembering.

"You mustn't come back down then, Sarah, this is it now. Without this stone around your throat your sanity is in jeopardy. The Moon and her ravens won't be far behind; look, the light is nearly gone. She will be able to scramble your memory in seconds."

"Surely now is the time I need it most then," Sarah panicked, gazing up through the branches to catch a glimpse of the darkening sky, petrified that if she so much as breathed she would be exposed. Every hair on her body was erect with fear. "Will she be able to see me?"

"No, you're within the branches of the Tree of Life. The Moon can't touch you while you're up there," Archie soothed. "But unless you hurry up and eat that apple, the tree will disappear and you will be left stranded on the beach. Then you really will be in jeopardy." He stared out at the horizon, "The Moon is neither dead nor alive; she has no soul as such, she's incapable of any emotion beyond anger. Her intent is to twist and wipe out treasured memories and replace them with fear and shame. She is the mind's poison; she can infect and demoralise anything living. But when it comes to you, Fee, her desire roots far deeper, it stems from a deadly hatred that originated centuries ago."

"Don't call me that, Arch ... please, I'm Sarah, your cousin. Felicity is only a part of who I am – or who I was."

"It is what you asked me to call you a long, long time ago," he said gently. "When we tried to run ... we were going to change our names. You said you wanted to be Felicity."

"Well I don't want it any more. And anyway, what do you mean by deadly hatred? Why does the Moon hate me so?"

Before he could reply, a screech turned their attention to the top of the eighty-foot cliffs behind them, where a black figure had appeared, silhouetted against the sky.

"Get the apple, Sarah!" Archie shouted.

Unthinking, she leapt into the branches above her where the apple dangled. The tree held firm as she scrambled up the thinnest part of it and grasped the fruit. It fell into her hand and clutching it, she scurried back down the trunk to where she felt safer and more protected by the tree's breadth.

"Have you got it?" Archie asked.

"Yes, I'm back close to the main trunk again," Sarah called back.

"Just stay there then. Don't move," Archie ordered, holding out his hand to where he thought she was, in a clear stop signal."

"I won't."

He nodded and turned away to stare up at the image looming on the rock face. "I don't know what she's going to do, but remember one thing for me, Sarah, no matter what happens," Archie said, and she found that he was speaking to her telepathically again, his voice gentle, yet sounding urgent in her head.

"Will it help if I do?" she cried, hugging the tree trunk.

"I think so."

"What is it?" Sarah asked, her gaze fixed on the black figure far above the beach.

"Even when it seems the Sun has gone out and all around you is black and empty, the Sun is always with you, remember that. You may not always know him, but be assured he is always with you, even at night, because if he wasn't, we would never be able to see the Moon. She is merely a reflector of his light. She has no light of her own. Like a thief she takes everything she has from others; she's not only a thief, she's a coward too. She only threatens under the cover of darkness when she knows it's safe for her to do so. Just try to remember that the Sun will help you if he can, like he helped me."

"But he's gone down now," Sarah whispered sadly, not understanding how the Sun could help when she could no longer see him. She could, however, see swarms of great black ravens hovering above the figure at the top of the cliff. "What about you?" she cried in panic, as the witch-like figure flew down to the beach, its cloak flying out behind it like ragged wings. As it reached the sand at the foot of the cliffs, three great, slavering dogs materialised beside it.

Sarah screamed. "Archie, oh, Arch, be careful!"

"I've told you, she can't do anything to me, I am dead. I am a spirit; not really here at all. She's not interested in me. You were one of her stars and as far as she's concerned, you belong to her."

Transmuted as Chanthira, the Moon, her ravens and her dogs diving swiftly on their prey like giant phantom bats, swept past Archie and swooped in on the tree, closing the gap at speed.

Sarah screamed again, as she saw Archie dive beneath the shelter of a great orange-coloured rock at the foot of the cliffs, but she saw that he was watching Chanthira and her creatures and his voice sounded in her head, calming her.

"It astounds me to see the Moon fully incarnate for the first time. When I journeyed through Transit I battled with her in my head and she almost drove me mad. She made me into a ghost, forced to witness my own wake. I thought I was lost and were it not for Kriss I might have been, yet in all those tribulations I never had the misfortune of actually dealing with her in person. Don't worry, Sarah. She is ignoring me, her attention is solely on the tree that neither she nor I can see, but she senses that you are there. You have to let me go, Sarah. Say goodbye and eat that apple." His voice faded to be replaced by another; a harsh screeching croak that tore into Sarah's ears.

"You may have the apple, Missy, but you need to bathe in the Transitional Sea to regain new life," screeched Chanthira angrily, peering sightlessly into the tree, her withered eyes searching for its branches, her ravens hovering, plunging and swooping in on Sarah from every angle and yet unable to penetrate the foliage they could neither see nor feel.

"I may not be able to see you now, Missy, but I have all the time in the world and no agenda at all. Take your time, for as a mortal you cannot live for long on a rotten apple alone. Eventually you must come down from that tree and then you will be mine again."

Her three, bull-sized hounds howled up at Sarah from beside their mistress, streams of foaming, drool hanging from their beards, their tongues lolling red. Chanthira stretched out her fingers, extending inch-long fingernails, like claws and feeling in front of her for the tree, but her hands passed straight through it, as though it were a ghost tree or a hologram. Her hooked nose twitched to smell the air; her black and grey robes flying wildly in the wind, her power illuminating around her in an aura that gleamed whitish-grey, as the night drew in.

The incarnation of the Moon terrified Sarah. Chanthira was everything that embodied her childhood nightmares of a wicked witch. In appearance, she was much like the three hags in the black hole, though bigger, more solid, more horrifying. Sarah wondered why the Moon favoured the look of a crone when she had the power to be anything she chose.

"Just because I can't see doesn't mean I can't hear your thoughts, Sarah," hissed Chanthira. "I choose to be a crone for you because it is what frightened you most as a child. You used to see my face pressed to your bedroom window in your nightmares, didn't you? And even when you tried to scream and wake yourself up, there was no escaping my face."

Sarah gasped. As a child she had indeed had a recurring nightmare of a witch at her bedroom window. It used to come in the depths of the night when the rest of her family were so deep in slumber it had been almost impossible to rouse them. She would scream for her parents and sometimes they would come and calm her, saying it was just a vivid dream, but Sarah had always believed it was so much more than that; the dreams were so real and always the same. Often when she woke, Sarah had been unable to dispel the tangible feeling of evil that surrounded her. She had known she was awake and lying in her bed, yet had felt paralysed, unable to breathe, her chest heavy as though something was pressing down on it trying to suffocate her. Next would come the whispering voices and then dark shadows swooping in around her. Finally the face would appear at the window.

Now, staring down at Chanthira, Sarah recognised the face of her nightmares and shuddered, terrified.

"Don't let her bully you," Felicity whispered in her head. "She's messing with your mind. You've taken on the Fates and won, you can do this. She's playing mind tricks on you. You are not a frightened child anymore, Sarah, you're a grown woman. You must fight her, not physically but mentally. Don't let her in, don't reminisce, if you do she has the power to drag you back to that memory and once she does that you're done for. She has the power to make you remain in that memory as a terrified child for all eternity. What's happening now is not a dream, nor is it a game. This is the moment when the colour of your world has the potential to change from dark back to light, from death to life, from anger to acceptance. Fight her!"

"How am I supposed to do that from up here? Grace told me I had to get to the sea, but she didn't tell me how. Can I fly, Fee?"

"The Moon can fly faster! You have to eat that apple first and it's rotting as we speak."

"I'm not leaving here without saying goodbye to Archie," Sarah said sharply.

"I can hear you two talking you know," screeched Chanthira. "Ahh ... Archie Fletcher," she snarled. "Is he still hanging around like a bad smell?"

Sarah gasped, realising she had stupidly given away Archie's presence. Suddenly the atmosphere changed and a bitter chill filled the air, catching in her chest and making her cough. She knew the Moon was attempting to force her out of the branches. Whatever she'd said, Chanthira would not have the patience to sit and wait, but would use all the black magic tricks she had up her sleeve. Sarah, consumed by fear, afraid that she might be sick, waited for the next onslaught.

The ground began to tremble and high above the beach the cliff face quivered. Great rocks broke away, crashing down with almighty thuds, to form miniature craters in the sand; even the mystical tree shuddered. Sarah screamed, squeezing her eyes tight shut. Undulations pulsed up through the ground like an earthquake and around the tree the ravens cawed, the dogs howled and Chanthira cackled with unholy glee. Not daring to open her eyes, Sarah hugged the trunk of the 'Tree of Life' and prayed.

"Oh God please keep me safe, please take me home. I just want to go home," she whispered under her breath.

"Call the dogs off!" boomed a familiar voice.

Sarah's eyes flew open and she gasped at what she saw. A man, taller than the thirty-foot tree itself, stood beside it. He was HUGE: his fingers the size of cucumbers, arms the size of tree branches and a staff longer than three pole-vaults put together. He was even bigger than Cyclops, but it was not Anian's shambling friend who had made her the sword, it was the man who had saved her from the black hole and the Fates: her St Christopher transmuted as a giant. His red cape blowing out behind him in the wind, he stood hands on hips, confronting the Moon and her hounds from Hell. Slowly the rumbling began to lessen, the ground stopped shaking and the bitter chill in the air seemed to ease.

"He's left the Fates," Sarah's mind pounded, "but he's not the same, he's so much bigger and more powerful."

"His mission is to protect you, Sarah, whatever it takes. You have reached your target and now he must ensure that you return home safely," Felicity explained. "He is dedicated to helping travellers, it's what he does."

Wide-eyed, Sarah listened to the Moon shrieking at the saint, "You don't frighten me, Christopher; you never have done. You were always an indecisive boy, never knowing whose side you were on. First you're on mine ... then you're on theirs. Where does your alliance really lie?"

Kriss raised his staff high above his head menacingly then, with full intent, he struck Chanthira sideways throwing her violently towards the cliffs. She turned in mid-air and flew like lightning back to him, her expression impassive, almost bored. "Do you think me a fool, Christopher?" she said scornfully. "You cannot trick me as you did the likes of Renshaw. You may have got Archie Fletcher safely over the bridge, but you can have him and welcome. It is Felicity I want and you'll never have her. She's mine and you know it. She has always been mine, ever since she tried to bargain with God and took her own life to follow her lover. She will always be one of my stars and there's nothing you can do about it. I merely take back what is rightfully mine. She escaped me the last time through her trickery, she won't do that again!"

"Archie and Felicity are soulmates; they belong together," Kriss said, standing over the Moon, his massive feet astride in a standoff stance. "Let them be. The game is over now."

Chanthira sighed, "Why do you always let me down, Christopher? I wanted so much to be proud of you." She shook her head, "Surely sending Sarah home to Earth will take them further apart? At least here in Transit there is only the bridge between them. They can wave to each other," she cackled.

"Better a world apart for a lifetime, than a bridge apart for eternity," Kriss retorted.

Chanthira moved out from between his legs and began to swell, growing bigger and bigger until she matched the giant's size. Then she stood nose to nose with her rival. "You are such a disappointment in comparison to my girls, you know," she hissed, white spittle flying from her lips.

Kriss did not react; he stood firm, his face devoid of emotion, which seemed to rile Chanthira all the more. Clinging to the trunk, Sarah watched as the Moon continued to inflate herself, like a swelling balloon, until she was twice Kriss's size, towering over him, dwarfing the 'Tree of Life' and the cliffs that edged the beach.

"Call yourself a giant? You think you are so clever. You know nothing, you foolish boy! You are of even less use to me than your three sisters."

"How dare you?" Kriss's voice rumbled like thunder. "I hate you for hiding those women away. They are not girls anymore that you hide in that black hole where the sun will never shine, have you not seen them of late? They are withered and ancient, white and senile. You cannot compare me to them. You have brainwashed them into controlling all life, strangling all freewill. Why should I care about being a disappointment to you? You are nothing to me but a sick crone, who chooses to mess with people's minds. You are a destroyer of confidence, creativity and freedom. For centuries you've been happily destroying Sarah's spirit with the most lethal form of emotional abuse. Well now it has to stop." Kriss moved his great hand to point in the direction of the tree, making Sarah wonder if in fact he alone could see it and therefore her.

"You cannot tell Felicity who to love and who not to love," he boomed, any more than you can tell me whose side I am on. We both know the answer to that question anyway. I know who I am and exactly where I came from and I owe absolutely no attachment or allegiance to you. Your mind tricks don't work on me anymore old woman. You can do nothing but untwist already twisted memories and for that I would be grateful," Kriss roared.

As he was speaking his body enlarged to equal Chanthira's in size, his face was scarlet with rage, his eyes bulging as he stared hard at the woman in front of him.

"Have you quite finished young man?" Chanthira murmured, her voice hushed and all the more sinister.

"No, I have not," Kriss yelled. "You were there every step of the way, guiding Sarah down that aisle to Joseph Jackson, forcing her together with a man who was nothing but cruel and abusive to her. Why?"

"Now, now, Christopher, I don't think we ..." Chanthira started to say.

"Oh but I think we do," Kriss continued. "You persuaded Sarah Belmont's father that Joseph Jackson was a good match. You took to destroying the girl's happiness because in one of your many incarnations your own life was so pitiful and you were loathed by everyone who knew you. You could not bear to see someone as young and beautiful as Sarah enjoying the love of a handsome young man. You needed to inflict your humiliation on someone else and who better than the daughter of the man who admitted you to the House of Correction?"

Hearing these words, Sarah was so surprised that she almost fell out of the tree. The images of her dreams flew through her mind and she saw behind Chanthira's swollen features the face of another. "Mistress Grey," she whispered to herself her eyes widening. "She was you!"

The Moon swung round and looked down, her eyes scanning the beach. "I can still hear your thoughts Sarah, even if I cannot see you," she hissed. "Yes, it was me. I can travel across the dimensions of time. I can be anything I want to be: a Thai barwoman, a governess, a witch at your window or the big cheese in the sky; take your pick. But know this ... I watch over you night and day, no matter what world you live in, there is no place for you to hide. I am the keeper of your emotions and your mind."

"Oh, give it a rest woman!" Kriss hollered. "Sarah, when you get home ..."

"She's not going anywhere," screeched the Moon.

Drowning out Chanthira's angry wail and her howling dogs, which had joined in the chorus, way below their titanic mistress, Kriss continued, "Ensure that when you look at the Moon, you understand that it is not an evil witch relentlessly searching time and space for you, it is but a giant rock and that is all. A dead, lifeless gigantic rock that steals the Sun's light and controls nothing but the tides!" Kriss stared hard at Chanthira, his eyes unblinking. "As Mistress Grey you were admitted to the House of Correction for theft and prostitution, but what they never managed to convict you of was murder," he said. "But a murderer you were and are!"

"Why must you try my patience, Christopher?" wailed the Moon. "You know what I could do to you. I gave you life and I can just as easily take it away. I believe my serpent has not quite finished playing yet. You thought that fool Joseph had managed to get rid of it didn't you," Chanthira shouted. "No chance ... in fact it was I who called it off. I wanted to see if the fairy could still fly," she jeered, looking roughly in the direction of the tree. "Seems it still can," she snapped. Then her voice changed, becoming soft and seductive. A high-pitched ringing seemed to pierce Sarah's ears, as Chanthira's voice ricocheted inside her head. "You know, Sarah, every second you linger here the closer you are to coming home with me, back into the sky where you belong. You've unfurled your wings, practically transformed back into Felicity. You do know that Felicity is your spirit-self? She loves being here in Transit, you know. Possibly not being with me, but the rest of it is like a blissful, lucid dream to her, a dream in which she has all control and can fly."

The Moon's insidious whisper grew softer and softer and Sarah felt herself growing weaker and weaker. "It's like a dream in which you know you're dreaming," the words continued. "A conscious dream, where for Felicity anything is possible, even reuniting with her lost love - for didn't you know Sarah? Archie Fletcher was Felicity's lover. She wants to stay here, don't let her fool you. She needs you far more than you need her. She is a very mischievous little star, Sarah, but she is a dead star. She needs you to give her form and shape. She doesn't want you to go back down to Earth again. Think back, Sarah: wasn't it Felicity who convinced you to jump to your death? She got you here. She has more control over your actions than you realise."

"Don't listen to her Sarah, not for a second do I want to stay here. She tries to divide us. She's playing mind tricks again. I am you. Keep hold of your sanity, you can't fight against yourself, you'll go mad. Don't give her power by listening." Felicity's voice shrieked in Sarah's head.

"Keep control of your thoughts, her magic is very powerful."

Raising her arms in the air, her face creased with fury, the Moon cupped her hands to the heavens. A current of high voltage, shot from her fingertips, turning the sky blacker than ink and filling it with electric energy. The ground beneath them, once again, began to tremble, throwing sand into the air around them and from it emerged the shape of the serpent.

Kriss was thrown backwards into the air, his staff flying away from him, as he landed hard on his rear, his size rapidly diminishing. Scrambling around on the beach, trying to wipe the grainy sand from his eyes, he searched for his stick to gain some control.

"You will NOT leave here, Sarah," the Moon wailed, as the dual-headed serpent launched itself at Kriss, swiping his staff even further away from his hand.

Unarmed, Kriss rose to face it; his bravery immense. "Take me instead," he shouted. "Please, I will serve you in her place, just leave them alone. Get rid of the serpent and have me back instead."

"NO!" Archie screamed, stepping forward from the shadows of the cliff. "Kriss, what are you saying? You can't!"

Sarah gasped at the sight and sound of Archie's panic and letting go of the tree trunk, she scurried down a branch or two, ready to come to his aid.

Chanthira whirled round at Archie and grinned, baring nothing but gums and brown lumps for teeth, aside from her canines, which were long and sharp like those of the rabid dogs that sprang up snarling at her feet. She hissed wildly at Archie, as though he were vermin to be exterminated and extended her fingertips in his direction.

"Mother, don't!" Kriss yelled. "Leave him be, he's no use to you, he's dead. If you try to harm him Transit will destabilise ... you cannot mean to do this ..."

"Mother?" Sarah whispered, aghast.

Kriss shot a look at Archie and another in the direction of the tree, "I fear so, but I don't have time to explain," he said, returning his gaze to the hag in front of him. "But let me just say that I chose to live the life of a protector, helping those who come to the river to cross in safety. There's nothing worse than for a good soul to be roaming lost and searching for meaning." Kriss raised his eyebrows, pleading for their understanding. "Just like I chose to abandon my mother when I realised who and what she was. Through my own determination to do well and spread hope, I became an honourable man, a saint no less. I made it my mission to counteract this corrupt woman's wickedness. But I will bow to you, Mother ... I will go with you if you will leave my friends alone."

The serpent's coils surrounded the Moon and her hounds stood firm, leaning against her legs, protecting her. The venomous snakeheads both faced Kriss, forked tongues slithering out intermittently under the full command of its mistress as she sneered at her son.

"You say that as though we should feel sorry for you, Christopher. Well I don't. You are a traitor."

"I am no traitor," Kriss cried.

"You betrayed me, your own mother!"

"It is no betrayal to deny evil. I will do everything in my power to protect Sarah's life, I will not let her down and if that means taking her place as your slave then so be it. I cannot erase your crimes, Mother, but I can choose to forgive all that you have done."

"But I don't want you Christopher, I never did. I don't like boys. You made it so easy for me to dump you when you betrayed me, but you make it incredibly difficult for me to control my firmament every time you loiter in Transit. I never want to see you again. I wish I had never set eyes on you!"

Watching Kriss through the branches Sarah saw his face crumple and tears spring to his eyes, as though this giant of a man had been reduced to a small boy, yearning for the love of his mother and never receiving it. As she watched, Kriss shrank to a regular-sized man and stood as though defeated, his head bowed.

"Stop it!" he screamed, the hurt harsh in his voice. "I can see right through you. You're a scary, horrible old crone, trying to use your mind tricks on me still. Demoralising me and torturing me the same as you always did." Tears splashed from Kriss's eyes to the ground, puddled and sank, leaving small indentations in the sand. "My actions, what I do helping others, are my only true belongings and blessings and whatever you say, I will forgive you. I will forgive, I will forget and I will go with you. You will pay one day for all you have done, for Karma always catches up with you when you least expect it. But like I said, you will not be taking Sarah with you. Instead you can have me."

"I can't believe you're her son, Kriss," Sarah whispered, still struggling to cling onto the branches. "How can someone so good spring from someone so evil? What happened in all her ancient life to make her this way?" Kriss made no reply, his gaze still fixed intently on the witch that was his mother and it came to Sarah that he was deliberately holding Chanthira's attention to distract her.

Archie was now nearly directly beneath the tree, creeping forward inch by inch. He looked up blindly and beckoned to Sarah. "Quick, climb down while Kriss is keeping her occupied," he said into her mind.

"I can't it's too dangerous," Sarah called softly.

"She's got into your head already; you're in danger up there now. The tree will only hide your physical body, it can't hide your thoughts," Archie whispered.

Still clinging to the rotting apple, Sarah slowly lowered herself down from the tree into Archie's arms, her feet finding the beach. "It's good to see you again," he grinned.

Then everything happened in split seconds. In a wild frenzy Chanthira flew at them, but the hissing serpent, its jaws snapping with venom, entwined her body hampering her movement. Her hounds pounded forward to attack. Sarah screamed, cowering into Archie, the smell of rotten lion flesh filling her nostrils as she buried her head into his hide tunic. At the same moment, Kriss threw himself across the beach and grabbed his staff, tossing it like an enormous spear at the closest dog. It struck the beast and pierced its middle, the force of it flinging the dog's broken body backwards bringing down the one directly behind it. Two down; one still charging.

"Hold on," Archie whispered into Sarah's ear. "Aura bright, propel my yellow light, aura bright, propel my yellow light. Please God keep Sarah safe, please keep her safe," Archie chanted, his head pressed into Sarah's, squeezing her with all his might.

The giant hellhound came at the pair of them, drool frothing from its fangs, its claws exposed ready to rip apart its prey. As it leapt a giant ball of yellow light encircled Archie and Sarah, and she knew instinctively that as long as Archie held strong, inside that bubble they were safe. The dog's claws could not tear it; instead, as it pounced it rebounded off the yellow shield as though it had hit a brick wall. The beast yelped in pain and fell away, its legs broken.

"Now, RUN!" Archie ordered, leading the way. Surrounded by her twin-cousin's yellow aura, her hand clasped firmly in his, Sarah kept her head down and ran. Jumping over the wounded dogs they fled down the beach to the water's edge. The sky was black, thunder rumbled above them and bolts of fork lightning shot to the ground all around them. Gazing out at the sea, Sarah saw thousands upon thousands of ravens swarming above the shoreline like a black cloud.

"What do we do?" she begged, terrified.

"Wait," Archie whispered, pulling her close. "Kriss will help us and my aura, which the Angel of the Rainbow bestowed on me during my transition, will protect us. I haven't used it for a while, but it seems like it's still working," he grinned at her.

Behind them, the Moon had turned her back on the saint and was heading rapidly down the beach, coming closer and closer, the monster serpent still coiled around her body.

"What's going to happen?" Sarah whispered, quaking with fear.

"I don't know," Archie replied.

Then there was an enormous shout and they heard Kriss cry out, "Mother, as a child I wanted your love. Why did you push me away? You may not want me, but I forgive you and you cannot turn your back on my forgiveness. Even the most immoral and warped creature cannot do that. You have to accept forgiveness; it is written."

Chanthira did not turn to look at him, but paused on her way to the ocean where Sarah and Archie huddled closer together. "You are no son of mine," she shouted, her voice dripping with contempt. "Your forgiveness means nothing."

"There is no need for you to say such things," Kriss said. "Your evil intent for misery is more acidic and more toxic than even I believed." As he spoke his voice was growing stronger, his body beginning to swell again.

"Believe it; I will not yield," Chanthira shouted, walking on. "I do NOT accept your forgiveness. I do NOT want you. I turn my back on you and everything you stand for."

"So be it, but like I said, the most immoral and warped creature cannot turn its back on forgiveness, not even you, Mother."

Standing straight, Kriss held his arms apart and raised his hands to the sky, his face intent, his eyes closed as though he were praying to an unseen deity.

With a wild roar, the dual-headed serpent lifted its two heads and hauling its great body from the protective coil encircling Chanthira, whipped round and sank its teeth into her neck. She opened her mouth and screamed; a loud, deafening, screeching scream that made even the sea tremble. Then she began to shrink and as she did, the serpent stretched one of its jaws wide and swallowed her whole in one large gulp. As though its mission had been accomplished, the monstrous creature slithered back into the sand and disappeared from sight as if it had never been.

Sarah and Archie stared at one another then back up the beach at Kriss, not quite believing what had happened or that the immediate danger had gone. In the dim glow of starlight, they watched the saint walk towards them, his red cape billowing around him.

He smiled down at them. "No one, not even she, can refuse to be forgiven. She was swallowed by her own evil. Now you must go Sarah, and quickly. Remember that Chanthira was simply a manifestation. The Moon herself won't be gone long, she will find another form and there are plenty more evil creatures of the air, sea and land that she can manipulate. My forgiveness has weakened her temporarily, but on its own it won't get rid of her completely. I fear it would take much more than that."

Sarah turned quickly to Archie. "I won't leave you here, Arch. I can't," she gasped, the large mouldy apple still clutched in her hand.

"I wish I could come back, but like I told you, I really can't," Archie stared intensely into her eyes. "You have to go right now, time's run out and your soul is passing into the shadow world. Don't waste this life you've been given, Sarah. You must live it with all your being."

Sarah didn't move, her eyes filled with tears as she shook her head.

"Listen," Archie said with force, gripping her shoulders, trying to shake her out of her obstinacy. "I wish I could go home with you, back to Eversley Avenue right now and have everything back the way it used to be. I'd love to see my mum and dad, ride my bike, enjoy another Christmas, rather than living a snippet of a life here and a moment there. But I can't. And besides, Nanny would be more than upset if I didn't go back to her and Granddad! I'd never hear the end of it," he grinned.

"Nanny and Granddad? They are there too?"

He nodded, "Of course, and everyone else we ever loved and lost."

Sarah smiled through her tears, "But I don't want to lose you again," she whispered.

"I won't be lost. Anyway, things we lose frequently have a way of finding us again at some point in time," his grin broadened. "You must go back," he insisted. "You'll find me again, I promise."

"What is my life without you in it? It's been unimaginable," Sarah pleaded, wondering if her experiences in Transit would help her somehow. How would she know if her cousin was safe? After the hideousness that had just occurred, how could he ever be safe? The Moon was not dead. It would be torture never knowing if Archie made it back to the other side. And even if he did, could anything that had happened make his absence in her life easier to swallow? The constant lump in her throat and hole in her heart were still there. Could her knowledge of his spiritual existence really ease her physical pain? Her mind sizzled with questions, each leading onto the next.

Archie hugged her, "So many questions! You can talk to me any time, you know, aloud, or even in your thoughts, I'll hear you as I'm doing now. You may not hear me reply, not always, but, if you listen carefully you never know, you just might. Everything happens for a reason, Sarah. You must know that by now," Archie comforted. "You have to face this fear of living without me. You can do this. Go and live ... and achieve. Pursue every dream you have with passion, until you're content it's been accomplished and exhausted. There's no other way to live. Don't live in the past, it'll only bring pain. Treasure each day as though it were your last. Cherish our memories ...

and at the same time, feel safe in the knowledge that one day we'll make plenty more. It's good for us to face our fears. In your last life you refused to live a life without me and that is what caused all the problems we have experienced since. You must not do that this time. People die all the time and things change every day, just like the seasons do. Every future is unknown."

"So our meeting now has happened for a reason?" Sarah asked.

Archie nodded, "I'm sure it has."

"I've come to hate the world, Arch. Without you, the grief is unbearable. I've a hole inside me that won't heal, a pain, here," she clutched her chest, "like a knife twisting inside."

Archie pressed his index finger to Sarah's lips, silencing her. "Love is everlasting remember. We made a promise, come what may. But now you must live, not for me, not for our past, but for you now and all those on the Earth-plain who love you. I don't belong on a pedestal; you will love again and your unborn children will heal that hole. Believe me. And when you live, remember this ... this moment, right now is our truth and it's our story. You made a deal with me to tell it and that deal will give you strength and passion to carry on." Archie's hands gently cupped Sarah's face. "Bring back the zest in your life, Sarah, the zest that always sparkled so brightly in your eyes; have purpose in all that you do. Because, like the Sun has said, what you do now has the potential to bring back meaning and purpose to everyone. Everything you do touches someone, somewhere and don't be afraid. One thing I've learnt since I've been watching over you all is that all of you are so troubled by grief and the mere thought of death that you have forgotten how to live."

Sarah stared at him imploringly, her gaze shifting from one side of his face to the other. "What about you?" she asked, big fat tears tumbling down her cheeks. She knew the end was very near now.

"I'll go back ... back over the bridge," Archie explained. "It's busy on the other side just like it is on Earth, but without all the grief."

"But how will you climb the cliff? I flew you the last time."

"So you do remember," he grinned. "Kriss will help me, he's an amazing man, larger than life," Archie smirked and turned to wink at his friend, who had walked a little way away to give them some privacy and stood waiting.

"I love you," Sarah whispered.

Archie smiled. "I know – and I love you back."

"A wise man once told me that love is the only reason for our existence." Sarah looked down and fumbled with the apple rolling about in her palms, its skin getting softer and browning with every second that ticked by. "He said it is the answer to everything."

"This very wise man didn't happen to be called 'Old Nick' did he?"

Sarah giggled through her tears. "Yeah. You know, I never really thought much in depth about death, not really, not until I had that weird dream about you. You'd signed up with the Army and gave me that letter. Do you remember? That was when I started to pray... for you."

She paused, thinking. The memory of that time had always remained very fresh in her mind, haunting and panicking her from the moment it happened. A breeze across the sea ruffled her sand-encrusted hair and Archie raised his hand to lift a curl off her forehead. "I was never sure who I was praying to before," she said. "So ... if there is a God over there where you're going, do you think he'd mind if I pray to you rather than Him? You're far more real."

Archie laughed heartily, revealing his chipped front tooth. "Not that I've met Him yet, but I'm sure He wouldn't mind. I don't believe we'd have found each other if there wasn't a God or some sort of deity: a creator ... or cosmos. Maybe God is just a great big secret never to be fathomed, one that talks to us through songs, letters and dreams."

It was Sarah's turn to laugh this time, a nervous laugh. Time was still ticking; Archie's eyes pressing her. He reached down to take her hands and pulled them up to her face, "Eat the apple, Sarah; it's time to go home. Please, do it for me."

And Sarah, who could never refuse him anything, pressed her teeth into the moist apple. The skin punctured and juice oozed out, dripping down her chin. "I'll let you go this time, Archie ... with a full heart and I promise I will try to live without you."

"Thank you," Archie whispered. "I'll look in on you from time to time." Raising her hand to his lips, he pressed a kiss on her palm and then let her go, walking backwards away from her.

Sarah closed her fingers around his kiss, which she could still feel warm and comforting in her hand. The cool waters of the sea lapped around her feet, as she too took a step backwards into the waves.

The ravens still swarmed the skies above, screeching and squawking. As she made her final farewell, one swooped down on her. Archie paused on the shoreline, pressed his lips together in frustration then waved his arms at the ravens and roared like a lion at the top of his lungs.

This closing sight of Archie in his lion hide bowled Sarah over. Stricken with grief she dropped to her knees in the ocean, raising her arms to protect her head from the bird's attack. Hot pain shot into her hand where the raven stabbed her with its serrated beak, blood spurting and flowing down her wrist. She could hear Archie's distant yells, but she suddenly felt faint and dizzy and her hearing made them sound weak and distorted. The apple she still clutched tumbled from her hand and rolled over her fingertips into the water. She had already taken a large bite, but did she need to eat all of it to return home, she wondered, as she wobbled from her knees onto her hip, slipping sideways, the water now up to her chest. The sand beneath was soft and unbalanced her. It was as though she were sitting in a basin of quicksand. She was sinking into it; only her neck and shoulders were above water now. The sea was ready to take her as it splashed and sprayed around her head. This was it then; the whole thing had been a trick and she was going to drown.

She cast a final glance back at Archie and then, quite suddenly, the beach vanished and her head went under.

CHAPTER TWENTY FIVE

AUGUST 2003
WHEN THE STUDENT IS READY, THE MASTER APPEARS

Sarah came awake to find her head resting in thick, wet mud, muttering to herself incoherently, "Arch...? Where...?" She tried to move, but nothing seemed to work, none of her limbs would obey her. Was she even alive? The memory inside her head of what had just past came flooding back: the feeling of sinking into the sand; watching Archie walking slowly back up the beach, until her head was submerged and she could no longer see him. Her panic about drowning that was the last thing she remembered. Where was she now?

"I should have stayed with you, Arch," she murmured, "but if I had, what future would there have been? Should I have forced the issue? Stayed in Transit with you, only for us both to become lost souls? But at least then we would have been lost and roaming together."

Lying there, barely conscious, Sarah thought through the decision she appeared to have made, to eat the apple and return to the Earth-plain, for as the smog and reek of petrol fumes found their way into her nostrils, she was certain that was where she now was, even if more dead than alive; so not drowned, at least. Maybe she could have tried to find a way to trek back in time to heal that fragment of her broken heart? Would it have helped, pushing for what her alter ego, Felicity, really wanted? What was it that she, Sarah Walker, wanted? She wanted to live; she knew that for sure. She wanted to live more than she had ever lived before and she wanted to savour every moment ... every breath. She had no idea where the will and want to live sprang from, but she could feel it deep in her guts, in her heart, in the gaping hole that still insistently burnt in her chest as she lay there, a foot deep in sludge. She knew that burning hole would never leave her, for that hole was Archie and he would always be part of her. There would always be a portion of her that would long for yesterday, the good old days, but today would be the greatest day she had ever known. She had to live for today, if for nobody else but for herself. If she had stayed locked in the past she would not have lived to see her children ... that is, if she had children. She had to live to pass on Archie's story as he had so innocently asked when he was just fourteen. She had to live to find out who she should pass it to. She had to write the story in his memory; a life that had so much meaning and purpose and love, for no matter how distant or tragic that love was, even gravity could not drag it down.

Tentatively, Sarah tried again to move, but all she could manage was to twitch her fingertips.

"Miss Sarah," a soft voice called from somewhere above her. She could hear footsteps squelching through the mud towards her as her thoughts continued to gather in her head.

"Oh thank Buddha ... I have found you," the gentle voice muttered.

"In another life, I'd be able to stay, Arch," Sarah whispered to the mud, her eyes only half open as the footsteps and the voice got closer.

"Miss Sarah," the accent was Oriental. "Are you okay?" A gentle hand brushed her matted, mud-encrusted hair from her face. She felt sick, her mouth was caked with dried blood and her body ached. A strong arm wrapped around her shoulders, sucking them free of the sludge. She allowed the man to pick her up, hoisting her like a rag doll into his arms.

"Archie ... I'm sorry," Sarah mumbled. "I can't replace you, not even with a zillion dreams." A surge of emotion rose from her belly into her head. She curled into the person who cradled her, trying to protect herself from grief again, deep sobs growling inside.

"Come, Miss Sarah, you come with me," the sturdy arms holding her squeezed her tightly. As she was lifted she saw around her a deserted riverbed; black mud oozed out of the bank where she had been lying and here and there were clumps of reed, but everything was blurred, she was delirious, too weak to react in any way at all. She had no choice but to allow this man to take her, whoever he was, yet he sounded kind. The tone of his voice was strangely familiar, he was most certainly Thai, but she felt safe in his arms. Forcing her eyes open she focused on the flat features right in front of her and recognised her taxi driver.

"I let him go!" she cried unthinkingly, looking up into Niran-Atid's wrinkled and toothless face, then rubbing her chin on his shoulder to wipe away a smear of mud that threatened to invade her mouth.

He smiled a gummy smile, seemingly unfazed that she was making his clean, if drab clothing muddy. "Of course you let him go, Miss Sarah. It was written that you should."

Sarah looked into his deep brown eyes and a small smile appeared on her face too. "How did you know where I was?" she asked.

"There is an old Buddhist proverb, Miss Sarah," Niran-Atid replied, his smile broadening as he began to pound his way up the river bank to the road where his taxi waited.

"What is it?" Sarah asked.

"When the student is ready, the master appears," he said, looking down at her as he walked, his eyes twinkling with untainted happiness.

'Where did he find it?' Sarah wondered, at his age, he would no doubt have lost loved ones and lived through great hardships. Why and how was he so happy? She failed to see past his eyes. They were so wise and good. And he was also implausibly strong for so short and slender a man. Then for the briefest moment, the web of wrinkles around his eyes seemed to smooth and disappear. Sarah stared at the old Thai Buddhist's face and saw that he was not old, but ageless. The sunshine of the day seemed to radiate from his eyes making them shine golden instead of brown and a familiar voice seemed to exude through them, serenaded by the soft strains of an otherworldly orchestra.

'I watch over you every minute of every day Sarah, for I am the Sun; I am the Spirit of Understanding. My light can help cast away shadows ... shadows of your past. Your past caught up with you in the end didn't it?' The voice paused; Sarah drew in a small breath. 'Every choice you made was yours alone. Your determination and guts has taken you far. You should be proud of yourself. Your journey was ambitious. Nonetheless, it is now complete and you survived. Remember what I told you Sarah ... the story you now tell not only has the power to restore faith in your life - but it will restore faith in the meaningfulness and purpose of every human's journey.'

Suddenly, the sounds died away, the illusion vanished as quickly as it had appeared and Niran-Atid's brown eyes regarded her from their nest of crows feet. "Come now," he said, placing Sarah gently on her feet and opening the taxi door. "We must get you to a hospital. Call your parents, tell them you are safe. Then I take you to refuge."

Sarah held tightly onto the door, her feet and legs not quite strong enough to keep her upright. Niran-Atid quickly took hold of her again and Sarah momentarily rested her weary head on his bony shoulder, glimpsing the river behind them as they fleetingly hugged. Her eyes focusing far better now, she looked upriver and caught a glimpse of the giant suspension bridge from which she had fallen. She drew in a short, sharp breath as the fall replayed in her memory. "In another life I'd have stayed," she whispered.

Lowering her into the front passenger seat, Niran-Atid helped her pull her legs round and strapped her in, then closing the door, walked slowly around the bonnet and climbed in the taxi beside her. "Music?" he asked, turning on the engine; cool air-conditioning slowly filtered through the vents.

Every part of Sarah's battered body seemed to hurt. Trying to ignore the pain she rested her head back on the headrest and shut her eyes. "Niran-Atid?"

"Yes?"

"Where is this refuge you want to take me to?" Sarah whispered; her throat as dry as sandpaper.

"North ... way up north," he said. "I show you on map when we get you to hospital. Refuge safe; Bhuddist teacher help your mind heal and learn who you are."

"I think I know who I am," Sarah said, not really understanding what he meant, though comforted by his promise of safety. "But I'm not sure what happened to me. There's no way it could have been a dream. I know I fell from Phra Pin Klao Bridge nearly a week ago and went to this weird place. And then I met ... I met ... I can barely remember ..." Shaking her head she tried to rearrange the thoughts that only moments ago had seemed so fresh and clear. "I was there; I know I was there. It was a place called ... oh," she wailed, "I don't remember what it was called."

"Did you eat the apple?" Niran-Atid asked with a quizzical look, slipping the taxi into gear.

"What?" A fleeting memory of a browning apple flashed into her mind, the feel of its juice running down her chin. "Yes, but how ..." Sarah opened her eyes to stare at Niran-Atid, "How did you know?"

"Then you will remember nothing," he explained, ignoring the question. "Miss Sarah, you have much to learn. At refuge, we help you learn. In some stories you hear that the apple give you knowledge, but in your story it take knowledge away from you. You will only remember what you need to remember, the rest will all be gone in a matter of moments, like dry sand slipping through your fingers." He lifted a hand off the steering wheel, fingers splayed then suddenly he clenched his fist. "The harder you try to grasp it, the faster it go."

"Archie was there," Sarah insisted. "I know he was there."

"Not anymore," Niran-Atid smiled, shaking his head. "He is gone, and you, Miss Sarah, fell off the Phra Pin Klao Bridge only yesterday."

"That can't be true," Sarah frowned, but the harder she tried to focus on anything the more confused she felt. The moment seemed to be slipping away from her as every second passed. Sarah panicked. "Archie asked me to write his story, but how can I if I can't remember anything?"

"Music?" Niran-Atid asked again.

Sarah shrugged, "Whatever. Niran-Atid, I have to know what happened. I can't forget. We went through so much trouble to remember, I know we did, even if I can't remember what."

"Your head may forget, Sarah, our minds are good at filtering in and out light and dark thoughts and memories. But your heart ... your heart is a muscle and muscles have fabulous memory. They know every pathway and every twist in that pathway ... your heart will never forget. Now, music?"

"Sure," Sarah agreed, not really bothered whether the radio was on or not, mystified by what this old man seemed to know and completely awed by his apparent wisdom and absolute serenity.

Niran-Atid fumbled about with the radio for a moment and tuned into someone rambling away in Thai. Sarah couldn't understand a word and the jumbled language only jumbled her thoughts all the more. She thrust her head back and closed her eyes again. She was so tense, even her fists were clenched. She tried to relax and as she did her palm opened, inside was a crumpled up scrap of paper.

"What's that?" Niran-Atid asked, peering into her hand as he pulled the car out onto the road then fiddled again with the radio and beamed with satisfaction. An English singer began to sing the first line of an overwhelmingly apt song, "A long, long time ago, I can still remember how that music used to make me smile ..." the taxi driver warbled, singing along.

Sarah smiled sadly as the song continued to enfold around them in the car, a memory bounding in with every chord: of love, family, warmth and togetherness - and then a pang of grief so piercing it made her gasp, for everything had changed.

"You okay?" Niran-Atid asked, placing a concerned hand on her shoulder as with the other he manoeuvred the taxi out into the traffic.

Too full of emotion to speak, Sarah nodded and looking down, un-crumpled the paper in her hand. Inside was Archie's St Christopher medallion and scrawled on the paper in a familiar hand was a one-line note:

I will miss you, more dearly than these written words can say.

Arch

~ The End ~

If you liked Waiting Game, you'll love Dead Game

When Lance Corporal Archie Fletcher's plane plummets into the Persian Gulf during the Second Gulf War, even his wild imagination could never have primed him for the adventure he must now undertake. With guardian angels, a cursed centaur and mythical saints, Archie battles his way through a feral land called 'Transit'. But 'Dead Game is no easy feat. The fantasy will sweep you away to a parallel world where you will follow Archie's fateful story full of courageous imagination - confirming that knowing deep within us all that the adventure of life must go on.

Shortlisted for the People's Book Prize 2013

Available now from Ghostly Publishing
(www.ghostlypublishing.com)
...and all good book shops priced

£8.99

Coming later in 2013:

End Game

Find out more at
www.ghostlypublishing.co.uk

And connect with me on Facebook at:
www.facebook.com/GhostlyPublishing

Lightning Source UK Ltd.
Milton Keynes UK
UKOW041651270213

206903UK00002B/21/P

9 781909 587250